Ravel lowere[...]he nar-
row indentati[...]cage,
cupping a bre[...]ling it
with his tongue[...]pple gently into his
mouth.

Anya breathed deep as heated desire flooded through her, spiraling downward. With her eyes tightly closed, she reached out to him, stroking with sensitive, questing fingertips along the muscles of his arm and over his chest. He caught her hand, guiding it to the thrusting length of him that was yet satiny in its smoothness. She accepted that invitation, exploring, lost in unexpected delight.

Time ceased to have meaning. The coals of the fire pulsed, softly crackling. Their bodies were gilded with gold and red and silver, awash and throbbing with their own internal heat. . . .

Also by Jennifer Blake
Published by Fawcett Books:

LOVE'S WILD DESIRE
TENDER BETRAYAL
THE STORM AND THE SPLENDOR
GOLDEN FANCY
EMBRACE AND CONQUER
ROYAL SEDUCTION
SURRENDER IN MOONLIGHT
MIDNIGHT WALTZ
FIERCE EDEN
ROYAL PASSION
SOUTHERN RAPTURE
LOUISIANA DAWN
PERFUME OF PARADISE
THE NOTORIOUS ANGEL
LOVE AND SMOKE
SWEET PIRACY
SPANISH SERENADE
JOY AND ANGER

By Jennifer Blake
Writing as Patricia Maxwell:

BRIDE OF A STRANGER
DARK MASQUERADE
NIGHT OF THE CANDLES
THE SECRET OF THE MIRROW HOUSE

PRISONER OF DESIRE

Jennifer Blake

FAWCETT GOLD MEDAL • NEW YORK

A Fawcett Gold Medal Book
Published by Ballantine Books
Copyright © 1986 by Patricia Maxwell

Library of Congress Catalog Card Number: 86-90735

ISBN 0-449-14765-7

Manufactured in the United States of America

First Trade Edition: September 1986
First Mass Market Edition: December 1991

Chapter One

🦋 🦋 🦋 *It was a glittering and fantastic spectacle.*
The St. Charles Theater blazed with gaslight from the great
Gothic chandeliers of wrought iron with their milk-glass globes.
The wooden floor that had been laid over the parquet area had
been waxed to a high gloss that reflected not only the warm
pools of light, but also the white plastered pillars with their
gilded decorations of acanthus leaves, the crimson velvet of the
stage curtain, the urn-shaped balustrades of the boxes, and the
lyre designs in the domed ceiling. Silken streamers of red and
green and gold had been looped from the dome down to the
upper tier of boxes. They swayed gently in the rising heat given
off by the burning gaslights, as if moving in time to the measured
lilt of the waltz being played by the orchestra.

Dancers whirled around the floor clad in silk and velvet and
lace, and with their eyes gleaming with pleasure through the
slits of the masks covering their faces. Here a girl garbed as
Medieval Lady with pointed, veil-draped headpiece was part-
nered by a Bedouin in flowing robes. There a Monk with a cross
swinging about his knees was paired with a lady in the guise of
a Vestal Virgin. Promenading on the arm of one of Iberville's
Dragoons was a lady with a powdered coiffure and a red ribbon
about her neck denoting an aristocrat of the French Revolution.
Cloth of gold shimmered. Feathers floated and drifted from
headdresses. Stones of paste vied in sparkle with the restrained
glint of real jewels. The air smelled of perfume, with also a faint
hit of camphor in which many of the costumes had been packed
away until this Mardi Gras season. There was the subdued roar
of merriment and conversation in voices lifted to carry above
the music. Over the gathering hung a faint air of daring, a sense

1

of risqué pleasure, as discreet flirtations were conducted behind the anonymity of concealing disguises.

Anya Hamilton, watching the crowd from where she stood against one of the great columns that supported the dress circle boxes, smothered a yawn. She allowed her dark lashes with their auburn tips to close. The smoke and the smell of partially burned gas from the lights were giving her a headache, or perhaps it was the tightness of the tie of her ecru satin demi-mask. The music was too loud, though the hollow shuffle of feet on the temporary wood floor, combined with the chattering of voices, nearly drowned it out. It was still early in the evening, but there had been too many late nights for Anya in the past weeks. This was her fifth *bal masqué* since coming to New Orleans shortly after Christmas, and she did not care if it was her last, though she well knew there were nearly two weeks more of them to go before the blessed respite of Ash Wednesday.

Mardi Gras had once been a pagan festival celebrating fertility and the rites of spring. Named in those early days the Lupercalia for the cave where had been held the celebrations surrounding the worship of the god Pan, deity of the land of lovers called Arcadia, it had evolved into an excuse for debauchery and licentious conduct during the time of the Romans. The early Christian fathers had tried to stamp it out but, failing abysmally, had incorporated it into the rituals of the Resurrection. Mardi Gras then was decreed to be the last day of feasting before the arrival of Ash Wednesday, which heralded the forty days of Lenten fasting preceding Easter. The priests had called their festival in Latin *carnelevare*, a word that could be loosely translated to mean "farewell to the flesh." It was the French who had named it Mardi Gras, literally Fat Tuesday, for their practice of parading a *boeuf gras*, or "enormous bull," through the streets as a symbol of the day. It was also the French, under Louis XV, who had popularized the weeks of opulent festivities in advance of the final holiday, and the tradition of the *bal masqué*.

Anya had a grudge against the Gallic race for the last. It wasn't that she disliked the masked balls, not at all. She always enjoyed the first one or two of the winter season, the *saison des visites* as it was known in New Orleans. But she saw no reason why Madame Rosa and Celestine had to go to every such affair to which they received an invitation. It must have been her Anglo-Saxon heritage that deplored such prolonged merriment; to her it was expensive, it was boring, but most of all, it was exhausting.

"Anya, wake up! People are staring!"

Anya lifted her lashes with irony behind the warmth in her eyes that were the ink blue of northern seas, turned her head to look at her half sister Celestine. "I thought they had already been staring all night at my ankles, at least according to you."

"So they have been and still are! How you can stand there with every man that passes ogling your lower limbs, I don't understand."

Anya flicked a glance over the other girl, dressed as a deliciously voluptuous shepherdess with a great deal of her softly rounded bosom showing, then looked down at her form that was completely covered except for her bare ankles that were a scant two inches below the hem of the doeskin costume that turned her into an Indian Princess. She picked up one of her thick braids that had the rich golden russet brown hue and patina of polished rosewood. Flipping the end in a derisive gesture, she said, "Scandalous, isn't it?"

"It is indeed. I wonder Maman allows it."

"I am masked."

Celestine gave a ladylike sniff. "A demi-mask, scant disguise or protection."

"An Indian woman with her skirt down to the floor would be ridiculous, and well you know it. Since I had to wear a costume, I prefer it to be authentic. As for Madame Rosa, she is much too good-natured to try to constrain me."

"What you mean is you haven't the least regard for her wishes, or for those of anyone else!"

Anya smiled at her half sister, her manner coaxing. "Dear Celestine, I'm here, aren't I? Don't be cross, it will give you wrinkles."

Instantly the younger girl's frown smoothed. She went on, however. "I'm only concerned for what the old ladies will say about you."

"It's sweet of you, *chère*," Anya said, giving the other girl the endearment heard a thousand times a day among the Creoles, "but I fear it's too late. They have been exercising the ends of their tongues on me for so long, it would be a pity to deprive them of the diversion."

Celestine looked at her elder half sister, at the smooth oval of her face, the sparkle of her eyes through her mask, her straight nose, and the warmth of the smile that curved her perfectly molded mouth. With worry in her brown eyes, she looked away, glancing around the room. "So far they only call you eccentric. So far." Abruptly she stiffened. "There, that man. You see how he stares? That's what I mean!"

Anya turned her head to follow the direction of her half sister's narrow gaze. The man Celestine spoke of stood on the first balcony tier across the room, with one hand braced on a Corinthian column and the other on his hip. He was tall and broad, an impression heightened by his costume of black and silver representing the Black Knight, complete with floor-length cloak and visored helmet covering his head and shoulders. He was a powerful figure and a romantic one in a rather dangerous way. So complete was his disguise that there was no hint of his identity; still, the glinting silver crossbars of his helmet were turned in her direction.

It was unnerving, that steady, faceless appraisal, almost as if it held a threat. Anya felt a ripple of unease that was allied to an odd awareness of herself as a woman. Her pulse quickened and she felt a singing tension along her nerves. It grew until, with a swift indrawn breath, she tore her gaze away. "Is he staring? I can't tell," she said mendaciously.

"He has been watching you for the past half hour."

"Smitten, no doubt, by my dainty ankles?" Anya thrust out her foot, displaying an ankle that, though slender and well turned, had too much strength to give the proper appearance of fragility. "Oh, come, Celestine, you are imagining things. Or else, you like the looks of the knight, since you must have been watching him while he was watching me. Shocking! I should tell Murray."

"Don't you dare!"

"You know I wouldn't, though the timing is perfect. Here he is."

Beyond Celestine, Anya had caught sight of a fresh-faced young man. He was dressed as Cyrano de Bergerac, but had removed his long-nosed mask and left it dangling around his neck. Of medium height, he had thick and curly light brown hair, ingenuous hazel eyes, and a smile that creased his tanned cheeks into dimples of consummate charm. At the moment, he was making his way along the edge of the dance floor carrying, somewhat precariously, two cups of lemonade.

"Sorry to be so long," he said as he relinquished his burdens, one to each lady. "There was a crush you wouldn't believe around the lemonade bowl. It's this heat. I can tell you we never had anything like it in February in Illinois."

Anya tasted her lemonade. She refused to look toward the balcony where the Black Knight had stood, fastening her attention instead on the couple beside her.

Murray Nicholls was Celestine's fiancé. Their courtship had not been a long one, but the betrothal period had been protracted. For once Madame Rosa had risen above her natural indolence to put her foot down. She did not believe in marriage between strangers. Love was an emotion that took time to be recognized and firmly established. It was not a storm of feeling that came like the one of the hurricanes of autumn, leveling everything in its path. They must be patient.

Patient they had certainly been. It was over eight months since Celestine had received her betrothal bracelet, and still there was no talk of a wedding date, though the trousseau, with its dozens of everything from sheets to nightgowns, was almost ready.

To Anya's eyes, the young pair were well suited. Celestine, like her mother, was dark haired and dark eyed, with a smooth white complexion improved at the moment with white pearl powder, a rounded form and face, and a gentle expression—when she was not concerned for Anya's good name. She was sweet and sentimental, and required in a husband a man who was soft-spoken and kind, one with a sense of humor to tease her out of her occasional crotchets and gloomy moods. Murray Nicholls appeared to have the proper qualifications, in addition to being the possessor of a good degree of intelligence and reasonable prospects as a clerk in a law office where he was preparing for his own entry into the profession. It was difficult to understand why Madame Rosa was so insistent on delay.

Anya recognized with wry self-knowledge that her own approval stemmed from the fact that Murray reminded her of Jean François Girod. Jean, her own fiancé until his death, had been just that open and fresh of countenance, just that charming and sunny of manner, and he would have been about the same age Murray was now, in his late twenties. Jean might have been a tiny bit slimmer, a bit shorter; he had been scarcely an inch taller than she was herself, though she could not be called petite as she towered nearly three good inches above Celestine, who was of average height. The eyes of the two men were different also; Jean's had been a deep, velvety brown. Still, the hair was the same, as well as the quick manner and the suppressed air of high spirits.

It has been those same high spirits that had killed Jean. His death had been so senseless; that was the one thing that Anya could not forgive. It had been in a duel, but not some grandiose meeting for the sake of honor. Instead, he had died because of a maudlin and drunken jest.

Jean and five of his friends had been returning from a card game out near Lake Pontchartrain late one night. They had spent long hours sitting around a gaming table in a smoke-filled room, wagering with bored abandon, drinking deep. It had been a night with a full moon and, as they passed the field with the pair of live oak trees known as the dueling oaks, the moonlight had made such dancing patterns of light and shadow across the grass under the trees that they were entranced. Someone suggested that they match swords, since the stage was so beautifully set for a duel. They piled out of their carriage and drew their weapons in reckless gaity. When the fight was over, two of their number lay dead with their blood staining the grass. One of them had been Jean.

The waltz that was playing came to an end and a contredanse began. Celestine drank the last of her lemonade and glanced at Murray, one slippered toe tapping the floor. Anya reached out to lift the girls' cup from her hand. ''I'll take care of that; you two enjoy yourselves.''

''Will you be all right?'' Murray asked.

"I'll probably go and doze with Madame Rosa and the rest of the chaperones."

"Such a waste," he said with a flashing grin.

"You're too kind," she mocked gently. "Go along with you."

A Negro waiter in uniform appeared with a tray to take the cups. Anya smiled her thanks and he moved silently away again. Still she stood where she was, watching her half sister and Murray Nicholls dancing among the other gaudily costumed couples. At twenty-five, she was only seven years older than Celestine, but sometimes she felt immeasurably more ancient. Sometimes she even felt older than Madame Rosa.

She glanced over her shoulder toward where her stepmother sat in her box that, with the raised floor, was nearly on a level with the dancers. Attending the older woman was her faithful *cavalier servente* Gaspard Freret. A dapper little man as thin as his chosen lady was stout; a writer of theater and opera reviews and fountainhead of the latest *on-dits*, Gaspard had been looked upon with tolerant amusement by Anya and Celestine for the past several years.

Anya had come to think, however, that he was something more than a nonentity. For one thing, he was a master swordsman and excellent shot, necessary skills for a gentleman in a city where the duello was an institution and a man might receive a challenge at any moment. For another, he seemed to have considerable standing among the city officials and business institutions, and had given Anya excellent counsel on a number of occasions concerning investments. Lately Anya had also begun to suspect that it was on Gaspard's advice and with his support that Madame Rosa had decreed the delay in the nuptials between her daughter and Murray.

The older pair were dressed as Anthony and Cleopatra, though Madame Rosa as the Egyptian Queen wore the deep black of mourning, doubtless, Anya thought with wry humor, for the death of Caesar. Madame Rosa had not left off her black for as long as Anya could remember, not since the deaths of her twin sons, Anya's half brothers, in infancy, certainly not since Anya's father had died seven years before.

Madame Rosa had been her father's second wife. Nathan Hamilton's first, Anya's mother, had been a planter's daughter from Virginia. He had met her while traveling from his home in Boston into the South, searching for land on which to establish himself as a businessman-planter. He had found Virginia a closed enclave of proud families living on depleted acreage, but he discovered there the woman he wanted to marry. After the wedding, he tried to make a go of managing a section of land given to the couple by the bride's father. It had not been profitable. After several years of effort, he finally, against the wishes of his in-laws, sold out and moved on to New Orleans with his wife and five-year-old daughter.

The land along the Mississippi River and its tributaries was rich due to frequent flooding that left the topsoil of the nation's heartland behind it, but the choicest plots had long ago been taken. While on a tour of the countryside by steamboat, however, Nathan chanced to sit in on a poker game. When he rose from the table, he was the owner of six hundred acres of prime delta land less than three hours' traveling time from New Orleans, along with 173 slaves and a house named Beau Refuge. His pleasure was short-lived. By the time he took possession of his land, his wife was ill with a fever, and died soon afterward.

Being a practical man and a sensual one, Anya's father had, when his period of mourning was over, looked about him for a woman who would make a home for him and be a mother to his young daughter. He settled on Marie-Rose Hautrive, whom he called Rosa, a young woman past the freshness of first youth at twenty-two and still unmarried. He courted her in the teeth of the opposition of her family: he had wealth, but to the French Creoles *la famille* was all-important, and what could one know of the family of a blue-eyed *américain* from so barbarous a place as Boston?

Plump and placid, too placid to attract suitors less determined, Madame Rosa had been a perfect stepmother. She gave Anya love and warmth and wrapped her in the luxurious comfort of her massive bosom and the home she made for Anya and her father. She sometimes complained gently of Anya's conduct as she was growing up, but never scolded, and certainly never attempted to discipline her. Her tactics stemmed from indolence in part, but also from an innate shrewdness. Anya's loss of her mother and doting grandparents at the same time that she was uprooted from her familiar home in Virginia had left her prey to violent nightmares. The indulgence she received because of them, combined with being treated like a small princess by the slaves who had come with the plantation her father had won, had made her willful and wild. Madame Rosa soothed her fears and gave her security. She did her best to make her a biddable young lady, and had succeeded well enough until the deaths of the two men closest to Anya, those of Jean and of her father.

Nathan Hamilton died of injuries after a fall from a horse just two months after the death of Anya's fiancé. Then double tragedy propelled Anya into a fierce rebellion. She was only eighteen, and it seemed that her life was over. If living and loving could come to an end so soon and for so slight a reason, then it would be as well to use the hours allowed precisely as one pleased. If such terrible things could happen to people who followed all the stifling rules dictated by the church and society, while men like Ravel Duralde, who had killed her Jean, went blithely on their way flouting every canon of decency, then what good was conforming? She would do so no longer.

And so she had discarded her petticoats and sidesaddle to ride astride over her father's plantation in a long divided skirt of soft leather worn with a man's shirt and broad-brimmed hat. She read books and periodicals on farming methods and, when she found her father's overseer unwilling to listen to her ideas for improvements, fired him and took on the job of running the plantation herself. Sometimes she argued with the men who were her neighbors about the theories of breeding horses and swine, a subject a lady should know nothing of, much less speak about in mixed company. She learned to swim with the Negro children, braving the treacherous currents of the river, and could not understand why drowning was thought preferable for a female to engaging in such an activity. She tended the ills of the plantation slaves, male as well as female, helping the elderly woman who served as nurse to set limbs and sew up cuts, as well as deliver babies and aid the women who had attempted to rid themselves of unwanted children. And she listened to the hair-raising tales of the shifts of love and desire, hate and assault that took place in the slave quarters after dark. The female slaves taught her a number of interesting facts, in addition to several tricks of self-preservation.

While in New Orleans during those years, she had fallen in with a crowd consisting mainly of young married couples, many of them Americans. They were a fast lot who thought it splendid fun to go for moonlight sails on Lake Pontchartrain, visit the cemeteries at midnight where the ghostly mausoleums in plastered brick and white marble shone like cities of the dead, or else drive at a gallop down Gallatin Street on a Saturday night, watching for the ladies of the evening who adorned the balconies and open windows, or who plied their wares on the street. They dared not drive slow on such pilgrimages because of the danger; there was on average a murder every night of the year on that short thoroughfare, and that was counting only the corpses that were discovered. It was an accepted fact that there were many other men who wound up in the river, the only rule of the street being that a man must dispose of his own victims.

With this group of friends Anya had spent a great many nights eating in the finest restaurants of the city, partaking liberally of wine with each of the many courses. Sometimes they would go on to some soirée or ball, or if some other amusement did not appeal, entertain themselves by thinking up ludicrous dares and wagers. Once Anya was persuaded to steal an operatic tenor's nightcap.

It was the custom for opera companies to arrive in the city for runs lasting three to four weeks. The tenor of the company then in town was flamboyant and vain, with a high opinion of himself as a ladies' man. He was also known to be more than a little balding. The dare had begun as a joke about the kind of nightgear such a Lothario might wear to hide a tonsorial deficiency always covered while on stage by a wig.

The man was staying at the Pontalba apartments that were then newly finished, the first of their kind in the United States. They were constructed with ornate wrought-iron balconies overlooking Jackson Square, the old *Place d'Armes* of the French and Spanish regimes. To do the deed, Anya persuaded her coachman to drive under the tenor's balcony late one night. Dressed in boy's clothes, she swung to the top of the carriage, then pulled herself up onto the balcony that led to the man's rooms. It was a warm night, and she depended on his windows to be open. What she had not made allowance for was the possibility that he might not be asleep, or alone in his bed.

Nonplussed, but dauntless, Anya stole into the bedchamber and snatched the nightcap, a splendid affair of velvet and gold lace, from the tenor's head while he labored in the throes of passion. Whirling with her prize, she ran for her life.

The tenor bellowed and gave chase. So magnificent was the capacity of the opera star's lungs that his shouts awakened the building. As Anya was driven away at breakneck speed, lying flat on the roof of her carriage, the Pontalba balcony was lined with spectators. She had not, by the grace of God, been recognized, but the story had spread so quickly of the stolen nightcap that at the next performance the poor tenor was laughed from the stage. Anya had felt such guilt for the man's public embarrassment that she had sharply curtailed such escapades, and finally dropped the company of the married crowd altogether.

Anya glanced back toward the dancers in the theater ballroom. They were growing noisier, the effect of the iced champagne punch being served up along with the lemonade in the refreshment room. This was a public ball for the benefit of one of the city's many orphanages, with entrance by subscription. As a result, the guest list was less than exclusive, including anyone who might have the price of a ticket. The air of license seemed to be growing as the night advanced. It was not surprising.

The contredanse came to an end, and after a moment or two, another waltz began. It appeared that Celestine and Murray were going to remain on the floor for it. Anya pushed away from the column, making her way toward Madame Rosa and Gaspard, trying to discover some way to frame a request that they go home.

There was a flicker of movement above her. A dark shadow spread, swooping, and from the balcony overhead a man in costume leaped, to land with springing lightness on his feet before her. His cloak settled around him, swinging in heavy folds about his heels.

With her nerves jangling, Anya drew herself up, staring at

the Black Knight. The helmet he wore was real, as was the plate armor cuirass molded to the muscles of his chest, but for ease of movement the rest of his armor was constructed of black metallic cloth cut and stitched in a clever design that looked very like the real thing. His cloak was of black velvet lined with cloth of silver.

"May I have this waltz, Mademoiselle Sauvagesse?"

His voice echoed hollowly from inside his helmet as he made his request, giving her the title that went with her costume. The deep timbre had a familiar ring, though she did not think she knew it well. It seemed to vibrate through her, touching a resonant chord inside. She did not like the sensation, nor the feeling of being caught off guard. Her voice was cold with annoyance as she spoke. "Thank you, no. I was just leaving the floor."

As she stepped away from him, he put out a gauntleted hand to catch her arm, detaining her. "Don't refuse, I beg of you. Such opportunities as this come seldom, sometimes only once in an overlong life."

His touch, even through the heavy glove, make the skin of her arm tingle with the prickling rise of gooseflesh. She stared at him, trying to pierce his disguise, disturbed by a peculiar and unwilling awareness. "Who are you?"

"A man who desires a single dance, no more."

"That's no answer," she said sharply. She thought he had hesitated over his choice of words. It made them seem as if they held a meaning hidden from her. She tried to pierce the bars that made up the visor of his helmet, but could catch no more than a jet glitter where his eyes should be.

"But can't you see? I am a knight painted black, a dastard, the foe of good and master of evil; an outcast. Won't you take pity on me? Allow me to bask in the warmth of your favor; dance with me!"

His tone was light and his touch the same, not at all restraining, she discovered, though she would have sworn a moment before that the hold was unbreakable. For a breathless instant she was assailed by a sense of overwhelming, inescapable intimacy. So disturbing was it that she jerked her arm free, turning away once more. "I fear it would not be wise."

"But when have you been that, Anya?"

She swung back toward him so quickly that her long thick braids flew out to strike soft ringing blows against his metal cuirass. "You know me?"

"Is that so strange?"

"I find it more than odd that you can recognize me while I am masked, yet you still remain unknown to me."

"You knew me once."

It was an evasion. "If this is a guessing game, you must hold me excused; I don't care for such play."

Ste stepped quickly around him. This time his hand shot out to capture her wrist, and it was not a light clasp. She was whirled back against him so that her shoulder landed hard upon the metal that covered his chest. She stared up at him through the slits of her demi-mask, her eyes wide and startled as she recognized the superior strength he held in leash, and also the sheer radiating force of him as a man. Her pulse began to throb. A soft apricot flush rose to her cheekbones, and her eyes darkened slowly to deepest cobalt with rising anger and the strange distress that increased it a hundredfold.

The man in black stared down at her with a tight feeling in his chest. His gaze caught and held for a long instant on the delicate color of her face, the lovely and smooth contours of her mouth. He was a fool; if he had not known it before, he knew it now.

His voice rasped as he spoke. "It's such a small thing I ask; why could you not have the grace to grant it without getting into a ridiculous wrangle?"

"I'm glad to see that you realize it is ridiculous." Her rage was no less biting for being quiet. "It will be less so if you will let me go, at once."

Before he could comply, before he could answer, there was a stir behind them and the sound of quick footsteps. Murray Nicholls, his face flushed and his hands clenched, appeared beside them. His tones stiff, he asked, "Is this man troubling you, Anya?"

The Black Knight breathed a soft imprecation before he released Anya's wrist and stepped back. "My most sincere apologies," he said. Inclining his head in a bow, he turned away with a swirl of his cloak.

"Just a minute," Murray called, his tone harsh, imperative. "I saw you molesting Anya, and I believe there is an explanation due."

"To you?" The voice of the man in black was as hard as granite as he turned back.

"To me, as a man who will soon be as a brother to her. Shall we step outside where we may discuss it in private?"

Celestine, standing a short distance away, made a sound of dismay that she smothered by raising her hands to her lips. Anya glanced at her, aware as was the other girl of the implications of the words of the two men. Duels had been fought many times over much less than had just occurred.

"Really, Murray," she said, moving to put her hand on his arm, "there is no need. It was a simple misunderstanding."

"Please stay out of this, Anya." The face of Celestine's fiancé was pale and his voice unusually stern.

Anya's temper, held precariously until that moment, left her control. "Don't take that tone with me, if you please, Murray Nicholls! You and Celestine are not yet married, and you have no responsibility where I am concerned. I can fight my own battles."

He paid no attention, but made a curt gesture that indicated he expected the black-costumed man to follow as he pulled his arm from Anya's grasp and walked away. The Black Knight hesitated, then, with a movement of wide shoulders that might have been a shrug, moved after the younger man, overtaking him in a few long strides.

Celestine tottered toward Anya, clutching her hand. "Oh, what is going to happen? What are we going to do?"

Anya hardly heard her. "Damn men," she said with unaccustomed heat. "Damn them and their stupid pride and their idiotic pairing off like fighting cocks."

The girls were joined almost at once by Madame Rosa and Gaspard. The older couple had seen the contretemps from where they were sitting. Gaspard had thought the matter had a most serious appearance and feared his presence might be needed, but he had, it seemed, arrived too late. Neither by word nor tone did he indicate that Madame Rosa had delayed him, still Anya knew it must be so, and was sorry. There might have been something he could have done; Gaspard was not only well versed in such matters, he was, above all else, extremely diplomatic.

They stood in a close group as if for mutual comfort as they waited for Murray to return. As the time passed, a terrible coldness grew inside Anya. She could remember so well the morning she had been told Jean was dead. The man who had killed him, Ravel Duralde, had come to tell her. He had been dark and handsome, perhaps three years older than Jean and his closest friend, though not of the plantation aristocracy. On that occasion, his face had been gray and his eyes filled with pain as he tried to explain, to make her understand the reckless euphoria, the sheer *joie de vivre*, that had led to the moonlight duel. She had not understood at all. Looking at the man, sensing the vibrant life that flowed so strongly within him, knowing of his reputation as a superb swordsman while Jean had been merely competent, Anya had hated him. She could remember screaming at him in her shocked grief, though she could not recall the words. He had stood gazing at her, his face dazed and without defense; then he had gone away. From that moment, the mere thought of dueling had roused Anya to instant rage, a rage so great she could scarcely control it.

Suddenly Celestine gasped with her hand over her heart. "Thank God. Murray. There he is, and alive."

"Did you think they would fly at each other at once?" Gaspard asked in his precise tones, his distinguished features expressing shocked surprise. "That is not the way an affair such as this is conducted. There must be seconds chosen, weapons collected, arrangements made. It will be at least the dawn, and possibly twenty-four hours more, before the duel can commence." Catching the glance of asperity sent him by Madame Rosa, he added hastily, "Of course, we do not know that the matter will come to such a painful necessity."

Murray Nicholls's face was greenish, with a fine sheen of perspiration across his forehead and upper lip. His smile was less than a success, and there was false heartiness in his tone as he reached them. "Well, that's settled. Celestine, *ma chérie*, shall we dance?"

"But what happened?" the girl asked, her gaze searching his features.

"Men don't discuss these matters."

"Quite right," Gaspard said, nodding his approval.

"In any case," Murray went on, "it came to nothing. Let's speak of something else, if you please."

Anya stepped forward with a frown between her winged brows. "Don't act as if we were simpletons. We were here when it started; it's useless to pretend that we know nothing. Are you going to meet this man, or not?"

"Perhaps it would be better if we took the ladies home," Murray said to Gaspard, ignoring Anya's question. "I believe they have been made a little overwrought by the incident."

Célestine, her gaze on the hand Murray held at his side, asked in a rush, "What is that you are holding? It's a card, isn't it?"

Murray glanced down at the strip of pasteboard in his hand, then with an abrupt gesture tried to stuff it into the pocket of the doublet of his costume. The card flipped from his fingers, fluttering to the floor.

It was a calling card of the sort one man gave to another in order that his opponent in a duel might know where to send his seconds to arrange the details of their meeting. Of heavy cream-colored stock, richly engraved, it was a damning piece of evidence. There would be a duel.

Anya knelt quickly to pick up the card before Murray could retrieve it. Rising slowly to her feet, she stared at it. The blood drained from her face as the name sprang out at her in strong black lettering, the name of the man in the costume of the Black Knight who had invited her to waltz, the man whom Celestine's fiancé would meet on the field of honor for her sake.

The man who had killed her fiancé with a thrust to the heart on a moonlit night seven years before.

Ravel Duralde.

Chapter Two

🜲 🜲 🜲 *"Where you are going?"*

Anya halted with a violent start as the question came to her from down the dark gallery. She recovered quickly, turning toward the dim figure of her half sister seated in a rocking chair a few yards away. "Celestine! What are you doing still up?"

"I couldn't sleep. My thoughts whirl around in circles until I think I shall go mad. Oh, Anya, Murray will be killed, I know it! He's no match for a man like Ravel Duralde. I'm so afraid."

"Don't upset yourself again. I thought Madame Rosa gave you a sleeping cordial."

"I couldn't drink it. I feel quite ill with nerves. But what of you? You can't be going out again, not alone and at this hour."

It was bad luck that she had been caught, Anya thought. She had meant to slip quietly away, leaving a note with some excuse. And yet, a spoken lie could not be worse than a written one.

"There has been a message from Beau Refuge, some problem among the hands. I'll only be gone a day or two."

Anya glanced over the gallery railing into the courtyard below. The coachman would be waiting for her in the *porte cochère*, the passageway that allowed the carriage coming from the stables in the far rear of the court to exit from under the main bulk of the two-story house into the street. She had sent her instructions, and he would not fail her. Still, she must hurry; it was getting late.

"But you can't leave, not before the duel," Celestine protested.

"You know how I feel about such meetings. I can learn the outcome at Beau Refuge just as easily as here."

"But I might need you."

17

"Don't be silly," Anya answered in a rallying tone. "It will probably end in nothing more than a scratch for one of them, a show of blood for the satisfaction of their ridiculous honor."

"That isn't how it was with Jean."

Anya stiffened there in the darkness. If Celestine would only let her go, there might be no duel. "I know," she said shortly.

"I didn't mean to remind you." Celestine's voice was soft with contrition in the darkness.

"Never mind. I would stay if I could, but I really must go. It's so warm, too warm for this time of year, and the wind is rising. There will probably be a storm by daylight, and I'd as soon not be caught on the road."

"You will at least try to return in time?"

The meeting between the two men would not take place for over twenty-four hours, at dawn of the following morning. That much Murray had revealed, as well as the fact that the delay was at his request. His chosen second, a good friend, was out of town and would not be returning until tomorrow afternoon. The delay was not an unusual occurrence, but it was one for which Anya was profoundly grateful, one on which she placed her dependence.

"I'll try, that much I will promise."

In a rush, Celestine came to her feet and moved toward Anya to catch her close for a quick hug. "You are the best of sisters. I'm truly sorry if I hurt you."

"You didn't, imbecile," Anya answered, but her tone was gentle, and she returned the affectionate clasp before moving on across the gallery to the stairs that descended to the courtyard.

It had been a long time since Jean's death had brought Anya the instant pain that it had in the beginning. It sometimes seemed like a betrayal that she now felt only numbness. Often she wished that it did still hurt, that she could feel something so she could be certain that her softer emotions were alive. Most of the time, she was only too well aware that the pain had turned to anger, an anger directed toward the man who had killed her fiancé, and that the love she had felt had turned to hate.

Still, there were moments in the dark hours of the night when she feared that she was a fraud, that she was only playing the part of flamboyant Anya Hamilton, an eccentric and venturesome female dwindling into spinsterhood while dedicated to the memory of a dead fiancé. She felt then a kind of terror, as if she were trapped behind a mask of her own making. And yet she knew beyond a doubt that to remove it would make her acutely uncomfortable, like appearing naked in public.

The carriage was waiting. She stared at it critically in the flaring lantern hanging in the *porte cochère*. It was a simple black landau like a thousand others, neither better nor worse, with nothing to call attention to it. The horses that pulled it were sound and strong, but not showy in any way, not even carefully matched. It would do.

She called up a quiet order to the man on the box, then gathered her heavy cloak of dark blue wool around the costume she still wore and climbed inside. She patted her cloak pocket to be sure her demi-mask was there, then sat down, leaning back on the leather seat. The carriage jerked into motion. She sat staring out the window, seeing nothing. Her mind drifted, and she allowed it free rein, not wanting for the moment to think of what she was about to do.

Jean. His family, staunch Creoles, had owned the plantation that adjoined the land her father had won at poker. They had resented the presence of the Americans, and there had been little communication between the two pieces of property, though there were a number of paths as well as the main river road connecting them. Regardless, each family had always known what the other was doing, whether they were ill or well, when there was a cause for grief or celebration. The reason was simple; most of the slaves of the two places were related by blood, and it was their constant visiting back and forth with news that had created many of the worn paths.

Then one morning while out riding, nearly two years after Nathan Hamilton had taken possession of the plantation, Anya escaped the stableboy who acted as her groom. She allowed her pony to wander in the direction of the other plantation, craning her neck in curiosity to see what might be seen. She was not paying attention to her progress, and soon became lost on the winding trails.

It was Jean, a truant also, who found her. He took her home with him, introduced her to his *maman* and his *père*, to his *grand-mère* in her lace cap and his Tante Cici, who was confined to her chair with a bad leg; to his cousins who lived with them, and his Scots tutor, who had been searching for him since breakfast.

His family carried on over her as if she were the most intrepid of young females, to have traveled the few miles separating the two places alone. They fed her bonbons and *dragées*, or candy-coated almonds, and allowed her to sip a small glass of wine. They sent a messenger to Beau Refuge to relieve the anxiety of her father and stepmother, but insisted that she stay for lunch. A holiday was declared, education not being considered a matter of vital importance, and she and Jean and his many cousins played games and rode in a cart pulled by a pet goat, sang and danced to the music played by Tante Cici. Finally, Jean, being all of ten or eleven years old himself, escorted her home, staunchly determined to support her as she explained to her papa how she had come to stray so far. Long before that day was over she had loved him. She had never stopped.

Once at Beau Refuge, Anya invited Jean in to meet her father and mother and baby Celestine. But though Jean had told her about his aunt's bad leg and about one of his younger cousins who was "slow," as well as explaining the presence of the older gentleman who was a friend of his father and who lived with his family in a guesthouse with a barn owl in the attic and wrote books about ghosts, she did not tell him about her Uncle Will. That came much later, when she knew beyond a doubt that he would not desert her once he knew.

William Hamilton, Uncle Will, her father's brother, had arrived one day without warning. Younger than Nathan by a year, his wife and two children had been killed when their house caught fire in the middle of the night. Uncle Will had saved himself, but could not forgive himself for not saving his family. Since Nathan was his only relative living, Will had come to be with him, and to settle in a place where there were no reminders of the tragedy.

At first he had seemed all right, though he made little effort to throw off his depression of the spirits. But always he would moan in his sleep and cry out. Then came days when he would lie and scream until he was hoarse. He began to roam the house at night, beating the walls with his hands. Once he tried to cut his wrists with a kitchen knife and, when Nathan stopped him, attacked his own brother. It was after he broke the lock of the cabinet where Nathan kept his guns, threatened Madame Rosa with a fowling piece, then shot himself in the foot with it that Anya's father confined him.

It had been the practice at the time to confine those for whom life had proved too much, the insane, in the parish jails throughout the state, there being no other facilities, though since then a special hospital had been built at Jackson to contain them. The jails had not been an ideal solution, for the unfortunates were often preyed upon by other prisoners, or else were a danger themselves to the weaker inmates.

Nathan Hamilton had not been able to support the thought of that kind of life for his brother. He had prepared a room for him in the building that housed the cotton gin at Beau Refuge, a stout structure some distance from the house, so that his cries would not be a disturbance. A fireplace had been installed for comfort in winter, as well as high windows with strong iron bars for air. It had been furnished with a bed, an eating table and chair, an armchair, armoire, and washstand. It also had a leg shackle with a long chain that was attached to a stout bolt set into the thick wall beside the bed.

There in that room above the gin, with a pair of strong servants to tend to his needs, Uncle Will had stayed for four long years. He had endured his confinement without complaint for the most part, though sometimes he begged to be set free in the swamp with a gun and a knife. Then one night he managed to hang himself with a rope he had made, inch by patient inch, season after season, by twisting into threads the cotton fibers that drifted into his room, and twisting the threads into a rope.

The room was still there at Beau Refuge. Like everything else at the plantation, it was kept in order; the floor swept, the bed ropes renewed, the lock and the shackle oiled, and the fireplace chimney kept free of birds' nests. Now and than baled cotton was stored in it when space became scarce. Once an unruly slave bent on beating his woman to death was kept there until he calmed down. It was empty now.

The carriage rolled through the city and turned into a dark

street near the outskirts. Here were rows of narrow shotgun houses, so called because a shot fired through the front door of the house would go completely through the two rooms placed end to end and exit out the back door. Before one such house, the carriage drew up. Anya got down and moved quickly to climb the narrow steps and knock on the door.

It seemed a long time before there was an answer. Then a bolt was drawn and the door opened a cautious crack.

"Samson? Is that you?" Anya asked.

"Mam'zelle Anya! What you doin' here this time of night?"

The door was drawn open, and in the light of the carriage lanterns could dimly be seen an enormous Negro man. His head barely cleared the doorframe, and his shoulders and arms bulged with muscles that had come from pounding hot iron in his job as a blacksmith. His voice as he spoke held disapproval not unmixed with suspicion, and he peered beyond her toward the carriage that waited.

"I need to talk to you, and to Elijah. Is he here?"

"Yes, mam'zelle."

"Good," she said, and when Samson's brother, a man larger if possible that Samson himself, appeared, she began to outline what she wanted.

They did not like it; that much was plain. Anya could not blame them. It could not be denied that what she asked would be dangerous. Still, they did not deny her. She had known she could depend on them, no matter the hour or the nature of the request.

It was Samson and Elijah who had tended her Uncle Will. In order to help pass the time of their vigil, Anya had shared her school books with them, teaching them painstakingly to read and write by drawing with a stick in the dirt. Later, after her uncle's death, the pair had been given jobs in the blacksmith shop. But they yearned for the freedom they had read about in the history books and in the tracts passed out by the abolitionists. They thought they could make their own way, earn their keep in the blacksmith trade.

As Anya's father lay dying of the injuries from his fall from horseback, the two men had come to her. They asked that mam'zelle intercede for them, that she beg the master to free them. It was still possible then for a man to free a slave by will on his death, and so Anya had agreed. Not only had she spoken to her father, but later, when Samson and Elijah opened their own blacksmith shop, she had told everyone she knew of the delicate and intricate patterns of wrought iron for gates and railings and cornices created by the big men. They had prospered, and they had not forgotten.

It troubled Anya that she must ask them to risk so much now. It could not be helped, however. She would protect them insofar as she was able, no matter what happened.

A short time later, with Samson and Elijah clinging to the rear of the carriage like footmen, the driver turned the vehicle back toward the center of town.

It was growing late, still with everything that had happened, it was only just after midnight. The gas streetlamps on Canal Street and St. Charles Street were burning brightly, and the mule-drawn omnibuses that rattled up and down the thoroughfares were most of them more than half-full. Many of the balls held that night were only just now ending, and the carriage traffic was thick as the guests made their way homeward.

On a street corner Anya saw a Charley, or constable of the city police, in his painted and numbered leather cap. He stood slapping his short club, known as a spontoon, into the palm of his hand as he talked to a pair of men dressed in the flamboyant fashion favored by most professional gamblers. As Anya watched, one of the gamblers thrust what looked like a wad of bills into the pocket of the constable's coat.

She looked away, her lips curled in disgust, though she was not surprised. New Orleans, one of the richest cities in the United States for many years, had always attracted its share of political scavengers. The current crop of government officials, however, was the most corrupt and venal in living memory. The party in power was the Native American party, known derisively as the Know-Nothing party for the constant refrain of its officials when accused of wrongdoing. So blatantly irregular were the methods they used to come to power and keep themselves there, hiring thugs to attack registered voters of the opposition party and registering names from tombstones for their own party, that people had begun to despair of a political solution.

Some said that behind the Know-Nothing party was a cabal of powerful men who had made themselves rich by manipulating the situation. These men never sullied their hands with the foul business of running the city, nor were their identities known to more than a few, but they had installed as their tool a New Yorker named Chris Lillie who had brought with him a whole new bag of dirty tricks from Tammany Hall.

The situation had grown so bad that something had to be done. There were persistent rumors of men gathering in quiet places to organize a citizens' group, calling themselves a Vigilance Committee. It was said they were arming themselves, and that there was a strong possibility of a general uprising to enforce fair elections when next they fell due, in early summer.

The police force was the tool of the Know-Nothings. Their laxity, their habit of spending their time on duty in the nearest barroom, was also a byword. At that moment it was something for which Anya was grateful, another factor she had taken into her careful calculations.

As the carriage reached Dauphine Street, the bright lights and homeward-bound revelers were left behind. The gaslight streetlamps did not extend this far. The houses were shuttered and dark except for a vagrant gleam of lamplight in some upper room. The shops were closed. Quiet blanketed the buildings, broken only by the occasional barking of a dog or howling of a cat. The carriage lanterns made strange patterns of shadow and light on plastered walls as they gleamed through graceful designs of iron railings and window grills, shifting as the carriage moved. The beams probed into the gateways of dark courtyards, searching out the dark leathery leaves of palms and banana trees in the shadowed recesses.

Anya leaned forward to open the small window under the driver's seat. "Slowly, please, Solon," she called.

The pace of the carriage slackened. Anya let down the glass of the large side window and put out her head, staring intently ahead.

Then she saw it. The empty phaeton carriage, with the horse's reins anchored to the banquette by an iron weight, was where she had expected to find it. With an expression of grim satisfaction on her features, she gave another quiet order, then sat back once more.

Her landau continued to the next corner and turned right on St. Philip Street. Halfway down the block, it drew close to the banquette and came to a stop. The vehicle rocked violently as Samson and Elijah jumped down from the back. Their large forms melted away into the darkness. Solon, on instructions, got down and doused the carriage lanterns, then climbed back up to the box. A solitary horseman passed by them in the street from the opposite direction, keeping to his far right to avoid the open gutter that channeled down the center. Stillness descended.

Anya had guessed right. Ravel Duralde was with his current mistress, an actress who had been appearing at Crisp's Gaiety Theater until it closed down a few weeks before. He had left his carriage around the corner as a gentlemanly gesture toward appearances, but should soon be leaving the woman's rooms that were located over the small ground-floor grocery shop beside her landau. The only exit was the gate guarding the alleyway that led from the courtyard shared by both grocery and the rented rooms. Anya could see the wrought-iron gate in the dimness. It was tightly shut. The windows of the rooms above the grocery were dark.

Celestine, and even perhaps Madame Rosa, would be aghast to think that Anya knew enough of the clandestine affairs of Ravel Duralde to be able to find him on such a night. She was not exactly comfortable with the knowledge herself, and yet the career of the man who had killed Jean had for some time provided a certain morbid interest for her. To hear of where he was and what he was doing had been irresistible to her, rather like the compulsion to press a bruise to discover the extent of injury. Knowing of his vices made it all the more satisfactory to despise him.

In the early days, just after the duel, she had rejoiced to learn that Ravel had joined the second Lopez filibuster expedition to Cuba in August of '51, because she had hoped that he would be killed. It had seemed only right that he should have been captured in that ill-fated attempt to take the Spanish island. When he was sentenced to a dungeon in a far-off Spain, Anya had not expected to hear of him again. But he had returned almost two years later, lean and dangerous and very much alive.

The addiction to gambling he displayed after the Spanish episode had seemed promising; many young men had begun on the road to disgrace that way. But Ravel seemed blessed by Lady Luck; he could not lose. He prospered, then went on to build a fortune based on speculation financed by his earnings at the faro tables. It appeared almost as if the money meant nothing to him, however; as if he willed his own downfall. Abandoning Mammon, he joined yet another filibuster expedition, going this time with the charismatic dreamer William Walker to Nicaragua in '55.

But he returned from that one also, arriving back in New Orleans in May of '57, not quite a year ago. He was a defeated man, cast out of Central America with his leader, but it had not shown in his manner. He had also been unharmed, though he had passed through fierce fire in numberless battles.

Ravel had not signed up for the second Walker expedition the previous fall. Some said it was because of his mother, widowed now, and not well. Others less charitable said it was because he had disagreed with Walker about the proposed site of the landing. In either case, he had spared himself another defeat, and possibly a court appearance with his leader since Walker was at present under indictment for violating the laws of neutrality. Ravel's luck had held.

Anya had not really wished him harmed; she was not of a vindictive nature in spite of the antagonism she felt toward this man. Her own virulence sometimes shocked her, for no one else had ever roused such heat in her. She was normally of a warm and even disposition, not given to brooding or holding grudges, yet it seemed that there should be some retribution.

Anya leaned to crane her neck, staring up at the shuttered windows of the second-floor rooms of the actress. Unbidden, there came to her mind a picture of what was surely taking place behind those shutters. The bodies entwined, the straining muscles and overstretched senses, the creaking bed ropes were so vivid that her breath caught in her throat. She threw herself back against the seat and clenched her hands into fists, forcing the images from her. She cared not at all how Ravel Duralde amused himself. Not at all.

The actress, Simone Michel, was young and attractive in an obvious fashion. Anya had seen her in several roles earlier in the winter, and thought her not bad in her chosen profession, though lacking the polish that experience would bring. The woman also lacked the hardness of the females who had been some years in the theater, even if she could not be described as virginal. It was always women like this that Ravel Duralde had chosen to take to bed in the past, women of a certain experience and only a few easily satisfied expectations.

Surprisingly, he had not, so far as Anya knew, given a *carte blanche* to one of the attractive free women of color who were paraded for young men of fortune at the quadroon balls. It might be that such a liaison had too much of an air of permanency. The quadroons, with their mothers who had been there before to guide them, had their expectations; they required guarantees of at least a semipermanent relationship with a high degree of security.

Such reflections brought Anya to a central question. Why, given his usual choice of women, knowing her past antagonism toward him, had Ravel Duralde approached her at the ball?

That question had teased her all evening, hovering persistently at the back of her mind. He had known who she was, even masked; that much he had made plain. She would have sworn that in the past he had gone out of his way to avoid her when she was in New Orleans. Certainly she herself had seen to it, insofar as she was able, that they never came face to face. Why, then, had he violated what had been almost an unacknowledged pact between them? Why had he asked her to dance?

There came the tread of footsteps. Firm and even, they sounded from inside the courtyard, approaching the gate. Anya took her mask from her pocket and slipped it on. She opened the carriage door and stepped out onto the banquette, then paused to raise the hood of her cloak so that it lay close to her face on either side, concealing her hair. She twitched the edges of the cloak in place down the front, then swallowed on a sudden tightness in her throat, searching her mind for the words she had planned to say. Panic brushed her as her brain failed to produce them.

He was coming closer. His shadow preceded him, thrown by the light from a distant door left standing open. It appeared black and enormous and menacing. Abruptly the door was closed. The shadow disappeared. All that was left was the dark, moving form of a man. Anya took a step forward, leaving the protection of the carriage. She took another, then another.

The gate creaked open.

What was she doing?

The silent cry rose full-blown inside her. Panic beat up into her chest in a smothering wave. She could not do it. This was a mistake, a fatal mistake.

There was no time to question, no time to draw back. She took a deep breath, then spoke in tones as low and seductive as she could make them. "M'sieur Duralde, good evening."

He went still as she materialized out of the darkness. It was not the stillness of fear, however, but of swift and incisive thought, a prelude to action. The night wind stirred the short cape that fell from his shoulders, and she realized that at some time in the past few hours he had changed from his costume into evening dress. In one hand he held a cane and top hat.

Ravel Duralde heard the sound of her voice, a sound that had haunted his dreams through a thousand wakeful nights, and felt his stomach muscles tighten. He could not mistake it, any more than he could mistake her straight, slender form or the tilt of her head there in the dimness. There were few things that could bring a woman like Anya Hamilton to accost a man like him at this time of night. Attraction to him was not one of them, nor was concern for his health. An explosive mixture of rage and desire seeped into his veins, mingling with the kind of embarrassment that he had not felt since he was sixteen, the embarrassment of being discovered coming from an assignation. No one except this woman could have the power to make him so vividly aware of his shortcomings.

When he spoke, the words had the hard crack of a whip. "What in the name of living hell do you want?"

Anya was startled by his vehemence and its underlying irritation. She stared for a long moment into his eyes that were as black and fathomless as the strong coffee of the Creoles, eyes that, with his dark hair, lean face, and aquiline nose, gave him the look of a Spanish ascetic. She thought that in a moment he would turn from her and be gone. Where were Samson and Elijah? She took a hasty step closer, reaching out to him. "I only wanted to speak to you."

"For what purpose? Have you been sent to plead for Nicholls? Have you come to persuade me that, being the less worthy of the two, I should back down?"

His ability to recognize her was infuriating. She abandoned pretense, allowing her voice to rise. "And if I have?"

"You of all people should know the futility. How can you think to appeal to my better instincts when you are so certain I have none?"

"There is always the possibility that I'm wrong." She risked a glance behind him, but could see no sign of the two for whom she waited.

"So cool, so unmoved. What would you wager against the possibility? What have you to stake that will compensate for my loss of honor?"

"Honor," she said, her tone scathing. "It's only a word."

"A concept, rather, one very similar to dignity, or to chastity. If you fail to value one, does that mean you have no regard for the others?"

"What do you mean—?" she began.

The words were snatched from her lips as he reached out a hard arm to encircle her waist, dragging her against him. His mouth descended upon hers with punishing force, and with the strong fingers of his other hand he imprisoned her face, forcing her to accept his kiss.

She made a small sound of distress, pushing at him with her hands that were confined in the folds of her cloak. Abruptly the pressure eased. His lips, warm and firm, brushed hers in a wordless apology, and with the tip of his tongue he soothed their sensitive, burning surfaces. Gently then, he tested their softness, seeking the sweetness within.

A distraction had been needed; a distraction had been gained. It must not be lost, not now. Anya forced her taut muscles to relax, allowed her lips to part a mere fraction, since it seemed to be what he wanted. Smooth-nubbed, his tongue slipped into her mouth, its warmth touching the fragile inner lining. She drew in her breath as sensation flooded her. It was as if, against her will, a locked gate somewhere deep inside had been opened. Rich languor seeped along her veins. Her heartbeat quickened. Her skin seemed to glow with internal fire. There was a heaviness in the lower part of her body. Conscious thought receded. She wanted, with piercing, frightening intensity, to be closer to him. With a soft murmur, she pressed nearer. Hesitantly, she met his tongue with her own, touching and retreating, touching and twining, permitting greater, deeper access.

Without warning, there was a muffled thud. Ravel's head snapped forward under the blow. Anya felt the throbbing sting as her bottom lip split; then she was sent staggering backward, off-balance as his weight plunged toward her. With a strangled cry, she caught him, and an instant later the weight was removed as Samson and Elijah grasped his tall limp form, hauling him back upright.

His head fell forward, lolling on his shoulders, and his long legs buckled at the knees. There was a creeping stain, black in the dimness, fast spreading down onto the white of his shirt collar and his cravat. His hat of gray cashmere and his ebony cane had fallen to the banquette. The wind caught the hat, bowling it out into the street.

Anya raised a trembling hand to her mouth. "He isn't dead? You haven't killed him?"

"Seeing what he was up to, we mighta hit him a bit hard," Elijah admitted in a base rumble.

Samson grunted agreement. "It'll be better for the long ride."

"But he's bleeding so."

"Scalp cuts always bleed. We'll take his shirt off for bandages. If you'll hold the door, mam'zelle, we'll git him inside the carriage before somebody gits curious."

"Yes," she said on a sudden shuddering sigh as she looked around with the bemusement fading from her eyes. "Yes."

With more speed than care, they bundled Ravel Duralde into the landau. Anya climbed in and slammed the door. The vehicle jerked into motion, so that she was thrown across her prisoner as he lay on the seat. In the brief moment she rested upon him, she felt the lean and hard masculinity of his body. Hurriedly, she pushed off of him and knelt at his side. She slipped her hand under his head to test the extent of his wounds, and the warm wet feel of the blood in his hair sent sick remorse flooding through her.

She had been criminally overconfident. She should have known it would be no easy thing to kidnap a man and hold him prisoner. Her plan had been simple. She would distract Ravel for an instant, allowing Samson and Elijah to stun him with a blow from behind. They would bind his hands and feet if need be, put him in the carriage, and the deed would be done.

It had worked. And yet there was little pleasure for Anya in the fact. As they set out for what looked to be a nightmare journey to Beau Refuge, Anya could only castigate herself for her failure to take into consideration the things that could go wrong.

Samson, riding inside with Anya while Elijah sat on top with the driver, helped her strip the cape and frock coat from Ravel. With fingers that had an annoying tendency to tremble, Anya removed his cravat and slipped free the studs of his shirt, then held his inert figure to her in the rocking vehicle while Samson dragged his shirt down his arms. By the time they had torn the garment into bandaging, Ravel's blood had stained not only the leather seats, but her cloak and the front of her Indian costume. The wounds were bleeding so copiously that she had ordered the carriage stopped within a block or two in order for Elijah to light the carriage lanterns once more, as their bright glow was needed in order to see to dress them. Finally, with Ravel Duralde's head in her lap to cushion his injuries, they drove on into the night.

He lay so still and lifeless; his weight was so heavily inert upon her thighs. Beneath the bronze of his skin his face was pale. It was a strong face, she discovered, with a broad forehead, thick, dark brows, and high cheekbones that sloped into lean cheeks. His eyes, set deep in their sockets, were thickly lashed. His mouth was firm, with sensual curves, chiseled edges, and small, sickle-shaped smile lines at the corners that served to soften the severity of his features. His chin was square, and smoothly shaven, though with a faint blue-black shadow under the skin. His hair, where it was not covered by the thick bandage, was close-cut to prevent its thick waves from becoming curls, though it still made whorls behind his ears and on the nape of his neck, and fell onto his forehead in a short crisp curl.

What if she had killed him? It did not seem possible that a man so forceful and virile could die so easily, and yet there were few injuries more serious than those to the head. She should not care, still as much as she might despise him, she did not want to be the cause of his death.

Reaching under his cape, which they had wrapped around him, she placed her hand over his heart. It beat with strong regularity against her palm, giving her some reassurance. His skin was warm and supple, covered by a triangular mat of soft hair that was faintly abrasive to her fingertips. Beneath it she could feel the bands of muscle that wrapped his rib cage. Her touch lingered upon them. Involuntarily, she smoothed her palm in a slight, circular motion. The tip of her forefinger touched one of his small, flat paps. She jerked her hand back as if she had been burned, and in the dimness a flush mounted from her toes to her hairline. She felt as guilty as if she had been caught out in some act of promiscuity. It was long moments before she could convince herself that the impulse that had made her stroke him had been a simple desire to soothe that she might feel toward any injured person, longer still before she could relax again.

The carriage jolted and bounced on its springs. Time and again Anya was forced to catch her prisoner close, to reach across his wide shoulders and clasp him in her arms to prevent him from being thrown to the floor. His long legs sprawled across the seat, one of them bent at the knee and banging against the far door, the other stretched between the seats. She was wedged into the corner, hardly able to move. She grew stiff, and her back and arms ached from trying to hold him. All feeling left her thigh on which his head lay.

She looked across at Samson. His head was back and he was snoring none too gently. It was as if she were alone with Ravel Duralde; his life was in her hands. It was not a responsibility she wanted. She had brought it on herself, however, and could not avoid it.

If he died, it would be her fault. She would stand condemned for murder. There would be little she could say to escape prosecution; she would be lucky if she were able to prevent Samson and Elijah from being hanged. To have the deaths of three men on her hands would be a devastating thing. Rather than live with that knowledge the rest of her life, it might be better to pay the ultimate penalty herself.

Suppose someone had seen them. Suppose someone had recognized the carriage, or perhaps had identified Samson and Elijah. The size and strength of the two Negro men made them memorable; she should have thought of that. Even now, the police pursuit might be forming, coming after them. They might be overtaken on the road with Ravel lying lifeless and covered in gore in her lap. The whole story would come out.

Anya had been careless of the opinions of others, even rather wild on occasion, but she had never been involved in anything truly scandalous. If it should happen now, with Ravel Duralde, the furor would be great. This was not something that Madame Rosa could explain away to her friends as being the result of youth or grief. Her stepmother would be devastated, and Celestine too ashamed to show her face. Murray would be a laughingstock if it became known that his future sister-in-law had prevented his opponent from keeping their appointment on the field of honor.

No. She must not think such things. Things were bad enough in all truth, but not that bad. She had her prisoner. She was on her way with him to Beau Refuge. She had only to hold him for a little more than twenty-four hours, then everything would be as it was before.

She looked down once more at the still figure in her lap. She had never been this close to a man before, not for this length of time. Her father had loved her dearly, but had never been a demonstrative man. Jean, the perfect gentleman, had seldom touched her for longer than it took to help her down from her mount or carriage. He had sometimes given her swift hugs for the pleasure of it, or to comfort her, but had always released her at once. She never knew if he was afraid he would hurt or frighten her, if it was himself he feared, or if possibly it was the dictates of convention that restrained him.

It was also true that no man had kissed her as had Ravel.

Jean's caresses had been brief, almost reverential, filled with warm and boundless affection but little passion. They had involved only the quick pressure of his mouth on her cheek or lips; never had they gone deeper. She had thought them satisfactory, even exciting, until tonight

The relationship of one human being to another was curious. She disliked this man, even hated him; she despised everything he stood for, everything he was. Still, because both she and Ravel had been special to Jean, because Ravel had sought her out tonight, and later taken it into his head to chastise her with a kiss; because she had injured him and made him her captive, and because they shared this long midnight ride, there was a peculiar bond between them. It was disturbing to realize it, and she would have repudiated it if she could. Still she could not help wondering if Ravel would feel it when he woke, or, feeling it, if he would acknowledge it.

The wind, steadily rising, rocked the carriage and whipped the branches of the trees overhead. It seeped in through the cracks around the doors and windows, bringing with it a taste of rain. Thunder rumbled far away, a growling, ominous sound. Onward the carriage rolled.

At a point nearly halfway to the plantation, they stopped to rest and water the horses at a low tavern. There was no one on duty except an old Negro man, who drew water from a well to fill the horse trough, then brought out a glass of sour wine for Anya and mugs of weakly fermented sugarcane juice for the three men with her. To keep the tavern servant from coming too close, Samson served Anya. Even so, she kept Ravel covered with the carriage blanket. When the man went away, she tried to pour a little of the wine down Ravel, but it ran from the corner of his mouth.

Lightning was flashing in white brilliance before they were ready to travel once more. There was no question of putting up for the night, not with their prisoner, though the elderly servant did his best to persuade them. "You going to be soaked," he told the men on the box, shaking his grizzled head.

They knew it, but there was no help for it. Pleading urgent business, they set out once more. The rain began to fall before they had gone three miles. It began as fat, heavy drops, changing quickly into a torrent that swept toward them in wind-chased sheets. It drummed on the carriage roof and slapped against the windows. It chased in distorting rivulets down the glass, obscuring all vision. It channeled in runnels along the road, splashing as the wheels rolled through it. Behind it came a cold wind to add to the misery. Their pace slowed to a crawl. The coachman, Solon, had traveled that road countless times since he was first set up on a carriage box as a groom, and so followed the winding road by instinct and the faint gleams of the lanterns. Waterlogged, hunched against the chill, enduring, they crept on through the night.

The dawn was watery and overcast. Light rain still pecked relentlessly against the carriage roofs, falling with heavier splatting sounds as the vehicle passed under the limbs of the evergreen live oaks. Suddenly from the box above, Anya heard a rich and bitter cursing. Samson woke from his second nap of the night. Her eyes wide and her heart beating heavily in her chest, she nodded to him to find out the trouble. He opened the small front glass, calling out, "What's the matter?"

It was Elijah who answered, his tones thick with disgust. "Back there when we went under that last oak, there was a big ol' hoot owl going to roost that used us fo' his privy. Wasn't a nice thing for him to do!"

Samson roared with laughter. Anya bit her lips, trying not to grin. It was such an anticlimax compared to her fears that she could not prevent the rise of amusement, though she knew it was not funny to the men on the box. There was still the trace of a smile on her lips when, a few yards further on, the carriage turned into the drive of Beau Refuge.

Chapter Three

ﷺ ﷺ ﷺ *Beau Refuge was built in the Creole style,* one developed in the warm climate of the West Indies, with its windstorms and driving rains. Two stories high, with an attic lighted by dormers, it had a hipped roof that spread in wide overhanging eaves to cover the galleries on both front and back. The lower floor was constructed of bricks that had been coated with plaster to protect the soft clay from which they were made. Whitewashed cypress was the material of the upper floor. Brick pillars supported the gallery floors, with graceful turned colonnettes, connected by a sturdy railing, reaching from the pillars to the roof. Set back beneath the gnarled and moss-hung branches of live oaks that had been old when the first Frenchman settled in the Mississippi Valley, the house gleamed ghostly pale in the first light of dawn.

Anya directed the carriage first to the main house. Samson got down and rang the bell. When the housekeeper, Denise, who lived in dormer rooms with her son Marcel, came to the door, Anya alighted and went inside. A short time later, she emerged with a ring of keys. Climbing back into the carriage, she directed the driver toward the outbuildings to the rear of the main house.

They rolled past the carriage house and stables, then turned down a snaking roadway that was also lined with live oaks. On either side among the ancient trees were the smokehouse and cooperage and blacksmith shed, the barns and chicken houses, the great plantation bell on its stand before the small church and nearby dispensary, and the slave cabins, where smoke was beginning to rise from the chimneys into the cool and misty morning air. At the end of the road was the cotton gin.

A large building of gray weathered cypress, foursquare and

solid, it sat on the edge of the open fields. There was an enormous open doorway in each end, taking up half of the gin's width. At the right end was the entrance where the wagons piled high with picked cotton were driven inside to be unloaded. On the left was the exit where they were driven out again. The machinery inside, silent and cold and glistening with oil at this time of year, bulked like some metal monster in the dimness, reaching up into the loft. The greater portion of the loft was used for storing the baled cotton until it could be loaded onto wagons and hauled down to the river to meet the steamboat. One end, however, had been walled up to form a small room that was reached by a separate set of railed stairs. It was here that Anya's Uncle Will had been kept for so many years.

The carriage pulled up before the loading platform inside the open building. Anya got down and mounted the stairs to unlock the door of the room while Samson and Elijah lifted Ravel down from the carriage seat. She stood for a moment looking around her at the old, drab building with the cotton lint clinging to the roughhewn boards and hanging in gray strands from the spider webs and dirt dauber nests in the corners. The air was damp and chill and smelled of crushed cottonseed, rancid oil, sweat, and wet earth. It was not a place she herself would like to stay for long; it was as well Ravel Duralde's enforced sojourn would not last above a day or so.

As the two black men maneuvered Ravel's long form through the small carriage door, they bumped his head against the frame. The unconscious man groaned, a low, husky sound.

"Careful," Anya said in sharp concern.

"Yes, mam'zelle," Elijah and Samson said in unison, though the two men looked at each other in what appeared to be relief at the sound of life from their burden.

With all the gentleness of nursemaids handling a newborn, they carried the tall gentleman up the stairs to the small landing fronting the doorway of the room. Anya hung the key in its old hiding place, behind a lantern on a hook, then pushed open the door with its small grilled window and stepped before them into the room. She moved to the bed and fluffed the cotton mattress that had been folded toward the foot for airing, pulling it back down flat on the bed ropes.

There was a thick gray light filtering through the three high windows in the wall above the bed, but it was not bright enough to allow them to see well. As Samson and Elijah placed Ravel on the mattress, Anya stepped over to the lamp on the side table beside the fireplace, shook it to see how much oil it had in it, then searched out a box of phosphorus matches from the table's drawer. It took the third try to find one that was not too damp to strike, but finally the lamp was burning with a bright yellow flame. She picked it up, bringing it to the bed, where she stood staring down at the man who was her prisoner.

His coat had been discarded as being too soaked with blood to be useful, and his shirt had gone to make the rough bandage wrapped around his head. The evening cape around his shoulders had fallen aside, leaving him naked to the waist. The lamplight cast a golden sheen across his harsh features, softening their lines, and gave the sculptured planes of his chest the look of having been cast in bronze.

She had expected to feel some triumph at this moment. Instead, she was aware only of being tired and on edge and defensive. She was also, as she looked at Ravel Duralde, assailed by a feeling that was very like remorse. Lying unconscious, completely still, the man exuded such strength and masculine force that it seemed regrettable that he should be brought low by what was admittedly a base attack.

She dismissed that instant of introspection with an impatient shake of her head. It could not be helped. He had brought it upon himself. Over her shoulder, she said, "Elijah, would you please build a fire? And then go to the house and help Denise and her son bring quilts and sheets to make the bed and water to be heated. Samson, I think any chance of escape is unlikely at the moment, still it might be wise if the leg shackle was put on him."

"Very wise, mam'zelle," the man answered, and reached for the leg ring and its chain that was coiled on the floor.

She went on. "After that, I expect it would be as well if the pair of you rested a little while, then took mounts from the stable and started back to New Orleans. Most men in this situation would feel more than a little vindictive toward those who laid hands on them. M'sieur Duralde may not be one of them, but I would rather not take that chance."

"What of you, mam'zelle? If he would be angry with us, he will be much more than that with you."

"I'm a woman; he is a gentleman. What can he do?"

Samson only stared at her with his dark gaze steady in his broad face.

Anya looked away over the Negro man's shoulder, aware of the rise of color to her cheekbones. "I'll keep out of his reach once he wakes, you can be sure of that. But you must see that I can't leave until he regains his senses? I'm responsible. If he doesn't rouse by midmorning, I may have to send for a doctor."

"How can you do that?"

She made a brief gesture with one hand. "I don't know. Maybe I'll tell him that we found M'sieur Duralde on the side of the road, or that he was inspecting the gin machinery and fell. I'll think of something."

"And when Duralde comes to himself?"

"Then I will leave him alone, only sending someone, probably Denise's son Marcel, to release him toward noon tomorrow, when all possibility of his reaching the dueling ground in time is safely over."

"You must take care. It's true he is a gentleman, and yet—not entirely."

"What a snob you are," she said, a smile rising in her eyes.

"You understand what I say?"

She sobered. "Yes, I understand. And I will take care."

Later, when the two men had gone, when the water had been brought and heated and the cuts on the back of Ravel's head cleaned, neatly stitched, and bandaged once more, Anya sent the housekeeper and her son who had helped her away, then sat down beside Ravel.

Time passed. The sky was overcast and brooding with the threat of more rain, still the light increased until the lamp was no longer needed. Anya got up and blew it out, moving it back to its table. Returning to the chair beside the bed, she noticed the dried blood still crusting the side of Ravel's face, the edges of his hair, and his neck. It was unsightly, and probably uncomfortable. For something to do, as much as anything else, she brought a basin of water and a cloth and, perching on the side of the bed, began to wash away the blood with gentle strokes.

The service, she told herself, was one she would have performed for an injured animal. There was no contradiction in her impulse to make an enemy more comfortable.

His skin, though browned by the sun, was olive in tint, the legacy of his French and Spanish lineage. As she smoothed the cloth over it, she allowed her mind to wander to other aspects of his heritage.

La famille, family background, family honor, the purity of the bloodlines, was the major concern of most of the older Creole women. Many of them claimed descent from the sixty *filles à la cassette*, the casket girls, so called because they had brought with them to Louisiana their trousseaus, given to them by the Company of the Indies, in a small trunk or casket. These girls, most of them orphans of good family, had been carefully chosen as brides for men of character among the early colonists. Their reputations for piety and charity, and as faithful wives and nurturing mothers, were admirable, and had remained so through the years.

But before the *filles à la cassette* had come the correction girls, women rounded up from the prisons and correction houses of France to be sent out to Louisiana against their wills as wives in order to prevent the men from running in the woods after the Indian women. These correction girls had been troublemakers from the beginning, reluctant to work, contentious, avaricious, often immoral, and anxious for one thing only, a chance to return to France. It was a drollery often pointed out that while the casket girls had been extremely fecund, founding innumerable families, most of the correction girls, by some strange coincidence, seemed to have been barren; few in Louisiana traced their lineage to these first women to arrive.

Ravel Duralde, or rather his father, was one of the few.

This was not the only source of the feeling that Ravel was not quite what he should be. There was also the fact that his father, before his death, had belonged to the cult of the Romantics. The elder Duralde had left the church to become a freethinker, and had spent his time writing novels peopled by ghosts and strange ethereal women. His labors had barely sufficed to keep him in pen nibs, and so he had taken his wife and children into the country, forcing them to live in a crumbling ruin of a house on the charity of his old friend M'sieur Girod, the same man who had been father to Jean, Anya's fiancé.

It was on the Girod plantation that Ravel and Jean had become friends, a friendship that had continued even after Ravel's father had died and his widow, rather than staying on as she was urged to do, had returned with her son to New Orleans. Ravel's mother, a woman of practical Spanish blood, had not declined gently into perpetual widowhood as was the custom. As a final sign of the lack of breeding in the family, she had, after the indecently short interval of less than two years, married again. Her husband, Ravel's stepfather, had been a fellow Spanish Creole, a Señor Castillo, who was a *maître d'armes*, a master of fencing and swordplay, and who kept a *salle* in Exchange Alley where he taught these manly arts.

It was a canon of the Creole code that the only accepted occupations for a gentleman were those of doctor, lawyer, or politician. A man might invest in various kinds of commercial establishments, but he did not toil there. Young Duralde had not only been his stepfather's star pupil, but had often himself crossed swords in practice with the young bucks who patronized the *salle d'armes* in order to improve their expertise, and likewise their chances on the dueling field. It was this near-professional skill that made his killing of Jean so unforgivable, so like murder.

Ravel's hand lay against her hip as she leaned over him. It troubled her there and, transferring her cloth to her left hand, she reached down to pick it up, meaning to fold it across his chest out of the way. She paused a moment with her fingers curling around his palm. It was a well-shaped hand, with long, tapering fingers that hinted at strength combined with sensitivity. They clasped hers in a loose yet warm hold that was oddly disturbing in its intimacy. What would it be like, she wondered, to be touched by them in a caress? There were women who knew, many of them.

His fingers twitched, closing for an instant in a firm grasp before relaxing once more. Anya quickly placed his hand upon his chest and drew back, waiting, hardly breathing. A moment later, Ravel sighed and made a stifled sound of pain. Long moments passed without change. Anya leaned to rinse the cloth she was using in the basin on the floor beside the bed, then began once more to wash the blood from the hair in front of his temple.

Slowly, Ravel lifted his lashes to stare up at her. He allowed his gaze to rest upon the clear oval of her face, her softly parted lips, the intense sea blue of her eyes. The image of her features did not fade, nor were they distorted by fear or hatred. With a great effort, he raised his hand and touched his fingertips to the curve of her cheek. She was real, alive. A puzzled frown drew his brows together.

He whispered, "Anya?"

Anya was still, as if held by some strange compulsion. She saw the disbelief in his face and felt tightness gather in her throat. She met his dark, questing gaze, felt the pain it held like an ache in her own being. Guilt inundated her in a surging wave.

No. She must not succumb to such sentimentality merely because Ravel Duralde was injured. The guilt here was not hers alone. She jerked her head back and came swiftly to her feet. She picked up the basin of water and carried it across to place it on the table near the fireplace.

Desolation rose like a dark tide in Ravel's eyes before his eyelids fell, shielding his expression. When he lifted them once more, his gaze was blank, protected, more clearly aware. He looked around the room, silently assessing its features.

He spoke finally, the words quiet, abrupt. "The cotton gin."

Anya turned to look at him in surprise as she wiped her hands with the cloth she had wrung nearly dry. "How did you know?"

"I came here once, with Jean, when we were boys. We climbed a ladder to look in the window at your uncle."

"Yes. Yes, I suppose so."

She remembered, though she had tried to forget. It was the year she had met Jean. They had played together that summer, she and Jean and Ravel, along with half a dozen of Jean's cousins near the same age. Ravel had been slightly older, a thin, dark-haired boy with arms and legs too long for him, but who moved with the casual, effortless grace of a half-grown panther. His father had died that August, and she had not seen him again for several years, though he and Jean had attended the same schools, keeping up their acquaintance. There had been a few soirées, a ball or two, where he had put in an appearance during the period of her engagement to Jean, but in truth, other than the entertainments of the Girods, he had not been invited many places.

"Would it be too much to ask how I got here? I seem to remember meeting you on the banquette, and then—nothing."

She watched him a long moment, trying to decide if he had failed to mention the kiss out of a wish to save her embarrassment, or if he had truly forgotten it. The nerves strung through her body were so taut that it seemed they must begin to fray like overstretched rope. Inside her chest was a leaden weight of doubt and apprehension that was not helped by the steady search of his black gaze.

Finally she said, "I brought you."

"That is fairly obvious. What exercises my mind is, how?"

"I rendered you unconscious and put you in a carriage."

"You?"

The skepticism in his tone brought the rise of irritation. "Is that so impossible?"

"Not impossible, but highly unlikely. Never mind. I will accept that you had accomplices, and can even guess at who they were."

"I doubt that."

"Judging from the ache in my head, it was your father's blacksmiths. I did hear, I think, that you had seen that they were freed and found them employment in the city."

"You believe I would involve them in something like this?"

"I don't think you would involve anyone else."

"You are at liberty to think as you please." He could not know, and she would admit nothing.

"Even if I am at liberty to do little else?"

His lips curled at the corners, but Anya did not make the mistake of thinking he was amused. She gave him a level look. "Now that you are awake, perhaps you would like some brandy for your headache."

"I would prefer whiskey, neat, but not now. Why, Anya?"

"Surely you can guess." She crossed her arms over her chest in what she recognized and deplored as a defensive gesture.

He watched her, his eyes bleak. "You think you can stop the duel."

She returned his gaze, and her voice was firm as she answered. "I don't think it, I know. I am going to stop it."

Anger flared white-hot into his face. He raised himself to one elbow, grimacing, lifting a hand to the bandage around his head, then letting it fall. "Do you think you can behave like a hoyden for the rest of your life and get away with it? What are you doing, trying to ruin yourself?"

"You're a fine one to lecture!"

"None better, because I know what I'm talking about. I've watched your wild career for years, watched you deliberately break every rule of ladylike behavior, watched you turn yourself into a female farmer, burying yourself on this plantation. It won't help; it won't bring Jean back!"

He had watched her. There was no time to consider the implications of that admission, nor did she have any inclination to in her anger and distress. "There would be no need for me to bury myself if you had not killed Jean!"

Pain swept across his face. His voice was low, ragged, as he answered. "Don't you think I know that?"

"Then you can hardly be surprised that I want to save Murray Nicholls from the same fate."

"That is another matter entirely. I must meet him."

"Not if I can help it. And I can." Her lips were a firm line in her face as she glared at him.

He held her gaze for a long moment, then whipped aside the quilts that covered him and surged upward, swinging his feet off the bed to stand. He took a step, and the color drained from his face. He swayed. As he swung back toward the bed, the leg shackle wrapped around his ankles to throw him off-balance. He fell full length, crashing into the bed, sending it slamming against the wall. His torso struck the mattress. He held to it, dragging it half off the bed as he slid to a sitting position on the floor.

Anya ran to him, kneeling, putting out her hand to catch his shoulder. "Are you all right?"

His breathing was harsh and heavy. It was a moment before he opened his eyes, and when he did they were filled with such black rage that she recoiled.

"Should I be?" he asked, his voice rasping as he clamped shaking hands to his head. "God!"

She got to her feet and stood over him, her body stiffly upright. "I'm sorry about your head. It wouldn't have happened if you hadn't kissed me."

He lowered his hands, sending her a skeptical look from the

corners of his eyes. "I would be interested to hear how you expected to chain me up like a dog without it. What was the alternative, a nice glass of wine with knockout drops?"

"There might have been, if I had thought of it, but I didn't have long to plan. As it was, they weren't supposed to hit you so hard."

He was still for long moments, then he gave a soft sigh and pulled himself slowly up. She reached to help him, but he did not even glance at her hand. She retreated, clasping her fingers tightly together before her.

He turned to sit down heavily on the edge of the bed. "All right," he said, his voice quiet, "maybe I deserved it. You have made your point. Now you can let me go."

"I will let you go at noon tomorrow."

"Noon?" he asked, frowning, then an instant later his face cleared. "I see. You realize, don't you, that if I fail to appear on the dueling field I will have not a shred of honor left? You know that I will be called a coward, that I will be a laughingstock?"

The reasonableness of his tone made her uneasy, but she refused to show it. "You are Ravel Duralde, the idol of the callow young men just out on the town, a man who has gone to the field of honor a dozen times and killed his man at least three of those times out. You can always say you were ill, detained. The courage of other men might be doubted, but not yours. As for your precious honor—"

"Don't," he said, the word softly incisive.

"Very well, but don't talk to me of how important it is for you to attend this duel!"

"But what is it you hope to gain? The meeting will only be postponed."

She made a swift, impatient gesture. "Oh, come, I've seen Jose Quintero's dueling code and heard men quoting the *Nouveau Code du Duel* of the Comte du Verger de Saint Thomas. A duel at which one of the contestants fails to appear cannot be held again."

"Nicholls and I could meet later, for a different cause," he pointed out.

"There is no reason why you should. You hardly know Murray, and may never come in contact with him again. Anything that he may have said to provoke you was meant only to protect me. He feels responsible, since he will soon be a member of our family.''

When he spoke, his tone was hard. ''So I understood. And how will Nicholls feel about a prospective sister-in-law who has created one of the biggest scandals ever to break over New Orleans? That is what it will be, you know. You can't honestly think that you can keep me here without the knowledge becoming public property!''

''I think I can, for a short time. You are hardly likely to complain; you would become that laughingstock you spoke of. And if it's the servants who are worrying you, only my house-keeper and her son know, and they can be trusted not to talk.''

He lay down and stretched out, supporting himself on one elbow. His voice soft, he asked, ''And what of when the time has elapsed and you deign to release me?''

A faint frown drew her brows together. ''I don't know what you mean. You will be free to leave, of course.''

''Suppose I decide not to go?''

''Why should you stay?''

''Oh, I can think of a reason or two,'' he said softly, his dark gaze resting on her lips, moving down over the soft fullness of her breasts, the narrow span of her waist, and the curves of her hips displayed by the soft draping of the stained doeskin costume she still wore. ''A woman desperate enough to go out and kid-nap herself a man should be stimulating company.''

''Desperate! Don't be ridiculous.'' Her heartbeat increased, thudding heavily against her ribs.

''It is ridiculous? What would you do, Anya, my love, if I were to walk into your house and make myself at home at your table, in your bedchamber, in your bed?''

''I am not your love,'' she said, her eyes narrowing. ''Step one foot in my house uninvited, and I'll have you thrown out so fast you'll have to send for your shadow!''

''Who will do the job? Your servants? It would mean the life of any slave who should touch me. The blacksmiths? Assault is a serious charge even for free Negroes. Murray Nicholls? But if all this is to protect him from my wrath, it would be defeating the purpose to expose him to it. Who then?''

The temerity of the man was infuriating. That he would seek to frighten her while lying flat on his back with her needlework in his scalp defied belief. And yet, there was in his long body as he reclined on the bed a sense of power only temporarily subdued. His cape had fallen away when he tried to rise, and he was bare to the waist; still, he made no attempt to cover himself, permitting her to gaze as she would at the corded muscles of his arms and shoulders, the flat planes of his chest marked by the copper-colored rounds of his paps, the fine, curling black hair that narrowed from the triangular furring on his chest to a thin line as it disappeared under the waist of his trousers. Unprincipled, rakish, intensely masculine, he exuded a threat that was far from subtle.

Anya's stomach muscles tightened. Never had she been so aware of a man before. Never. Nor could she ever remember being so disturbed, so unsure of herself and a situation. She did not like it. With slow emphasis, she answered him, "I will do it myself."

"Would you care to explain how?"

"I have a pistol, and I know how to use it."

A faint smile touched Ravel's lips. She was quite a woman. Most others of her sex that he knew would have stammered and blushed and run away at the suggestion he had just made, or else fluttered their lashes in a coy pretense of misunderstanding or in blatant invitation. Of course, such women would never have dared attempt to hold him prisoner. Admiration had its limits.

He said, "I have been shot at before."

She lifted a brow as she selected a new means of defense. "Tell me, are your threats an example of the honor that you refuse to have called into question? I was warned that you were not quite a gentleman. I see why."

"Since you are not quite a lady," he drawled, "it hardly matters."

"Not a lady? That's ridiculous!" The taunt had touched a nerve, one made more sensitive by self-doubt.

"On the contrary. Show me, if you can, an etiquette book or ladies' journal that covers this situation. What might the heading be: 'The Proper Way to Interest a Man'?"

"I don't want your interest," she said in waspish tones. "I only want to hold you for a few hours."

His voice dulcet, he said, "You may hold me for as long as you please."

"That isn't what I meant!"

"Isn't it? With some women it's necessary to guess what they want. But I remember; you don't like guessing games. We could cease playing and begin in earnest."

She drew herself up, looking down at him with cold hauteur. "It's plain that the blows on the head have addled your senses. You need rest. I will leave you to it."

"You would leave me without food and water? I could do with breakfast."

That he was hungry was a good sign. "I will send it," she said over her shoulder.

The faint click of the chain was her only warning. She glanced back to see him easing from the bed. As swift as a doe scenting danger, she leaped away, plunging across the room, hitting the wall near the door with a hard, jarring crash.

There was no need to go farther. She knew exactly the limits of Ravel's chain, for a semicircular depression was worn in the floor at its outermost limits, caused by years of her uncle's pacing. Even if Ravel stretched out the length of his body, he could not quite reach her. The arrangement had been planned that way. The man being held could draw near to the fire in the room's fireplace but not reach the flames. He had access to the bed, the armoire, and the eating table, but not the lamp on the side table between the fireplace and the door. His comfort was assured, but so was his safety. And the safety also of whoever might enter to tend the fire, bring food, or see to his comfort.

Anya was trembling, her heart beating high in her throat. Her eyes were dark blue with angry fright as she stared across the room at Ravel Duralde. He had subsided back onto the bed, supporting himself on one elbow. He looked at the trench worn into the floor and the length of the chain that he held in his hand where he had picked it up to prevent it dragging. He lifted his black gaze to Anya where she stood.

His voice deep and even, he said, "Next time."

There would not be a next time, not if she could help it. Anya made that silent vow as she marched away from the cotton gin. She would not go near the man another time. He was not seriously injured; he could not be if he had an appetite. If he was not hungry, if the pretense had been no more than a ploy to gain sympathy, then it would serve him right if she did desert him. She would send the whiskey for his headache and something for him to eat, and that would be the end of it. She did not care if she never saw him again. Let Denise and Marcel tend to the man.

He was not that easily dismissed, however. She could not stop thinking of him and the things he had said, not while she bathed the grime of the night away in a tub of hot water, not while she lay in her bed with the curtains drawn and the quilts up to her chin, trying to rest after being awake all night.

Would he really do the things he threatened? Would he force himself into her house, her bed, if he were freed? He could not be so vindictive. Could he?

It didn't seem likely. If he had not been more of a gentleman than she had been led to expect, he would have cursed her roundly for the predicament in which he found himself. She had been waiting for that, but it had not come. Perhaps he had been too weak for such a violent reaction? Perhaps he was saving his strength for the vengeance he preferred, the one he had outlined?

Even if he were, she must release him. She could not keep him locked up a moment longer than necessary. The rest of the house servants and the field hands would soon discover his whereabouts, if they didn't know already after all the problems and extra trips back and forth to the cotton gin created by his injuries. The news would fly from plantation to plantation and all the way to New Orleans faster than a man on a good horse could ride. It was amazing, the speed and accuracy of the news on the slave grapevine. Her good name would be in jeopardy, as Ravel had said.

She must take care for Madame Rosa's and Celestine's sakes. Despite Ravel's accusations, ruining herself was not part of her plans.

Was she burying herself as he had said?

She could see how it might appear that way, but she enjoyed riding over the plantation, seeing after the crops and animals and the people who lived and worked on the place. She did not care for parties and idle gossip, the endless round of visits and entertainments where the same faces were seen day after day, night after night. She had no aptitude for doing Berlin work in colored wool or fashioning flowers out of wax or weaving ornaments out of hair carefully saved from her nightly brushing. She enjoyed fine clothes and the search for the items to complement them as much as the next woman, but could not bear to sit in the salon waiting for callers, looking like a dressed-up doll, or else lying at ease eating chocolate bonbons and reading novels. She liked to do things, to see things accomplished. To her, it was the idle ladies with nothing to do who were less than alive.

It made her uneasy to think of Ravel Duralde watching her, knowing so much about her. Why should he do that, unless it was out of guilt for the way he had interfered in her life? If he had not killed Jean, she would be a young matron by now, probably with three or four children. Her time would be spent supervising the nursery and her house, planning meals for her husband, seeing to his comfort, occupying his bed. She would have grown rather fuller of figure, no doubt, from childbearing, and perhaps quieter in her manner. The only thing she would know of what was happening in the fields or with the selling of their crops and animals would be what Jean chose to tell her. Her dependence for news and opinions of events would be entirely on him.

She frowned up at the gathered silk lining of the tester above her bed. Such a quiet round of days might well have been stultifying. But she would have had Jean, of course. They would have talked and laughed and played with their children, and at night they would have slept side by side in their bed.

She tried, just for a brief and rather shamed moment, to think of what it would have been like to lie in Jean's arms, to make love. The image would not come. Instead, she saw the lean features and broad chest of Ravel Duralde.

She flung herself over in the bed, pushing at her pillow. He was out there in the cotton gin. Her prisoner. She had captured the Black Knight, the premier duelist in New Orleans, the man they had called El Tigre when he fought with the phalangists of William Walker in Central America.

She had caged the tiger. But how could she let him go? How could she?

Anya knelt on the ground, reaching into the flower bed to grasp handfuls of the crisp winter grass that threatened to choke the verbena. Nearby, in this back garden of Beau Refuge, a young Negro boy of twelve or thirteen speared at dead leaves as if the rake he was wielding were a lethal weapon. The verbena bed fronted a row of spirea in full bloom, with arching branches of white as fine and full as egret plumes. Beyond the end of the lacy gray-green growth of verbena with its purple flowers was a row of daffodils whose yellow trumpets were just opening. A wind with a moist chill in its breath waved the spirea branches and set the daffodils to dancing on their stems.

"Joseph," she called, "watch out for the bulbs."

"Yes, mam'zelle," he said, but continued to mangle the stems of the daffodils as he searched out leaves.

"The yellow flowers, be careful of them!"

"Oh, yes, mam'zelle!"

The housekeeper Denise, coming along the brick path that led from the house, stopped beside Anya with her hands on her ample hips. The wind flapped her apron and the knotted ends, like cats ears, of the kerchief tied around her head. "You'll never make a gardener of that boy."

"I don't know; at least he's willing."

"His mind wanders from what he should be doing."

"His is not the only one," Anya said, a rueful smile on her lips as she nodded her head toward several sprigs of verbena she had managed to pull up with the grass.

"Humph. It's a wonder there's any flowers left in that bed." The housekeeper lowered her voice. "And if it's the man in the gin on you' mind, it's that one I come to talk to you about."

51

at the yard boy, then rose to her feet, moving
hat is it?''

e don't eat. When I went for the tray with his noon meal
just now, he was lyin' there with his face to the wall. He hadn't
touched his food, and he didn't answer when I talked to him.''

A frown appeared between Anya's eyes. "Do you think he's
worse?''

"I couldn't say, but it don't look good.''

There was disapproval in the housekeeper's voice. Massively
built, the woman had the high cheekbones and deep-set eyes of
the Indian warrior who had been her grandfather. Her grand-
mother, in a bid for freedom some ninety years before, had run
away, taking to the woods. There she had found shelter with the
Choctaws. She had lived with them for a time, but, discovering
that having her freedom did not make up for the loss of the
company of her own kind and the amusements of the plantation
and New Orleans in the winter, she had returned to her old
master. There had been a child born of her sojourn, however,
and Denise was the child of that child. Because of her Indian
blood, the other slaves in the quarters said that Denise had "red
bones.'' It gave her distinction, and added luster to her reputation as a woman with a temper.

With her soft lips tightly pressed together, Anya considered
the situation. She had not meant to go near Ravel Duralde again.
"I suppose I had better see about him.''

She gave a few instructions to Joseph, then moved off toward
the cotton gin. Her strides were firm, kicking out her skirts in
front of her, though she recognized the faint tremor along her
nerves as apprehension. Her thoughts played cautiously with the
fear that Ravel might be developing brain fever or some kind of
inflammation from his wounds, but she was by no means sure
that a major part of her disturbance wasn't from sheer reluctance
to face her prisoner.

The sky was overcast, banked with low clouds. The wind was
out of the north. Anya pulled the coat she wore, an old frock
coat of her father's that she had saved for outdoor chores, about
her more closely as she looked around at the heavens. They
needed a south wind to bring back the warmth from the gulf,
though it would probably mean more rain. It would come, per-

haps in a few hours, perhaps in a day or two. Hopefully, by the time it did, Ravel would be gone.

The cotton gin was dim and deserted, a brooding hulk of a building. Anya took down the key of the room from where it hung on a strip of leather behind the pierced tin lantern. She turned the key in the heavy lock, then as a precaution, one always observed by her father, hung the key back up before pulling open the door.

It was dim in the room, and rather chilly. The fire had burned down to a bed of pulsing red coals. Ravel turned from the wall onto his back as she entered, but only lay watching without speaking as she stirred the embers with a poker and put three or four sticks of wood on the fire. The split oak caught with a muffled roar. Straightening, she placed her back to the leaping flames, clasping her hands behind her to warm them.

She met Ravel's black gaze, and held it with an effort. "Do you have fever?"

"Not that I know of," he said evenly.

"Why didn't you eat your food?"

"Beef broth, coddled eggs, and custard? I'm not an invalid."

"I would have thought," she said, restraining her worry and irritation with an effort, "that you must have eaten worse things while you were in prison in Spain."

"Frequently. This isn't Spain." He lifted his leg and the chain links of his shackle clanked together with a cold sound. "I swore when I was released from the Spanish dungeons that I would die before allowing myself to be chained again. Strange how things work out."

It was a moment before she spoke; then she said slowly, "I hadn't thought of what a reminder this must be."

"Yes," he said, his voice dry, "but you don't intend to remove the shackle."

"No."

He turned his head, staring up at the ceiling. "Your compassion is overwhelming."

"Surely you didn't expect anything else?"

"I didn't expect to be kidnapped, either."

"For that," she said firmly, "I have no apologies. I will send you something else to eat." She stepped away from the fire, moving toward the door.

He pushed erect in a fluid movement. "Don't go! Stay awhile, talk to me."

With her hand on the door, she paused. "There is no point. We can only disagree."

"It doesn't matter. Anything is better than—" He stopped. He let himself back down on the mattress, his face expressionless, a mask of hard control. "Forget it."

Was it real, this dislike of being confined that he showed, of being left here alone, or was it a trick? She weighed the question carefully, her teeth set in her bottom lip. There were many who could not bear small, close places or to have their freedom of movement restricted; her father had been one of them. After Ravel's enforced stay in Spain, it would not be surprising if he were the same. He was being confined at her instigation, for no real fault except the high-handed temper that had caused him to challenge Murray. Did that not make him in some peculiar fashion her guest? In which case, wasn't it her responsibility to entertain him? That she despised him made no difference to that obligation. A hostess was often forced to amuse people she cordially disliked.

With stiff reluctance, she turned and moved to the armchair of split and faded brocade that sat in the corner, drawing it away from the fireplace so that it faced the bed with the back to the door. She sat down. Ravel turned his head to stare at her a long moment. Finally he shifted, sitting up and leaning with his back against the wall. Whether from manners or the coolness of the room, he pulled a quilt up and draped it around him like an Indian's blanket. Drawing one leg up, he rested his forearm on his knee.

Anya glanced at him, then away again. There was another reason she had acceded to his request, she told herself. It was curiosity, an irresistible desire to see what other weaknesses the man might reveal. She leaned her head back, allowing her gaze to move once more to the man in the narrow bed.

"Was it so bad in prison?" she asked quietly, almost at random.

"It wasn't pleasant."

"You were—mistreated?"

"No more than in any other prison," he said with a small movement of wide shoulders. "I was kept alone in a cell for two years. The worst of it was the feeling that the world had forgotten us, those of us who were sentenced and sent to Spain. But it was better than the alternative."

"Which was?"

"Death by firing squad."

"Yes," Anya said with a faint shudder. It was a moment before she went on, and then her tone was reflective. "They are strange men, the leaders of the filibuster expeditions like the ones to Cuba and to Nicaragua. Why do they do it?"

"For glory, for greed, because they are driven like the explorers by a need to conquer something, to prove themselves. It would be hard to find two men more different than Narciso Lopez and William Walker, and yet they both wanted to carve out empires, and have the privilege of turning those empires over to the United States."

"With themselves as the leaders."

He inclined his head in agreement. "Of course. That's only human nature."

"Could they really have done that?"

"About Lopez, I'm not sure; Spain has a strong presence in Cuba. But Walker certainly could have. He was president of Nicaragua for some months. All Washington had to do was give him official sanction and some sign of military backing. Congress and the president failed to do that, in spite of previous encouragement. They gave a lot of reasons, but in fact it was Northern monied interests, and Cornelius Vanderbilt in particular, that swayed them. The moment when intervention could have been successful passed. Walker failed."

"I believe I read that it was a ship of the United States Navy, under a Captain Paulding, who shelled Walker's men and finally captured him. Did that really happen?"

"It did indeed."

"But why? Walker and his men were Americans."

"A bagatelle. The government meant to disassociate the United States from the undertaking so that Vanderbilt could continue to do business, to run his steamers through the Nicaragua route from the Atlantic to the Pacific Ocean. Paulding exceeded his orders officially, but probably not unofficially. I believe they are going to give him a medal.''

There was bitterness in his voice, and also a hint of hardships endured and tragedies remembered. Anya said slowly, ''I can see what Walker hoped to gain, but what of the others, the men who fought?''

''They went for the promise of land, grants of hundreds, even thousands of acres, and for a fresh start in a new country, on a new frontier. There were also those who went for the sake of the fight, the excitement of it. And as always, there were a few who went to escape hanging here.''

''And you? Why did you go with them?''

''I went,'' he said with deliberation, ''to escape my own personal demons.''

''Meaning?''

He turned his head, his dark eyes shadowed with torment. ''Surely you can guess?''

For a short while there had been something very like a truce between them. It was gone. ''The duel.''

''The duel,'' he repeated. ''I killed my dearest friend. On a moonlit night when the world was cool and beautiful and touched with silver, I pushed my sword through his body like a pin into a butterfly, and watched him die.''

She drew in her breath, tried to speak, then had to stop and clear her throat of the lump of anger and pain that had gathered there. ''There must have been more to that night than that.''

He was quiet. He looked down at the chain on his ankle, picking up the links and letting them drop so that they made a musical clinking in the silence.

''Well?''

''I could tell you, but I doubt you would believe it.''

''There have been many things said about you, but I've never heard that you were a liar.''

''A damaging admission. Take care, or you may find something to approve.''

There was a raw edge to his voice. She chose to disregard it. ''We were talking about the duel.''

''It might be best if we didn't.''

"Why?" she asked, her voice hard. "Is there something you prefer that I not know?"

"No, I—"

"Something that reflects upon you?"

"No!"

"Some reason for that stupid contest besides the one given out?"

"It was a mistake to mention it. Let it go."

"I can't!" she cried, leaning forward, her eyes dark blue and luminous with unshed tears. "Don't you see I can't?"

"Neither can I."

He leaned his head back with a sigh, staring at nothing. At last he went on. "It's nothing so different. There were the six of us, the moonlight, the empty dueling field under the oaks. We paired off. It was a simple contest of skill, at first. We were all a little tipsy, perhaps some of us more than a little. There was a great deal of laughing and slipping around in the dew. Then I pinked Jean in the arm. Jean flared up in a rage. I never knew before that night that he resented my hard-earned skill with a blade, but apparently he did. More than that, I had ruined his new frock coat."

"His frock coat." She repeated the words as if they had no meaning.

"It may sound funny, a trivial thing, but men have died before for less. In any case, Jean wouldn't put his sword down, but demanded that we continue. He lunged, I parried and began a riposte, all the while talking to him, trying to make him see reason."

There was more; Anya knew it from the sound of his voice. She did not want to hear it, still it was as if she were driven to it. "And then?"

"There is a point in many moves of swordplay past which it is impossible to draw back. I was driving forward in a riposte, intending to nick him in the arm once more as a warning. He slipped in the wet grass, lurched toward me. My sword point caught—"

"Stop! Please."

Her breasts rose and fell with the swiftness of her breathing and her heart was beating so hard it jarred the bodice of her gown. Her hands were clenched on the arms of the chair. When his voice ceased, she closed her eyes. Still the image of the duel he had conjured up with his words burned in her mind.

"You did ask," he said, his voice shaded with weariness.

She lifted her lashes to stare at him with a cold and leaden feeling inside her. His face there in the dim room was pale, shadowed by a dark growth of beard on his chin, and with the faint glint of perspiration on his forehead. His black eyes were steady though the set of his mouth was grim.

"Your skill," she said, the words scathing. "Is that what you call your ability to kill other men on the dueling field? How does it feel to know that you can take a life at will? Do you enjoy it? Does it make you feel good to know that other men fear you?"

A muscle clenched in his jaw, then relaxed again. When he spoke, the words were even. "I have never sought a fight or killed a man if there was another choice."

"Oh, come! Surely you don't expect me to believe that."

"I repeat—"

"What of Murray? He would never have dreamed of challenging you, never in this life!"

"It's surprising what young men will do—if they think it will increase their prestige. Half the meetings I have had were with fools who thought it would be a fine thing to be able to say they had drawn blood from Ravel Duralde."

"So you killed them for their effrontery."

"You would have preferred that I had died instead?" he asked, then answered himself. "Foolish question; of course you would."

"I would prefer," she said, her tones hard, "that no one die in a duel ever again."

"A noble sentiment, but impractical."

Her eyes blazed with blue fire at his reply. "Why? Why is it so impractical to ask that men settle their differences without resorting to bloodshed? Is it so impossible for them to be reasonable, rational men and still have pride and honor?"

"I understand how you feel," he answered, his tones deep and curiously gentle, "but the custom of the duel has its uses. The threat of it curbs the excesses of braggarts and bullies, guards the sanctity of the family by discouraging adultery, and protects females from unwanted attention. It's rooted in the ideals of chivalry, a means of insuring that men live up to their better instincts, that they keep to the canons of decent behavior or face the consequences. And it allows them to take a portion of their protection into their own hands, without relying exclusively on a police force that may or may not be there when they are needed.''

That he would dare attempt to defend the practice of dueling to her sent cold fury racing through her veins. She controlled it, saying in sweetly puzzled tones, ''A primitive means of deciding the justice of an issue, surely? By might instead of right? What if it's the bully who kills his opponent, or the wronged husband who dies instead of his wife's seducer? And what is there in the code duello to prevent a man who is known to be superior with a sword or pistol from playing the complete villain, doing precisely as he pleases, even forcing himself upon any woman he chooses?''

He was not fooled. Bluntly he asked, ''A man like me?''

''Exactly.'' Her answer was grim.

''Nothing.''

Ravel watched the angry color rise into her face with a certain bemusement overlaid by savage satisfaction. If she expected him to accept her insults as well as the situation in which she had placed him, she was going to be disappointed. He wanted her to remain where she was, talking to him, with a longing that came as a severe shock; still, he was not ready to retain her company at any price.

Dear God, but she was beautiful, sitting there in her old coat that was too large for her, with her hair windblown and straggling from its knot on top of her head and her hands as grubby as any schoolboy's. He would like to draw her down beside him, to take down her hair and spread it out on his pillow like a shawl of rich, glowing silk, to press his lips to hers, warming them, melting their thin, tight line until they opened softly, sweetly, to him. Oh, yes, she was beautiful, a natural, desirable woman. She was also unattainable. Maddeningly so.

Ravel broke the silence, his tone abrupt. ''What have you been doing to yourself?''

''What do you mean?'' She scowled at him.

"You look worse than an Irish washerwoman in that ragged coat, with your hair in your face and dirt under your nails."

"I regret that my appearance offends you," she said with cold sarcasm. "I was working in the garden."

"Don't you have people to do that for you?"

"No one I trust in my verbena beds. Besides, I like it."

"As you like riding about the fields until you are so freckled no amount of the renowned Antephelic Milk will remove them?"

"The state of my complexion is not your concern!"

"It might be to your future husband."

"As I have no intention of getting married, it doesn't matter."

"You mean to live like a nun for the rest of your life? That's ridiculous."

She pushed to her feet, her voice rising. "Why is it ridiculous? I don't see you leaping into matrimony!"

"Men are able to arrange these matters without it."

"Oh, yes, certainly, but it isn't the same thing, is it? What of companionship and children and a home and—and love?" If the words she spoke were a trifle disjointed, she ignored it.

"What of them?"

"Don't they matter?"

"They matter," he said, "they matter a great deal, but as I am unlikely to have them—"

"Why should you be?"

"Perhaps it's because I am not quite a gentleman?"

His words were mocking, but carried also a lash of bitterness. Anya, hearing it, felt a surge of unwilling empathy. For all his bravado, for all the adulation heaped upon him because of his repute as a duelist and his success with women, he knew no contentment. He was, in his way, as haunted by the death of Jean as she herself. More, because of his birth, he was as firmly and forever outside the magic Creole circle of society as she was due to her *américain* blood.

She swung from him in agitation, pacing toward the window in the corner behind his bed. She did not want to look at him, did not want to acknowledge any common bond between them. She wanted to hate him, to blame him for what had become of her life, for its emptiness. She did not want to think of him as able to feel pain and remorse, hunger and cold, loneliness and fear, but rather to think of him as the Black Knight, armored in steel, a hard and insensitive killer. She did not want to admit that the sight of his long, lean body, his muscled shoulders, bronze features, and the black pools of his eyes made her intensely aware of him as an attractive man; she wanted instead to find him repulsive, twisted of soul and ugly.

She lifted her gaze to the small grilled window where beyond the glass the gray sky of early spring pressed close. She drew a deep breath and let it out slowly. When she thought she could speak without rancor or the tremors of distress, she turned toward the bed.

"I will send you something else to eat, perhaps potato soup along with a flank steak and a bottle of wine. Afterward, if you care for it, I might also order a bath. And I . . . may be able to find my father's razor and a strop to sharpen it."

He sat up, his gaze upon her narrowing. "That's most thoughtful of you."

"Not at all," she said, coldly polite. "Is there anything else you require?"

"A shirt wouldn't come amiss, if there is one available."

His tone was carefully neutral, not at all demanding. She supposed that after tearing his linen up for bandaging, the least she could do was provide some kind of substitute. Her tone colorless, she said, "Unfortunately, I gave most of my father's clothes to the man who had been his valet. Not long ago, however, I bought a supply of red flannel shirts for the field hands, if you would care to have one of those."

He smiled with real amusement rising to his eyes. "Do you expect me to be offended? Believe me, I will be too grateful for the warmth. The flannel shirt will be fine."

"Very well. I'll send it also." She turned away, moving toward the door.

"Anya?"

She paused, her back to him. "My name," she said stiffly, "is Mademoiselle Hamilton."

"You have been Anya to me for some time."

The low timbre of his voice sent a shiver along her nerves,

though she did not quite catch the words. She turned slowly to face him. ''What did you say?''

Without discernible hesitation, he said, ''You have been very kind. Would you be kinder still, and agree to have dinner with me later this evening? That hour of the day is always the worst.''

''I don't know. I'll have to see what else requires my attention,'' she answered. Swinging away, she let herself from the room.

She turned the key and hung it back on its hook, then went slowly down the stairs with her hand trailing along the rough cypress banister railing. Why hadn't she refused his request for her company? She had no intention of returning to eat with him, no matter how lonely and confined he might be, and she should have said so at once.

What was the matter with her? It was almost as if she didn't know her own mind, her own feelings. Usually when she decided on a course, she kept to it without misgivings, without this feeling of doubt and low spirits. She made her arrangements, followed them, and accepted the results, whatever they might be.

Not this time.

Granted, she had never done anything quite like this before, never involved herself in an affair with such potentially serious consequences. There had never before been a time when she felt in danger of losing control of the situation.

Until now.

It was possible that her doubts stemmed from the identity of her prisoner. She had hated Ravel Duralde for a long time, and hate was a powerful emotion. To have the object of it near her, at her mercy, could not help but affect her. The fact that she was disturbed by his presence should not be surprising, nor was it unreasonable for her to be upset by the violent swings in her feelings toward him. Though she had reason to despise him, she could also feel compassion for his predicament, and remorse for her part in it. What could be more natural?

More, she was a normal woman, quite capable of responding to a handsome and virile man in a purely physical way. It was a matter of animal forces, nothing more. It had no meaning. The feeling would disappear once she was away from him. She would forget that he had kissed her, forget the feel of his warm and mobile mouth upon hers, the strength of his arms about her, the hard length of his body against hers. She would.

By this time tomorrow, the ordeal would be over. Ravel Duralde would be gone. In the meantime, she certainly would not be eating her dinner at the cotton gin.

Anya finished weeding the bed of verbena. She and Joseph piled the leaves he had raked around the azaleas and camelias, the hydrangeas and winter honeysuckles and cape jasmines of the back garden. She pruned the huge old muscadine grapevine on its pergola in the side garden, and also the fig trees that grew behind the laundry, then put down the cuttings to root in a shady bed of sand beside the door of the detached kitchen building, where the dishwater as it was thrown out would keep them constantly moist. Now and then she stopped to breathe the fresh air of spring, to smell the wafting fragrances of the spirea and daffodils and white winter honeysuckle, and the rich scent of the yellow jasmine coming from the tangle of vines that grew along the fencerow near the house. She did not, insofar as she was able to prevent it, think about Ravel Duralde.

When the light began to fade, she dismissed Joseph and went into the house. Feeling grimy and gritty from head to toe, she ordered a bath brought to her room. She soaked in the hot, steaming water for a time, then lathered herself with fine-milled Lubin's soap perfumed with an extract of damask roses. She also rubbed the rich lather through her hair, enjoying the scent and silken feel of it. The smell of roses lingered upon her skin and among her tresses even after she had rinsed the soap away and blotted the water from her body with thick Turkish toweling, after she had dried the shining curtain of her hair before the fire.

She was not in the habit of dressing for dinner while alone at the plantation. When Madame Rosa and Celestine were in residence it was different, of course, but when there was only herself at the dining room table it seemed a needless labor to change into an evening gown. Often, she avoided the dining room altogether, preferring to have a tray in her room. On these occasions, she usually relaxed before the fire in no more than her dressing gown.

This evening, however, she felt an urge to dress formally, to look her best. It had nothing whatever to do with the slighting comments on her appearance made by Ravel, of course. She could permit herself a whim now and then surely? She had been most informal, even sloppy, all day; tonight she would have a *grande toilette*.

Denise served as Anya's maid. The woman had been her nurse when Anya first came to the plantation as a young, frightened girl without a mother. After so many years, Denise felt it her proprietorial right to dress Anya, and also to scold her and to worry over her. On this evening, the older woman helped her into underclothing and tightened the strings of her new empress corset. She lifted her quilted petticoats with their embroidered hems over her head, settling them into place for warmth and to prevent her cage crinoline from swinging like a bell. Next came the crinoline itself, an affair of five graduated sizes of hoops covered with cloth tapes, all together with straps. Over this went another layer of petticoats, also embroidered and edged with lace, and padding to prevent the crinoline's hoops from showing through like bones under her gown.

The gown itself was of bayadere silk in shades of pink to deepest rose red. It had been made up in France and imported by Giquel and Jaison on Chartres Street, the emporium where she had bought it. Very little had been required to perfect the fit, no more than a minor alteration of the bodice seams to make it conform to her slimmer waist. Madame Rosa and Celestine preferred to have their gowns made by their own dressmaker; they claimed that the workmanship was far superior. But Anya could not force herself to endure the endless fittings required unless absolutely necessary, and so bought ready-made garments when she could find them.

The neckline of the gown was cut low across the bosom, exposing a great deal of her neck and shoulders. In an attempt to distract from that expanse of pale flesh, Anya fastened around her throat a necklace of garnets. It was a beautifully designed piece of glittering, faceted stones, with a Maltese cross at the center surrounded by scrollwork and flanked by tiny tulips, fleurs-de-lis, and arrow points made of jewels on either side. Delicate, yet large enough to be showy, it had been given to

Anya by her father. It was not terribly valuable, the garnets being set in base metal with only a wash of gold, but she loved it.

Anya sat before her dressing table with a hairdressing cape about her shoulders while Denise brushed the long mane of her hair and put it up. Denise plaited and shaped a portion of it into a coronet, then brought the hair at the crown through the coronet and allowed it to fall in a smooth swath that curled over Anya's shoulders to lie in a fat, glossy ringlet. Denise drew out small tendrils of hair at the temples and in front of Anya's ears, and used a curling iron heated on a bracket placed over the lamp chimney to form them into fine curls. Satisfied at last, she moved about the room putting things away while Anya turned her attention to the array of bottles and jars on the dressing table.

Her hands were dry and rough from her yard work. She smoothed a soothing lotion known as Balm of a Thousand Flowers into them, then shaped her nails and buffed them to a gloss with a chamois skin buffer.

The Creole ladies of New Orleans had been accused by the American women of painting their faces. That was not strictly true, though they were known, on occasion, to aid nature somewhat. Madame Rosa had instructed Anya in that art as naturally as she had pointed out the importance of attention to her teeth.

Now to give her brows and lashes darkness and sheen, Anya applied a touch of a pomatum with her fingertips, then to even her skin tone used Lily White, liquid *blanc de perles*, smoothing it over her face. Deciding after a critical inspection that she needed a little color, she took a rouge paper from a small box, brushed it delicately across her cheekbones, then, after moistening her lips, pressed it to them also.

She sat for a moment surveying the results in the mirror. Satisfied, she tossed the rouge paper aside and wiped her fingertips on a cloth. She looked rather different than she had earlier. It was a pity, she thought, that Ravel Duralde would not be able to see how different, even if the change had not been made for his benefit.

As with most houses of Creole style, the principal rooms of Beau Refuge were on the second floor to protect them from the possibility of flooding, with the lower floor being little more than a basement built above the ground and used for storage and sometimes for servants' quarters. There was no hallway in the house. The galleries on the front and back served that purpose, giving access through the many pairs of French windows that opened onto them. In addition, the rooms opened into each other, so that if every window and door in the house was thrown wide, there was free circulation of air throughout, a great boon in the warm, humid climate.

There were nine large, high-ceilinged rooms in the house. Across the front was the library, the salon in the center, and the bedchamber used by Madame Rosa. The second rank of rooms included the dining room in the center and a bedchamber on each side, while across the back was Anya's bedchamber, a sitting room she claimed as her own, and another bedchamber that belonged to Celestine.

The decor of the house, redone at the time of the marriage of Madame Rosa to Anya's father, was in wheat-straw gold and olive green. There were heavy brocades at the windows and medallion carpets on the floor; chairs and settees were covered with silk, and the bed coverings were of ecru linen edged with heavy Valenciennes lace. Bronze-framed mirrors topped the fireplaces, and marble statuary was set in the corners of the rooms. The chandeliers were of bronze doré and Baccarat crystal. Sèvres porcelain graced the mantels and tables here and there, and the paintings and lithographs that hung on the walls of gentle pastoral scenes in gilded frames.

To reach the dining room, Anya had only to walk into the sitting room, turn right, then pass through the sitting room door into the dining room. The table sat ready, with her place laid, waiting for the meal to be served. No one was in sight however, nor was there any sign of food. She moved to the sideboard where a tray of decanters stood. After pouring a small sherry for herself, she wandered back into the sitting room and seated herself as was proper upon the edge of the seat of the wing chair.

The stiff pose was too uncomfortable to maintain. Unlike many young ladies among the Creoles, Anya had never been forced to wear an apple slat in her bodice to encourage rigid, upright posture. Careless of the possible wrinkling of her dress or the possibility of revealing her petticoats and crinoline, she leaned back in the chair, resting her head against the padded upholstery.

As she sipped her wine, she stared out into the darkness beyond the French windows. It was an uneasy night. The wind had changed its quarter, blowing steadily from the south. It waved the ancient arms of the live oaks so that they creaked and groaned in protest. Thunder rumbled in the distance, a low, threatening sound. Drafts of air finding their way into the room caused the flames in the lamps to flutter on their wicks, casting wavering shadows on the walls. The air smelled of kerosene and the rose-petal potpourri that filled a Chinese jar on the table beside her, of pollen from the trees that were beginning to bloom, and of the sulphurous taint of the coming storm.

There was a copy of the *Louisiana Courier* also on the table. Setting down her glass, she picked up the newspaper, scanning the columns, stopping to read an item from France holding up to ridicule the entourage of postillions, liveried servants, mounted lancers bearing small flags, and equerries thought necessary to accompany the young son of Louis Napoleon of France and his nurse for a carriage outing. She had passed on to a tale of Indian trouble with the Shawnees in the Kansas Territory, when Denise's son Marcel appeared in the door.

She laid the paper aside, saying with a smile, "Dinner at last? I'm starving."

Marcel was a grave and intelligent young man near Anya's age, with a slender frame, waving black hair and soft brown skin. There was enough of the Caucasian in his features so that Anya had been forced to wonder more than once if his father might not have been the man from whom her own father had won the plantation. Denise was reticent on the subject, claiming, when Madame Rosa asked her in forthright Creole fashion about the boy's parentage, that she could not name his father. Marcel was an excellent servant, quiet, efficient, and loyal. When he could be teased out of his habitual solemnity, he had a wide and infectious grin. There was never any indication by word or deed that when they were children he and Anya had run and romped together up and down the galleries of the house.

Tonight his face was even more sober than usual, and he did

not quite meet her gaze as he bowed. "I'm sorry, mam'zelle. Dinner is indeed ready, but I'm not certain where to serve it."

"Not certain? What do you mean?"

"I went just now to the cotton gin with a tray. M'sieur Duralde said to me that I must bring your meal also. He will not eat alone."

She got to her feet with a swish of skirts. "I see. Then he must go hungry. I will eat in the dining room as usual."

"Your pardon, mam'zelle. He also said that if you should refuse, he will be forced to set fire to the cotton gin."

She went still. Flags of color appeared on her cheekbones. "He'll what?" she asked sharply.

"I am to say for him that he regrets the necessity of the threat, but you must not doubt he will carry it out."

"But how—?" She stopped before the question was formed. She seemed to remember leaving the tin box containing phosphorus matches on the side table in the corner when she had used them to light the lamp the night before. Her Uncle Will had never been able to reach that far, but Ravel was a taller man, with longer arms and, perhaps, greater initiative. Somehow he must have found a way to knock the box from the table and pull it toward him.

"He has matches," Marcel answered helpfully. "He showed them to me."

"Why didn't you take them from him?" she asked in agitation.

"I thought of it, but he warned me not to try. He said, mam'zelle, that you must come and get them yourself."

Chapter Five

🦋 🦋 🦋 *Ravel stood at the window. With his height,* he could see above the sill, out into the windswept darkness. His face was silhouetted against the gray light, his expression pensive. He had mended his appearance since Anya had left him, taking advantage of the comforts she had provided; still the red flannel shirt he wore and the white swath of bandaging about his head, half-concealed by the curling crispness of his dark hair, gave him the look of a pirate. The chain of his shackle lay stretched across the floor, the steel links gleaming dully in the lamplight. It made a faint rattling as he turned with the opening of the door.

He stared at Anya, his dark gaze missing no detail of her appearance, from the gleaming coronet of hair on top of her head and the glitter of jewels at her throat, to the edging of lace on her petticoat that was visible as she held the rose-hued silk of her gown above the floor. A look of warm appreciation rose in his face, to be quickly replaced by sardonic amusement. He leaned his shoulders against the wall under the window and crossed his arms over his chest.

"Ravishing. If this magnificence is for my benefit, I am honored."

"I didn't expect to see you this evening, as you well know." Her answer was short. His effrontery was incensing. Her cheeks were flushed and her mouth set in a thin line as she lowered the hem of her skirt to the floor and threw back her shawl, draping it over her arms.

"How disappointing. You have other guests?"

The temptation to lie, to plead social duties as a means of

escaping, was strong. She conquered it with a severe effort. "As it happens, I don't."

"How fortunate for me." He pushed away from the wall. "Permit me to offer you a chair."

She took a quick step backward as he came toward her. "Stay where you are."

He stopped. His tactics earlier, he saw clearly, had been at fault. His voice quiet, he said, "If I have given you reason to be wary of me, I beg your pardon."

"That's a novelty, at any rate." She lifted her chin as she spoke.

She was one of the most desirable woman he had ever seen. If there had been a time in the past seven years when he had forgotten it, he knew it beyond a doubt now. The shape of her mouth, the curve of her breasts, the slender span of her waist enticed him. He wanted her as he had never wanted anyone or anything in his life. Honor was a paltry thing compared to that great hunger.

He lowered his lashes, indicating the table with a smooth gesture. "Won't you be seated?"

"I am here because of your base threat. I have no intention of sharing a meal with you as if your message had been an engraved invitation."

"You have to eat."

"Not with you."

"You have cracked my skull, taken my freedom, and compromised my honor. Your company for a meal doesn't seem much to ask in return."

"My view of the matter is somewhat different."

"How so?"

"It would be tedious to explain."

His tone dry, he answered, "I have no pressing appointments."

"Your dinner is getting stone-cold." Anya cast a look of irritation at the covered silver servers that had been spread out on the table. An aroma that was decidedly appetizing hovered above them. She felt her stomach shift, making ready to growl, and in haste she moved away from him.

"Don't be shy. You know you are panting to tell me what a blackguard I am for using such threats to get you here."

She sent him a brief glance over her shoulder. "I'm afraid that would give me scant satisfaction for what I feel at the moment."

"What would give you satisfaction, Anya?" he asked, his tone soft.

Something in his voice sent a quiver along her nerves. She moved away from him. At the doorway she had left open, Marcel stood, on guard, awaiting further orders. His face was expressionless, the face of discretion worn by all good servants. Should she send him away, or tell him to bring her own meal? Neither course was acceptable to her, and yet it would be awkward for her to hover in this manner while Ravel sat down to eat.

When she did not answer, Ravel lifted a brow. "What is it? You don't like having someone else's will imposed on your own? It troubles you to feel you are no longer entirely in control? Will it mend matters if I pledge my word to deliver the matches I hold into your hand immediately after dessert?"

She swung around. "You would do that?"

His slow smile was charming but enigmatic. "They will have served their purpose."

Circumstances sometimes changed plans. A tête-à-tête with Ravel Duralde was not what she had intended, still it might be worth it for peace of mind.

He watched her face. "The situation may be unusual, but there is no reason that we can't behave in a civilized fashion."

The words were sensible enough, and their formality should have been reassuring; Anya could not say that they lacked sincerity. And yet even as her brain counseled capitulation, her basic instinct was for caution.

"You can pretend that I am some doddering past acquaintance of your father's to whom you need be no more than polite. Except for an occasional request to pass the salt, you can ignore me."

Nothing was more unlikely. Still, it did not matter. She was hungry after her work in the garden, and it seemed suddenly the height of stupidity to allow pride and anger and this man's games to make her feel uncomfortable on her own property or to interfere with her evening meal. She gave a curt nod, then directed that the cold food be taken away and replaced with a fresh selection of hot dishes, for two.

Silence descended around them like a thick and smothering coverlet when Marcel had gone. The wind had died. The night stillness was sullen, waiting. The thunder that grumbled around the sky had a closer sound.

The light in the room was yellow, overbright. The lamp on the table beside the fireplace sent a spiral of black smoke toward the ceiling, burning with a hectic glow caused by a wick turned too high. Anya walked to the table and removed the lamp's soot-blackened globe, lowering the wick until the flame that danced upon it was blue and barely edged with yellow.

Ravel watched her, his features stern to conceal his satisfaction at the progress of events. The glow of the lamplight, reflecting in her face, gave her a strange, unearthly beauty, and he felt a stir of something like despairing desire in his loins. He suppressed it with ruthless care. She must not be made more wary of him than she was already.

He moved toward the eating table that sat in the corner and pulled it forward into the room, closer to the fire. He reached for the straight-backed chair that went with it, placing it on one side, then turned to the armchair near the hearth. Bending, he lifted the heavy, upholstered piece with ease, then set it down opposite the straight chair at the table.

Anya followed his movements, her gaze abstracted. The red flannel shirt she had sent him pulled taut across his shoulders and back as he bent, emphasizing the muscled hardness. His trousers, perfectly tailored for fit, fastened under the instep, clung with amazing fidelity to his thighs and the lean line of his hips. There was about him as he moved a dark and predatory grace. He was sleek and powerful and dangerous, with a faint intimation of some desperate need. Watching him, she was afraid that she had made a mistake in agreeing to his demand.

He turned toward her, indicating with a brief gesture the place he had arranged as he inclined his head. "If you please?"

The heat of a flush caused by her wandering thoughts about him rose to her cheekbones as she met his gaze. She lowered her lashes and, maneuvering her skirts with one hand to collapse the hoops of the crinoline and prevent wrinkling of the silk, sat down gingerly in the chair. He waited until she was ready, then shifted the heavy chair closer to the table. His hand brushed her arm, and she sent him a quick, startled glance as she felt the stinging heat of the contact.

His chain clanked over the floor as he stepped to the other side of the table and took his place facing her. She averted her gaze from him, though she could feel his upon her. The depth of her consciousness of him amazed her. She had never been quite so acutely aware of a man in her life, certainly had never felt this uncomfortable degree of perception with Jean. She tried to tell herself it was because of the circumstances, her antipathy for Ravel, the memories of the past that linked them and the peculiar circumstances of the present. She did not quite believe it. There was something in the man himself, something that had always affected her adversely, even in those long-ago days of her betrothal, when Ravel had been among Jean's friends.

The need to dispel the feeling was so strong that she unconsciously fell back on the formal graciousness of a hostess.

"We were speaking this morning of William Walker," she said with a cool smile. "Did you attend the meeting of the Friends of Nicaragua last week?"

Amusement for the ploy flitted across his face before he nodded. "I was there."

"Were you, by chance, one of the speakers?"

"As it happens, I was."

"Your sympathies are with Walker, I imagine."

Again he inclined his head.

"They are saying that he may be formally tried in court for violating the neutrality laws. Do you think he will be convicted?"

"It depends on where the trial is held. If it's in Washington, it's possible. If it's here in New Orleans, where he has his greatest base of support, the chance is slight."

"There has been a rumor lately about the men who fought with Walker in Central America. People are saying that they are the force behind this secret committee of vigilance."

His features hardened for an endless moment. His dark gaze

was probing, assessing as he studied her. The suspicion that closed in upon him was blighting, but must be considered. "You are remarkably abreast of events."

"For a woman, you mean?"

"There aren't many of your sex who interest themselves in what is happening outside their family circle."

"I enjoy knowing what is taking place, and why. Is there anything wrong with that?"

"Hardly. It's just surprising."

His comments were no more than an attempt to distract her from her original question. She smiled artlessly, saying, "But about this Vigilance Committee, do you know anything of it?"

"Vigilance against whom, or what? Do these rumors say?"

"Against the corrupt officials and police force of New Orleans who were bought and paid for by the Know-Nothing party."

"I see. And you approve of that goal?"

The lash concealed in that question was surprising. Anya lifted her chin. "I can't say that I disapprove. It looks as if someone is going to have to do something."

He was wrong. He must be. A smile curved the strong lines of his mouth, rising to brighten his eyes. "I should have known a woman so ready to take unconventional measures to get what she wants would not condemn others for doing the same."

She was not given a chance to form an answer. Their conversation was interrupted by the return of Marcel bearing an enormous silver tray covered with dishes. He placed before them a seafood gumbo rich with shrimp and crab and sausage in a spicy, dark brown roux. He had also roast chicken with cornbread dressing and oyster sauce, venison steak with rice, and a selection of cheeses. There were small loaves of French bread wrapped in a white cloth, and for dessert blackberry cobbler made with berries put up the year before and served with clotted cream. To drink there was white wine in crystal goblets, and coffee that was kept hot by supporting the pot in a silver cradle over a burning candle.

Marcel poured the wine and placed the bottle aside. He checked one last time to be certain that they had everything, from silverware and china to the saltcellars with their tiny spoons. He bowed. "Is there anything else, mam'zelle?"

"No, thank you, Marcel. That will be all."

"Shall I stay to serve you?"

"I believe we can manage."

"Perhaps I should send the carriage for you in a half hour, in case it begins to rain."

"That won't be necessary. I don't believe it will start so soon."

The instant the answer was made, Anya regretted it. Consideration for the people who served her, people who might be tired and hungry themselves, was so ingrained that she had not paused to seriously consider the suggestions Marcel was making, and the reasons behind them, until it was too late. Marcel, perhaps instructed by his mother, had meant to offer her the protection, slight though it might be, of either his presence or the imminent arrival of her coachman. She could not now change her mind without making her distrust of her prisoner obvious. It was with great uneasiness that she watched Denise's son bow himself from the room.

When he had gone, she took a deep calming breath. She was letting her imagination run away with her. She was in no danger. The man sitting across the table from her was chained. What could he do?

And yet he had threatened her. In addition, it did not seem likely that a man like Ravel Duralde would so easily resign himself to being kept a prisoner. Or that he not make some serious attempt to escape in order to uphold his honor by appearing on the dueling field at the proper time. She must take care.

Her appetite had vanished. She managed to eat her gumbo, but could do no more than push her chicken about on her plate. She sipped her wine, glad of something to do to occupy her hands, as well as for the sake of its warmth to banish the chill inside her.

She searched her mind for something innocuous to talk about, but could discover nothing. The silence was broken only by the clatter of silver and the booming of thunder drawing slowly nearer.

Ravel was aware of the constraint, but seemed to find satisfaction in it. He ate with a certain ruthless precision, pulling the small crusty loaves of bread apart with his strong fingers, slicing the chicken so that the meat fell cleanly from the bone, spearing the venison steak to transfer it to his plate. Anya poured coffee for them both. When Ravel had finished his dessert, he leaned back with his cup in his hand, watching her over the rim as he sipped at the strong brew.

Finally he set the cup down. His tone thoughtful and yet accusing, he said, "What about love?"

Anya's cup wobbled on its saucer. Hastily she placed it on the table. "What do you mean?"

"You said earlier that you weren't interested in marriage and children. But what of love? Do you seriously intend to remain a virgin all your life?"

The Creoles had little reticence about private matters. Anya had heard women describe in mixed company the embarrassments and hilarities of their wedding nights, and list in excruciating detail the dreadful pangs and difficulties they had suffered during their confinements. Madame Rosa complained to all and sundry about the horrors of the change of life through which she was currently passing, receiving a full quota of sympathy from Gaspard because of them, and Celestine was as likely as not to tell her Murray that the reason she did not feel well enough to go driving or walking was because of her monthly courses. Creole ladies tended to find the Anglo-Saxon reluctance to discuss such things in public vastly amusing. It was only natural, was it not? But Anya had never quite managed to rid herself of her notions of personal privacy.

Frowning, she said, "That is no concern of yours."

"Oh, I think it is. I am responsible for your being alone now."

"You need not let it trouble you."

"I think I must. Because of what happened one night seven years ago, I am what I am, and you are also as you are. Whether you recognize it or not, there is a bond between us. It's something neither of us wants, but it is a fact."

Lightning crackled above the cotton gin, flashing hard at the windows in an eerie white glare. Thunder boomed hard upon it, and rumbled away into the night. Immediately afterward came the first spattering drops of rain on the roof. The fire hissed and crackled as raindrops fell down the chimney.

Gooseflesh rose on Anya's arms, in part because of the chilling sound of the rain, in part reaction to the words Ravel had spoken and the deep, prophetic rasp of his voice. The cotton gin seemed suddenly as distant from the main house and the quarters as the moon. Its isolation struck her like a blow in the pit of her stomach.

Her fingers were clenched on the handle of her coffee cup. She released them with an effort and crossed her arms over her chest, clasping her arms.

"You feel it, don't you?"

She had recognized the bond he spoke of, though it seemed to her to be a thing of mutual antagonism. Even that, however, was too personal to admit. "No," she said hurriedly. "No."

"You do, but you refuse to accept it. You are afraid of me, but you try to cover it with anger. Why? Why do you fear me?"

"I'm not afraid of you," she said, goaded into a reply she would not have made under ordinary circumstances, "I dislike you."

"Why?"

"That must be obvious."

"Indeed? If Jean had killed me that night, would you have blamed him in the same way? Would you have called him a murderer and an assassin, a mad dog who knows only how to kill?"

The words he spoke awakened echoes in her mind. Had she really said them to him that night he had come to tell her about Jean? They must have hurt him, that he remembered them so well.

"You don't answer. I take that to mean you would not. Your dislike must be personal then. Perhaps it's my background—or lack of it."

"Certainly not," she snapped, more disturbed than she would have liked to admit by the relentless questions and the direction they had taken.

"There is only one other possibility then. You feel the attraction between us that has been there from the beginning, long before Jean died. You feel it, but you are afraid to acknowledge it. You are afraid because it might mean that you don't have a proper regret for your fiancé's death.''

She came to her feet so abruptly that she jarred the table, toppling her cup and spilling the coffee across the cloth in a dark brown stain. She did not pause to see the damage, but pushed her chair back and spun away, moving toward the door.

The rattle of the chain warned her, but in her elaborate gown and layers of petticoats she was not swift enough to escape. He caught her from behind, clamping hard fingers on her forearm and swinging her around to face him. He grasped her other arm, holding her immobile.

She wrenched back against his hold, but there was more strength in his hard soldier's hands than she had ever encountered. Fury rose inside her. Through clenched teeth she said, ''Let me go!''

''Do you really expect that I will?''

Ravel held her heated gaze for a moment before allowing his own to drift over her flushed cheeks to the vulnerable curve of her neck and lower, to where the white curves of her breasts rose and fell in her agitation, filling the décolletage of her gown. The need to press his lips to that enticing softness was so great that a wave of dizziness mounted to his head. In the effort of control, his grasp tightened.

Anya drew in her breath in a gasp of pain. ''Bastard!''

His face hardened. Bending abruptly, he placed his arm under her knees and lifted her high against his chest. Her skirts, spilling over his hold, brushing his legs, flared out as he swung around with her. Her shawl slid from her arms to the floor. It twisted around his shackle, threatening to trip him for an instant, but he kicked it aside and strode toward the bed.

''No!'' Anya cried as she saw his purpose. She twisted in his arms, pushing at him, reaching with fingers curved into talons for his eyes.

He breathed a curse and flung her down on the thick cotton mattress. She thrust herself up, sliding away from him. He put his knee on the bed, catching her with one arm, forcing her back down with his weight as he lowered himself beside her. She beat at his head and shoulders with her fists. He winced as she caught him on the cheekbone, but immediately snatched her wrists, pinning one under his body while he brought the other down beside her face, thrusting his arm under her head to catch and hold it. Shifting, he brought his leg up over both of hers, stilling her movements.

She stared up at him with her eyes dark with wrath and fear she would not admit. His weight upon her chest made her breath come in hard gasps, and tremors of reaction shuddered over her, one behind the other. He watched her for long moments, his gaze fastened on her mouth. When he spoke at last, there was a faint thickness in his tones.

"Where," he asked deliberately, "is the key?"

"The key." The words as she repeated them held paralyzed disbelief.

A sardonic smile softened the harsh curves of his mouth. "Did you think I had designs upon your delectable body?"

That was exactly what she had thought. She lifted her chin. "Why should I not, since you seem to be capable of anything?"

His smile faded. The pressure of his grasp upon her wrist increased until there was no feeling in her hand. "It is, of course, an idea."

She searched his face, trying to discover if he was serious or if he was only trying to frighten her. She could feel the heavy beat of his heart against her rib cage, the powerful corded muscles of his body and the hard length of him as he held her. He wanted her; she was not mistaken in that, and yet he held his desire in firm leash. For the moment.

She moistened her dry lips with the tip of her tongue. "I—I don't have the key. It's outside."

"I know that the key to the door is left on a hook outside," he said, his voice soft. "I have had plenty of time to discover that much. What I require is the one to this leg shackle."

"It's at the main house."

"How convenient."

"It's true!"

"I wonder."

Holding her gaze, he moved his free right hand to the neckline of her gown. His fingers burned as he touched them lightly to the upper curves of her breasts. Slowly he inserted them under the rose pink silk, sliding them with infinite care toward the valley between the twin globes.

"Don't," she said on a gasp. "I told you I don't have it."

He made no reply, but plundered the secret and shadowed hollow that he had found, caressing the warm satin of her skin. "Not there."

Removing his fingers, he spread his hand over a rounded breast, pressing, stroking. He lingered as he discovered the bud of her nipple through the layers of cloth, caressing until it hardened under his skillful attention.

"What are you doing?" She strained away from him, struggling also against the slow seep of desire, like a gentle poison, invading her senses.

"Searching for the key," he answered her, the words absorbed as he directed his interest toward her other breast. Ignoring her attempts to evade him, he captured that warm, silk-covered mound, gently clasping, kneading, brushing the nipple with his thumb.

The blood throbbed in her veins. The surface of her skin was growing warmer, so that she felt as if every portion of her body were mantled with a flush. She had heard the word *seduction* all her life, but had never known until this moment how pervasive such a thing could be. Did he know what he was doing to her? Did he?

"Don't do this," she cried, a strangled sound.

He smoothed his hand down over her ribs to the narrow indentation of her waist, and lower to her abdomen. He grasped her skirts, drawing them upward. His breath warm at her ear, he said, "Let's see if you have a petticoat pocket."

"No—Yes, but there's nothing in it."

"Any lie to thwart me," he said with a sorrowful shake of his head.

"I promise—" The words were stifled by a gasp as he lifted her crinoline, pushing the hoops aside so they collapsed across her abdomen, and ran his hand along her thighs through the layers of petticoats underneath. "Ravel, please."

He reached lower still, drawing up the last petticoats, placing his hand on her bare knees, then sliding it upward over the silk of her pantalettes until it finally rested, warm and heavy, upon the small mound at the juncture of her thighs.

"So the key is at the house. I wonder what it would take," he drawled, "to persuade you to send for it."

"There's no one to send!"

"You could signal with the lamp. I'm sure your housekeeper will be on watch."

It was a threat. The question was, would he carry it out if she did not do as he suggested? Would he deliberately possess her if she did not secure his release? She would like to think that he would not, and yet there was about Ravel Duralde an unknown quality, a sense of behavior pushed beyond the normal boundaries, as if he might not recognize the same limits as ordinary men. It might be possible that he would take her refusal as an excuse to satisfy his own desires, above and beyond the issue between them. He might well feel it was his right to do so after the thing she had done to him, or at the very least a fitting revenge for it.

She discovered, with shock, that she did not want to put the matter to test. It was not fear, but rather that she preferred not to know if Ravel would rape her. But if she did not, if she failed to defy him, then it must mean the defeat of her plans. It would mean that Ravel, riding hard and fast through the night, could still reach New Orleans by daybreak, could still arrive at the dueling field in time to meet Murray.

It might also mean, after such a long and tiring ride, coming so soon after his head injuries, that the odds of Ravel being killed, instead of his opponent, would be greater. That too was something she did not care to see put to the test.

"Why?" she asked with tears of angry distress rising in her eyes. "Why are you doing this?"

"For honor," he answered, though the words were etched with the acid of self-derision.

"It can't be necessary for you to kill a young man like Murray Nicholls. Not for so slight a reason. Your honor can't mean that much to you."

"Can't it?" he asked in bitter tones. "How much does your virtue mean to you?"

"Not as much as a man's life."

The words hovered between them. Anya stared at him, her drowned gaze widening as she realized the implication of what she had said. She hadn't meant—or had she? In that confused moment, with her heartbeat pounding in her chest and the tight feel of reluctant response in her lower body heightened by his lean form resting heavy upon her, she could not be sure.

Outside, the thunder crashed and the rain poured down, sluicing over the roof and channeling in streams from the eaves, splashing on the ground below the windows. The sound was loud in the sudden stillness.

"My honor for your virtue, a fascinating exchange."

Even as he spoke, Ravel could not believe she would do it. She had hated him too much, for too long. When she did not answer, he went on. "I wonder if Murray Nicholls is worth the sacrifice, or if he realizes the depths of your affection."

"It isn't affection."

"What then? A simple concern for your sister's happiness?"

"In part," she agreed, her voice breathless.

"And what else?" he asked in goading tones. "The purest of altruism? The regard of one human being for the welfare of another? Will you believe me if I tell you that I am inclined to accept your offer—if offer it is—for the same reason?"

"For Celestine's sake?" Anya asked, confusion drawing her brows together.

"For yours. And because I lack the strength of will to refuse." He laughed, a husky, sardonic sound. "So much for honor."

By slow degrees, he released her, taking his hands away, levering himself up so that his weight no longer oppressed her. Anya rubbed her wrists to restore the feeling and circulation. He sat watching her, propped on one hand with his knee drawn up. She could feel his gaze upon her, considering, devouring in its intensity.

Her virtue for a man's life. Murray's or Ravel's, it did not seem so bad a bargain. She had no real expectation of marrying, so that purity for her wedding night did not greatly concern her. This one physical act would be quickly over, and as quickly put from her mind. The process was of no great importance; only the result mattered.

It was long moments before she could bring herself to look at Ravel. Still, when she finally sat up and lifted her lashes, her eyes were steady and darkly blue with determination.

"You agree? You swear you will make no attempt to meet Murray in the morning?"

How could he refuse? Loss of honor was a small price to pay for this boon, one he had never dared dream would come to him. But could he bear the hatred that must accompany the sacrifice? Would it suffice to still the pangs of conscience if he told himself she despised him already, could not despise him more?

"I agree," he answered, his voice deep.

Anya swallowed hard. For a moment she had thought he meant to repudiate her and the agreement. She had even dared hope that he might say she could go, that she need trouble herself over the duel no longer. She should have known better. What was he waiting for, then? If a blackguard he must be, then why could he not be one completely? Why could he not take her at once and have done with it? Hard, remorseless, the rain drummed on the roof above them.

"Well then?" Her voice came near to cracking with the strain that gripped her.

His lips curved in a slow smile as his dark eyes held her. "There is no hurry."

"Could you—lower the lamp?"

"I would rather not."

The soft glow through the soot-darkened globe was not that intrusive, but neither was it the darkness she craved. She did not insist, however. She drew a deep breath, then let it out slowly. She glanced over his shoulder toward the door, and the fire that was slowly dying in the fireplace, before looking back at him. "You—you will have to help me undress."

"Of course," he said gravely.

She shifted with stiff muscles, turning her back to him so that he could reach the row of tiny buttons fastening her gown. He did not begin on them at once, but closed his hands upon her shoulders, holding them, feeling the flesh and sinew and bones of her, quiescent under his palms, accepting his touch. His heart contracted in his chest, and lowering his head, he brushed the tender and vulnerable nape of her neck with his lips. So brief, so gentle was that caress that Anya sensed it rather than felt it. She tilted her head in inquiry.

Ravel removed his hands with slow reluctance, lifting them to her hair and probing with his fingers for the pins that held her braided coronet. He pulled them out one by one, tossing them to the floor so that they made a musical, tinkling sound. With swift movements, he unplaited her braid, spreading the silken strands with the waves pressed into them, draping them around her shoulders. Only then did he begin on the buttons.

Panic, suffocating, stomach-wrenching, beat up into Anya's mind as she felt his fingers so warm and sure upon the bare skin of her back. It was only by a supreme effort that she could force herself to sit still, to permit this encroaching intimacy. She had held herself inviolate for so long that she was not certain she could bear what was to come, regardless of all her attempts to reassure herself, not certain at all.

He did not wait for further permission, however, but when the gown was undone and the sleeves sliding down her shoulders, began to untie the tapes of her crinoline and petticoats, and to unlace her corset. Within a few short minutes he was drawing the layers of clothing off over her head and tossing them aside, as if plucking the petals from a flower.

When she was left only camisole and pantalettes, she swung back to face him. He reached out to catch the end of the blue ribbon that held her camisole closed at the top, and slowly untied the bow. The knot slipped free. The edges of fine lawn began to widen, exposing the gentle curves of her breasts, though the ribbon was still crossed. With the tip of one finger, he spread the gap a fraction. He drew in his breath with a soft hissing sound.

The soft lamplight touched her hair with red-gold highlights and gave the intense blue of her eyes the soft sheen of sun-touched mist on the sea. It gilded her cheekbones, leaving the triangular hollows underneath in shadow, and with delicate fidelity burnished the perfect globes of her breasts until they appeared sprinkled with gold dust and crushed pearls.

Anya looked up at him, wondering at his lack of haste, his apparent enjoyment of the process of removing her clothes. His face was intent, the corners of his mouth lifting in an expression of absorbed pleasure. He glanced up. Finding her watching him, he stopped.

His smile widened with a slow and sensuous lightening of his features. Shifting, he lay down, stretching full length. He clasped both hands behind his head. His gaze holding hers, he said, "My turn."

"You mean—you want me to undress you?"

"That's the idea," he answered in rich amusement.

She was aware, suddenly, of a peculiar excitement churning inside her, a rising feeling of recklessness that carried also a sense of freedom. She could touch him; he wanted her to touch him. There was nothing to prevent her from satisfying every curiosity she had ever known concerning men and the mysteries of the marriage bed. She had, thanks to the frankness of the Creole ladies, and also the slave women, a working knowledge of the male anatomy and the process that led to procreation, but there were gaps in her understanding of both. Those gaps would be filled this night.

Supporting herself with one hand, she leaned over him. Her fingers trembled as she reached for the bone buttons of his shirt. One by one she unfastened them. She drew the edges of red flannel aside, exposing the hard planes of his chest with its dark matting of hair. She trailed her fingertips through that curling growth in tentative pleasure, surprised at the crisp yet soft feel of it, and at the unyielding firmness of the bands of muscle underneath. She brushed his hardened paps, conscious of his indrawn breath of sensitivity in that area. She did not linger, but trailed downward over the flat, tight wall of his abdomen to tug his shirt from the waistband of his trousers.

He moved to accommodate her, then, as she freed the tail of the shirt, rose on one elbow to permit her to push it from his shoulder. She spread her fingers, smoothing her palm over his neck and upper arm, brushing the soft material from his firm skin until it was caught by the width of his biceps and his elbow. She leaned closer to him then, using both hands to pull the sleeve free.

Her breasts tingled, the nipples tightening, as she brushed his chest. She recognized suddenly the warm, masculine scent of him combined with the freshness of soap and the cotton-lint smell of the flannel shirt. She felt a loosening sensation inside her, and the slow rise of warm anticipation. She refused to consider it, however. Keeping her lashes lowered, she stripped the shirt from him and tossed it on the pile of her own clothing beside the bed.

He lay back down. Immediately, before she could lose her courage, she unbuttoned the front of his trousers. Opening the flap revealed his underdrawers of linen, so finely woven they were almost transparent. Uncertain how to proceed from there, she hesitated.

A grin crossed his face. With the toe of one foot, he prized off one of his half boots, then the other. They fell to the floor with thuds that were loud in the quiet. His movements swift, economical, he stripped down his knit socks, pulling them through the leg shackle before skimming out of trousers and underwear. These last two items, encasing the chain over which they were drawn, trailed also to the floor.

There was a scar on his thigh, a long, angry-looking slash. Anya stared at it, because so long as she did, there was no need to acknowledge his nakedness or to look elsewhere. In a show of concern, she reached out to touch the scar, though the moment her fingers came in contact with his warm skin her concern was abruptly real.

"How did you get this?"

"A Spaniard with a bayonet in Nicaragua."

"Did you—?" She stopped.

"Did I kill him? Yes, I did."

His voice was tight, as if he expected her denunciation. She said with quiet deliberateness, "You might have been crippled."

"It doesn't matter," he said, "not now," and discovered that he spoke no more than the truth. It didn't matter. Nothing mattered except the moment and the strange pact that held them together.

"No," she whispered.

He looked at her, his eyes black and opaque, with mysterious shadows in their dark depths. Quickly, almost before she realized what he was doing, he flicked open her camisole and removed it. His gaze kindled as it swept over the perfect symmetry of her tip-tilted breasts with their apricot pink nipples. With a sound in his throat that might have been a sigh of deepest satisfaction or the release of some deep-held disbelief, he put his hands on her shoulders and drew her across him. Her hair swung forward around them like a russet satin curtain. Glinting with fiery highlights, it enclosed them in perilous intimacy and the heart-catching scent of damask roses. Her breasts were flattened against his chest. He cupped her face with one hand, then slowly brought her nearer until her lips touched his.

His mouth, the chiseled and passionate molding of it was upon hers, and there was no hardness there, only a warm and sensual enticement, a firm entreaty. His tongue teased the sensitive and fragile curves of her lips, testing the line where they met. He found the small injury where his teeth had cut her as he had been struck the night before, and he soothed it with minute soft strokes. Enthralled by that tenderness, she permitted her lips to part, allowing him entry, and with tentative pleasure touched his tongue with her own.

In some distant recess of her mind, there was a feeble and puritanical protest at her cooperation in her own fall from grace. Conscience dictated that she submit; it did not require that she enjoy the submission. She would have liked to blame it on the wine that ran with heavy strength in her veins or perhaps some ancient feminine weakness, or even on Ravel's overwhelming strength. It was none of those things. The cause lay within herself, in the stirring of desire long unawakened, of needs long unfulfilled. It was an ungovernable instinct to accept this chance to experience life's most bountiful reward for the pain of living, this chance that had been thrust upon her.

Ravel tasted of coffee and the wild sweetness of the berries of summer. His mouth was warm and welcoming, the inner surfaces moist and smooth. Their tongues clashed, entwined with fine-nubbed grain against nubbed grain. His hands glided over her shoulders and down the slender line of her back, pressing her to him, moving lower to clasp her hips. His fingers sought and found the side button of her pantalettes, and he released them, sliding them down, following them with his hands upon her bare skin, kneading, sweeping in easy circles along her sides.

Beneath her, she could feel the long rigidity of him, an indication of the force of his desire for her. There was no haste in his movements, however, only a deep and sensual appreciation of the moment, as if he meant to impress the taste and feel of her upon his body, his memory.

Holding her to him, he turned with a taut flexing of muscles until she faced him on her side. He trailed heated kisses from the corner of her mouth and along the curve of her cheekbone. He pressed his face into the silken swath of her hair that lay along the turn of her neck, brushing the rich-colored strands with his lips before he raised himself and bent to draw her pantalettes down her thighs, freeing her of them. He lowered his head then, tasting her skin at the narrow indentation of her waist and along her rib cage, cupping a breast in his hand before encircling it with his tongue and taking the strutted nipple into the gentle adhesion of his mouth.

Anya breathed deep as heated desire flooded through her, spiraling downward, ever downward. With her eyes tightly closed, she reached out to him, stroking with sensitive, questing fingertips along the corded muscles of his arm and over his chest, drifting lower to the firm flatness of his belly. He caught her hand, guiding it to the thrusting length of him that was yet satiny in its smoothness. She accepted that invitation, exploring, lost in unexpected delight, and also in wonder at the generosity with which he offered himself to her.

Time ceased to have meaning. The rain clattered and drummed overhead and lightning flared in the room. The lamplight wavered and flickered, and the coals of the fire pulsed, softly crackling. Their bodies were gilded with gold and red and silver, awash and throbbing with their own internal heat. The sound of their breathing grew heavier, their movements more driven, less controlled.

Ravel's hands upon her were gently marauding, allowing no modesty as he sought out the secret and untouched source of her feminity. His slow and insistent caress there seemed to dissolve her very bones and send the blood racing in molten splendor along her veins. There was a heaviness in her limbs and a melting, abandoned sensation deep inside her. The muscles of her abdomen contracted in spasm. Her heart jarred in her chest. She arched toward him, wanting, needing to be closer, to become a part of him.

He pressed his hand closer upon her, a finger slipping between her thighs, insidiously, delicately penetrating. Circling, easing, he soothed that first stinging sensation, breaching her tightness with slow and delicious insistence. His close-held patience without limit, he eased the way, until with a soft and strangled sound she moved against him in mounting, undeniable rapture.

Drawing her to him then with her knee over the long, lean-muscled length of his thigh, he entered her, pressing, receding, gradually easing deeper and deeper still. There was an instant of burning pain, though before she could draw breath to cry out, it was gone, banished by his sweet and steady rhythm against her.

A soft sound of mingled relief and purest voluptuous gratification left her lips. As if at a signal, he gathered her to him and turned her to her back, raising himself above her. His chain, attached beside and above the bed, was twisted beneath her, around her thighs, binding them together, inseparably.

Anya scarcely noticed the additional bond linking her body to his. She strained upward against him, accepting the deeper angle of penetration in trembling ecstasy, without reserve. Her lashes quivered on her cheeks. Gooseflesh rose, tingling, along her skin. Her lips parted and she spread her hands, pressing her sensitive palms upon his shoulders, rubbing, clenching and unclenching her fingers.

In rich, fervid wonder, they moved together. Anya accepted the increasing urgency of his thrusts, absorbing their impact, letting them fuel the vivid and beatific grandeur inside her. It hovered, expanding, pouring through her in liquid heat, seeking an outlet.

She caught her breath on a smothered cry as it spilled over her. It was elemental, a storm of passion as tumultuous and unchecked as that which raged in the windswept night. Together they rode it, striving, reveling in its violence. Man and woman, locked in each other's arms, they rose above the petty reasons that had united them, seeking, finding the essential truth: from the prisons of themselves, the prisons life had made for them, this was the only escape.

Chapter Six

꽃 꽃 꽃 *The thunder rumbled away into the darkness.*
The rain slackened, then returned to fall with soft relentlessness, as if it meant to continue through the night. Anya and Ravel lay with bodies entwined, their ragged breathing slowly returning to normal. With gentle fingers, he brushed at a fine strand of hair that lay across her face, enmeshed in her lashes. He ran his hand down her arm and along her flank and, feeling the cool surface of her skin, reached to drag the quilt that covered the bed up over her.

Anya lay with her cheek against his shoulder. There was such confusion in her mind. She did not know whether she was glad or sorry for what had just happened; she only knew that she was content for the moment in the arms of the man who held her. Her body was replete and her mind relieved of a great weight. There was a peculiar wanton pleasure in lying naked against him, one she made no attempt to resist. In the back of her mind she knew she should feel soiled and used, uplifted only by a consciousness of the good she had done, but she could not quite capture that sense of martyrdom. Her major concern, she discovered, was not for the man she had saved, but for the one she might have harmed.

Her voice low, she asked, "Is it really true that some men may call you a coward if you don't appear in the morning?"

"Not to my face."

"What do you mean? That they won't say it in front of you out of fear, but may whisper behind your back?"

"Something like that."

She frowned. "What if there are those who aren't bashful,

90

some of the young men who want to meet you for the glory of it? Wouldn't it make a good excuse?''

''Possibly.''

She heard the grimness behind the noncommittal tone of his voice, and knew that his answer was less than forthright. It was not just possible, but probable, that other meetings would stem from this one failed appointment on the field of honor. Why had she not realized it?

She had not realized it because her concern had, until this moment, been for Murray and Celestine, for anyone and everyone except the formidable, undefeatable Black Knight. But she had defeated him, and now, suddenly, she was afraid for him.

She pushed herself up to one elbow. ''You would not go out of your way to challenge anyone who might slight you!''

He withdrew from her a little so that he could see her face. ''What do you require of me, that I permit your precious future brother-in-law to insult me?''

''Murray wouldn't do such a thing!''

''He did.''

''You must have misunderstood him, or else he didn't realize how touchy Creoles can be. He was only trying to protect me.''

''I did not fail to understand. I gave him an opportunity to explain, and he chose to take that as a reflection on his courage, for which he slapped me in the face with his gloves. I had no choice except to issue a challenge.''

''He must not have known who you were.''

''Should that have made a difference?''

She shook her head. ''I don't know. In any case, it makes none now since there can be no rescheduling of the meeting.''

''Suppose,'' he said, his gaze steady on her face, ''Murray Nicholls decides that my failure to appear is another insult, cause for a new meeting?''

''Impossible. The code—''

''The code prohibits men from meeting more than once over the same cause,'' he said, his tone weary. ''That is, when anyone pays attention to it. It also condemns crossing swords again after the drawing of first blood or the exchange of more than two rounds of fire, though I've seen men fight to the death or exchange fire five and six times, until one of them falls. But the code is silent on the question of an entirely different pretext for a duel, and there is nothing easier to discover."

She pushed slowly erect, staring at him in dismay. "You are saying that if you please, you can challenge Murray again?"

"For the last time, our quarrel was not of my choosing."

"You put him in a position where he felt he had to make a stand, which is the same thing," she accused him. "And now you mean to do it again!"

With controlled animal grace and splendid nakedness, he sat up to face her. "All I am trying to tell you is that another meeting is possible; I tried to make that clear once before, but you wouldn't listen. I will avoid it if I can, but I will not run from Murray Nicholls, not for you or anyone else."

Anya barely let him finish. "You made a fool out of me, letting me barter myself to prevent this meeting, knowing full well that you could go ahead with it as you pleased later! I should have known there was no honor in you, nothing but stupid pride in your reputation as the master duelist in New Orleans. Nothing must interfere with that, nothing, not even your word as a gentleman!"

Dark color rose in Ravel's face. When he spoke, the words carried a slicing edge of contempt. "I didn't begin the practice of dueling, and it gives me no pleasure to continue it. My one object when I walk out on the field is to stay alive with honor. I have pledged, and will pledge, to keep to the letter of the agreement made between us this night, but as memorable as the interlude has been, I don't intend to die because of it."

"You mean to kill Murray for revenge for what I've done," she said in choked tones, "to make him pay for the humiliation I've caused you!"

He looked at her, his expression bleak. "A fine opinion you have of me. I would give you my word to spare this man's life if at all possible, if he will allow it, but I doubt you would accept it."

She swung from him, sliding off the bed, bending to scoop up her clothing and scrape together her hairpins. With her things in her arms, she faced him. "No, I won't accept it. Nor will I let you go. One treachery deserves another, or so it appears to me. You can stay here and rot!"

He came up off the bed, but she was ready for him. She skipped backward the few steps that took her out of reach, beyond the length of his chain.

He did not pursue her, but stood with one knee resting on the mattress. As she started out the door, he said, "I still have the matches."

She turned back with the knob in her hand. "Burn the place down then. But you'll roast in it, because I intend to give the order to let it go up in flames with you inside!"

"You think your people will obey?" The look on his face was skeptical.

"I don't know," she answered with a scathing smile. "Why don't you try them?"

She stepped through the opening, then slammed the door behind her. She took down the key and turned it in the lock with vicious satisfaction, then hung it back in place.

Her clothes were spilling from her arms. She dropped them on the small landing and tried to sort them out in the darkness. The rain was louder here, falling beyond the open ends of the building. A cool wet wind whipped down the wagon drive. Anya shivered, though as much from reaction as from cold. Finding her camisole, she pulled it on, then searched out pantalettes and petticoats, donning them before struggling into her gown and crinoline. She could not fasten her buttons without half breaking her arms bending them backward, and so did not try. Twisting her hair up in a knot as best she could, she thrust her pins into it and at the same time stepped into her slippers and started down the rough steps.

At the doorway of the wagon drive, she threw her shawl over her head and tied the ends under her chin. Lifting her skirts and taking a deep breath, she plunged out into the night.

Water splashed underfoot, wetting her slippers before she had gone a dozen feet. The wind billowed her skirts like sails, holding her back, and blew raindrops into her face, so that she could barely make out the lights of the big house. She had no thought of turning back, however, but marched on with her teeth tightly clenched and her eyes narrowed. She did not want to see Ravel Duralde again, not now, not ever.

The man was a double-crossing, womanizing scoundrel. He

had taken advantage of her in the most despicable way possible. If she were a man, she would do her best to run him through with a sword.

She should have known better than to trust what he said. She did not know what had come over her that she had succumbed so easily to his wiles; she was not usually so gullible. He had even had her beginning to believe him, to think that she might have been mistaken about him all these years. She had wanted to believe it, God help her, had wanted to think that he was as haunted by Jean's death as she was, that he had lived with the constant specter of regret and remorse. She had pitied his years spent in a Spanish prison and had overflowed with compassion for his dislike of being confined. Worst of all, she had been enormously flattered by the thought that the desire he felt for her was greater than his care for his honor. What an idiot she had been! Just the thought of it made her want to scream.

A sound like a sob caught in her throat and she choked it down. She would not cry; it was too late for that. If only she could turn back the clock and be the way she had been that morning, whole and chaste, and with her self-respect intact. She could not. There was nothing to be done except forget the incident, put it behind her.

Your virtue for my honor—

Dear heaven, would she ever forget the things he had said, the way he had looked at her and touched her, the way she had responded to him? Would storms and the smells of cottonseed and lint and a warm male body always remind her? How long would it be before she ceased to feel as if she had been used like a woman of the streets? How long before she could learn to live with the fact that Ravel Duralde had taken her virginity, not out of passionate need or caring, but simply because he could not resist an easy conquest, a fitting revenge?

Denise was waiting, sitting in a chair in Anya's bedchamber. She got to her feet as Anya stepped in through the open French windows from the back gallery. Her gaze widened until her eyes were round and staring in her head as she saw Anya's wet gown opened down the back and her hair straggling from its makeshift knot.

"Mam'zelle, what happened?" she cried.

"Nothing of importance," Anya said, summoning a smile. She threw aside her shawl and began to take the pins from her damp tresses, letting them fall once more. "I would like a brandy, and a hot bath, if you please?"

The housekeeper did not move. "Did he attack you?"

"I would rather not talk about it."

"But, *chère*, you got to tell me."

Denise had been Anya's nurse, companion, and near as much of a mother as Madame Rosa had ever been. It was impossible to deny her. Anya gave a soft sigh. "He didn't attack me, at least not in the way you mean."

"He forced you?"

"Not precisely."

"But you went to bed with him?"

Anya moved away from her. "What does it matter? I'm all right. There's no need for concern."

"You are compromised, *chère*; he done this to you and he has to make it right. He's got to marry you."

Anya whirled back to face the housekeeper. "No! I won't have it."

She could just imagine what Ravel would say if he were told he must marry the woman who had abducted him. But even if he would agree, she had no wish to be wed to a man she hated, a man who would use such base means to get what he wanted.

"Are you sure?"

"I'm sure."

The housekeeper hesitated a moment, as if she would argue further, but then began to move toward the door.

"Denise, when you return you may begin packing for me. I return to New Orleans in the morning."

"With M'sieur Duralde?" the woman asked, her tone stiff with disapproval.

"Alone."

"You will leave him here, in the gin? But mam'zelle, you can't!"

"I can."

"Think of the scandal if people get to know! I understand you being mad at him, *chère*, but this ain't right."

"Maybe not, but I don't care."

"His people will be worried; they'll search for him. They may even call in the police."

"Let them."

"But *chère*—"

Anya sighed and let her shoulders sag. "I know, I know, and I will be back to set him free in a day or two. As for his people, I have been told it isn't unusual for him to be gone without notice for short periods; there should not be too much of a stir."

"He'll be fit to be tied, sure enough. He may go to the police himself."

"And admit he was held prisoner by a woman? He will not want to make such a thing public knowledge."

Denise gave a slow nod. "You might be right, but what if he decides to dish out justice hisself? He'll have plenty of time to think about it."

The thought sent a shiver along Anya's nerves. It was entirely possible, though it might also be that Ravel would consider what he had done already as ample repayment for her crime.

"I will worry about that when the time comes."

The housekeeper said no more, but went away to prepare the bath. Later, when Anya had soaked the chill from her bones and drunk her brandy, when Denise had packed her trunk, then lowered the lamp and taken her rain-soaked silk gown and mud-splashed petticoats away to be refurbished, Anya lay in bed staring into the darkness. The anger that had buoyed her up until this moment slowly seeped away. She was left with a great weariness of the spirits.

She felt betrayed. It was not just what Ravel had done to her that oppressed her, but a feeling also that she had been deceived by her own emotions. She had come very close to feeling compassion for him and even sincere admiration. More than that, he had awakened in her a degree of passion and desire she had never dreamed she could know. His tenderness, his generous concern for her pleasure, the exquisite care with which he had initiated her into the mystery of making love had been a revelation. She had come very near to liking him for a few short minutes.

How could she have been so wrong? How could a man she had hated for so many years convince her so easily to reassess her feelings toward him? It argued a blind spot of some kind in her nature that he had been able to do so. It made her wonder if, in some way she had not heretofore expected, she was susceptible to the blandishments of handsome men, that the overpowering strength of her own passions could make her forget reality. Or was it possible that it was only one man who could trigger those emotions, only one to whom she was vulnerable?

Her sole source of satisfaction was that, regardless of her supine behavior, she had not been weak enough to let Ravel go free. There would be no duel tomorrow, no matter what might happen in the future.

It was not much of a consolation. Slow tears, draining from the corners of her eyes, tracked down her temples into her hair. She turned her face into her pillow and wept.

The first thing Madame Rosa wanted to know when Anya entered the salon of the townhouse in New Orleans was what emergency had taken her from the city in the middle of the night. She was looking soignée in her usual plump and indulgent fashion, dressed in a morning gown of black silk and with a cap of white lace tied with lavender and black ribbon rosettes set with purple silk violets on her hair. She was having her usual cup of midmorning imperial tea, along with a few trifles to stave off hunger until noon, among them coconut bonbons, cream chocolates, and *dragées* on a crystal plate, with nearby a jar of English biscuits smelling strongly of vanilla, and beside that a plate laid with slices of Gruyère cheese, truffled sausages, small rounds of bread, and, as an aid to digestion, a few fancy dried prunes.

Anya removed her kid gloves and took off her bonnet, handing them to a maid. Moving to her stepmother's chair, she bent to kiss her cheek. "If you will pour me a cup of tea while I go to my bedchamber to wash my hands, I will tell you all about it when I get back."

"Certainly, *chère*, and I will put something on a plate for you. You have always been thin, but this morning you look positively peaked."

Madame Rosa, for all her indolence, was nothing if not observant. Anya knew she should have remembered and been prepared. Aloud she merely thanked her and continued through the salon to the more private rooms of the house.

By the time she returned, she had pinched some color into her cheeks and was ready with a glib tale of an illness in the slave quarters that Denise had feared was dysentery from polluted water but had turned out to be merely a highly contagious stomach ailment. To forestall further questions, she went on to ask what the older woman and Celestine had done in her absence.

At that moment, Celestine swept into the room. Hearing the question, she answered before Madame Rosa could begin to speak. "We have had the most frustrating time this morning you can imagine! High and low we have looked for a scarlet petticoat like the one worn by Queen Victoria at Balmoral, and have not been able to find such a thing anywhere. All we have had is stupid jokes about red flags to bulls and the trouble sure to be brought on by wearing such a garment. One buffoon even suggested that after being tossed by a bull, the petticoat should then be called a 'gored' skirt!"

"I remember reading about it somewhere," Anya said. "I suppose it's become the rage?"

"Exactly. Not only is every merchant in the city sold out, but there's hardly a piece of red flannel to be found anywhere, or a seamstress not already piled high with more embroidery work than she can handle. But Anya, it's such a cunning style! It's worn on the top of your crinoline, and the skirt of your gown is looped up on one side to show the fancy embroidered border at the hem in the most dashing manner."

Anya had to smile at her enthusiasm. "It doesn't sound like something Victoria would introduce."

"I believe," Madame Rosa said in her ponderous way, "that the idea was to enable her to lift her gown hem to protect it from the mud of Scotland, while showing something durable and commonplace instead of indiscreet white linen and lace. No one seems to think anything of pulling their skirts up quite high to keep them out of the dirt while they are wearing one."

"Men, I assume, are in favor of the style, then?"

"Extremely," Celestine said with a twinkling laugh.

"Gaspard considers it tasteless," Madame Rosa announced,

"but then so many women wear gowns with it that clash abominably with the red color."

"What else has been happening?"

"Goodness, Anya, you sound as if you have been gone forever instead of only two days." Celestine looked at her with wide eyes.

"Do I?" In truth she felt that way. It also seemed that she had changed in some fundamental way, so that her interest in such things as red petticoats was forced, merely polite.

Madame Rosa said, "I understand we missed a memorable performance by Charlotte Cushman as Mrs. Haller on the night of the *bal masqué*. We plan to remedy the error by seeing her as Queen Katherine in *Henry the Eighth* this evening, if you would care to join us?"

"I would enjoy that." Perhaps it would be a distraction from her thoughts, if nothing else.

"Oh, Anya, you haven't heard the news, have you?" Celestine suddenly exclaimed. "The most peculiar thing occurred; you won't believe it! Murray came around before breakfast this morning to tell us about it, since he knew I would be sick with worry. All our alarms were for nothing. The duel did not take place! Ravel Duralde failed to appear. No one seems to know why, or where precisely he may be. It's a great mystery."

"How—strange," Anya managed, keeping her lashes lowered as she sipped at her tea.

"Yes, indeed. It seems the man spoke with his seconds, asked them to act for him so that plans for the duel could be made, but has not been seen since. Murray is piqued. He feels that it is a deliberate slight, that Duralde considered him so negligible that he let the meeting slip his mind, leaving town without a thought of it. For myself, I don't care. I am relieved beyond measure that it is over."

"Yes, of course," Anya said, summoning a teasing smile with an effort. "You were so relieved that you went out shopping at once for a red petticoat?"

"Exactly," Celestine agreed with a bubbling laugh.

Madame Rosa entered the conversation. "The puzzle of the man's absence has not received as much attention as it might have due to the terrible news in the newspapers this morning of the explosion aboard the *Colonel Cushman*. The steamboat was near New Madrid en route to St. Louis. They say eighteen people were killed, but as yet there is no news of the survivors.''

"One of Murray's friends was on board with his wife and two children," Celestine added.

"The usual cause, I suppose?" Anya commented.

"Too much pressure," Madame Rosa agreed with a nod. "After the boilers exploded, the vessel caught on fire and sank inside twenty minutes. The passengers had to jump overboard. They say the *Southerner*, just ahead of them, turned around and came back to pick up those in the water."

"There was no one we knew on her, by the blessing of *le bon Dieu*," Celestine added.

"Yes, a blessing," Anya agreed, sipping at her tea. There were more tragic things in this world than that which had happened to her. She would do well to remember it.

And yet she could not forget. The memory remained with her as stubbornly as a winter cold, increased tenfold by Celestine's mention of Murray's view of the events surrounding the duel. It carried with it outrage and chagrin and a nagging sense of anguish that demanded some kind of action as an antidote.

Despite the cold and overcast day, she dragged Celestine with her for a bout of shopping for Beau Refuge, buying casks of Louisiana Isabella wine from the 1856 vintage, also boxes of bottles of Château Margaux from Bordeaux, several half bottles each of white and brown curaço from Amsterdam, and a box of Copenhagen cherry cordial. She bought cases of Worcestershire and walnut sauce, three barrels of cracknel biscuits, two barrels of sardines, and a chest each of imperial and hyson tea. She bought a dozen brass-bound churns for the plantation dairy, a bale of blankets for the storeroom for next winter, and for the dispensary a case of quinine and a barrel of castor oil.

Far from being satisfied with these wholesale purchases, she made a stop at Menard's on Old Levee Street, where she placed an order for garden seeds, from tomatoes and cucumbers and okra and several varieties of beans, to pineapple melons, muskmelons, and yellow-orange watermelons. While there she also ordered sent to the plantation enough privets and pittosporums to form a double lane a hundred feet long.

As they were leaving, Celestine made the mistake of mentioning Mardi Gras, and how much she would like to join the maskers in the street on the evening of the great day as the magnificent parade being spoken of in whispers rolled along the Canal Street and through the French Quarter. Anya at once directed the coachman to take them to the Royal Street shop of Madame Lussan.

The small brass bell attached to the door jingled musically as they entered. The ground-floor shop was long and narrow, heated by a small fireplace with a grate in which coal burned with a pulsing red glow. The interior was dim, lighted only by the front windows. In the firelit gloom the masks of devils, apes, bears, cyclopes, satyrs, and other creatures that lined the walls took on a grotesque and menacing realism. The satin of dominoes in black and gray and red hung here and there, gleaming as they moved in the faint draft that drifted down the shop. Spangles and paste jewels glittered from the other costumes that lined the walls. There were heaped trays of jet and brass buttons. Strings of shimmering fake pearls and glass beads in rainbow colors dripped from racks. Around the counter were loops of the fashionable gilt and silver ribbon-tape, and also waterfalls of gilt and silver tassels on cards. The whole place glimmered and shone like a pirate's treasure house.

Madame Lussan sat behind her counter sewing spangles on the bodice of a dress. She rose as they moved toward her, a plump woman with dark hair twisted into a tight knot on top of her head, bright eyes that missed nothing, and an eager manner.

"*Bonjour mademoiselles*, and how may I serve you this afternoon?"

"We wish costumes for Mardi Gras Day, but want something out of the ordinary," Celestine said.

"Doesn't everyone?" Madame Lussan said with sympathy. "How distressing it is to see yourself everywhere you look. My stock is most unique, I do assure. Even in the popular characters, the colors of the costumes or the details are different. They were carefully chosen in Paris, and are of the finest quality materials and workmanship; you need have no fear of them being destroyed by rain or a careless movement."

Celestine, looking around with sparkling eyes, said, "You have a large supply, the largest I've seen."

"Indeed. Since the fine parade of the Krewe of Comus last year, there has been great excitement about the day. So many more people are inquiring about costumes for Mardi Gras Day itself, instead of only for the balls, that I fear there will be a great crush in the streets."

It had been only a year before that a group of men calling themselves the Mistick Krewe of Comus had formed a club for the sole purpose of celebrating Mardi Gras in what they considered to be the proper style. Mardi Gras had, for the past fifty years or more, been marked by street masking and impromptu lines of decorated carriages filled with young men in costume and groups of knights of Bedouins on horseback winding through the streets. There had been no organization, however, and due to the rowdy conduct of the lower elements of the town, the day had fallen into disfavor—until the Krewe of Comus had come upon the scene. The Krewe was made up mostly of Americans, some of whom had belonged to a similar club in Mobile called the Cowbellions that paraded on New Year's Day. The group in New Orleans had selected Mardi Gras as the holiday for their parade, and had introduced a novelty called a *tableau roulant*, or rolling tableau. Brightly illuminated and highly colored, it featured a fantastic scene set up in tableau form on a platform built on wheels. This tableau was pulled through the streets with hundreds of other costumed figures following. The spectacle the year before had been fantastic, but was supposed to be even more stupendous this year, with many more of the rolling tableaux.

"Have there been many ladies inquiring for costumes?" Celestine asked.

Madame Lussan gave a quick nod. "A great number. The men are going to have to give way to the fairer sex, instead of expecting them to view the proceedings from a balcony as if it were a theatrical production. But I digress. Come, tell me, what is your dearest desire? Who would you choose to be above all else? That is what Mardi Gras is about, after all!"

Anya tore her eyes away from the mask of a goat with a long white beard, horns as red and as spided as those usually reserved for the devil, and a distinct leer in its glass eyes. "I have no idea what I want, or who I would like to be," she said with a smile. "My secret desires are hidden even from myself."

"It is usually so," Madame Lussan said with a shrug. "Permit me to show you a few items."

She turned and led the way toward the rear of the shop, saying over her shoulder as she went, "Will you be attending the ball at the Theatre d'Orleans tomorrow night? I have some truly elegant *grandees toilettes*."

Before they could answer, a gentleman emerged from one of the small rooms at the back of the shop, the retiring, or toilet, rooms where one went to try the costumes for fit. He carried his hat and cane in his hand and was smoothing his hair with his other hand. To Madame Lussan, he said, "The Cossack officer uniform will do excellently. You may send it at your convenience."

"Certainly, M'sieur Girod," the proprietress answered.

"Emile!" Anya exclaimed in pleased recognition. "When did you return from Paris?"

The young man came toward them with a warm smile lighting his face. Of medium height, he had tightly curling hair of a light brown cut close to his head, liquid brown eyes in a mobile face, and a clipped mustache in the cavalry style on his upper lip. His complexion was typically Creole, with an olive undertone to the skin and a faint flush of color over the cheekbones. He was Jean's brother. Born four or five years after Jean, he had been studying at the university in Paris for the past two years, the typical arrangement for the sons of the wealthier Creole planters.

He did not immediately answer Anya's questions, but took the hand she gave him, bowing over it with a Gallic flourish. "Anya, how happy I am to see you! I called at your townhouse yesterday, but was told you were away from home. How magnificent you look, the same goddess I used to worship from afar." He turned to Celestine, saluting her hand also. "And Celestine, we meet again; fortune is indeed with me. It was gracious of you to entertain me yesterday in your sister's absence. What fun it was remembering old times."

Emile, along with perfecting the Creole gentleman's habit of extravagant compliments, had achieved a certain polish in the years of his absence. Because the exchange of visits between Beau Refuge and the Girod plantation had slowed upon Jean's death, and because Emile had not been of an age to indulge in the social round of the winter season, Anya had not seen a great deal of him in the past few years. She remembered him primarily as the younger brother who had loved to tease her, and who had kept a pet crawfish, leading it around on a string or caging it in a glass case half-filled with mud in his room.

Now he went on. "I arrived back in New Orleans aboard the *H. B. Metcalf* by way of Havana a few days ago, and immediately went down on my knees to kiss the smelly mud of the levee. Ah, New Orleans, it's like no other place on earth! Paris is beautiful and cosmopolitan, with some ancient stone pile of historical significance on every corner, but dear old damp and warm and comfortable New Orleans is home."

"It isn't so warm today," Celestine said, drawing her shawl around her with a theatrical shiver.

"I am devastated to be forced to contradict a lady, but, believe me, compared to Paris in February, it's balmy! But do I understand you are choosing costumes? I will go away if I disturb you, or if you prefer to remain anonymous in whatever you decide upon, but it would give me great pleasure to stay. Who knows, I might even be of service?"

He was, indeed. He unhesitatingly vetoed a daring and yet rather childish pierrette costume for Celestine, suggesting instead a court gown of richly embroidered russet panne velvet from the period of Louis XIII that gave her delicately rounded face and figure a somber majesty. He argued with Anya over the various merits of a softly draped and wide-sleeved medieval gown from the Court of Love of Eleanor of Aquitaine, of a graceful long tunic and toga in fine cream wool edged with gilt tape and wide bands of regal purple ribbon that might have been worn by a Roman goddess, and of a Japanese kimono of heavy, finely embroidered scarlet silk complete with hair ornaments and a sandlewood fan. Emile seemed to prefer the romance of the medieval costume, while Anya leaned toward the exotic look of the Chinese silk. In the end, she compromised and chose the simplicity of the Roman costume, and caught Emile winking at Celestine as if to say that had been his choice all along.

Anya enjoyed Emile's company, his quick, laughing comments, his obvious pleasure in intimate female society, as well as the bittersweet memories he evoked of his brother, but she had another motive for encouraging him to stay with them. When they had reserved their costumes and left the shop, she invited him to return with them to the townhouse for refreshments. He accepted with all the amiability of a man with limitless time on his hands, declaring with disarming charm that he was unable to tear himself away from two such lovely ladies. On the short carriage drive they continued to exchange a rapid-fire banter, and were still laughing when they walked into the salon of the townhouse.

Madame Rosa looked up to greet them, laying aside a French copy of Trollope's *Barchester Towers* without haste. She did not rise to greet Emile, but remained as she was with her small feet in high-buttoned black shoes resting on a silk-covered stool. He came forward to kiss her hand instead of merely bowing, as she was a married lady, and, with his innate good manners, stayed beside her talking while Anya moved to ring for a servant and order tea and coffee, *eau sucre* and orange-flower water, along with a selection of cakes.

They talked of commonplaces until the servant had brought the tray of refreshments. At an indolent gesture from Madame Rosa, the tray was placed before Anya. Anya poured the orange-flower water for her stepmother, a concoction she could not stand herself, since the laudanum with which it was liberally laced made her sleepy, but one that was a great favorite among older women. Celestine took tea and Emile coffee. When Emile passed the other two ladies their cups or glasses and placed his own cup on a table beside his chair, Anya poured black coffee for herself and leaned back.

"Tell me, Emile," she said in a tone as lightly conversational as she could summon, "as a man-about-town you must have heard of the fiasco this morning of the failed meeting between Ravel Duralde and Celestine's fiancé. What are they saying in the cafés?"

Emile shifted in his chair, his face sobering. He was so long in answering that Anya spoke again.

"Oh, come, I know this is a subject that women usually avoid, but there is no point in pretending that we don't know about it."

He stirred pale golden sugar into his coffee with a small silver spoon, then gave a small shrug. "There are some who are saying Ravel Duralde wished to avoid the meeting because of the unhappiness he has already brought to the women of this family. Others claim his action was an intentional affront. Then there is a third group, including many of the men who served under him in Nicaragua, that has been searching high and low for him along Gallatin Street and in the Irish area called the Swamp, afraid of foul play. They claim that it is the only reason he would fail."

"And what do you think?"

"I have no reason to love the man," he said, his voice cool in contrast to its earlier warmth, "and it's true I don't know him well since he is several years older. However, nothing I have ever heard of him leads me to believe that he would run away from a fight or treat a matter of the duello so lightly as to stay away without good reason."

There was a stir in the doorway. Murray, his face flushed, stepped into the room. His manner was a shade belligerent as he faced the Creole. "Ah, but there you have the reason. Duralde is getting old and tired of fighting. He heard that I had some prowess with weapons, and did not care for the odds. He thinks that I will forget the matter, that it will blow over if he stays away for a time. He will discover precisely how wrong he is when he returns."

Anya sat staring at Murray with a frown gathering between her brows. His manner was unbecoming in her opinion, possibly out of a relief that he could not afford to express, and perhaps out of the fear that someone would sense it. It could not be that he did not realize his lucky escape. Ravel's reputation as a duelist was based primarily on his skill as a swordsman, but he was also a soldier, and considered deadly with firearms as well.

She leaned forward in her concern. "Surely there is no need to go to such lengths as to force another meeting. As reasonable men, there must be some other way to settle this ridiculous business.''

''Ridiculous?'' Murray asked, placing his hands on his hips. ''It was a question of an insult to you, a lady, if you will recall, Anya.''

''I recall the incident very well, and I have no memory of an insult. If you are at all concerned for my good name, or for Celestine's fears, you will let this matter rest.''

''I am sorry for Celestine's concern, of course,'' he said with a faint smile directed toward the other girl, ''however, I must question how your good name comes into the matter.''

''If you persist, everyone will begin to wonder exactly what it is Ravel is supposed to have done to me.''

''They already wonder,'' Celestine said, though her words were softly spoken.

''What do you mean?'' Anya asked, swinging to face her.

''Well, there are one or two who have made a point of trying to find out the cause of the duel, asking sly questions, particularly after you left the city on the same night.''

''The curiosity is natural,'' Madame Rosa said, ''but it isn't something that I like, this gossip and supposition about my husband's daughter. Anya is right; the business should be stopped.''

Murray gave them a smile of triumph. ''From what I have seen there is little need to worry. I could tell even on the night of the masked ball that the man did not want to meet me. Apparently he wants it even less now.''

The manner of Celestine's fiancé grated on Anya's nerves. She had to bite the inside of her bottom lip to prevent herself from pointing out his error in judgment to him. If Ravel had been reluctant to meet Murray, she knew with sudden clarity, it had had nothing to do with fear or with age. Ravel was not old, being only a little more than thirty, but by his own admission he was weary of fighting, and wary of senseless duels.

''I would take care how I spoke if I were you, m'sieur,'' Emile said with deliberation.

Murray stared down at him. There was a suggestion of a derogatory inflection in his voice as he spoke. ''Would you indeed?''

''It may be that you will wake up one morning and discover

that Ravel Duralde has returned. His anger has not until now been aroused. But have no doubt; if the things you have said here have also been expressed elsewhere, and if they should come to his ears, you will be called to answer for them.''

The words were firm, regardless of the flush that tinted the cheeks of Jean's younger brother. There was, Anya saw, a streak of iron in Emile beneath his mannered grace and florid compliments. That he should champion Ravel, a man who must be considered his enemy, seemed strange until she realized he was defending not the man but one of his own race against an *américain* and a Northerner.

Whatever the reason, she applauded his stand. It occurred to her suddenly that she was very close to taking Ravel's part in this quarrel. The realization so astonished her that she sat back silent and aghast in her chair. Was she that susceptible to the man whose arguements she had, against her will, allowed to sway her? It did not seem possible, and yet what other explanation could there be?

Murray, scowling down at Emile, said hardily, ''Sir, are you questioning my discretion?''

''How should I since you are a stranger to me?'' Emile answered, his gaze limpid. ''I merely seek to warn you.''

Madame Rosa, stirred to movement by the tension in the room, sat up. Her manner, aided by her size, took on a hint of the imperious. ''Gentlemen, if you please, quarreling is much too fatiguing; pray do not do so in my salon. M'sieur Nicholls, I beg you will be seated so that we may have save ourselves the trouble of looking up at you. Ah, very good. So amiable. Now, what may Anya pour out for you in the way of refreshment?''

Chapter Seven

🦋 🦋 🦋 *The amusements available in New Orleans* that winter season were many. In January the celebrated aeronaut Morat, veteran of seventy-one balloon ascensions, had been in the city to afford celestial views of the environs to anyone wishing to go up in his mammoth new balloon, the *Pride of the South*. The first female magician, Madame Macallister, wife of the late master of the art, had for the sake of her children taken up the wand and presented nights of magic including the aerial suspension of her assistant, Mademoiselle Mathilde, manipulation of a gorgeous magic cabinet, and the display of splendid paraphernalia for her varied experiments in mechanism, electricity, hydraulics, and pneumatics. At Spalding and Roger's Museum and Amphitheater on St. Charles Street, the elephants Victoria and Albert were entertaining audiences and giving the newspapers opportunities for humorous quips concerning the royal personages for which they were named. Also featured was the Human Fly, a man who walked on the ceiling with his feet up and head down, and the Siamese twins Chang and Eng. To compete, Vannuchi's Museum further along the street had imported a double-headed female child with four limbs who could sing, waltz, and play the harmonica but who, as the advertisement put it, "lapsed into a singular unity of persons as regards their animal functions." The museum also featured the miniature Venus, Mrs. Ellen Briggs, only thirty-five inches high, and Kentucky giantess Mademoiselle Oceana, the largest woman in the world, weighing 538 pounds.

In a more serious vein, world-renowned Louisiana chess player Paul Morphy had a month before he demonstrated his incredible prowess at the game by playing against two other players while blindfolded. Edwin Booth had received mixed reviews for his performance at Crisp's Gaiety Theater, before its closing, in the lead roles in *Hamlet, Richard III*, and *Othello, the Moor of Venice*. For February, there was the promise of a lecture by Thomas Forster, editor of the *Boston Banner of Light*, on "Spiritualism in the Trance State," and another on "Poetry and Song" by the Englishman Charles Mackay, editor of the well-known *Illustrated London News*.

For the music lovers, the opera season was in full swing, with the Theatre d'Orleans having already featured performances of *La Favorite* and Verdi's *Ernani*, with plans for Rossini's *Mosè in Egitto*. There had also been advance notice of a week of concerts to be given by the famous maestro Sigismund Thalberg on the pianoforte with accompaniment by the brilliant Vieuxtemps on the violin.

Art for the moment was represented by a showing of Rosa Bonheur's marvelous painting *Horse Fair*, a canvas that had previously been exhibited only in London and Paris. A large and ambitious work much praised by the critics, though with some caviling about minor details, it was on view in the Lecture Room of the Odd Fellow's Hall.

Anya and Celestine drove out to see the painting on the day after Anya's return, the last day of its exhibition. They stood before it in silence for long moments. Framed in heavy gilt, it was a view of a horse fair, or sale, in the Bois de Boulogne near Paris. It contained some twenty animals and twenty-five or thirty human figures, all beautifully alive and full of movement and color. The spire and rotunda of the famous Hotel des Invalides appeared in the distance. Clouds of dust stirred by the prancing hooves hung among the branches of the trees. The muscles and veins and contours of the horses were perfection. The costumes of the spectators were vividly colored and accurately depicted complimenting the bodies beneath them and their natural movement. It was a most pleasing and inspiring piece of work. If there were blemishes, Anya could not see them.

Celestine sighed. "I wish I could paint. I mean really paint, not just make daubs on china."

"It's just as important to appreciate art as to create it," Anya said, though she too felt the stirring of a kind of jealousy of the woman who had produced the masterpiece before them.

"Yes," Celestine agreed. "This reminds me, I must buy a valentine for Murray since Sunday will be Valentine's Day. They have a good supply at the booksellers on Canal Street, if you would like to stop by and look at them?"

It had been pointed out many times that the Creole passion for the arts was largely confined to music and dancing. In Celestine's case, it was obviously true. Smiling a little at her half sister's transparently brief moment of artistic fervor, Anya led her away to search for valentines.

Their sortie into intellectual pastimes did not end there, however. There was still the visit to the theater that evening to see Cushman. Anya was ready early for the simple reason that, lacking any other occupation, she had begun dressing far ahead of time. The salon where the party would be gathering beforehand, a room charmingly done with an eye to an appearance of summer coolness in shades of blue and with crystal ornaments sitting here and there, was empty when she entered it. Celestine was still in her bath, if the sounds of an off-key aria coming from her bedchamber were any indication, and Madame Rosa was undergoing the torture of having her hair pomaded and arranged by the woman who was hired by the month as hairdresser to the ladies of the house. Anya paused a moment, then moved to stand at one of the French doors that overlooked the streets. She drew aside the gold silk-brocade drapery and lace-edged muslin curtain that covered it, staring out.

Night was falling and the sky was colored gray and gold and pink above the rooftops. Pigeons wheeled in flocks, catching the last rosy light under their wings. The street below, beyond the narrow balcony that fronted the house, was dim, but not yet dark; the streetlamps had not been lighted. Now and then a glossy carriage pulled by highbred horses rattled past. A dog wandered along, sniffing at the garbage in the open gutter that ran down the center of the paved thoroughfare. A young mulatto with a white apron over her dress, a striped kerchief on her head, and a wide tray on her hip swung along under the overhanging balconies on the opposite side, singing of her *tout chaud calas*, or hot rice cakes, and of her creamy pralines rich with pecans.

A young boy balancing on his head a tray of woven rattan filled with perfect red camellias on short stems offered *belles fleurs* to nestle in the hair of the ladies or the buttonholes of the gentlemen going out for the evening.

The rest of the street vendors, the oyster man and the cream cheese man, the woman who sold greens and scallions and chives; the vendor of sweet milk and buttermilk and the man who peddled cheap red wine from a barrel; the broom man, coffee man, knife sharpener, and the man who fixed tin had all gone home, leaving only these hopefuls to wander the streets crying their wares.

At Beau Refuge, Marcel would be taking Ravel his evening meal. Anya wondered how the Black Knight had fared through the long day, and if he knew she had left the plantation to return to New Orleans. If he did know, he would doubtless be enraged at being left in his prison, chained to the wall. The imprecations he would call down upon her head would sear her ears no doubt, if she could hear them. He might even be plotting other ways of catching his keepers, Denise and Marcel, off guard and so win his freedom.

It had been nearly forty-eight hours since she had seen him. She wondered if his head wound was mending and if he found his solitary state oppressive. Not that she was losing sleep worrying over him; he deserved what had come to him, and probably a great deal more.

She thought of him, lying with his long body stretched out on the bed in that small gin room, with his feet crossed and his hands behind his head, of the slow and faintly mocking smiles that curved his molded mouth and reflected in his dark eyes. She thought of him reaching out for her, drawing her down beside him, his hands upon her warm and sure, his lips—

With a gasp she swung from the window. She raised her hands to her face, pressing them hard against the bones under the skin as she squeezed her eyes shut. She would not think about that, she would not. Such pleasures as he had given her she could find with any man. There was nothing unusual in her response to him, a man of his experience, nothing unusual at all.

The stern words quieted her mind, but did nothing for the

ache deep inside her. She had not been prepared for the storm of feelings he had aroused in her. She was herself, the same, and yet changed by it. It was as if some vital part of her had been taken apart and reassembled to a new design, with some essential element missing.

"What is it, *chère*? Do you have a headache?"

There was concern in Madame Rosa's voice as she came into the room. She wore her usual black, though softened by the magnificent amethysts and diamonds that winked at her throat and ears and on both wrists. Draped at her elbows was a shawl of soft black wool that she could pull around her shoulders if she felt chilled. She looked placid and yet distinguished in a peculiarly French fashion, though there glinted in the depths of her eyes a look of anxiety.

Lowering her hands, Anya attempted a reassuring smile. "Only a little one."

"Shall I order a glass of orange-flower water for you? It is best to deal with things before they become entrenched."

"No, no, I'll be fine. Perhaps I'm just hungry."

"It could well be; you ate little enough at noon." Madame Rosa glanced at the clock that ticked on the mantel. "Is that the time? We must sit down to our dinner soon if we are to make it to the theater by curtain time."

Performances in New Orleans were protracted, beginning at seven and lasting, with the inclusion of the farce or other light entertainment following the main performance, until near midnight. It was customary to have a simple meal before leaving home, then go to a more elaborate supper afterward.

"Will Gaspard and Murray be dining with us?" Anya asked, not because she wanted to know but because it was something to say.

"Gaspard will, and so will be escorting us to the theater. Murray could not get away in time. He will be joining us there." Madame Rosa moved to a settee and settled herself upon it as she spoke.

The taffeta of Anya's dark sapphire blue evening gown made a crisp rustling sound as she took a turn about the room. She paused at a side table to pick up the stereoscope that lay there, looking through it at a scene from the interior of the London

Crystal Palace with its palms and flitting birds. After putting it down again, she wandered to the small pianoforte in one corner, pressing down a note so that it chimed softly through the room. She glanced at her stepmother, then looked away again.

"I've been thinking of Ravel Duralde," she said, her tone carefully casual. "Tell me, how does he strike you?"

"I have always thought him a most unfortunate young man."

Anya sent Madame Rosa a flashing glance of surprise. "Unfortunate?"

"What else, when he was born to a recluse of a father self-centered to the point of madness, a man who must force the memory of a less than ideal family history upon the notice of the public? Then there is his mother, a woman of much sensibility and ill health. He grew up with heavy responsibility in such a family. And what must he do but add the tragedy of killing his dearest friend to these burdens? I pity him with all my heart."

"He killed Jean."

"You can't think he meant to do it, or that he has not regretted it more bitterly even than you? He has sought so long to escape it, in traveling, in war, in gambling, in women. It cannot be done, and now after so many years he must know it. His mother's illness is such that he has now to remain in New Orleans. He can no longer rove the world seeking forgetfulness, but must find it here, where he was born."

"First Emile defends him, and now you. It seems strange."

"Gentlemen of the same stripe have a tendency to protect each other and also their peculiar habits against outsiders; a slur upon one Creole is a slur upon them all. You must not take that to mean that Emile doesn't care about his brother's death, or that he has forgiven the man who caused it. Nor am I suggesting that M'sieur Duralde is a man one would wish to know socially, though there are many, particularly among the *Américains*, who do not look beyond his fortune."

"Isn't the Creole emphasis on lineage and social desirability a little ridiculous considering the soldiers and adventurers who established New Orleans?"

Madame Rosa shrugged. "I do not make the conventions,

only abide by them. Change is difficult, and also most fatiguing.''

The answer was honest at least. As far back as Anya could remember, that had been Madame Rosa's attitude. She was generous and tolerant and endlessly obliging, but there was a point past which she would not go, the point at which the effort seemed likely to exceed the benefit. She was not selfish, far from it, nor was she a hedonist, but she did tend to conserve her energy.

Now the older woman went on. ''In truth, it may be too late. M'sieur Duralde is a proud man who has suffered much. Resentment, for his mother's sake if not his own, would be natural. Even if Creole society would accept him as this date, he might well scorn it.''

It was of course possible; Ravel had pride. ''What of Murray? You have permitted him to become betrothed to Celestine, and yet as an American should he not be even less repectable than M'sieur Duralde?''

''This family is not all of Creole society, thank the good God; I am free to accept whom I please on a personal basis. Besides, if you will forgive my saying so, *chère*, as the wife of an American I was not the *crème de la crème* myself for some years. I have only redeemed myself by becoming a widow! Amusing, is it not?''

They were interrupted by the noise of a carriage arriving in the street below. Within a few short minutes Gaspard crossed the threshold of the room. A maidservant came from the back of the house, and he relinquished his hat, cane, and cape to her before treading toward them with his elegant, not quite mincing, stride.

He made them his best bow as he greeted them, then, flipping up the skirts of his evening coat, sat down near Madame Rosa. After every greeting and compliment suited to the occasion, he embarked on the kind of polite and easy conversation that requires a degree of finesse but little thought.

Gaspard was almost handsomely attired in a full-dress coat of solid black with silk lapels and silk-covered buttons worn with trousers of black elastic cashmere. Underneath it was a vest of silver-colored moiré silk embroidered in silver dots. His shirt, starched and ironed to a crackling satin gleam, had a standing collar encircled by a cravat of silver silk tied in a double bow. His boots were of patent leather with rather tall heels to give him added height.

There was always such an air of sartorial perfection about Gaspard that Anya and Celestine had often accused him of being Mr. Prettybreeches. The appellation had been invented in a moment of wit by the editor of the *Louisiana Courier* as a means of introducing items concerning proper dress for men into his newspaper, items suggested by this fictional gentleman. Gaspard took the teasing as a compliment, or else, with his usual polished address, pretended to do so. He was so good-natured, so attentive to Madame Rosa's comfort and well-being, so ready to be amused while at the same time supremely unaware that there was anything about himself that might be humorous, that Anya could not help liking him.

A short time later, Celestine joined them and they moved to the dining room. When their meals were finished, they descended to the carriage for the drive to the Saint Charles Theater.

The planking of the dance floor that had turned the theater into a ballroom the weekend before had been removed and the theater had taken on its proper character once more. The play, however, was slow moving and, perhaps because it was so familiar, uninteresting of plot. The first scenes held little meat for an actress of Charlotte Cushman's ability, being merely the detailing of why and how Henry VIII meant to be rid of his unwanted first wife, Queen Katherine. There was a certain entertainment in seeing precisely how ridiculous the actor playing Henry could behave as he strutted and postured about the stage, but the greatest amusement of the evening was to be had from training one's opera glasses on the occupants of the other boxes and anticipating the visits back and forth of the gentlemen during intermission. Murray's rather noisy arrival in the midst of the histrionics troubled no one.

Hardly had the curtain rung down after the first act and the gaslights on brackets between the boxes turned up than Emile Girod presented himself. Jean's younger brother was in fine spirits, and seemed delighted to be able to visit with them and display his best gallantries for the amusement of the ladies. They all discussed the actors, disagreeing amiably about the talent of the man playing Cardinal Wolsey, with Anya and Madame Rosa claiming that he was respectable, while Celestine and Emile declared him pedestrian. Gaspard, when appealed to, came down on the side of his inamorata. Murray, frowning in preoccupation at the young Creole who had possessed himself of the seat behind Celestine and sat leaning forward with his hand on the back of the young girl's chair, could not for a moment be brought to understand what they were arguing about. Emile, a sensitive young man, removed his hand at once and turned to talk to Anya.

The moment was awkward. To ease it Anya said, "What an egotist Henry was, ranting and raving about an heir for his throne, discarding one woman after another, ordering them put to death, and all for something that was probably his own fault anyway."

"Ah, but there was his son by his mistress," Murray objected.

"So the woman said, but who, pray, could prove it? The man was obsessed! Look at all the heartache he caused, to say nothing of the lives he destroyed and the damage he did to England by sowing the seeds of civil war. Men like him should be removed, no matter the means."

"Depose the tyrants?" Gaspard mused. "But unless you destroy them at the same time, they have a nasty habit of returning, worse than ever."

"A tidy assassination now and then would save everyone much grief," Anya maintained stoutly.

Madame Rosa pursed her lips. "Who should wield the sword? And would he not become a worse tyrant?"

"It's possible," Anya answered impatiently, "but if you were confronted with a murderer with a knife in his hand while you held a pistol, would you fail to shoot out of fear that you might afterward become a murderer yourself?"

"I agree with Anya," Emile said. "There are some men who deserve to die."

"Ah," Madame Rosa said, "but who should decide which ones?"

"That is the heart of the problem, certainly," Anya said. "I'm not really championing indiscriminate killing, but I still think it's a good idea to remove those who have caused harm in the past and have the potential to cause more, the legal murderers such as kings, corrupt police, and duelists who use their power and positions and skill for their own ends.''

"Duelists?" Celestine asked, puzzlement in her brown eyes.

"We all know there are some who are quite unscrupulous, who use the threat of their skill to manipulate others.''

"Such as Ravel Duralde?''

Anya felt the warm tide of blood flow into her face. She lowered her head, pretending to be concerned with the fastening of her glove. "I wasn't thinking of him in particular, but since you bring up the name, why not?''

"No, no, Anya," Emile protested. "You never used to be unjust.''

Gaspard studied her with a mingled look of surprise and speculation. "An interesting theory.''

"Such a weighty discussion," Celestine complained with a smile, "nearly as weighty as this play. Now we all know that if Anya had been queen in Tudor England, there would have been no problem. Henry would have suffered a regrettable accident while hunting, or else simply disappeared one dark night.''

Gaspard looked pained at the suggestion. "Once, perhaps, when she was younger and more volatile; now she is far too much the lady.''

"You can't know her at all well if you think so!" Celestine sent Anya a sparkling glance that slowly faded as she saw the flush spreading across her half sister's cheekbones.

Celestine could be as acute in an intuitive fashion as her mother at times. With a supreme effort, Anya said in mock chagrin, "I protest, I am being maligned.''

"I wonder—," Celestine began, her voice shaded with speculation as she looked at Anya in the shimmering gaslight.

"Ah, at last the curtain rises," Madame Rosa said, overriding her daughter, distracting her. But, though the older woman's smile was placid, the glance she sent Anya out of the corners of her eyes was thoughtful.

The evening wore on. The trial scene was satisfyingly dramatic, with many tears and much hand wringing, which Cushman performed magnificently. The farce, *Betsy Baker*, was a well-acted bit of froth. Anya's interest in it, not great at first, sharpened as it progressed. There was a dark-haired actress of opulent charms playing one of the bit parts. Her stage skills were less than impressive, but her shape, displayed in her scanty costume, was voluptuous. The program gave the name of the woman as Simone Michel. She was Ravel's current mistress.

Anya raised her opera glasses to her eyes, surveying the actress with more than ordinary interest. What was it men saw in such obvious creatures? Grasping, with scant intelligence and less virtue, what could they offer a man other than a warm body in his bed? Perhaps that was enough, all that most men wanted? Perhaps they preferred a woman who would not be hurt by their defection when they tired of her, one who would accept their parting gift, shrug, and go on to the next man? It might be less expensive for them, and less entangling, than a more lasting alliance. She would have thought, however, that someone like Ravel would have better taste.

When they left the theater at the end of the farce, they discovered that rain had fallen during the performance. The streets outside glistened, reflecting the gaslights in the water that sheeted the banquettes and ran like a millrace in the gutters, washing them clean. Carriages crowded each other, wheeling and backing, jockeying for position near the door as the drivers sought to get close so that the ladies would not have to trail their skirts of silk and satin and velvet in the wet. Horses whinnied and jibbed. The men on the boxes cursed their beasts and bawled insults at each other. Nimble-footed boys wove in and out through the melee, offering cheap umbrellas for sale at exorbitant prices.

Anya, Madame Rosa, Celestine, and Murray, along with Emile, stood waiting while Gaspard went further along to wave his cane at his driver in a command for the man to bring his carriage up. Madame Rosa had invited the young Creole to join them for supper, to "even their numbers," she had said, blandly ignoring Murray's lack of enthusiasm for the arrangement. Emile put forth the suggestion that he travel to the townhouse in the same way we had come to the theater, by the omnibus. Murray offered to do the same, so as to save crowding in the carriage and the inevitable crushing of the gowns of the ladies. Madame Rosa would not hear of it. It was beginning to rain again in a fine mist and looked as if it might pour at any moment. As a result, the waiting omnibuses were being filled to overflowing. The skirts of the ladies could surely stand a bit of crushing, since they were homeward bound.

Conversation after that was fitful as they waited, being primarily concerned with whether the ladies wanted to step back inside, and whether the inexpensive silk umbrellas being hawked would actually stop rain without dripping dye all over the buyer.

The downpour held off, and the carriage arrived. There was some hilarity as they squeezed into it, but finally Gaspard, Madame Rosa, and Anya were seated with their backs to the horses, while Murray, Celestine, and Emile faced them. They were still unable to proceed homeward, however, Two carriages had become entangled at an intersection some distance ahead of them, blocking traffic. Gaspard's coachman on the box of their own carriage inched forward until a side street was reached, then swung into it. Rather than following the long, slow-moving line of the detouring carriages, the man continued on for a few blocks hoping to get out of the congestion before turning back toward the Vieux Carré.

It was a great relief when the noise and confusion fell away behind them. They had left the area of the gaslights, and the streets here were quiet and dark. The houses were set back behind fences, closed in, the shutters tightly drawn, with only now and then a faint gleam of lamplight showing through their slats. Somewhere a dog barked, a sound with the monotonous persistence of a creaking gate.

The carriage slowed and turned into a cross street. Here the dwellings were meaner, with crumbling plaster, peeling paint, and sagging doors. Interspersed among them were small shops, butchers and bakers and cobblers, with now and then a barrelhouse from which spilled sawdust and lamplight and the smell of cheap whiskey. Men reeled along the banquettes, a few with their arms wrapped around hard-faced women wearing gowns cut so low they revealed their breasts to the nipples.

Celestine, staring out the window, reached to clutch Murray's arm in a tight hold. He patted her hand, though his manner was distracted. Gaspard, his lips pursed, leaned forward to tap on the pass-through window, urging his coachman to go faster. In anticipation of having the order obeyed, Anya reached for the hanging strap beside her as she sat in one corner.

Ahead of them, a ramshackle cart drawn by a mule pulled into the street from an alley. The man on the box above them swore, sawing at his reins, bringing his team to a halt so close to the cart that its broken-down mule kicked at the leader.

There came a thudding noise and the carriage jolted on its springs as a heavy weight landed on the back. At the same time, a man ran from the side to leap onto the step and wrench open the door. The driver of the rickety cart in front of them flung himself down from his seat, abandoning his vehicle, dragging a pistol out of his waistband as he ran toward them.

It was an ambush. Madame Rosa gasped and fell back against the seat. Gaspard turned to her in concern, grasping her hand. Emile, his face stern in the light of the carriage lanterns, twisted the knob of his cane and drew a slender and lethal blade, hissing, from the hollow staff. At the same time, he threw himself in front of Celestine to shield her. Murray, his face flushed with anger that might have been directed toward Emile as much as for the men converging upon them, thrust his hand under his coat and brought out a small, multibarreled pistol of the kind known as a pepper pot.

"Hold it right there, boys," the rough-looking man in the doorway growled. In his hand was a large Colt revolver, darkly shining, the bore waving slowly from one male passenger to the other. Gaspard and Murray and Emile went still, freezing into position.

Anya caught the sour animalistic smell of the man so close to her. The insolence of his voice, the incredible daring of this attack in the middle of the city brought the rise of virulent anger inside her. She did not pause to think. Clinging to the strap she held for purchase, she lifted her leg beneath the mound of skirts made by her gown and petticoats and collapsed hoop and kicked high.

Her movement was hidden until it was too late. The man yelped as her foot caught his hand. The revolver went flying, tumbling in the air. In that instant, Murray fired. The man in the door made a choking sound as he was thrown backward by the blast.

The cart driver, almost to the carriage, came to such a sudden stop that he skidded, stumbling, nearly falling on his face. He looked up, staring inside the carriage through the swirling, acrid screen of gun smoke. His skin turned a pasty white. "Mother of God," he croaked, then spun around, taking to his heels.

The third attacker did not tarry to look. He jumped from the rear of the carriage and pounded away into the night. The scrawny mule attached to the cart, startled into unaccustomed vigor by the shot, bolted, pulling the empty cart bumping and sluing behind him down the street. Within a matter of seconds, the street was clear and everything was quiet.

"Good shooting, *mon ami*!" Emile said with enthusiasm as he slapped Murray on the back.

"Is the fellow dead?" Murray asked, leaning to stare out at his victim, his face pale with what could have been either regret or fury.

"I should think so, at that range." Emile sheathed his sword cane and turned his attention to Celestine, who had begun abruptly to cry.

Murray, noticing his fiancée's distress and the way the young Creole had taken her hands and begun chafing them, reached to remove Celestine from his grasp and take her in his own arms. "I suggest we drive on then."

"Shouldn't we at least see if he's still alive?" Anya objected.

Gaspard was fanning Madame Rosa with the small black lace fan he had taken from her evening reticule. "We will inform the first policeman we see and let them deal with the matter."

"I'll look at him," Emile said, and, before anyone could protest, swung down. He knelt beside the sprawled figure on the street, feeling for a heartbeat. After less than a second, he got to his feet once more, wiping his hand on the handkerchief he took from his sleeve.

"Well?" Murray asked, his voice tight.

"Through the heart."

Emile, his attitude of nonchalance rather forced, stepped back into the carriage. The order was given to proceed. There was silence for some blocks.

Finally Gaspard said, "They grow bold, these ruffians."

"Why should they not?" It was Madame Rosa who made that ironic reply, a reference to the poor protection given in the last few months by the police, one that needed no explanation.

Gaspard nodded. "Indeed."

Anya sat staring out the window. Her hands trembled and there was a feeling of sickness in the depths of her stomach. Because she had acted, a man was dead. It had happened so quickly, but was no less final for that swiftness. In some peculiar way it seemed an omen. Could the same thing happen again? Was it possible that because she had involved herself in another dangerous situation, because she had abducted Ravel to prevent a meeting between him and Murray, another man might die?

She had thought she was acting to prevent a death. It might be that she would be the cause.

The following day, a Saturday, dawned bright and clear. Anya rose late, as did Celestine and Madame Rosa. The evening at the theater had been protracted enough, but afterward there had been much discussion over the small repast Madame Rosa had prepared. It had been the early-morning hours before the gentlemen had taken their leave, allowing the ladies to seek their beds.

Even then, Anya had not slept. Her thoughts had run in endless circles, always returning to the impasse of Ravel and what she was going to do with him. Regardless, when morning came and she finally closed her eyes, she was no nearer a solution.

At eleven o'clock a maid arrived bearing hot coffee. The girl's smile and greeting were so cheerful that Anya could have strangled her without a qualm. The coffee helped somewhat; still it was a great effort to drag herself from bed. The energy, fueled by rage and chagrin, that had propelled her since leaving Beau Refuge had departed. All she felt was a vast weariness and a fervent wish that she had never heard of Ravel Duralde.

Still his image hovered inescapably at the back of her mind. She tried to read and could not concentrate. She partook of a late luncheon, but had difficulty entering into the conversation over it with Madame Rosa and Celestine. She received a visit from Emile, but so distracted was she that she very nearly put the cornucopia of paper lace holding nougat candies he had brought her into a small vase as if it had been a nosegay. He snatched the candy from her and kissed the inside of her wrist. The action was so unexpected that she was disturbed for a few minutes by the fear that he had taken it into his head to pay her court. However, his manner as he joined Celestine in teasing her over the mistake was so boyish, so like that of a younger brother, that she dismissed the idea.

It was to seek some diversion from her preoccupation that she left the townhouse as the evening waned and walked toward the levee. Saturday was a day of departures in New Orleans, as many of the river packets and oceangoing steamers that jostled the riverbank four deep or stood out in the channel left on their regular runs. It was a favorite occupation of the city to stroll along Front Street and the levee to watch the activity as the boats and ships got under way.

Because of the fine day, there was much activity along the river's great curve that caused New Orleans to be known as the Crescent City. Stevedores rolled barrels up gangways and hoisted boxes and bales into holds as clerks stood checking off lists. Drays rattled up and down. A man carrying a portmanteau in one hand and holding his hat on his head with the other hurried along. Beside a man in the uniform of an officer of some western plains division of the army walked a woman in a traveling costume, with a baby in her arms and a small boy holding on to her wide skirts. Two identical young ladies in gray silk gowns covered by soft black wool capes edged with gray braid were being escorted by a venerable gentleman with a white mustache and beard and followed by an elderly Negro maid in cap and apron who carried a wooden jewel box. A trio of boys in short pants and bare feet were chasing a cat, dodging in and out among the long rows of barrels and sacks and the piles of trunks. Sidestepping the boys before sauntering on was a man wearing the white frock coat and broad-brimmed hat affected by the fraternity of riverboat gamblers.

The rice cake and praline sellers hawked their wares adding to the din of shouts and oaths that rose above the rumble of steam engines being fired up and made ready. The rich, sweet aroma of the confections hung on the air, blending with the sour stench of rum and molasses and rotted fruit, and the pervading smell of the woodsmoke that hung in a dark pall over the area, rising from the forest of smokestacks that stretched as far as the eye could see.

As the sun began to set and the hour of five o'clock neared, the tempo increased to a frenzy. Red sparks appeared in the belching black smoke. Lamps were lighted aboard the steamboats, sending out their golden gleams. There was a great stir and shifting along the levee as lines were taken in and positions were changed. The pound and thump and hiss of engines took on a purposeful sound. People emerged on the decks to stand by the rails, waving and calling.

The first packet gave a blast of its whistle, detached itself from the levee, and nosed into the river. Stalwart, majestic, with a half-moon hanging between its stacks and the last light picking out its name in gold on its side wheelboxes, it began to churn the yellow-brown waters of the Mississippi River on its journey upriver. It was followed by another and another, one behind the other like ducklings following their mother.

Anya, standing on the levee near where the twin spires of the St. Louis Cathedral pierced the evening sky, counted them off. There was the New Orleans to St. Louis passenger packet, the *Falls City*, and the Ouachita, Bayou Bartholemew, and Black River packet, the *W. W. Farmer*, heading for Alabama Landing, Point Pleasant, Ouachita City, Sterlington, Trenton, Monroe, Pine Bluff, Columbia, Harrisonburg, and Trinity. Behind it was the Lake Bisteneau packet *Empress* for Minden, Moscow, Boon's Landing, Port Bolivar, Griggle Landing, and Speing Bayou on the Red River, followed by the steamer *O. D. Jr.* for Donaldsonville. The steamers, numbering nearly a dozen leaving on this day alone, would make their ponderous way up the many rivers of the state that branched from the Mississippi, to all the small towns and landings, or to the big cities of the Midwest and the East, with hundreds of plantation stops in between. And each of them, at some time in the twilight or perhaps in the early morning after lying tied up for the night, would pass the dock at Beau Refuge where, riding above the level of the land, the passengers would be able to see the main house under its old oak trees.

Sometimes, if there were slave children sitting on the levee, the pilots of the boats would blow their whistles until the mournful blasts echoed over the fields for miles. If it should happen this evening, Ravel, lying in his room, might hear the sound and think of the men and women who were free to travel the river, to go where they pleased, when they pleased. Would he think of her then, and wonder where she was and what she was doing?

She should be at the plantation. That was where Ravel was, where the problem she had created lay and where it must be solved. The rage and humiliation that had sent her from him in such haste were spent. Running away had changed nothing. Somehow she was going to have to come to an agreement with Ravel, one that would allow her to release him without penalty. That could not be done while she was miles away from Beau Refuge.

She swung from the levee in sudden decision. If she hurried, she could be home before midnight.

Chapter Eight

The journey back to Beau Refuge seemed endless. The winter night closed in early. The road wound before them into dark infinity, relieved only by an occasional spark of light from a house set back from the road among the trees. The carriage jolted on its springs as they rolled through potholes and swayed as they rounded the curves. On the box, Solon the coachman whistled and sang to keep himself company and to rout the specters of the night.

Anya sat bolt upright, staring into the darkness. She was tired, but too on edge to doze away the time. The fears that haunted her were not of ghosts and goblins or marsh spirits, nor could they be banished by whistling. The closer she came to the plantation, the more certain she grew that when she arrived she would find Ravel was no longer a prisoner. He would have tricked Denise and Marcel in some way so as to gain his freedom. He would be gone, riding for New Orleans to wreak vengeance upon her and her people for the indignity he had suffered, preparing to challenge Murray, thereby retrieving his good name.

His escape might be the best thing that could happen; certainly she had no idea of what she was going to do with him if he was still there. And yet she could not bear the thought of letting him go. That would be to admit that she had made a mistake, that she should not have abducted him, should not have interfered in the affair between him and Murray. She would make no such concession. No matter how the matter turned out, she could not see how she could have behaved otherwise. To have done nothing would have been cowardly and supine conduct.

She might, of course, have spoken to Ravel in a common-sense fashion. She had an uncomfortable suspicion, however, that things would have ended in the same way. He was unlikely to have courted the social disgrace of failing to live up to the dueling code without a suitable recompense, one of his own choosing.

Your virtue for my honor—

She clenched her hands into fists, then slowly forced herself to relax them once more. Would she ever forget those words, those hours in Ravel Duralde's arms?

She would, if it killed her. What was so memorable, after all, about the kisses and caresses of a wastrel, a scoundrel, a murderer? It was not as if it were an experience she was going to repeat. It had seemed so shattering to her because it was her first time, because she had been unprepared for such an assault upon her senses, or for her own passionate response, because of the circumstances involved that had included the attempt to save a man's life. Given enough time, the emotional upheaval would be as nothing. Doubtless her wedding night, if she should ever choose to marry, would banish the last vestiges of remembrance. Certainly the possibility was as good an argument as she had yet encountered for being wed. Not that she needed to resort to such desperate measures. After her stay in town, she was able to view the incident with considerable detachment.

Regardless, when finally she stood outside the door of the small room in the cotton gin, her palms were damp and her knees were weak. The key as she took it down from its hook jangled in her hand, and she had to make the third attempt before she could fit it into the lock. She turned the handle and thrust the door open, then almost fell into the room as she tripped in her haste to step inside.

She came to such an abrupt halt that her skirts and the heavy hem of her cloak swirled around her feet. Her heart leaped inside her, then pounded on once more. Ravel lay stretched out on his side upon the bed with his head propped on one hand and a book in front of him. Even in repose there in the confines of that small room he appeared lean and dangerous. However, the white bandaging around his head, in such strong contrast to his bronzed skin, gave him a certain rakish charm. He looked up, and a smile, warm and yet shaded with irony, kindled in his eyes.

She was more lovely than he had remembered. Her hair caught

the lamplight in russet-gold gleams and her skin had the soft sheen of ivory silk. She had presence, the ability to command attention, and yet there was in the straightness of her dark blue gaze something unconsciously fine, unquestionably trustworthy. The lack of pretense about her made her rare among women. Her body had a slender but elegant grace, with high, gently rounded breasts and a narrow waist. Her skirts hid the shape of her hips, but he remembered their perfect curves well. She was a lady, of that there could be no doubt. Still, there was about her a hint of strength and the will to retaliate if she were injured, also of unpredictability, and a sparkle caught for an instant in the depths of her eyes that made her fascinating. He wondered if she realized her attraction, then decided in the next instant that she must know it well, that many men must have told her.

"I understood that you had returned to New Orleans. It must have been a hasty trip."

"So it was," she answered, moving to close the door behind her. Swinging back, she said with abruptness caused by relief and guilt, "Your head appears to be giving you little trouble."

"It's fine, so long as I'm careful about how I comb my hair."

His dry tone and the look in his eyes troubled her. She dragged her gaze from his, transferring it to the book he held, the extra pillows stacked on his bed, her father's chess set that was arranged on the table, and the tray beside it holding a bottle of wine and a plate of sandwiches covered with a damp napkin. "You seem to have made yourself comfortable during my absence."

He gave her a smile of singular charm. "Marcel has been seeing to my needs. I belive he feels sorry for me."

"Sorry for you?" Her voice echoed with surprise and a degree of wariness.

He closed his book and lay back on the pile of pillows with his hands clasped behind his head. "Apparently he thinks you are holding me here for your own pleasure."

"He thinks nothing of the kind!"

Ravel went on as if she had not spoken. "Naturally I tried to disabuse him of the notion—"

"Naturally!" The word was laden with scorn.

"But he seemed to feel that, as uncomfortable as my situation might be, it was the best chance for his mistress to acquire a husband.''

A dangerous light appeared in her eyes. "Why, you—"

"You mustn't blame him. He is only concerned for you."

"As there is no possibility of my ever accepting you as a husband, I won't!"

"Never?"

"Certainly not."

His eyes narrowed. "Ah, but suppose you are pregnant with my child?"

"There is always the English remedy," she answered with a lift of her chin.

He pushed abruptly to a sitting position. "You wouldn't."

The English remedy was the celebrated female pills supposedly prepared from a prescription of Sir James Clark, physician to Queen Victoria, and advertised as being able to "bring on monthly period with regularity." The warning against using the pills during the first three months of pregnancy, since they were "sure to bring on miscarriage," was so prominently displayed that they were commonly used as a specific for that purpose. Anya was by no means certain she could make herself swallow them should the need arise, but she had no intention of allowing this man to think he might have any hold over her.

"Wouldn't I?"

He stared at her for long moments. When he spoke, his voice was hollow. "Do you hate me so much?"

"Tell me why I should not."

There was a note in her own voice she did not like, one that almost had the sound of pleading. He did not appear to hear it, however.

"I never meant to hurt you."

"That is of course a consolation." She went on before he could say anything more. "But if you were able to appeal so successfully to Marcel's sympathies, why are you still here? Surely you could have persuaded him to let you go?"

"It could be I was in no hurry to leave."

"Oh, yes, you are enjoying your stay immensely. It is, in fact, a perfect rest cure?" She sent him a glance of solicitation that was scathing in its falseness.

"I was curious to see if you would come back. And of course I could not deprive you of the joy of telling me exactly in what ruins my honor now lies."

A flush rose to her face at his use of that word, and also at the memory of some of the remarks Murray had made. Her voice compressed, she said, "It will not be so bad, I think. There are many who speak for you."

"Are there?" He watched her with frowning interest in his dark eyes.

"Emile Girod, for one."

"Emile," he repeated softly. "He has returned?"

She nodded, not really surprised that he was aware of the movements of Jean's brother. Reckless, unprincipled, and unscrupulous he might be, but she had come to recognize that there was more to Ravel Duralde than appeared on the surface. It was confusing, when she wanted nothing more than to despise him with a whole heart.

He came to his feet with swift courtesy. "My manners are terrible, for which you may blame my surprise at seeing you again so soon. Won't you sit down, chère? And permit me to offer you some of this excellent wine?"

"Thank you, no," she said with meticulous politeness. "I have had a long journey, and I'm tired."

The chain on his ankle clattered on the floor as he moved to hold a chair for her. The sound affected her with an unpleasant sense of embarrassment.

"All the more reason for resting here a few minutes," he insisted.

She remembered suddenly his dislike for solitude. A good memory and ready sympathy could be burdens at times. She stood irresolute, torn between leaving and staying, knowing instinctively it would be better to go and yet unable to bring herself to be so insensitive. It was his calm patience that decided her. As he stepped to touch her arm, inclining his head in a small bow as he indicated the chair, she moved stiffly to accept his invitation.

The room was small, the night was dark, and the lamp that burned on the table made only a small pool of golden light. There in that bed against the wall she had lain naked with the man who moved now to take the chair across from her. The sense of intimacy between them was so strong all at once that it was as if her body, beyond the control of her mind, recognized him deep within its marrow and sinews. She could feel her pores expand, sense a deep relaxation inside her. She was aware with an intense familiarity of the planes and angles of his face. She knew without conscious memory the feel of the smooth and warm surfaces of his lips on hers, the texture of the hair that grew on his chest. She had felt his weight upon her, had taken him inside her, had fallen asleep against his muscled length, and her senses refused to disregard it.

"What are you thinking of?" he asked, his voice deep, his gaze upon her face.

"Nothing," she said hurriedly.

She thought for a moment that he would persist. Then, with a slight movement of his shoulders, he said instead, "I trust you had an uneventful drive this evening?"

"Yes, though last night was not so pleasant," she answered, and in gratitude for his forbearance and to aid the pretense of normalcy, went on to tell him of the attack upon their carriage as they returned from the theater.

"It was fortunate Nicholls was armed," he commented.

"Yes. He seemed to know exactly what he was doing."

A corner of his mouth lifted an instant. "Is that a warning?"

"If you care to take it that way."

"I am unmanned by your concern."

"I somehow doubt it," she snapped, annoyed by his obvious amusement.

"Well, perhaps not," he agreed, unperturbed, "not with a woman like you so near me."

She sent him a look of smoldering resentment for the innuendo. "Am I supposed to be flattered?"

"Interested, possibly. Do you have any idea how enticing you are, sitting there? Do you have any conception of the self-control it requires to prevent myself from reaching out and pulling you into my arms? I know how soft and sweet your lips are, and how your breasts fit into my cupped hands. I've seen the way your eyes turn into dark blue pools of desire, and the need to put that look there again is driving me slowly insane. I want—"

He stopped, biting back the words, closing his lips firmly.

Pushing back his chair, he got to his feet and moved away a few steps, his hand clasped on the back of his neck. Over his shoulder he said, "I'm sorry."

Anya stood and moved to the door, pulling it open. With her hand on the knob, she turned to look at Ravel still standing with his back to her, at the wide width of his shoulders beneath the red flannel of his shirt, the tapering of his lean waist and hard flanks under the close tailoring of his trousers, at the chain that anchored him firmly in his cell.

Her voice quiet, almost reflective, she said, "So am I."

Anya's regret was real and comprehensive. She was sorry she had ever conceived the idea of abducting Ravel, sorry she had injured him in the process, sorry that he had turned out to be a man of such devastating and complicated charm, and sorry that she had allowed herself to be swayed by his facile arguments to the point of giving herself to him, sorry that she could not find it within herself to continue the intimacy they had begun. It made no difference. She could not release him.

If she released him, he would in some manner continue his quarrel with Murray, the outcome of which seemed inevitable. If she did not, his presence at Beau Refuge must, when it became known, ruin her own good name. She was caught between two fires. There was more to it than that, however. She could not keep Ravel a prisoner indefinitely; it was impractical to think otherwise. The time would come when his patience would end and he would force his way to freedom, or else she would listen to the promptings of her own conscience and free him. The time for some decision, for finding some solution to the dilemma in which they found themselves, was short. There might be only another day or two at most. But what could it be? What could it be?

Morning came, and Anya was still no closer to an answer. She rose early and dressed herself in a plain gown of washed-out blue cambric without collar or cuffs, topped by a plain and serviceable apron. As she brushed her hair and coiled it in a knot on the nape of her neck, she stared in the mirror at the dark circles under her eyes. She looked like death's first cousin, but it hardly mattered. She was going nowhere, and if Ravel should find her less attractive that might be a good thing.

She fully intended to visit him again. It would be cowardly to stay away, however much she might prefer it. It was, she reminded herself, her duty to provide some means of making the time pass more pleasantly for him. That he could wish to see the woman who was holding him prisoner seemed unlikely, but since it apparently afforded him some amusement, she would allot time for him.

It was Sunday, she realized, as, leaving her bedchamber, she moved through the house where nothing was stirring. By law, it was a day of rest for the people on the plantation. She could have the carriage brought around and go to mass, but it seemed inappropriate under the circumstances. In any case, there was no legislation decreeing a day of rest for the plantation mistress.

Anya found the housekeeper, Denise, in the kitchen, where she was directing the cook concerning breakfast. While it was cooking, Anya went with Denise to the storehouse to hand out supplies of beans, salt meat, cornmeal, and molasses for each person on the place; then the two of them moved on to inspect the dairy, where cows were being milked and the previous day's milk and cream set out to sour for the making of butter and cheese, necessary tasks regardless of the day. Afterward, while Denise returned to the kitchen, Anya checked on the winter garden, when she made a mental note to order the last great heads of cauliflower cut for the kitchen, and to direct the making of rows for the seeds she had bought in New Orleans.

She was escorted from the garden by ten or twelve of the children on the place, who had discovered her there. Noticing that many of them had sores on their legs from flea bites, she took them to the small building set aside as a dispensary and spread ointment on the sores. Leaving them, she went in search of Marcel, who served also as her majordomo, instructing him to see that bright and early on Monday every cat and dog on the place was dipped for fleas, their sleeping places cleaned and sprinkled with lime, and that sulphur was burned in the cabins.

Still she was not done. Ravel had put his foot through one of the sheets that had been placed on his bed, and Denise feared that the weakness caused by mildew from the damp climate might have invaded a dozen or so more. She was quite right, as it happened, and Anya spent half an hour making out a list of linen to be ordered when she returned to New Orleans.

When the task was completed, she was still in time to walk with Marcel as he carried a tray containing both her own and Ravel's breakfast of *café au lait*, hot rolls, sugar-cured ham, and blackberry jam out to the cotton gin.

Anya unlocked the door of Ravel's room and pushed it open, then took the tray from Marcel. With a smile and a nod of dismissal for the man, she stepped inside.

The small, high windows gave little light. The day was overcast, with only now and then a gleam of sun, and so the room was dim and filled with shifting shadows. Anya could just make out the shape of Ravel's long body under the covers of his bed, lying on his side with his back to her. The top of the sheet made a sharp angle across one bronzed shoulder, and the tousled thatch of his hair was black against the white of his pillowcase. He did not move as she entered. She stood irresolute for a moment, then stepped quietly to the table to put down the tray.

The fire had burned down, allowing the room to grow cool. She scraped back the ashes to find a few coals, laid slivers of pine pitch kindling over them until they caught, then added larger wood until flames leaped high up the chimney. There was a draft through the open door, and she moved to close it.

The food was getting cold and she was hungry. Anya waited a few minutes to see if the crackling of the fire would rouse Ravel. When he did not move, she squared her shoulders and walked to the side of the bed. There were men, so she had heard, who could sleep through anything from a thunderstorm to having the house fall down around their ears, men who had to be bodily dragged out of bed. She was prepared to do her duty toward her guest, but had no intention of starving while he slept.

She stared down at the man in the bed, studying the lines of the muscles in his shoulder and neck that, even relaxed, had the look of leashed power, the sculptured strength of his sun-browned features, and the thick black fringe of his lashes resting on his cheeks. There was about him in that moment a peculiar sense of guarded vulnerability, as if even in sleep it was necessary to protect himself from possible pain. Watching him, she felt her throat tighten. Deep inside her there was an odd twisting sensation that she recognized as an unremitting compassion. What an idiot she was to feel such a thing for the man who had killed Jean and who would kill Murray if he could. What an idiot.

Reaching out her hand, she put it on Ravel's shoulder and gave him a quick shake. Like the swift and sinuous lash of a cracking whip, he turned, swung, caught her wrist. A hard arm encircled her hips, and in an instant she was hurtling dizzily through the air. She landed on her back on the mattress, falling so hard that her teeth snapped together with a sharp click and the air left her lungs in a gasp of shock. Hard hands fastened on her wrists, imprisoning them on each side of her face. A hard thigh clamped across her knees, and she was held immobile. Her gaze wide, stunned, she stared up into Ravel's coffee-black eyes that glinted with devilish laughter and satisfaction.

"Good morning," he said.

Anger boiled up inside her. She clenched her hands into fists, straining against his hold, wriggling and twisting as she tried to free herself. Her struggles were worse than useless, for she could feel her skirts that had been bunched around her knees working higher. Panting with rage and effort, she subsided.

"That's better," he said, his voice rich with amusement.

She glared at him, setting her teeth. "Swine! Let me go."

"Ask nicely, and I might."

"I'll see you damned first!"

"As you like," he said with a lifted brow. "I enjoy having you in my bed myself, but I had the idea you found it a little uncomfortable."

She gave him a waspish smile. "You would have felt foolish if it had been Marcel instead of me."

"No doubt. But I would know your footsteps in a crowd of thousands. There was no chance of a mistake."

"You would know— It was a trick! You weren't asleep at all!" The idea that she had been feeling sorry for him while he was lying in wait to trap her made her feel hot with chagrin from head to heels.

"How could you think I might be, with the noise you were making?"

"Some men sleep hard." The words sounded almost defensive, even to her own ears.

"If I was one of them, I would have been dead a dozen times over. To cut the throat of a sleeping man was a favorite sport in Nicaragua. On the ship transporting prisoners to Spain, as well as in the dungeons before we were put in separate cells, any man who slept too sound woke up stripped naked—that is, if he woke at all."

"Very well," she snapped, "I stand, or rather lie, corrected. If there is a reason for this farce I would as soon hear it now, so that I can get up and eat my breakfast."

"Oh, yes," he said, his voice soft, beguiling, "there was a reason."

She saw herself reflected in the black pupils of his eyes, saw the warm sheen of desire that surfaced there. Then his head came down, blotting out the light, and his mouth covered hers. His lips were firm and tasted faintly of coffee. His lean cheek had the clean smell of shaving soap. Dimly Anya realized that Marcel had made an early trip to the cotton gin with wake-up coffee and shaving water, one that had gone unmentioned. An instant later, such vagrant thoughts dissolved in a tide of purest sensation.

Warm, his mouth was warm, and his movements were guided by sure and vital instinct. He explored the molding of her lips with slow pleasure, gently testing the split that had all but healed. He brushed them with the lightest of touches, tasting the moist corners and tender surfaces with the tip of his tongue, delicately awakening their sensitivity as he probed the limits of her resistance. He traced the indentation between bottom lip and chin, and slowly circled her mouth with a trail of kisses so searing that against her will her lips parted in surprise at their heat.

He took instant advantage of that moment of weakness, molding her mouth to his, pressing inside. He explored the porcelain-hard edges of her teeth and swirled in sinuous play around her tongue with his own, stroking the delicately grained top and flicking across the incredible smoothness underneath before easing deeper, as if he would take possession. He savored the fragility of her mouth's inner lining, and drank of her sweetness.

Anya's heart thudded as piercing pleasure crept along her veins, fed by his careful expertise. Who had taught him this patient art of wooing? It did not matter. She was aware, as never before, of the quick current of life that flowed through her. Deep inside she felt a slow flowering, and burgeoning need to be held closer, to forget place and time and the identity of the man who held her, to lose herself in this new and incredible magic.

Ravel, sensing her acquiescence, released her left wrist to cup her face in his hand, tracing with his blunt fingertips the curve of her cheek, the turn of her jaw as it descended into the line of her neck, and lower to the swell of her breast. Gently he clasped the round globe that jarred to the beat of her heart, his thumb brushing the peak through cambric and lawn until it rose to a tight bud of anticipation. She lifted her free hand to his hair, threading her fingers through the thick waves, holding him, increasing the pressure of his kiss.

What was she doing? Distress and self-accusation rippled through her with the force of a tidal wave. She clenched her fingers in his hair, pulling. He drew a quick breath of pain as she tugged at his stitched scalp. As he released her lips, she turned her head sharply away. In the same instant, discovering her right wrist was only loosely held, she wrenched it free and heaved at him with both hands.

He was thrown off-balance, toppling backward to teeter on the edge of the bed. As he grabbed at the post of the bed to save himself from falling, Anya thrust herself up, sliding, scrambling over him. Ravel recovered, lunging after her. He caught her foot, and she tumbled to the floor, landing on her outstretched hands. She kicked out at him, striking him in the stomach. He grunted and let her go. She rolled away in a flurry of skirts, but he clutched at her, coming up with a handful of apron. In a single fluid and silken movement, she jerked free the tie at her waist, leaving the apron a limp prize in his hand as she surged to her feet.

He came up off the bed, balling the apron into a wad, tossing it into a corner. Magnificently naked, his mouth curved in unholy enjoyment, he stalked after her with his chain scraping the floor in grating echo to his measured treads. His need for her was all too evident. With his lower body pale in contrast to his upper torso that had been colored teak brown by some tropical sun, he seemed half man, half beast, infinitely menacing. Fear she had not acknowledged until that moment leapt along her nerves. It ran over her in a quick shiver, lingering in her knees. She stumbled backward, feeling the heat from the fireplace close behind her.

His lips twitched. At the same time, she saw in fleeting dismay what had amused him. She had moved in the wrong direction. He was between her and the door. The chain that held him so firmly attached to the wall should have given her room to pass, but Ravel's longer arms made that a chancy proposition. She might skim past him, if it were not for her full skirts. It was far more likely that he would catch her by that fullness, or else they would flare like tinder as she crowded near the fireplace.

She retreated deeper into the corner. Her hip brushed the table where the tray had been set, shaking it. The dishes rattled, and the drinking glass, turned upside down on the neck of the carafe, chimed with the sound of a bell. The water. Hard upon the thought, she reached for the carafe, snatching aside the drinking glass, spinning to send the contents in a sparkling, liquid arch toward Ravel.

He gasped out a strangled oath as the icy water splashed over him. With his hair dripping and rivulets running down his face, pooling in the hollows above his collarbone and trickling down the curling hair on his chest to the flat plane of his abdomen, he stared at her. His voice harsh with shocked wrath, he demanded, "What did you do that for?"

The strength of his surprise was an indication of how blameless had been his intentions, how scant her danger. Concupiscence there had certainly been, but the peril had been in large part in her own mind, prompted quite possibly by her fears of her own reaction to him. The last thing she could do would be to admit it, however.

"It seemed to me," she said with a lift of her chin as she placed the carafe back on the table, "that your ardor needed dampening."

"Oh did it indeed? And what of yours?" He looked around him and, catching sight of his shaving water in the bowl on the washstand, started toward it.

"Ravel! You wouldn't," she exclaimed as she saw his purpose. The water, scummed with soap and a floating black powder of beard stubble, had long since cooled in the chill morning air.

"Wouldn't I?"

He picked up the bowl, turning with it. There was a gleam

in his eyes as he moved toward her, dragging his chain. Water still beaded his skin, standing among the myriad tiny bumps of the gooseflesh that covered him. She pressed against the table behind her, holding out a hand as if she could ward off the promised drenching, keeping her gaze on the dull water that lapped gently in the gold-rimmed bowl.

"You—you can't. You are a gentleman."

"I thought that was in doubt."

"No, not really—"

"Any lie to save yourself."

If she made a quick dash, she might reach the door in time. But any sudden move could also trigger an instant deluge. He would not miss; she knew that without question.

"I was persuaded otherwise at first, but no longer."

It was true, what she said; she discovered that fact with wonder. She went still, her gaze blank as she stared at him.

"Prove it."

"How? I may as well try to prove that I am a lady after what I have done."

He had frightened her, he could see that. She was pale and in her eyes was a lingering wariness. But she was no longer alarmed, nor did he sense the basic contempt that had allowed her to treat him as negligible, a man who could be taken by force and shunted aside to assure the safety of those for whom she cared. His need for retaliation seeped away. Turning, he set the bowl of water on the floor, then moved to take from the foot of the bed the dressing gown of black wool with claret silk lapels provided for his use by Marcel. He shrugged into it, lapping the edges and pushing the gilt buttons into their holes with quick movements.

Over his shoulder, he said, "Some things need no proof. But one thing is certain, my—ardor is certainly damp."

It was an olive branch of sorts. It seemed suddenly of great importance that she say the right thing, something neither challenging nor provocative, but completely prosaic. "And your breakfast is getting cold. While you dry yourself, I'll take it and have it reheated."

"Never mind," he said, his smile rueful and yet warm as he turned, "I'm only grateful your hand didn't fall on the coffeepot.

As for breakfast, I'll put it by the fire for a few minutes; it will be fine.''

She moistened her lips. ''Actually, it's also my breakfast.''

''I am honored,'' he said, his voice dry. ''Of course you must do as you please.''

''I'm sure it will be all right,'' she said, and turned abruptly away, minutely adjusting the tray on the table.

They sat down to eat a short time later. While the coffee and rolls warmed, the room had been tidied: the shaving water poured away into the slop jar, Anya's apron rescued from its corner and folded neatly, the puddled water on the floor mopped up with a length of toweling, the bed made and the table, to make room for their meal, cleared of the chess set and books that had been stacked upon it. They had worked together to achieve that neatness, still there was constraint between them. In silence they spread butter and jam on their rolls. The tinkling as they stirred sugar into their coffee was loud. Anya sipped at the dark brew, and it was an effort to prevent the tightness of her throat from betraying her with swallowing noises.

She could not recall ever being so on edge with a man before, nor so aware of his every movement, of the way the muscles tensed in his jaws, the fine black hairs that grew on his wrists, the grace and strength of the shape of his hands. She had also never held a man prisoner before, or been intimate with one; betrayed one, or been betrayed by one. To be comfortable with Ravel was too much to expect; it should be enough that they were no longer antagonistic toward one another. It should be, and yet she could not help wishing that the strain could be eased.

Ravel touched his napkin to his mouth, then dropped it beside his plate. He leaned back in his chair, his fingers toying with the rim of his Sèvres coffee cup. He stared at her a long moment with a slight frown between his eyes.

''Tell me something,'' he said at last.

''Yes?''

''Why are you here? I don't mean to sound blunt or unwelcoming—God knows I am glad of the company—still, visiting as if I were an invited guest is the last thing I would have guessed you would do.''

''I didn't intend it.''

"I'm sure."

She glanced up at him, then back down at the fleur-de-lis design in the pat of butter that she was destroying with a tine of her fork. "In the first place, it is hardly proper, and in the second it can only call attention to the fact that you are here."

"That makes sense."

She threw down the fork. "What has happened between us makes a mockery of proper behavior, and your stay has been protracted past the time when it can be hidden. You can't remain here much longer; soon you will have to return to New Orleans. There must be a way to enlist your help in putting a stop to any meeting between you and Murray. There must be, but I don't know what it is. In order to find it, I have to discover what kind of man you are."

"You could ask."

"When would I know when I had the right answer?"

The angles of his face tightened, then relaxed again. "Do you play chess?"

"What?"

"There is a great deal to be learned about a person from how they play games of any kind, but especially from chess."

"I used to play with my father," she said slowly.

"And will you play with me?"

It occurred to her to refuse. He had spoken as if he were a master of the game, and it was unlikely she was a match for him, though she had sometimes, not often but sometimes, beaten her father. Still, that was not the reason. If she could discover something of his strengths and weaknesses during the test of strategies and maneuvers, then he could do the same for her own. Why he should wish to, she could not imagine, but she did not make the mistake of thinking that his suggestion had been made at random, or from a desire to be accommodating. He had a reason, and she would give much to know what it was before she sat down across a chessboard from him.

She met his dark gaze above the ruins of their breakfast with trepidation and excitement crowding in her mind. Slowly she smiled. "Yes," she said. "Yes, I will."

Chapter Nine

✻ ✻ ✻ *Chess had ceased to be a game for intellec-*
tuals and become the rage in Louisiana. With the advent on the
world scene of the chess champion from New Orleans, Paul
Morphy, people in the state who had never sat down to a chessboard in their lives suddenly began to find it a delightful pastime. Ladies in the *haut ton* bought special game tables with
boards inlaid in the tops, or set out chess sets in their salons
with pieces on various squares to make it appear that there was
a perpetual game in progress. Young ladies speaking of knights
and castles were not always engrossed in the medieval period,
and it was not uncommon for an elderly gentleman, taking his
handkerchief from his pocket, to shake out a captured pawn or
two.

The chess set that had belonged to Anya's father was Venetian
and nearly two hundred years old. It had a board of ebony and
ivory in satinwood, and pieces of silver and bronze on bases that
were inlaid with lapis lazuli and mother-of-pearl and trimmed
with gold. Each piece was carefully fashioned, a small work of
art, from the imperious queens to the pawns that looked like
foot soldiers. As a child, Anya had played other games with
them, pretending that they were families with many brothers, or
arranging royal weddings. It had given her pleasure to handle
them then, and still did.

While Anya removed the breakfast dishes, Ravel pulled on
his clothes, then they both set up the board. She put more wood
on the fire so that they need not be distracted by the need to
replenish it and, when Marcel came for the remains of breakfast,
sent a message to Denise with directions for the noon meal to

be served in the gin. Finally she and her prisoner sat down facing each other at the table with the board between them.

Their play was cautious at first as they took each other's measure. Anya's father had been a sober player who went by the book, one who preferred the classic games. Anya had little patience with such moves by rote, tending toward a cavalier but watchful style with sudden brilliant forays into enemy territory. Ravel's play, she discovered as the morning advanced, was both classical and daring, but also with a degree of concentration and Byzantine calculation she had never before encountered. His ability to predict her moves far in advance was annoying in the extreme. She did not pretend to be an expert at the game, but the ease with which he was able to achieve check and mate the first time put her on her mettle. She settled down to make it a bit more difficult for him.

The morning passed with amazing quickness. Noon came, and still they played. They ate cold meat and bread, fried cauliflower and fried fruit pies without taking their eyes from the board. The rivalry that had sprung up between them was friendly, but intense. Neither gave quarter or asked for it, nor did they take an unfair advantage or expect one.

Ravel, Anya had plenty of opportunity to discover, was generous in victory. He did not gloat, nor did he point out her errors unless she asked. He took her pieces from the board matter-of-factly, without triumph or vindictiveness. When she thwarted his schemes, he was admiring of the strategy even at his most irritated, and when in midafternoon they battled to a draw, there was wry satisfaction in the smile he gave her across the board.

It was then Anya realized that in the heat of the contest she had forgotten the purpose of it. She wondered if Ravel had done the same, or if the manner in which he had played had been designed to give her a good impression of his character. There was no way of knowing. It also crossed her mind to wonder what he had learned of her, what she might have given away. She could think of no reason why it should matter, and yet it did.

"This has been a pleasure," Ravel said, leaning back in his chair. "With practice you could be formidable."

"It's kind of you to say so."

"I'm not being kind. And I appreciate the sacrifice of your time today."

"You make me sound like a martyr, when all the time it's you who—" She stopped, reluctant to remind him of his imprisonment.

His voice soft, he said, "If this is martyrdom, then you should have men beating down your door to endure it."

Anya gave him a straight look. "Next you will be saying that it was a privilege."

"Some portions of it," he said promptly.

Color flared into her face as she took his meaning. She refused to acknowledge her discomfiture, catching at the first thing that came into her mind as a distraction. "It must be growing inconvenient. I understand your mother lives in New Orleans and is not in good health. If you would care to write out a message, I will see that it reaches her."

"There is no need."

"No?"

"I sent one yesterday."

"I see. You bribed Marcel."

"He was careful to read the note first to see that it did not compromise his position as my guard."

She shook her head. "It isn't like him."

"I did tell you that he felt sorry for me."

"You played on his sympathies."

"Only a little. It seemed necessary."

"I'm surprised you thought to relieve your mother's mind."

A hard light came into his eyes. "You think that you have more concern for the woman who bore me than I would be likely to show?"

"I'm not certain what to think about you." She held his dark gaze, though it was an effort.

"Now, that," he said, "is progress of a sort. Shall we play again?"

Marcel brought them afternoon coffee along with fruitcake and marzipan. It was an excuse, Anya thought, for checking on her and the trend of their game. The coffee was welcome. The mental exercise of staying ahead of Ravel had taken such a physical toll that she needed the stimulation.

It was not long after she and Ravel had finished the last of the dark brew in the silver pot, draining their second and third cups, that the man across from her reached into his trouser pocket and took out a hairpin. He turned it over and over in his long fingers with an idle motion as he contemplated the pieces of the chessboard, as if he were hardly conscious of what he was doing.

A hairpin. Her hairpin. She must have missed it that night, left it behind in her flight from his bed. Such a hairpin could be used to pick a lock if one were patient and relatively skillful, or at least so it was said. She had tried it once without success as a child on an armoire she had suspected of being filled with New Year's Eve presents. It would not be surprising if Ravel knew the secret after his years in prison.

But if he did, why hadn't he used it? Why was he still sitting opposite her with a shackle around his ankle? Why had he not released himself, overpowered Marcel, and made good his escape? Could it be that he had his own reasons for waiting?

What they could be she hardly dared consider. A strong possibility was that he had been waiting for her return, waiting until he could catch her off guard, until he could achieve the particular vengeance he craved.

Her scalp prickled as the idea sank in. She stared at him, at his hard ascetic features that were relaxed now, even touched with wry humor. Sensing her gaze, he looked up at her, and a ghost of a smile flitted across his lips.

The conviction came to her abruptly that he knew exactly what he was doing. The display of the pin was like a chess move. He was waiting for her countermove, waiting with interest and a certain cynical enjoyment to see what form it would take.

No. She was being entirely too fanciful. He was not the kind of man to resort to petty revenge; she would swear to it.

There was nothing to indicate that his vengeance would be petty, of course. He had already exacted a considerable price for his incarceration. If he should attempt to take the same coin again, would her resistance deter him? This time she would resist, with all her strength.

There was one way of discovering how aware he was of what he was doing. She lifted her hand to smooth at the tendril of hair escaping from the knot on the nape of her neck. Reaching out with her other hand toward Ravel, she said as lightly as possible, ''You found my pin. It's so vexing the way they disappear. May I?''

He glanced down at the pin he held, then back up again, his smile widening. ''You need it? Sorry, I can't oblige.''

''Whyever not?'' She feigned surprise, though her heart began to increase its beat against the wall of her chest.

''Call it sentimentality. To you it's a hairpin, a useful object. To me it's a keepsake. Men, like your own sex, sometimes cling to the things that evoke pleasant memories.''

A furious accusation hovered on the tip of her tongue. It died unspoken. There was an expression in the depths of his black eyes that sent a shiver along her nerves. She was assailed by uncertainty combined with a sudden debilitating need to believe him.

She was a fool. Her returning fury rushed in upon her like a tidal wave. Her voice tight, she said, ''Nonsense!''

''You think so? How little faith you have in yourself, *chérie*. But if your need for pins is so great, I might, just might, be persuaded to give this one up.''

''Yes?''

''Yes. For the proper recompense.''

''And what,'' she asked in dawning suspicion, ''might that be?''

He pretended to consider. ''We might begin with a kiss, freely given.''

''Begin?''

He was laughing at her, toying with her in full recognition of the fact that he had the upper hand, and knew that she realized it. The knowledge, instead of weakening her resolve, only served to strengthen it.

''Forgive me,'' he said with exaggerated politeness, ''but it has become an ambition of mine to taste the sweetness of your lips without coercion from me.''

''You don't call this coercion?''

He lifted a brow, his gaze limpid. ''In repayment for a pin only? It's surely a mild form, one you are free to repudiate if the prize isn't worth it.''

He knew precisely what he was doing. But why? Why?

"If that's all—," she began.

"Ah, well, if we are speaking simply of what I would like, it would be to feel your body against mine, pressed close from chest to ankle, every soft yet firm curve, without restraint."

Heat flowed through her, radiating from the deepest recesses of her body, rising to burn on her cheekbones. With what hauteur she could muster, she said, "You expect a great deal."

The smile in his eyes kindled. "I would like to see you take down your hair and shake it free. I would like to have you turn your back to me for aid with the buttons of your gown, asking my assistance in ridding you of the surfeit of clothing you wear. It would be my pleasure to lift it away, layer after layer as if penetrating to some ancient mystery. And when you were down to your white and shimmering skin and nothing more, I would like you to turn to me, unblushing, and step into my arms as if you belonged there."

He stopped, his lips closing in a firm line, as though he had said more than he intended. The silence between them was taut, laden with torn emotions and things left unspoken, unasked.

Anya's tenuous control snapped, abruptly, like the breaking of a twig under strain. She surged to her feet and, in the same motion, reached to snatch the pin from Ravel's fingers and whirl from the table. He came upright, but before he could disentangle his chain from the chair's legs, Anya was halfway across the room.

She faced him, backing toward the door out of range of the chain. Her voice was breathless as she spoke. "The price was too high. You should not have been so greedy."

"You are an unprincipled witch."

His words lacked the heat she expected. "I have learned to be."

"At my tutelage? I should be flattered."

"But you aren't, are you?"

"No. Are you surprised? Never mind. I have your measure, chère Anya. Next time I will know what to expect."

Anya gave him a level look, her eyes as dark as ink. "If there is a next time."

Swinging around, she left him standing beside the table as

she let herself from the room. Still his words, soft with confidence, followed her.

"There will be," he said. "Oh, yes, there will be."

The February dusk had fallen early. A smudge of soft blue and gold lay in the west, but there were moving shadows under the trees and in the sharp-angled shades cast by the outbuildings. Somewhere a dog barked and pigs grunted and squealed as they were fed. A field hand lying resting on the porch of his cabin while his woman cooked their supper played a Jew's harp with a haunting, mournful sound. His dark shape was half-hidden in the dimness as Anya passed, though he lifted a hand in greeting.

Fruit trees were budding and blooming behind the cabins, and the grass was beginning to turn green again. The cool air carried a hint of the sweet scent of spring. The short sub-tropical winter this far south would soon be done. In two days it would be Mardi Gras, the beginning of the meatless days of Lent. The *saison des visites* would be at an end, and though Madame Rosa and Celestine would remain in the city until after Easter, Anya would be released to see to the planting.

The barking dog yelped and was silent. A faint breeze rustled the leaves of the live oaks overhead with the sound of stealthy footsteps. Anya, her head bent as she placed her hard-won hairpin in the knot on her nape, paused in what she was doing, coming to a halt. She lowered her hands, at the same time turning to look back the way she had come, aware of a distinct unease. The field hand had got up and gone inside. The church, with its bell off to one side, looked small, shrunken in the uncertain light. The nursery on her right was empty, the babies and small children home with their mothers on this day of rest.

Further back down the road, half-hidden as it curved, the gray bulk of the cotton gin was silent, lifeless. Not a glint of light showed, though the windows on the back would be spilling their lamplight into the gathering night. Ahead of her as she swung back, the big house was also dark, the colonnettes of the upper floor at the rear gleaming pale and insubstantial in the dimness. Denise usually left a lamp burning in Anya's back bedchamber as well as downstairs when she was out; surely the housekeeper did not think she meant to stay the night at the gin?

An oversight, that was all. The outdoor kitchen, separate from the main building, was brightly lighted. At any moment she would see the glow of the lamp moving, being carried from it toward the big house. She would see Marcel coming to meet her perhaps, or else Denise bustling about, carrying food into the house for her dinner. Perhaps it was not as late as she thought. She was on edge from her unsettling encounter with Ravel; her imagination was running away with her. But it had been years since she had last felt nervous of the dark or anything that moved in it at Beau Refuge.

They came at her from behind the carriage house. There were five of them. Their clothes were gray and shapeless, their hair shaggy when it was not covered by dirty, floppy, and sweat-stained hats. They were big and brawny, with the broken noses and gapped teeth of the kind of thugs who prowled Gallatin Street near the river. They were sure of themselves and of her, for their grins were wolfish as they swept down on her, and their arms were spread wide as if they were shooing baby chicks.

In the house lay possible safety, a weapon, Marcel to stand beside her. The men were between her and that goal, however. Back the way she had come lay the bell that when rung would peal out a call for help, signal an emergency that would bring the hands running toward the sound. It was her best chance.

She whirled, lifting her skirts high. She was fleet from years of racing with Jean in tomboy games and from the exertions of riding and walking over the plantation. The men cursed and pounded after her. She could hear their heavy footfalls, their grunting breathing. She sprinted harder.

One of her slippers came off. She stumbled and kicked off the other. They were gaining on her. A sharp ache pierced her side. The air rasped in her chest with every breath. Tears of effort blurred her vision. The church was ahead of her. The bell post. The bell. Its rope.

She reached out her hand, caught the rope. The impetus of her forward motion sent it clanging against the side of the bell. Discordant, so loud it ached in the ears, the noise vibrated in the air.

It was not repeated. Rough hands clamped bruisingly on her arms and shoulders. The bell rope was jerked from her hand, the clapper caught, silenced. The single loud peal might have been caused by no more than a young boy jumping up to slap at the clapper.

Anya was hauled around, her arms twisted behind her back until a scarlet haze of pain spread over her vision, stilling her twisting struggles as she caught her breath against it. A rough-clad arm with the hard feel of an oak limb cut across her middle, compressing her lungs, while one breast was caught in an aching grasp. She smelled sweat and stale tobacco and foul breath as the man who held her growled in her ear.

"Where is he? Where's Duralde?"

Shock held her silent. She could not think. It was only the shafting pain as her breast was slowly squeezed that made her gasp out, "Who? Who do you want?"

"Don't play dumb. You know. Duralde."

"What makes you think I would know?" The pain had eased for an instant, but that calloused hand held its hard grip, a palpable threat. Anya twisted her head, catching a glimpse of the man who held her. For an instant there seemed something familiar about him. The impression vanished before she could grasp it.

"A little bird told us," one of the others said, and laughed, a grating sound.

"Quit stallin'." The first man jerked her arm up higher so that her shoulder and elbow joints creaked, streaking pain into her back and arm. "We ain't got all night."

"He isn't here," she gasped. "Really!"

Had Ravel sent a message to these men as well as to his mother? Or had there ever been a note of concern sent to the woman who bore him? Had it been to his vicious crew all along? No matter how it was done, she would be damned first before she would help him in his escape.

"I'll bet she'd show herself right helpful if we was to throw her down and lift her skirts."

"Lord God, I hope she don't squeal soon, so's I get my turn," another said, rubbing at the front of his greasy trousers.

The rage and disgust and striving that churned in her mind clashed suddenly with horror. The suggestion, so casually spoken, was not idle, not meant simply to frighten her into compliance. It was all too real. She kicked backward at the man holding her, surging forward against his grasp. For her pains her arms were wrenched so hard that she snapped upright again, rising on her toes with her teeth set hard in her bottom lip to keep from crying out.

Her hair had been loosened by her struggles, uncoiling, sliding down in a shower of pins. A fourth man, one somewhat cleaner than the rest, stepped forward and sank his fingers into the silken mass, closing them in a tight fist. "Nice," he said, his tone slick, his mouth wet, his voice thick with lust and an Irish brogue. "As nice a piece as I've ever seen."

"Back off," growled the man who held Anya, apparently the leader of the pack.

The other ignored him, running his hand down the swath of her hair so that it cascaded over her other breast. He rubbed his palm over that fullness. "Very nice indeed."

"I told you, back off."

"You go to hell, Red!"

The two men glared at each other and the air crackled with the threat of violence. The others in that group eased back, giving them room.

In that moment of inattention, a man stepped from the shadows. He was slim and tall and dressed in the white coat of a servant, and in his hands he carried a chased dueling pistol. Marcel's voice was strained, uneven, but the pistol he bore was steady as he called out. "Let mam'zelle go!"

"Jump 'im!" The leader swung Anya so that she covered him even as his voice cracked out the order.

There was the rush of booted feet, the click of a hammer as Marcel's pistol, perhaps primed in haste, misfired. Marcel was thrown to the ground. There came the sodden thud of blows as the men crouched over him, their arms rising and falling.

"Stop, oh, stop," Anya cried.

"Here, that's enough! Let him up."

Marcel was hauled erect. He could not stand straight, but bent over with his hands at his belly. His face was cut and bleeding and one eye already swelling shut. The look he gave Anya was despairing, shamed.

"A real hero," the leader growled. "Tell us where Duralde is, boy, and we'll maybe let your mistress go."

"No—," Anya cried, the word choked off by the slice of pain.

Marcel raised his dark brown gaze to her face. "I am sorry, mam'zelle, but what else can I do?"

Together Anya and Marcel were half-dragged, half-pushed toward the gin. Anya stumbled along, tripping over her skirts and petticoats. Her hair slid forward into her face as she was jerked back and forth. Her skin crawled with loathing for the men who pulled at her, mauling her, groping at her with their hands in the darkness. Helpless anger grew inside her, seething, searching for an outlet. She longed for a knife or a club, a weapon of any kind and the chance to use it. She wanted to kick and claw and bite, no matter how little good it would do, no matter the cost.

Her chance came as the leader was unlocking the door. He released her into the charge of one of the others, using both hands as he manipulated the heavy key in its padlock. That man misjudged her strength. His grasp was loose as he reached to catch her chin, bending toward her with his mouth loose and open for a kiss. She snatched her wrist free and brought her forearm up under his chin in a swift, hard thrust. His head flew back with an audible snap. Immediately she slammed her fist into his nose. He made a strangled noise and staggered back. She spun around, ready to run, but the leader blocked her way, his rust red hair hanging in a rough curtain from under his bowler hat. Behind the man, the door of the small room swung open and she glimpsed Ravel rising from the chessboard, a tall, broad shape against the lamplight.

"Damn wildcat bitch," the leader called Red spat out. "Git in there where you belong." He caught her arm in a grip that made the bones grate together, and slung her with vicious force through the open doorway. The door slammed and the lock grated.

Anya staggered across the floor, falling with her hair whipping around her like a bright silken flail. Ravel moved with oiled swiftness, and she was caught against a hard chest, held, sheltered until she caught her breath with a sob of rage and pain. Her face a mask of fury and her body trembling with convulsive shudders, she pushed from him, backing away until she came up against the wall. She put her palms against it for support, holding to its stability as the tremors shook her and salt tears beaded her lashes, catching the lamplight as they quivered.

"What is it? What's happening?" Ravel felt his blood congeal in his veins as he saw how pale and disheveled she was. He started toward her and she slid sideways along the wall.

"Stay away!"

Ravel stopped. She was so distraught that she did not realize he could not reach her. He watched the knowledge register with her, saw her draw a deep, shuddering breath as she fought for composure.

"Anya, tell me!" he said, his voice low and throbbing.

"As if you didn't know!" Her eyes were as hard as cobalt porcelain.

"I don't, I swear it."

"They are your men, doing your bidding. Command, master, and they will obey."

"They aren't mine." He put his hands on his hips, willing her to listen to him, to believe him.

"They asked for you. How else could they know where you were unless you sent for them?"

"The grapevine, someone you told in New Orleans possibly; how the devil should I know? But they have nothing to do with me."

Anya didn't believe him. He could not reach her, and would not so long as he was held by the chain. He didn't like that. He would say anything to persuade her to come closer. "Why did they ask for you, then?"

"I have no idea."

"You lie."

"You took my word once."

"I was wrong."

He would not plead. "How many are there?"

"Enough."

"Four, five? Are they armed?"

Anya gave him a scathing glance. He seemed so in earnest, as if the information were important, but she would not be taken in, not again.

Ravel tried once more. "If they are my men, why didn't they release me?"

"I can only assume you wanted it this way."

"Think, Anya!" he urged. "If I had wanted to keep you with me against your will, a raging mistress, I could have taken you at any time in the past twenty-four hours. There would have been no need for reinforcements."

It was true. "You had no idea I would be returning when you sent your message."

"In which case my instructions should have been different."

A stillness came over her as her mind moved in swift and cogent thought. "Why else would they be here? What purpose could they have?"

There was one, but he preferred not to voice it. "A very good question. Have you no ideas?"

"None," she said shortly.

"What are they doing now?"

"I don't know."

She moved toward the fire, holding her hands out to the blaze. She was chilled to the bone, the effects of reaction to what had happened. The movement brought her closer to Ravel, within reach if he cared to make the effort. It was perhaps, a sign that she no longer feared him, if he cared to take it that way. It did not mean, Ravel well knew, that she believed him completely. There was in her manner the same skittishness as a doe scenting danger. If he made a wrong move, she would turn on him in an instant.

He moved to lean against the bedpost with his arms crossed over his chest. Silence fell. Together they strained to hear, to gain some hint of what might be taking place beyond the confines of the small room. There was no sound.

Robbery attempts against plantation houses were rare, in spite of their isolation. Southern men in general were excellent shots, since a great deal of their time was spent hunting, and they were notoriously short of temper when it came to trespass upon their lands or their good natures. In addition, it was not unusual to find three or four superior shots among the servants, men whose job it was to keep the tables at the main house and in the quarters supplied with wild meat. Anyone unwise enough to challenge such prowess usually found more trouble than they could handle.

Anya, as she had told Ravel, was a fair shot, as was Marcel, but they had been caught by surprise. The men in the quarters could be depended on to come to the aid of their mistress; Anya did not question that loyalty. They would, however, need a leader. Even if they learned what had taken place, it was unlikely that they would risk interference without specific instructions. Marcel could lead them if he were free, or even Denise. But nothing was less likely than that they would be allowed to do so.

If the purpose of the men was simple theft, perhaps they would ransack the main house and leave with their spoils. Or if the slaves, the most valuable commodity on the place, were their object, maybe they would take them and go. It seemed unlikely they would do either one. They had asked for Ravel. Somehow, someway, he was at the root of their presence, no matter how he might deny it.

The minutes slipped past, becoming an hour. The evening twilight left the sky and darkness descended. Neither Anya nor Ravel made a move to light the lamp. Shadows filled the room, thickening until the only light was the flickering red glow of the fire. Anya sank down to sit before it with her elbows propped on her knees and her chin in her hands, staring into the flames. After a time she closed her eyes.

Ravel stood watching the firelight dancing across the pale and shadowed oval of her face with a grim smile on his own features. The demon that had hounded him for seven years had caught up with him at last. He had killed Jean, and out of guilty grief had invited death. It had not come to him, despite countless battles with comrades falling around him and years spent in prison. He had played recklessly, enticing ruin in the gambling dens, only to emerge enriched. He had sought distraction in the arms of women, and found attention that he did not deserve or require. He had gone his way alone, but discovered that his self-sufficiency drew friends and acquaintances to him. He had, in fact, walked the world daring its dangers, and always returned unscathed. Until now. Until he had seen Anya Hamilton across a ballroom and recognized, suddenly, the form of his demon.

He loved her, had loved her for years. He had seen her at the masked ball, and he could no more stop himself from approaching her than he could stop breathing. He had felt that if he was not allowed to touch her, if only for a moment and behind the shelter of a disguise, then the rest of his life would be dust and ashes.

His abduction had been quite a shock; he would be the first to admit it. The daring of it, the thoroughness, and the reason had been so enraging that if he had been able to put his hands on her when he first regained his senses he might well have done something he would have regretted. Later, when he had had time to think, it had seemed a heaven-sent opportunity. The meeting with Nicholls in New Orleans could wait. Discovering ways to force Anya to come to him, to talk to him and accept him for what he was, just a man, he was content. If it had not been for that moment of weakness, when he had succumbed to the temptation to have her at any price, he might have been able to walk away when the time expired and she decided to let him go. It was no longer possible. He would not willingly leave her, nor would he permit her to escape him. Not when this ordeal was over. Not ever.

There came a soft scatching at the door. Anya opened her eyes with an effort. There had been too many late nights with little sleep for her, and too much strain. She felt drugged with weariness and fireglow, sore in every muscle and joint from the mistreatment she had received. She did not think she could move.

A faint smile touched Ravel's mouth. Thrusting himself away from the bed, he moved as close as he could to the door. The soft scratching came again as he neared.

"What is it?" he asked, his voice low.

The cover for the small grille in the door was pulled aside. The answer came in a woman's sibilant whisper with the sound of the patois of the slaves, though the words were couched with an attempt at refinement that identified one of the maids from the main house. "Marcel sent me. He could not come himself for being locked up with Denise in his room. He said to tell you and mam'zelle that the men do nothing for now but eat and drink. They wait for the one they call the boss."

"I see."

"I better go back now, 'fore they miss me."

Ravel thanked the girl and they heard her quiet footsteps retreating down the stairs and out of the gin.

Anya clasped her arms around her knees, watching Ravel as he stood so broad and tall in the dimness. It was incredible, but suddenly she wanted to believe he had nothing to do with these men. She was seized with a swelling tightness inside her chest that threatened to cut off her breathing. To banish it, she cleared her throat, saying in husky tones, "What does it mean?"

He turned toward her, and the firelight reflected red in the back of his eyes. "I have no idea."

She heard the uncompromising hardness of his tone, but it roused no answering fire inside her. She turned away, staring into the sinking fire. Who might the boss be? She tried to think but her brain refused the effort. There seemed no clue on which to base a supposition. The only thing that was apparent was that it could not be Ravel.

She heard the clank of his chain as he returned to the bed. The ropes under the mattress creaked as he lay down. It seemed a long time later when he spoke again. "There's no more wood for the fire."

He was right. They had used the stockpile of logs in the room during the day, and Marcel had not replenished it. There was still a deep bed of coals glowing red with heat, but the damp cold was creeping in around the windows and under the door and she had lost her shawl.

"You'll be chilled through if you stay there on the floor. Come to the bed. You can wrap up in the cover."

"I'm all right, thank you."

He swore softly. "You are the most obstinate woman I've ever known."

"Because I question your word or fail to fall in with your every suggestion? If no woman has ever done that before, then you must have been very spoiled."

"I had intended to be the soul of chivalry and let you have the bed to yourself," he drawled, "but if I have to come and get you, then I refuse to be responsible for the consequences."

"You will forgive me if I say that seems like a somewhat frivolous threat under the present circumstances?"

"Tell me a better time. If you watch and wait for trouble, it's likely to come. If you ignore it, it may well pass you by."

"Being a prisoner isn't exactly something you can ignore," she said, her tone cross.

"No?"

One moment he was lying relaxed, the next he was on his feet and crossing with long, swift strides the distance that separated them. Before she could do more than throw up a hand to ward him off, he was upon her. He caught her arm, placing it around his neck, then thrust one hand behind her back and the other under her knees. She cried out in surprise, kicking as she was lifted against the hard surface of his chest; then as she met his somber gaze she went as still as if she had been made of marble.

His arms were like steel chains around her. The beat of his heart jarred through them both, arousing throbbing echoes that Anya felt deep inside. There was an expression in the black depths of his eyes that brought the warmth of a flush to her cheekbones. As the seconds ticked past and she failed to protest or to struggle, the color deepened, becoming fiery. Her only defense was disdain, and she lifted her chin, silently daring him to comment.

His lashes flickered, lowering like dark shields. He stepped to the bed and placed one knee on the mattress, lowering her to the resilient surface. Lying down beside her with his weight on one elbow, he reached to pull the quilts up over them.

Chapter Ten

🜨 🜨 🜨 *Anya's leg was lying in disturbing intimacy* against that of the man beside her in the bed. She shifted, holding herself stiff as she tried to place a little distance between them. It was impossible. The sag of the bed ropes tipped her slowly back toward him. As she relaxed, her hip and thigh were molded to his once more. She tried again. The result was the same.

It was difficult to maintain an air of hauteur while being pressed against a man's side, absorbing his warmth. She had not realized how chilled she had become. The reaction to the heat of his body against her cool flesh, even through her leather skirt, sent a shiver over her.

"What is it?" he asked.

"Nothing."

She closed her lips tightly on the word. Clasping her hands over her abdomen, she placed her elbow against his ribs to support herself. He turned on his side in an effort to accommodate her. The movement caused her to roll toward him. Hastily she put her hand on his chest to hold herself off. If she was not careful, the treacherous mattress would have her on top of him.

With a sound of irritation deep in his throat, he took her hand and placed it on his side, slid his arm under her head, then reached to draw her against him so that their bodies braced each other. She was also pressed to him from breast to ankle.

"There, is that more comfortable?"

It was, of course, on a purely physical level. Otherwise, it was extremely trying. Through set teeth, she said, "You are insufferable."

"Agreed," he said gravely.

160

"It doesn't seem to trouble you."

"No."

His apologetic tone was so patently mocking that she retreated into silent dignity. The blood was racing in her veins and she feared he could feel the jarring of her heartbeat. Her chill had vanished, to be replaced by a radiant warmth that came from within. Her breathing quickened, becoming deeper. She was angry, she told herself, that was all. Who wouldn't be?

Ravel wanted her. The need of her was like a fever in his blood, and yet something restrained him. It was only in part the resistance he sensed in her. That might have been overcome, if it had not been reinforced by a sense of time running out. There might never be another night like this one, another time when they could be together without hindrance, without an audience. He wanted suddenly to know everything there was to know about her, her thoughts, her feelings, her dearest hopes and wildest dreams. He wanted to hold and understand the essence of her. He just wanted to hold her.

"What, no more insults?" he asked, his voice wry and yet shaded with something like pain.

She shrugged, but unconsciously her fingers spread over his side, gently holding in a gesture that might have been a need for support or an impulse to comfort.

"Tell me," he went on, "does it ever trouble you, having the responsibility for the support of Madame Rosa and her daughter on your shoulders, plus that of the people in the quarters here?"

His question and the reflection that lay behind it seemed to indicate a truce. It might be safest to abide by it. "Sometimes. At others, I like it."

"Do you ever wish there was someone to share it, that there had been a brother to grow up with you, to take some of the load now?"

"Jean was my brother."

She had not meant to say that, it had simply come out. It was true, though. Recognizing that fact, she felt a giving sensation inside her, as if she had let go of some truth that she had been holding.

It was a moment before Ravel answered; then he said, his voice soft, "He was also mine."

The words, the way they were spoken, so hopeless of understanding, accepting of what was past, brought a hard constriction to her throat. It was a moment before she could speak. "He wasn't perfect, we used to quarrel sometimes, but he cared about people. He would be upset, if he knew—"

"If he knew what has happened to us, what I have become?"

"And what I have done to you."

His breath was warm against the top of her head. She thought she felt the brush of his lips upon her hair, but that was, of course, unlikely.

He said, "Is that how you judge your behavior, by whether Jean would approve?"

"Not exactly, and yet I can't think of a better measure."

There was a silence. Ravel, as if driven, broke it. "Do you ever think of doing something different, something besides shuttle back and forth between here and New Orleans, besides see after this place and follow Madame Rosa and Celestine from one entertainment to another?"

Her mouth twitched in a brief, humorless smile in the deepening darkness of the room. "I used to think of traveling, of going slowly from one country to another until I had covered the whole of Europe, and then beginning on Asia and Africa."

"What holds you back?"

"Madame Rosa is a prey to sea and carriage sickness."

"And being a young woman and unmarried, you cannot go alone."

"It isn't done," she agreed.

"There are many things," he said with amusement threading his tones, "beginning with abducting men and ending with your position at the moment, that are not done by a properly brought-up young woman."

She started to speak, then stopped. She raised her head and sniffed. She took a breath, and another, and one deeper than before. "Is that just the fire dying, or do I smell smoke?"

Ravel pushed himself up on one elbow. Before he could speak, a faint and flickering orange-red glow began to light the room. The smell of smoke, combined with the acrid odor of kerosene, grew stronger. Somewhere a man gave a shout, a hoarse, jubilant sound. When it had died away, they could hear the soft, muted crackling of flames.

Ravel whipped off the cover and surged to his feet. Anya scrambled after him. By the time they were standing upright, the noise of the blaze had taken on an angry, devouring hum. The reflection of the leaping spires of fire danced on the walls and ceiling. Smoke seeped in around the windows, gathering in the room to form a gray and breath-catching cloud.

"It's the gin, they're burning the gin," Anya said in disbelief. The men who had attacked her had set fire to the cotton gin, knowing the two of them were locked inside.

Ravel made no reply. He slipped his hand into his trouser pocket, bringing out a small object, then lifted his chained leg and set his foot on the bed. Bending, he inserted the object in the lock and began to manipulate it.

The hairpin she had snatched from him so short a time before was not the only one he had found. She should have known he had let it go too easily. She made a sound through her nose that was a cross between thankfulness and disgust.

He sent her a quick glance. "It's amazing, the skills that can be learned in prison."

"So I see. I trust it also works on the door?"

There was a quiet click and the leg shackle sprang open. Ravel removed the thick ring and flung it aside. "Of course."

"Of course." She looked at the window where tongues of fire were licking past the glass, trying to get to the dry cypress shingles of the roof. "You might have used it to release us a bit earlier."

"I didn't think it would be necessary," he told her over his shoulder as he moved with oiled quickness to the door and knelt at the keyhole. "I rather expected to have the privilege of a visit from the boss first."

"You wanted to see him?" The smoke in the room was growing thicker. Anya lifted the hem of her gown, using it to cover her nose and mouth. There seemed to be more air near the floor and she went to her knees beside Ravel.

"Call it curiosity. I'd like to know who else wants me dead."

"Else?"

"Besides you."

She stared at him with smarting eyes, blinking against the sting of the smoke. "I don't want that at all!"

"You must admit it would solve your problem of what to do with me."

"You can't really have thought I had anything to do with the animals who put me in here?"

"That part could have been their mistake."

"It wasn't," she said, and ruined the icy effect of the words by choking and coughing in the middle of them.

Ravel, with his head inclined toward the door in a listening attitude, made no reply. Seconds passed that seemed hours. The old building was burning like tinder soaked in turpentine, going up so fast that fires must have been set at several points. The heat was increasing and the smoke growing black, boiling into the room in a dark and smothering fog. Anya wiped at the tears streaming from her eyes with her skirt. When she looked up again, Ravel had his hand on the door handle, trying it.

He paused, turning to her. His eyes were red rimmed, narrowed against the smoke, and there were smoke-tears gathering underneath them in the hollows above his cheekbones. "I never dreamed you would be in real danger; it just didn't seem possible. I'm sorry."

Questions crowded Anya's mind in a confused tumble, but this was no time to sort them out. She only shook her head and rose to her feet, plunging out into the fresh air at his gesture as he threw the door open. Ravel was right behind her. With an arm at her waist, he swept her down the stairs.

They had gone no more than a half dozen steps when they heard a yell. One of the thugs, bullet-headed and barrel-shaped, came on a run from outside. He stopped in the wagon drive below them and raised a rifle to his shoulder. His face was contorted and his mouth open as he squinted along the barrel.

Moving with the quick reflexes and easy strength of the great hunting cat, El Tigre, for which he had been named, Ravel vaulted over the railing, springing down upon the other man. The pair went sprawling in the dirt of the wagon drive. There was a grunted curse, the sound of bone crunching under bone. The man with the rifle lay still.

Ravel crouched over him an instant, waiting, then rose with animal grace. He moved to the open end of the building, angling to one side for the cover of the wall. He looked out, quartering the night that was colored orange with flames, searching it with his eyes. The only thing that moved nearby was the branches of the trees whipped by the hot vortex of the fire, though there was a stirring further down the road.

Anya joined him. Keeping her voice low, she said, "The others?"

"It seems they were so sure of us they left only one guard while they went on to other things, like rounding up the slaves."

Slave stealing was common, though it was more usual for them to be enticed away one at a time, with promises of freedom, than to be taken at gunpoint. The demand, and the price, was high in Texas, and the border was no great distance away.

"Do you think they heard the guard call out?"

"We won't wait to find out." Returning to the fallen man, Ravel scooped up the rifle, then caught Anya's hand and started back down the wagon drive.

Anya took a few steps. Feeling the hot blast of the fire, seeing the yellow flames, she stopped. "That guard, he's still alive. We can't leave him."

Ravel gave her a straight glance. He did not bother to remind her that the man would have killed them both. Turning back, he went with swift economy of movement to strip off the guard's greasy suspenders and bind his arms behind his back. He made a gag with the handkerchief he took from his own pocket and tied it in place with a piece of the man's shirt, then grabbed an arm and began to drag the unconscious guard toward the rear entrance to the gin.

The wind was roaring down the wagon drive, carrying with it billows of smoke filled with fragments of burning ash and soot. The heat was so intense that it parched the skin of their faces and seemed to sear its way into their lungs. Overhead, there were small rivers of fire flowing along the rafters of the unsealed roof. There was a humming, thumping noise in the gin machinery as the upper gears and main drum absorbed the heat. The fire rumbled and crackled and spat. Through the open doorway of the room they had left, they could see that the bed had burst into flames and there was smoke seeping up through the cracks in the floor.

It was the regularity of the thumping sound in the machinery that drew Anya's attention. At first she could see nothing in the smoke-filled inferno that the gin had become. Then she saw a movement at the back of the platform running down the side. She stopped.

There were two people lying bound and gagged there, one of them kicking at the upright beams that held the machinery. It was Marcel and Denise.

Ravel and Anya were beside them in an instant. Ravel tore the gag out of Marcel's mouth, while Anya did the same for Denise. The manservant croaked out, ''My pocket—knife.''

Flaming bits of wood were raining down all around them by the time the ropes were cut and enough circulation restored that Marcel and Denise could stumble out of the gin. It was as well that the rear entrance of the long building was deserted. They made no attempt at concealment, but threw themselves headlong into the night, not stopping until they had reached the deep shadows under a live oak tree. They let the guard fall to the ground and bent over, drawing deep breaths to the depths of their lungs of the blessedly cool and untainted night air.

When he was able, Marcel told them what had taken place. The man they called the boss had come in his carriage. He had not stepped down, but called the leader of the men out to him. His orders given, he had turned around and driven away back toward New Orleans. The men had immediately tied up Marcel and Denise, then gone to round up the slaves in the quarters, making ready to haul them away while the hours of dark still lasted. The men had carried the two house servants out to the gin; they were the ones most likely to be able to identify them, they said, so they would burn with their mistress and her prisoner. The gin had been fired and a single man left on watch while the others loaded the slaves in the wagons and ransacked the house.

The thought of the people she had worked with and cared for so long, the older ones, the children and babies, being hauled away like so many head of cattle made Anya feel ill. Almost to herself, she said, ''We have to stop them!''

Ravel turned his gaze toward her and slowly she lifted her lashes to meet it. He wondered if she realized the plea that lay deep in her eyes. He gave a hard nod. "We will need other weapons."

"Everything is at the main house under lock and key—unless they have already been taken." The hunting rifles and handguns that had belonged to her father were prized goods, easy to sell in New Orleans. The muskets and silver-chased fowling pieces, relics scorned by the crooks who infested Gallatin Street, might have been left behind.

"Cane knives?"

"Yes. They are in the tool shed, but it's locked."

"Let's see," Ravel said, his teeth gleaming white in the tight grin that lighted his smoke-grayed face.

A short time later, Ravel and Marcel had armed themselves with the cane knives, the long, wide-bladed, and lethally sharp knives used for cutting cane and also for clearing underbrush. Denise had taken a hoe for protection until she could get her hands on a butcher knife from the kitchen. Anya had seized on a short-handled sledgehammer since she had always hated the vicious-looking cane knives. With the greatest stealth, they circled wide around the slave quarters, coming up on the rear of the big house. Denise left them there, moving with the silence of her Indian ancestors to the separate kitchen building. She returned just as quietly a few moments later, carrying a knife with a blade that had been sharpened so many times it was as thin as a stiletto.

Standing concealed among the fig and pomegranate trees in the back garden, they watched the shadows of the men against the lamplight as they crossed from room to room in front of the upstairs French doors. There appeared to be only two of them. That meant two were still down at the quarters. A harnessed wagon belonging to Beau Refuge stood on the drive at the end of the walk leading from the back gallery of the house. In it were several bulky sacks. The sight of them, with their implication of leisurely picking and choosing among her possessions while she herself was supposedly roasting in the gin fire, made Anya's blood beat high in her veins. Her grip on the hammer she held tightened.

For long moments there was no sign of movement from the upper floor. The men must have carried their depredations toward the front of the house, where the salon and Madame Rosa's bedchamber were located. His voice low, Ravel said, "Now."

They moved swiftly toward the back stairs that led from the ground floor to the upper gallery, giving access through the French doors to the main rooms. The doors leading into the middle room, the sitting room, stood open. One by one they eased inside. Ravel crossed to station himself to the left of the doorway opening from the sitting room into the dining room at the center of the house.

Anya took the right side, opposite Ravel, and grasped her hammer with both hands. Denise moved quietly to stand in the doorway leading to Celestine's bedchamber on the left. Marcel flattened himself against the wall, merging into the shadows of the corner farthest from the small lamp that burned on a side table, a position giving him a view into the dining room.

The men must return through the sitting room to reach the back stairs that gave access to the waiting wagon. To do that, they would have to come through the door Anya and Ravel guarded. The minutes inched past. Thumps and jolts and the sounds of doors and drawers being opened and shut could be heard. The men were in no hurry. It seemed an eternity before the manservant made a brief, warning gesture.

Footsteps. They were firm and heavy, as if the man who approached was burdened. A faint shadow, cast by lamplight from the dining room, crossed the threshold. Anya lifted her hammer, brought it down.

Before it landed, the hammer struck a glancing blow on the butt of the rifle Ravel was swinging toward the back of the man's head. The double blow of hammer and rifle, neither solid, still sent the man staggering to fall on his face. He dropped the bag he carried. A silver sugar bowl spewed from it across the floor, whirling like a top.

From the dining room, the second man yelled, dropping his bag. He pulled a pistol from his coat pocket. Ravel spun, reversing his rifle, fanning the hammer to cock and fire in one smooth motion. The second man was thrown backward by the blast of the shot. Dark gray powder smoke blossomed in the room.

The first man had been no more than stunned. Even as the shot rang out, he picked himself up and sprinted for the door. Marcel ran forward, swinging his cane knife in a shining arc toward the juncture where the man's head and shoulder came together. It struck, sank in. The man screamed and tumbled headfirst out onto the gallery, to lie in a fast-spreading pool of blood.

Denise gave the dying man a meager glance, then stepped further into the room where she had been concealed. She emerged a moment later with a rifle in each hand. "Look what I found."

The weapons had been propped against the bed, apparently left while the men turned out the drawers of a dressing table, then forgotten in their search for spoils. Ravel took one in exchange for his that must be reloaded and Anya accepted the other, while Marcel knelt to search through the pockets of the two dead men for ammunition. The sound of the shot would draw the other thugs, and they must be ready.

"M'sieur, mam'zelle," Denise called from where she had stepped out onto the gallery.

It was time. The men were coming. Ravel was first through the door, with Anya behind him and Marcel, hastily closing the breech of his rifle, behind them. They moved down the railing, where the light from the sitting room would not silhouette them as such perfect targets.

There was only one man. The other had stayed with the slaves. He came on up the middle of the drive from the quarters, his head lifted as he caught the movement on the upper gallery.

Ravel lifted his voice, calling, "Hold it right there, friend!"

The man shied like a horse finding a snake under his feet. His rifle boomed as he dropped into a crouch and scurried toward the trees.

The bullet buzzed overhead with the sound of an angry wasp. Beside Anya, Ravel raised his rifle and fired. She did the same. The twin shots exploded. Dirt was kicked up between the feet of the man on the drive. Something plucked at the sleeve of his shirt so that he yelled a curse and dropped his rifle. Ducking, weaving, he gained the cover of the trees and went crashing back toward the quarters. Seconds later, there came the sound of running hoofbeats.

"Let's go after them!" Marcel said, ready to head for the stairs.

Ravel shook his head. "We would never catch them; besides, they are just hired hands. It's the boss I want. But we have a few things to take care of here first."

A few things, such as releasing and calming the slaves, containing the gin fire so that it did not spread to the roofs of the outbuildings, the quarters, or the main house, and burying the dead. They worked through the hours of the night into the dawn.

Ravel was everywhere, cutting the ropes that made a cordon of the slaves, hoisting a crying child to his shoulder the better for it to find its mother, organizing the men into a bucket brigade to get water to the buildings most in danger, beating out flames with a wet burlap sack.

Anya treated cuts and burns, passed out sugar lumps to the youngest and most frightened children, set the oldest ones who were getting in the way to watching for sparks in the dried grass and undergrowth, and sent a delegation of older men to see to the bodies in the big house. With several of the women, she went to tend to the man left trussed up with suspenders behind the gin. He was gone. All that was left was the twisted suspenders lying in the grass to show that he had worked his way free and fled.

It was only as dawn was streaking the sky, and the gin was reduced to a pile of smoking black beams and gray ash dotted with a few red embers, that Anya and Ravel made their way back to the house. They pulled themselves step by weary step up the back stairs and across the gallery to the sitting room. Inside, they started toward a settee to sit down, then looked down at themselves and decided against it. Covered with dirt and soot, their faces gray with fatigue and smeared with smoke-grime, they looked at each other and began to laugh. It was the ridiculousness of their appearance that triggered their mirth, but beneath that was the exhilaration of having cheated death and destruction, and the sheer pleasure of breathing, feeling, living.

Denise found them moments later as they gasped with laughter, leaning weakly upon each other in the middle of the sitting room. She put her hands on her hips and cleared her throat. "When you two are finished," she said as they turned toward her, "there's water heatin' and tubs waitin' for the both of you."

For Anya, it was heaven to lie in the water and feel its silken heat against her parched and bruised skin, to breathe the scented steam and allow the muscles clenched tight throughout her body to slowly relax. There were sore places everywhere and small burns she could not remember receiving. Her hair was singed in places around her face, and the clothes that lay heaped on the floor where she had stepped out of them had so many holes burned into them that it looked as if they had made a feast for moths.

But as the labor and pain and distress of the last hours melted away from her and her brain rested quiescent, the same harrowing questions rose to the surface to haunt her. Who was the boss? Who had tried to kill Ravel, and her? But most of all, why?

It had to be someone who knew or suspected that Ravel was at Beau Refuge, that much was obvious. Celestine and Madame Rosa might have begun to guess he was there, but they were naturally above suspicion. She did not think Gaspard and Murray were quite so perspicacious. In any case, Gaspard was far too fastidious to stoop to such a thing, even if he had a reason for it, and Murray had no real grudge against Ravel either, despite the duel. Even if Murray were afraid to meet him, he would be too concerned with the obligations due his honor to ever jeopardize it by such an act.

There was Emile, of course. Jean's younger brother was something of an unknown quantity after his years in Paris, still, if he was at all like Jean, he would have far too much reverence for life to treat it so lightly. If he had, perhaps, conceived a belated urge to avenge the death of his brother, she thought it more likely he would find some pretext for a duel himself rather than resort to hired killers.

But whom did that leave? Someone who had gotten wind of Ravel's presence through the servants' grapevine? It might have happened that the news was out, but wasn't it too much of a coincidence to suppose that anyone who had heard would also have reason to want him dead?

Her own involvement in the danger she put down to sheerest accident. She had seen the thugs and they had thought it best that she didn't live to talk about it, just as they had tried to silence Denise and Marcel. The ransacking of the big house and the other depredations had probably not been part of the original plan, but had sprung from the fact that the men thought her out of the way.

What did that leave, then? She could think of nothing else. It was a question she must discuss with Ravel.

That he could have thought she might have some connection with such a plot against him still incensed her. But that someone had tried to take advantage of what she had done to Ravel, the vulnerability that she had caused, was even more enraging. It had been the trick of a coward and a cold-blooded killer. She despised the very idea, and wished there were some way of making Ravel realize it.

An opportunity to try came within the hour. She was sitting on a chaise lounge before the fire, drying her long tresses, when she heard footsteps. They came from outside on the gallery, and she thought from the measured tread that it was Ravel. Her first thought was of some new problem. She glanced down at her dressing gown of white flannel trimmed with lace-edged batiste flounces. It could hardly be called alluring, being much more concealing than most ball gowns. She rose to her feet and moved to the French doors, stepping outside.

He was standing with his hands braced on the railing and his head turned away from her, staring toward where the remains of the cotton gin sent lazy spirals of smoke into the sky. His hair was damp and curling and the clothing he wore, though clean, was of the rough material issued to the field hands. It made no difference. The square set of his shoulders and angle of his head marked him as one who was his own man and, indefinably, regardless of the accident of birth and her own prejudices, a gentleman.

He turned his head and the morning sun molded the angles of his face in golden light, glowing in his eyes. A slow, heart-wrenching smile curved his lips.

"Is—something wrong?" she asked, suddenly breathless.

He shook his head. "I was just looking one more time to be sure the fire had not broken out before I leave."

"Leave?" She had known he would go, but not so soon.

"I have to go back to New Orleans, you must know that."

"You could rest first. Surely a few more hours can't matter?"

She moved toward him, and he caught his breath. The sun, striking through the white garment she wore, outlined her body in a lambent glow, giving her a look both angelic and seductive. He felt a slow ache twisting in his belly, and though he wanted to look away, could not force himself to do it. He stood as if mesmerized as she came closer, and in his head there was a faint and dizzy singing.

When he did not speak, she moistened her lips, disturbed by something in the air, and also a deep warmth she felt rising inside her. "I suppose I should go, too; Madame Rosa must be told what has happened. We could travel together."

"It might be best if I went alone."

A clouded look came into her blue eyes. "Of course, if you prefer it. I can't blame you, after all. I—know it's a little late, but will you accept my apology?"

She reached out to touch his hand where it rested on the railing, and that gentle contact burned him more fiercely than any ember. The morning breeze caught the ends of her hair, wafting them toward him like fine and fragile tethers. He felt the folds at the hem of her dressing gown brushing his trousers legs, smelled the fresh and heady scent of her. They were delicate enticements, nearly as potent as the sweet curve of her lips, and his memories.

"For what?" he asked, his voice deep, wryly self-derisive. "It's been my pleasure."

Ravel put his hands on her arms, drawing her closer until she was pressed against him, her soft curves and hollows molding to the hardness of his form. He closed his arms around her, pressing her against him. As she stood quiescent in his embrace, he rested his cheek for a moment upon the silken center parting of her hair. He was taking advantage of her remorse and weariness, the stunned effect caused by the fear and violent death of the night just past. He knew it, but could not help himself. There had been so much death, of friends, of hope, of promise. He needed to hold her, to seek in her something he had found nowhere else, the reaffirmation of life. Just once more, just once.

His arms enclosed her like iron bands, an unbreakable hold. Anya made no attempt to free herself. Beneath the soft material that covered her from throat to ankles, she wore nothing. Her awareness of her naked state was acute, giving her a feeling of seductive vulnerability. She wanted him. That desire was as deep and undeniable as it was unlikely. Where it came from she could only guess; perhaps from emotions long dormant that had been awakened by this man, from the fierce joy of having cheated death, and something more that was too close to the quick to be examined.

There was a comforting rightness in leaning on his strength, feeling it surrounding, supporting her. For the moment that was something she needed with an edge of desperation, that she wanted as a shield against the problems that hovered around her, against her fears, her mistakes. There was in the passion that joined man and woman a great and unexpected boon. It was forgetfulness.

He drew back, searching her face, questioning. She stared up at him, her eyes wide in her pale face. She had nearly killed this man. But he was alive, they were both alive.

They moved as one, turning toward the open French door that led to her bedchamber. Inside, her bed loomed large with its carved mahogany posts and elaborate headboard and tester by Mallard, its high, soft mattress and white lace drawnwork coverlet. It was too pristine, too virginal. The chaise with its graceful rolled back and pale green silk brocade upholstery beckoned.

Anya sat down upon it, lying back, shifting to give him room. He did not take it, but instead knelt beside her. The flannel dressing gown she wore, held only by a pearl button looped by a braided frog of white silk at the throat and another between the breasts, fell open to reveal the long length of her legs. They shone with an opalescent gleam in the firelight, and he put his hand upon a slender thigh, smoothing, brushing aside the soft folds of material to trace upward to the curve of her hip. His face absorbed, his concentration upon what he was doing, he slipped free the loops that held the dressing gown closed and spread the edges wide.

Her breasts were like carved alabaster, blue veined, coral-rose tipped, perfect in their symmetry. He cupped them in his hands, leaning to taste their sweet essence, brushing his lips down the fragrant valley between them, before trailing lower across her abdomen in a path that meandered, sliding over the narrow, inward curves of her waist, circling, finding the softly cushioned mound at the apex of her thighs. Gently, with generosity that was near reverence, he sought the wellspring of her most exquisite pleasure, tracing with warm lips and gentle adhesion to that ultimate source.

She was beguiled, caught in such a maelstrom of desire and aching yearning that she felt naked in soul as in body, without protection, stripped of subterfuge. There was magic and a hint of possessiveness in his touch, and for the moment she had no wish to deny either. Her hand had a faint tremor as she closed her fingers upon his shoulder, kneading the muscles, awash in sensations so vivid with pleasure that they carried an intimation of anguish.

Melting, she was dissolving in liquid heat deep inside. She had no will, no strength, no purpose beyond this joining. Her blood ran scalding in her veins, and acid tears gathered under her lashes. His caresses deepened. Frantic need beat up into her mind and she clutched at him, her nails biting into his shoulders.

With a lingering caress, he left her. She heard the quiet slide of his clothing as he removed it and dropped it to the floor. The side of the chaise gave as he joined her upon it; then he was covering her, his legs hard and faintly rough with curling hair as his knee pressed between hers. She felt a probing, then his strong and careful entry.

So great was the relief and the pleasure that a long shudder rippled over her and she gave a gasping cry. Mindlessly, with her eyes tightly closed, she rose against him. The force of the passion that gripped her was astonishing, embarrassing, and with eyes tightly closed, she turned her head from side to side. For long moments he catered to her need, surging, receding, filling her again and again.

His movements slowed, ceased. His voice deep, throbbing, he said, "Anya, look at me."

The words came to her as if from a great distance, a plea and a command. The effort to comply was great, not the least because it warred with her own shamed reluctance. Slowly her lashes lifted. Her eyes were dark, half-blind as she stared up at him.

In his face was concern and leashed desire and something so near love that it could serve as an excellent counterfeit. There was in addition something more, a sureness that carried benediction for them both. She caught her breath as the sense of desperation that had gripped her eased, faded away, leaving only her great and enveloping need. She smoothed her hands along the corded muscles of his arms and the flat planes of his chest, enjoying with a deep and heretofore unknown sensuousness the faint grating of the coating of hair, the firm resilience of his skin, the board hardness of his abdomen and belly just above the point where their two bodies were coupled.

Her gaze had followed her questing hands. She looked back up, her features soft with surprise and grace though her eyes were still slumberous. He lowered his head and took her lips. His arms trembling with strain, he began slowly to thrust into her again. Anya, a small sound deep in her throat, rose to encompass him, taking him deep within her, holding as if she would never let him go. With mingled breaths and taut sinews they strove.

It was a conflagration, rich, warm, consuming. It took them into its fiery heart, drawing them deeper and deeper still. Gladly they plunged, seeking surcease, repletion, the supreme consummation.

Instead, they found glory, intangible, ephemeral, beyond price, the perfect completion.

Chapter Eleven

Anya and Ravel left for New Orleans within the hour. They did not travel separately; after what had taken place between them, the possibility was not even mentioned again.

Their behavior was most circumspect in front of the servants. Ravel waited for her downstairs and gave her his arm out to the carriage. He helped her inside and got in after her, taking the opposite seat with his back to the horses. They pulled away from the house to the cries of good-by from half the people from the quarters, most of whom, on learning that the horses and carriage had been ordered, had found some excuse to ease up toward the main house. It seemed they wanted to get a good look in the daylight at the man their mistress had been keeping locked in the gin, the man who had done so much the night before to prevent their being carried off and to save Beau Refuge from burning.

Anya thought Ravel bore the inspection, the craning necks and hoarse whispers, with commendable restraint. He seemed hardly aware of it, his attention turned inward as if grappling with some private problem. He returned the waves with a brief smile, his posture in his seat relaxed and yet slightly aloof. It was only as the miles churned away beneath the wheels of the carriage and his withdrawn attitude remained the same that she realized it was not a pose.

By slow degrees, the warmth she had felt in his arms began to cool. It seemed there would be no private acknowledgment of what they had shared. It must have meant little to him if he could dismiss it so readily. She swallowed on a hard knot in her throat and gathered the tatters of her own dignity around her, turning her head to stare out the window. There was little to see except stretches of fields lying fallow under the weak February sun, interspersed with thick woods floored with the dark green spikes of palmetto and hung with vines showing tender new growth.

As they neared New Orleans, Anya suggested that Ravel direct the driver Solon to his lodgings, or wherever he wished to stop. He inclined his head in silent agreement and did as she indicated. The carriage wound through the city, pulling up finally at a commodious house on Esplanade Street.

Fairly new, an acquisition since Ravel's rise to prosperity, it was of two stories, built of brick covered with cream plaster, and finished with graceful window arches and Ionic columns that gave it the look of a Roman villa. Set back under a pair of oaks, it was enclosed by a wrought-iron fence and had a formal front garden with paths outlined with box shrubs and planted with massed beds filled at the moment with pansies in full bloom.

The carriage came to a halt before the gate of the fence. Ravel turned to Anya. "I would be grateful if you would come inside for a moment. I would like to present you to my mother."

There was reserve behind the words, almost as if he expected her to refuse for reasons that had more to do with who he was than with what had occurred at Beau Refuge. Anya hesitated, torn between a desire to leave him and have done with this episode and curiosity to see the woman he spoke of with such softness in his voice. It was possible, too, that an explanation for Ravel's absence would be required, one Anya would be expected to give to Madame Castillo. She would rather face the Gallatin Street thugs any day, but she was not a coward. She would go.

Ravel directed Solon to the kitchen, where he would find food and drink and a place to rest after his long drive, then took Anya's arm. As he opened the gate and closed it behind them, she had the odd feeling of being coerced, almost as if she were being led like a captive to his home. The recent events had affected her mind more than she had realized. She must not allow such fancies to take root, or she would become as mad as her Uncle Will.

The interior of the house was American in style, with rooms

opening off a central hall, but very French in feeling with its subdued colors and graceful, beautifully made furnishings. It was also extremely quiet. Ravel had not rung for a servant, but had opened the door with his own key. No one came to greet them or offer assistance with wraps and hats. The ticking of a great cabinet clock standing in the hall was loud, doleful. It chimed the half hour, and the sound seemed to echo endlessly through the silent rooms.

"If you will step upstairs, I'll show you to a room where you can wash your hands while I go in search of Maman. Don't hurry. It will be better, I think, if I take the time to make myself a little more presentable before she sees me."

Anya had no objections. He was still wearing clothing from the Beau Refuge storeroom, clean enough since it had replaced that which had been scorched beyond repair during the fire, but hardly fitting for a gentleman. She could not blame him for wishing to change. And naturally anything he might do to lessen the number of questions she herself was called upon to answer must have her approval.

She moved ahead of him up the wide, curving stairs with their mahogany treads covered by an Oriental runner. At the end of the upper hall, he stepped ahead of her to open the door to a back bedchamber. She moved inside. He inclined his head, and with a few brief words to indicate that he would return for her shortly, he shut the door upon her and went away.

Anya stood listening to his footsteps receding down the hall with a frown between her brows. After a moment she shook her head, as if to rid herself of the unease that gripped her. Removing her bonnet and gloves, she looked about the room.

It was a pleasant chamber, very feminine in feeling, with walls painted palest blush pink, an Aubusson carpet on the floor in shades of rose, cream, and green, and embroidered muslin curtains under rose silk draperies lavishly hung with rose red fringe and tassels at the windows. The decorative leitmotif was cherubs. The small figures could be seen holding back the mosquito netting of the tester bed, lying on the fireplace mantel, hanging on the wall. Some were of marble, some of carved and painted or gilded wood; most were quite old and valuable.

Anya removed the dust of travel and tidied her hair, then sat down to wait in a slipper chair. The bedchamber, for all its softness, was oppressive to her. It took only a moment for her to discover the cause. Unlike the rooms she was accustomed to, it had only one door, the one leading into the hall. There was no access to the outside other than a pair of windows, and no connecting rooms. It gave her a closed-in feeling that was similar to that which had been caused by the small room in the cotton gin. It was a distinct relief to hear the quiet knock as Ravel returned.

He did not wait for her to open the door, but turned the silver knob and stepped inside. Anya came slowly to her feet. The man who advanced into the room might have been a stranger. He wore a frock coat of deep charcoal gray with light gray trousers, a white waistcoat, and black cravat. He had removed his bandaging, and his hair was well brushed, lying in sculptured waves over his head. His half-boots were polished to a mirror shine, and the watch chain that looped across his flat abdomen had the rich gleam of purest gold. His face was stern, the eyes as hard as obsidian.

"My mother isn't in," he said abruptly. "This is her visiting day."

"I see." Anya lowered her lashes, afraid he would see the alarm that was rising inside her. She moved to the bed where she had placed her bonnet and gloves. "Perhaps another time then."

"You could wait."

"I think not. I need to talk to Madame Rosa, and there are other things that must be done."

He made no reply. Though she moved toward him, he did not give way to permit her to approach the door. She came to a halt. With a coolness she did not feel, she lifted a brow in inquiry.

At last he spoke. "Suppose I said to you, 'Don't go; stay here where it's safe.'"

"Safe?"

"Someone tried to kill you."

"Because of you." She started to step around him, but he moved to block her way.

"Maybe. Maybe not."

She stood still. "What do you mean?"

He watched her with care. "Are you sure you don't know? It

occurs to me that what you did may have been part of a larger scheme, that once your part was played, you were no longer of use. You were expendable.''

"You can't believe such a thing," she said as his meaning crept in upon her. "You can't think that I deliberately took you to Beau Refuge so that you could be killed!"

"Can't I?"

"You must be mad!"

There was no relenting in his face. "I'm beginning to wonder."

"It makes no sense. If anyone wanted you dead, there are plenty of assassins in New Orleans."

"A telling point, but the fact remains that you did drag me to Beau Refuge and we were nearly killed, both of us. Whoever made the attempt may try again. I would prefer that they don't succeed."

His dry irony was lost on Anya. "So would I! Listen to me, if you please. There was no scheme! I thought I could stop the duel by seeing to it that you did not appear when the time came. That's all there is to it! I have no idea where those men came from or why, but I had nothing to do with them or with whoever sent them."

"It was a coincidence, in fact, that they came when they did?"

"Yes!" she cried, her voice throbbing with anger and apprehension. He was so tall and broad. In all the time she had known him, even when he first discovered that she had had him chained, she had never seen him look quite so forbidding.

"I'm not a fool," he said softly.

"Nor am I a murderess!" She took a deep breath, struggling for control. "The best way to prove that it's so is to find out who wanted you dead, and why. To stand here arguing about it is only wasting time. Unless of course you know who it might be?"

His answer was indirect. "It will be best if you stay here until I can be sure."

"I can't stay here; it's out of the question!"

A faint smile touched his lean features. He took a step toward her. "I think you can."

"If you are doing this for revenge," she said, her blue gaze stormy as she gave ground, "let me tell you I consider it more than a little excessive."

"Meaning that I have already had my—satisfaction? It may be that I consider it incomplete."

The implication, coupled with the raking look he gave her and the sudden warmth in his eyes, was unmistakable. The color drained from her face as she absorbed the shock. "You mean you—you want me, even though you think I tried to have you killed?"

"Perverse of me, isn't it?"

"Demented! As demented as staying chained to the wall at Beau Refuge when you could have gone. I thought it was honor that had kept you there. What was it in truth? This need for revenge? The pleasure of ruining my good name by lingering? The prospect of forcing yourself on me again?"

"Forcing, Anya?" he said, his voice rough as he reached for her. "There was no force used or required. There was only this."

He pulled her against him, his fingers biting into her arms as he captured her mouth with his. His lips were hard, burning in their demand for surrender. She struck at him with her hands that were trapped between them, twisting, struggling. He released her arm, sinking his fingers into the thick coil of hair at the nape of her neck to hold her immobile. Still she fought him, though the pressure of his mouth lessened, his lips moving upon hers with insistent, devastating tenderness.

It was so familiar, so frighteningly familiar, the deep, hot burgeoning of desire inside her. She did not want it, would not succumb to it or give him the satisfaction of knowing he could arouse it. She could not fight him and herself at the same time. She went still, concentrating on subduing the treacherous impulses while she stood as lifeless and cold as a statue in his arms.

He released her so abruptly that she nearly fell, might have if it had not been for the grasp he retained on her elbow. The urge to strike out at him was so great that she trembled with it, but something, perhaps his hold on her arm, perhaps the expression in his eyes, prevented it. They stared at each other, their breathing jagged, loud in the tense quiet.

Ravel curled his free hand into a fist as he slowly brought his needs under control. He wondered if she knew how close he was to taking her there on the floor. Another word, a single gesture of defiance—

God, he was as mad as she called him. How much of what he had said to her did he believe? He hardly knew himself. He only knew that he would do anything to hold her with him a little longer. Anything. And if she hated him for it, so be it. At the back of his mind, scarcely acknowledged but beckoning, lay a solution to his dilemma. To broach it would, however, be most unwise; it would give her an advantage he was almost sure she would not hesitate to use. Almost.

"If my presence and my touch are so distasteful to you," he said, his voice tight, "why did you visit me in my prison? Why didn't you leave me out there alone?"

Her answer, dictated by impotent rage, came unbidden. "Because I was sorry for you!"

No, she would not hesitate. His grip on her arm closed harder and harder until suddenly she paled, wincing. He flung her from him, swinging away, heading for the door.

"You will never get away with this!" she cried, taking a step after him. "Solon knows I'm here."

He spoke over his shoulder. "Your coachman is locked in the stables and your carriage out of sight."

"You're a fool if you think you can keep the fact that I'm here a secret. It will be all over the city in twenty-four hours."

He turned at the door, his face grim. "Has it occurred to you, Anya, *ma chérie*, that, fool though I am, that might be my purpose?"

The door closed behind him. There came the rasp and click of a key turning in the lock.

Revenge, that was what he had meant. He was going to complete the ruin of her name begun at Beau Refuge. Anya went swiftly toward the door and, knowing it was useless, turned the silver knob back and forth in frustration. She stopped. No. It could not be. His mother lived here with him, a more than adequate chaperone. In fact, a visit to his home, his mother, could conceivably shed some aura of respectability on his sojourn at the plantation. It would also give rise to speculation about a match between them.

The idea was insupportable. It was also laughable. Ravel would never think of marrying her, not after what she had done to him. The conventions meant little to someone like him. If she was compromised, he would doubtless consider it her own fault, not his. Certainly if it had been his intention to do the honorable thing he must surely have said so before now.

Unless his motive had nothing to do with honor? Vengeance would be equally served, perhaps better served, if he forced her to marry him. To be wed to him, Jean's killer, a man who had taken her virginity by a trick; he must know she would hate it. He wanted her, she knew that. How he would enjoy being able to save her good name, prevent her from dwindling into a spinster because of what he had done. At the same time, he would gain the respectability he had never had by the alliance with Madame Rosa's stepdaughter, and force her into his bed quite legally. Revenge indeed!

She felt sick with rage, and her own idiocy for getting involved with Ravel Duralde. Sick, and with a strong inclination to put her head down somewhere and weep. She leaned her forehead against the door panel for a long moment, closing her eyes tightly against the acid seep of tears into her lashes.

Then with a deep breath she drew herself erect. She would not stand for it. There was no power on earth that could make her submit to so debasing an arrangement. She would far rather face the whispers and the tittle-tattle, the inevitable ostracism that would come. What did she care for society, for parties and balls and the trivial round of amusements? She had Beau Refuge. She liked her own company. She would survive.

But Madame Rosa would be appalled, and Celestine would feel the shame as her own. What Murray would make of the scandal she could not think. He was not so bound by tradition as the Creoles, and yet he was a most conservative young man. Murray and Celestine, so young and in love. There might be protection for them in a marriage between Ravel and herself. There would no longer be cause for a duel, and, in addition, a meeting between men so closely related was unlikely.

Unlikely, but not impossible. In all probability that was where Ravel was going now, to find and challenge Murray. No doubt settling that affair was the urgent business that had brought him back to town. It could not be permitted. Somehow, someway, she must stop it. In order to do that, she must first find the means to escape. This was a bedchamber, not a room designed as a prison. There had to be a way out.

The simplest method must be eliminated first. Anya dropped to her knees before the door, placing her eye at the keyhole. If the key was in the lock, she could slip something, a piece of cloth or paper, under the door, push the key out of the hole from this side with a buttonhook or nail file if such a thing could be found, then when the key fell on the cloth outside, draw it back toward her under the door.

The key was not in the lock. Ravel must have taken it with him.

She rose and made a quick circuit of the room. The windows here on this second floor were not quite far above the ground due to the high ceilings of the house, typical of the warm climate, but were also barred across the lower halves with iron grilles. The grillwork was primarily decorative, but might have been installed by a previous owner for the safety of a child. It was ornate, but had a substantial look.

She returned to the door. She had watched Ravel pick the lock at the gin. It had not appeared too difficult, and pins were one thing she had with her in abundance. Drawing one from her hair, she got down on her knees once more and set to work.

It was not as easy as it had seemed. The mechanism was stiff and unwieldly, refusing to yield to the pressure she was able to exert, or else her knowledge of how a lock worked was faulty. She should have paid more attention to such matters, but how was she to know it would ever be useful? She threw the pin down in frustration, and pulled herself to her feet with her hands on the knob. She had sat so long on her legs that they tingled from lack of circulation, refusing to work. She was growing hungry, too. It was well-past noon and she had not eaten. At least she had not starved Ravel! So great was her sense of ill-usage that she picked up a cherub in pink onyx, strongly tempted to throw it out the window just for the satisfaction of smashing something.

Out the window. Though the bottom half was covered by a grille, the top was not. She had only glanced at the windows through the muslin curtains, assuming that since the house was fairly new and had many American features the windows were double sashes. Now she moved to jerk the draperies open and pull the muslin curtains underneath to one side. With the filmy fabric out of the way, it was easy to see that the windows were casements. They opened on hinges, swinging into the room, leaving the entire expanse free and uncluttered. All she had to do was climb over the grille. That was, of course, if she could find some way of letting herself down to the ground.

There was an obvious solution. Whirling to the bed, she threw the pillows and bolster aside and stripped back the coverlet and quilts. The sheets were of linen, monogrammed at the top hem, gratifyingly strong. She tugged the top sheet from the mattress, holding it up, wondering if it would not be better to tear it in half.

The knob of the door rattled, was twisted back and forth. Anya hurriedly bundled the sheet in her arms, turning toward the bed. There was no time to remake it. What Ravel would say when he saw what she was doing, what action he would take, she did not like to think. The key was being inserted in the lock, scraping as it was turned. The knob began to move.

The woman who stepped into the room was tall and elegant, if rather thin, and dressed in a visiting costume of soft velvet trimmed with gray and pink striped ribbons. Her hair, drawn back in lustrous waves, was black with wings of white at her temples. Her eyes were dark and quick with intelligence under rather thick brows, dominating a face that seemed to gain strength from the fine lines of humor and pain around the eyes and about the mouth. Her age might have been no more than forty, though common sense suggested it must be nearer fifty, perhaps more. The resemblance to Ravel was unmistakable.

The woman's entrance was swift, impetuous; then as she saw Anya her footsteps slowed. Her face pale, she said in soft distress, "If I had not seen it for myself, I would not have believed it."

"Madame Castillo?"

"You have it right."

"I'm Anya Hamilton."

"I am aware. This is really too bad. This time he has gone too far."

Anya moistened her lips. "Perhaps I should explain—"

"There is no need; I have eyes in my head. The arrogance of

him, the sheer unprincipled gall. That he could do it at all is shocking, but that he would dare while I am under the same roof makes me long to slap him!''

"If you think," Anya said, her temper kindling, "that I am some loose woman your son has brought here to embarrass you, or that this is an episode of simple lust, I take leave to inform you—"

Madame Castillo's expression changed rapidly from concern to blank surprise to amusement. She gave a choke of laughter. "Simple lust! Oh, *chère*, if only it were."

"You are aware then of—of what is between your son and myself."

"In part, and the rest, knowing Ravel, I can guess."

The message he had sent from Beau Refuge must have been more comprehensive than he had indicated. An uncomfortable flush rose to Anya's face. "I can't blame you for being angry for what I did—"

"Oh, I'm not angry. Anything done to prevent a duel in which my son is involved must have my blessing—even if his continued good health was not the purpose."

"Then your disapproval is for his keeping me here?" Anya said slowly, a trace of surprise in her tone.

"Not, perhaps, the fact, but the method seems lacking in finesse."

The older woman tipped her head to one side, her gaze upon Anya direct, relentlessly appraising. She was no easier to understand than her son. Did she mean that she had no objection to Anya despite the abduction, that her annoyance was with Ravel's flouting of the conventions? Or was she saying that she understood and applauded Ravel's deeper purpose, to pressure Anya into marriage, but deplored the way he was going about it? In either case, it made no difference. There was only one point of importance at this moment.

"You will let me go then?"

Madame Castillo smiled. "I doubt that I could stop you; you appear a very determined young lady. Of course, it might be best for the peace of this house if I were to go away and close the door, permitting you to make your way out the window. My conscience won't allow it, however; I should never forgive myself if you fell. And so you are free to go, if that is what you want.''

Anya tossed the sheet she held on the bed, searching out her bonnet and gloves where they had been thrown to the floor as she removed the coverlet. She stood, tying the bonnet of sea blue velvet set with nodding egret plumes on her head, smoothing on her kid gloves.

Of course it was what she wanted. How could it not be? To be free at last of Ravel Duralde, never to cross his path again, was her dearest wish. It was unreasonable of her then to think of him as he had been that morning, splendidly naked, with his hair damp and curling on his forehead and his eyes black and lustrous with passion. *"Look at me, Anya—"*

If she left now she would never again feel his caresses, never see the sudden flash of his laughter or the intent concentration of his thought processes as they played chess or solved problems together, never again lie replete and languorous in his arms. If she were to marry him, no matter how or why, she would have those things.

But there was nothing to say he wanted to marry her at all. The suspicions she harbored might be no more than tortuous fancies without foundation. Because she found his chess moves complicated and filled with clever entrapments did not mean that he must proceed in that manner in the situation in which they found themselves. He was a man of the nineteenth century, not some Byzantine ruler from the ancient world plotting confusion to those who had injured him. She would go home, back to Madame Rosa's house, and that would be the end of it.

She did not truly expect that it would be. Nor was it.

The problem was not the necessity of explaining everything to Madame Rosa and Celestine. As the matter was discussed over an early tea hastily prepared for Anya, her half sister cried and fumbled with her vinaigrette in a storm of sympathy and indignation and foreboding, but Madame Rosa remained reassuringly sanguine. There would be talk, a great deal of it, but so long as Anya and Ravel conducted themselves in a suitable manner, it would pass. To aid matters, she would have Gaspard drop just a hint here and there about a visit by M'sieur Duralde to Beau Refuge to inspect some—what? Horses? Mules? Of how he had become ill of an unknown and possibly contagious fever so that he had insisted on keeping well away from the main house until he recovered. And of how grateful they all were that he was on hand when the gin went up in flames. Anya might have to endure a few prying questions and suggestive remarks, but if no more serious consequences developed, they should be able to launder this particular piece of linen in private.

The oblique reference to consequences referred to the hope that Anya was not pregnant. What she would do if she should be was a question Anya refused to consider. She had spoken blithely to Ravel of taking the English remedy, but she preferred not to put her resolve to the test. The time might come when she would be glad for Ravel to marry her, whatever his reasons.

Because of that, and because she could not prevent herself from thinking of what had happened, the question that had haunted her from the beginning remained with her, preventing her from making an end of the affair. Gaining in importance from minute to minute the longer and harder she struggled with it, was the puzzle of what sort of man Ravel truly was.

It was not the only question, of course. The more she thought of the things he had said to her, the more puzzled she became. He suspected her of being involved with the men who had tried to kill him, a not unreasonable surmise in view of her abduction of him. And yet there seemed something more behind his suspicion. What could it be? The duel and its cause appeared central to the matter, but surely he could not think that Murray would choose so low a means of avoiding a meeting, or that she would help him if he had? Nor did it make sense for Ravel to suppose that, if she had aided Murray, he would then have turned on her and ordered her death. It was ridiculous.

But what else was there? There must be something she was missing. Her need to know was so strong that she could think of nothing else. She could not relax, could not rest. She felt only a terrible need to find the answers she sought someway, somehow, and soon.

Where was she to look? Whom was she to ask? What questions should she use to discover the information she needed? She didn't know but she would find out. It seemed sensible to suppose that the best way to learn about a man would be to ask those who knew him. There were three people who came immediately to mind. The first of these was his mother, but Anya had spoken to her, and it was unlikely that she could or would reveal more than she had already. Of the other two, the most important was Emile. He had been out of the city, but he must have some idea of Ravel's character, the esteem in which he was held by the men who knew him, or else could find out. The final person was the actress Simone Michel, Ravel's current mistress.

With Anya, to decide on a course of action was to embark upon it. She sat down at once at the *escritoire* in her sitting room and wrote a short and carefully worded note asking Emile to call upon her. Ringing for a servant, she dispatched the missive as soon as she had folded and sealed it.

Her messenger had hardly left the room before a knock came. Anya called out her permission to enter, then as she saw who it was, sprang to her feet in quick apprehension.

"Marcel! How did you come to be here? Is something wrong at Beau Refuge?"

"No, no, don't alarm yourself, mam'zelle. Nothing is wrong."

As he came forward, Anya saw that his arm was in a sling of black cloth, a color so nearly matching his coat she had not seen it at once. She indicated it now. "You look far from right."

He gave her a smile as he shook his head. "My wrist is broken, just a small crack in the bone, or so the doctor said. I didn't feel it until after you had gone this morning. I was only an hour behind you on the road, but I had instruction from Maman to go straight to the doctor, without troubling you until I was sure of the problem."

Anya made a sound of impatience for such scruples. "The doctor looked after you all right?"

"Indeed he did, once I mentioned your name."

"You must stay here with us for a few days, until you feel well enough to return to the country."

"You are kindness itself, mam'zelle," he said, "but this is a mere nothing. I'm well enough to return now, unless you have need of me here?"

He deserved a rest, though it might be difficult to make him take it unless he could also feel useful. A plan began to form in Anya's mind. She seated herself once more at the *escritoire*.

"Please sit down, Marcel," she said. "There is something I would like to discuss with you."

Emile arrived within the hour. When Anya swept into the salon, she found him sitting on the settee with Celestine, regaling her with outrageous compliments and teasing remarks while Madame Rosa sat fanning herself gently, smiling as she watched the young pair. Celestine blushed and laughed, but her behavior had the pretty circumspection becoming in one betrothed to another man.

Such an audience for her interrogation was not what Anya had envisioned. She allowed several minutes filled with banter and the exchange of the latest news to pass. Finally, she turned to Emile, saying quite frankly, "There is a matter that I need a man's opinion on, if you don't mind, *mon cher*. Perhaps you will be so kind as to walk with me to the square and back?"

"It will be my pleasure," he agreed at once. He rose with inherent good manners, giving no sign that he was reluctant to depart with her. Still, Anya had the feeling that he would rather have stayed talking to Celestine. It was troubling that he should be developing a tendre for her half sister, but it seemed that was the way of the world. Love was seldom convenient, parceled out in exact proportion to those who had need of it.

The square was the old Place d'Armes, now beginning to be called Jackson Square after the equestrian statue of General Andrew Jackson donated by the Baroness Pontalba a few years before when she had turned the old parade ground into a park. Strolling around the square had always been a pastime of the people of New Orleans. It was even more enjoyable since the cathedral had been rebuilt with new, pointed steeples and the upper floors of the buildings on either side, the Presbytère and the old Spanish Cabildo, had been given new facades. The Pontalba apartments, where once Anya had snatched the nightcap of the operatic tenor, ran at right angles to the other buildings. The apartments were long structures of red brick with galleries graced with wrought-iron railings and slate roofs. On the lower floors were select shops in the Continental manner, while the upper floors housed some of the most distinguished families and famous visitors in the city. The park in the center, planted with lush flowers that flourished in the near-tropical climate, was enclosed by a fence of wrought iron. On the fourth side of the square, beyond a street where horses pulling carts and carriages stepped at a quick pace, lay the levee and the river.

Anya and Emile took a slow turn about the square, glancing now and then into the shop windows where fancy goods were displayed. The air was pleasantly cool, with a fresh breeze from the river that fluttered the ribbons of Anya's bonnet. The cool sunlight of the waning afternoon slanted through the buildings, gilding the wrought iron, casting long blue shadows across the streets. Emile kept up an easy and general conversation, swinging his cane with a jaunty air as he walked. He glanced at Anya now and then, but gave no sign of impatience, seeming quite willing to wait for her to broach the subject that had brought them there herself. His attitude reminded her so much of Jean that it made it easier to turn to him at last.

"What would you say, Emile, is the best way to know and understand a person?"

He gave a quick, inquiring look. "It would depend on the person."

"A man, say, of some reputation. If you did not want to depend on the public view of him, what could you do?"

"I suppose the best way would be to talk to him."

"And if you could not do that?"

"Then you could speak to those who know him."

"Precisely what I thought. At the theater a few days ago, you defended Ravel Duralde. Could you tell me why?"

"I felt he was being unjustly maligned."

"Yes," she said, her gaze intent on his face, "but what made you think so? The accusation, if I remember correctly, was of cowardice, or at least a reluctance to meet my future brother-in-law on the field of honor. What led you to believe it was false?"

"One gains an impression." He made a slight helpless gesture.

"How," she persisted.

"From what other men say, how they say it."

"What do they say of Ravel?"

"Anya, you ask the impossible. I couldn't begin to tell you."

He was avoiding the issue, she knew it. Why should he? Was it the natural male reluctance to discuss another man with a woman? Or was it that he had some knowledge he wished to keep from her?

"Has there ever before been anything strange about a duel in which Ravel was a participant?"

"Not to my knowledge. Most occurred when he was younger or elsewhere, primarily Central America. I understand the duello was a favorite way of settling disputes there."

"What of his other activities? Have you ever heard that he trifled with other men's wives, or was associated with any kind of enterprise that might be dangerous?"

"Anya!"

"Well, have you?"

"No." He touched his thin mustache in a quick, nervous gesture.

"Where does his money come from, then? Isn't it strange that he has become so wealthy overnight?"

"It came originally from gambling. Ravel has since used a combination of skill, acumen, and luck in the financial arena to increase his holdings." He came to a halt, exasperation in his face as he turned to her. "What is this, Anya? What are you trying to say?"

She looked at him, studying him feature by feature. To trust or not to trust? It was a strange choice, one usually made on faith, not fact. She said frankly, "I want to know who would want to have Ravel Duralde killed."

"What do you mean?"

His gaze was narrow, almost defensive. Anya felt a moment of chill. She had thought to tell Jean's brother the truth, but suddenly it did not seem best. It was possible he might take it upon himself to become the protector of her good name by calling Ravel out. That was the last thing she needed. Falling back on the fiction Madame Rosa had suggested to explain Ravel's presence at Beau Refuge, she went on from there to describe the arrival of the gang of thugs and the fire.

"So you see," she ended, "the obvious question is, who hired those men, who is the boss who tried to kill Ravel?"

Emile Girod heard her out in grim silence. He held her steady regard a long moment; then he looked away. "I don't know," he said, his voice hard, intent, "but it isn't me."

Chapter Twelve

🔆 🔆 🔆 *Emile and Anya, after an aimless turn or two,* had wound up in the narrow passageway that lay between Chartres and Royal streets and ran three blocks from Canal Street to the front of the St. Louis Hotel. This short street, known as Exchange Alley, was where most of the *salles d'armes*, or establishments for the teaching of the art of fencing, were located. In the quiet that fell between the two of them, they could hear the sharp clang and snick of blades being crossed. So fine was the afternoon that the doors had been left standing open to cool the exertions of the gentlemen at their practice, and the sounds rang out clearly along the stone-paved pathway.

Hearing them, Anya suppressed a shiver. They reminded her of Ravel, of his expertise and her fear of it that had led her to where she was now. It was strange, so much ringing clatter and scraping, so much sweaty striving, for the purpose of wounding each other.

Since dueling with pistols had become the fashion with the advent of the Americans, however, the *salles d'armes* had lost a degree of their appeal. The development of power in the wrist and grace of motion were no longer of supreme importance. The young men of the city were just as apt to be found perfecting their aim at the shooting galleries on the lower levee as matching blades in Exchange Alley. Nothing, it seemed, could lessen the appeal of dueling itself, not even the danger of arrest for a pastime that, though immensely popular, was illegal. The police were inclined to look the other way under normal circumstances, particularly if their palms were properly greased, but there were enough people who were offended by the noise and danger of the ritualized killing to force them to act if the offense was too blatant.

With only the briefest pause, Anya said to Emile, "Certainly you didn't try to kill Ravel; the idea is absurd."

"There are some who would say I had reason." Emile touched his neat mustache in a nervous gesture.

"After all these years? I was not hinting at any such thing. I was only asking for your help."

He shook his head, his soft brown eyes still troubled. "I will be glad to help you in any way I can, Anya, but I'm afraid I've been out of the country so long that I am worse than useless."

There was reluctance in his voice. She was not surprised; men were ready enough to apply themselves to their own intrigues, but did not like to be drawn into those of women. Perhaps she should have gone to Gaspard. No. It was unlikely that Madame Rosa's patient escort could, or would, keep such a request from her, and for the moment Anya did not care to trouble her stepmother with worries over what she was doing.

A flight of pigeons fluttered down from their perch on a building ledge to settle in front of Anya and Emile. They waddled around Anya's skirts searching for crumbs. Their legs were bright red and their neck feathers shone with dark green and blue gleams of iridescence. The birds were the descendants of pigeons brought from France many years ago. As tender squabs they were considered a great delicacy by the Creoles, an unfailing aphrodisiac. Doubtless some of them were being baked somewhere at the moment, for it was time for preparation of the evening meal. Borne on the air were the rich smells of dinner cooking in both private and public kitchens, of seafood steaming, gravies browning, and onions and garlic sautéing in butter; of bread baking and the sweet creamy scent of sugar and milk and nuts and bottled fruits being slowly turned into dessert.

A magnificent black horse pulling an open victoria clip-clopped past. The gait was not too fast, not too slow. The occupant of the vehicle was a woman dressed in deep green. Her hair was a shimmering blond, her face exquisite, her shape perfection. She looked neither to the right nor to the left. Her afternoon gown was fastened at the throat and at the wrists, and

in her hand was a small parasol edged with fringe. Her appearance, in fact, was most discreet. And yet she was not a lady.

How Anya knew she could have not said. Perhaps the woman
reclined a bit too languidly on the carriage seat. Perhaps it was
the fixed and meaningless smile on her lips, as if she were too
willing to please. Perhaps it was the faint shoddiness of the
clothing of her driver. Whatever the reason, Anya could tell.
And she was reminded of Simone Michel, Ravel's mistress. It
was not that the two women looked anything like each other;
the similarity was in the attitude.

Staring after the carriage, Anya said slowly, "Never mind. I
think I know who might be better able to answer my questions,
if you will bear me company while I speak to them?"

He agreed readily enough. They turned back down Exchange
Alley as a shortcut to take them in the direction Anya wanted to
go. The paving stones beneath their feet, great slabs of slate
rock that had been brought to the city as ballast on ships, slanted
toward the center for drainage. They were also uneven, so that
it was necessary for Anya to watch her step. Emile gave her his
arm for support, and she accepted it not because she needed it,
but because she did not want to reject his overture, leaving him
to wonder if she did suspect him after all.

Above them loomed buildings hung with balconies of wrought
iron or inset with arches or pedimented doorways set flush with
the banquettes. The mingled shouts and rattle of swordplay,
bouncing between the plastered brick walls, reverberated around
them with a sound sometimes musical, sometimes so rasping it
tore at the nerves. The sun no longer penetrated to this narrow
alley. It was cooler here and a bit dank, the light growing dim-
mer with the advance of evening.

At the other end of the alley a man entered, followed by a
crowd of small boys. He was of average height, thin to emaci-
ation, with a dark line of mustache that drooped past the corners
of his red mouth. His eyes were feverishly bright and his cheeks
flushed. He was obviously ill, and yet he moved with the spare
elegance and strength of a born swordsman. One of the boys
behind him carried his cane as if bearing a holy relic, while the
others pushed and shoved, jockeying for the positions at his

sides. A towheaded tot smaller than the rest clutched at his coat-tail and was gently reprimanded.

"Who is that?" Emile murmured.

"Luis de Salvo, or so he calls himself. He arrived only a few weeks ago, but has established himself as one of the greatest of the *maîtres d'armes*, though he has an old injury in the lungs that troubles him. His swordplay is like lightning, and there is a special corner of the St. Louis Cemetery filling up with his victims. Soon he will have to copy Pépé Llulla, and buy his own graveyard."

De Salvo turned toward one of the fencing halls and paused at the short set of steps before the door. Retrieving his cane, he distributed a few coins to his young escorts, which sent them scampering as the younger ones tried to keep their booty from the bigger boys. The master swordsman climbed the steps and disappeared through the doorway. Immediately there were calls of greeting and good-natured banter from inside.

Anya and Emile drew even with the door of that *salle*. The sound of a voice rang out. If he had not spoken, Anya might not have noticed Murray in that place. As it was she turned her head and saw him standing in the circle around de Salvo. His head was thrown back as he laughed at a comment of one of his companions. He leaned on a buttoned foil, holding it with the ease of one familiar with the weapon.

How long had Murray been learning to fight with a sword? Was it an interest of long standing, or had he taken it up after he had so narrowly missed having to meet Ravel? It was disturbing to see him there, mingling with men who had, most of them, handled a blade of some sort since they were children. What was he thinking of? Celestine would be upset if she learned of it.

Anya would not have him think she was spying on him, however. Averting her gaze before she could draw his attention, she walked on beside Emile.

They talked of this and that, idle commonplaces. while they made their way toward St. Philip. As they neared the rooms of the actress located above the grocery, Emile began to look uneasy. He glanced from Anya to the grilled gateway ahead of them that led to the back court entrance. It was so obvious that he suspected he was going to be involved in an unpleasant confrontation between women that Anya had to compress her lips to keep from smiling.

"Anya, this is not—not *comme il faut*," he said as she paused beside the iron gate and waited for him to open it.

"No, but I see no alternative. You yourself said I should talk to those who know him, and who better than his—"

"Yes," he said hastily, "but you should know nothing of this woman, much less visit her."

"Shocking, isn't it?" She looked at him squarely, a challenge in her eyes. "I would have thought your years in France would have cured you of such provincial notions."

"I assure you the canons of behavior for females of good family are just as strict there. In Paris there are only two kinds of women, ladies and those who are not. They do not mix on a social basis."

"This isn't a social call. However, you may leave me if you like."

"You know I can't do that."

The sulky tone of his voice made him seem very young. She tilted her head. "Is it your own reputation that concerns you?"

"Certainly not," he said, his face registering his disdain for the question.

"Then," she said gently, "let me worry about mine."

She reached for the gate handle. With an imprecation under his breath, Emile forestalled her and opened the grilled closure, standing aside as she entered. She could feel his disapproval like a weight as he followed behind her down the paved walk and into the courtyard. Here grew a few shrubs and a redbud tree that was a froth of reddish purple bloom, but the leaves of fall still littered the ground, drifted into the corners. To the rear was an arched opening through which could be seen a staircase leading up to the gallery that ran around the court. With her skirts sweeping the dead redbud leaves into eddies, Anya headed toward it.

A maid opened the door to them. She had the coloring and self-assurance of a quadroon, and the cap and apron she wore were of fine muslin trimmed with lace. She took Emile's hat and sword cane and Anya's visiting card and invited them to be seated in the salon, then went away to consult with her mistress.

Anya looked around her with interest. The salon seemed suffocatingly full of crimson plush. It hung in generous swags at the windows, covered the settee and chairs, and was present in several fat ottomans sitting here and there. The remaining furniture was of dark and massive wood heavily carved in spiky and uncomfortable-looking Gothic designs. Bric-a-brac overflowed the tables and crowded the shelves of a huge étagère, from crystal ornaments and daguerreotypes and tintypes in tarnished silver frames to boxes covered with seashells, from molting feather fans and curling theater programs to antimony cups and pin trays embossed with the names of famous spas and theaters. The room was fairly neat, but there was about it the dejected air of most places where the occupants are transients. The attempt to impose a personal stamp upon it with the collection of souvenirs of past travels and meager triumphs seemed too revealing, oddly pathetic.

Anya seated herself on the edge of the settee. Emile, apparently too ill at ease to follow her example, stood at her side. They waited.

After long minutes, the door into the other rooms of the house opened. It was not the actress who emerged, but the maid. The girl carried a folded square of paper in her hand. She did not speak but, flashing a nervous smile, hurried through the room and out the front door. Her footsteps clattered down the stairs and died away. Anya and Emile looked at each other with raised brows but did not speak. The minutes ticked slowly past. Finally, the door opened once more.

Simone Michel sailed into the room in a gown of plum brocade decorated with coils of black braiding. Her dark hair was carelessly dressed, piled in a mass of curls that made her appear as if she had just left her bed. The curves beneath the brocade were opulent, the arms and shoulders gracefully rounded. The actress's face, without stage makeup, seemed softer and yet at the same time more determined. The sensuous fullness of her mouth was curved in a tight smile, and in her large and luminous eyes was a militant light.

"Forgive me for keeping you waiting, Mademoiselle Hamilton," she said, "I was just dressing to go to the theater. Would you care for a glass of sherry? I'm sorry I can't offer you more, but I wasn't expecting visitors."

Despite the politeness of the words she spoke, their tone was brittle, demanding an immediate explanation. Hearing them, Anya, who would have been happy to come at once to the point, felt in herself a distinct unwillingness to be pressed by this woman, or to allow her to control the visit.

She said pleasantly, "We have not met, Mademoiselle Michel, but I have seen you on the stage in several roles this winter. Permit me to compliment you on your success and also your considerable skill as an actress."

"Thank you." The reply held a note of surprise and no small degree of wariness.

"I don't believe you are acquainted with Emile Girod. He is a dear friend, recently returned from Paris." She indicated Emile with a brief gesture.

The young Frenchman did not let her down, but stepped forward to execute a perfect bow over the hand of the actress. "Delighted, mademoiselle. I am at your service."

Anya did not give the woman time to reply. "I don't believe we will trouble you for refreshments, though it is kind of you to offer when we have descended upon you unannounced. We were out walking, enjoying the afternoon—so very mild and agreeable, don't you think—when I had an impulse to see you."

"I see," the actress said, though it was plain from her stiff tone that she did not. Moving to a chair, she seated herself, spreading her skirts around her.

Anya hesitated, eyeing the other woman. The superior manner she herself had assumed suddenly seemed wrong. It was not going to help her cause if she made an enemy of the woman. They could sit here and exchange supercilious remarks for hours without approaching the point where they could be frank with one another.

"No," Anya said, relaxing her upright posture, shaking her head with a wry smile, "and how could you? The fact is, I have a problem, and I thought you might help me with it. It concerns a mutual acquaintance, Ravel Duralde."

"Ravel?"

The actress was still wary, as if she were afraid of being accused and upbraided.

"Not twenty-four hours ago someone tried to kill him."

Simone gasped, her hand going to her throat as her eyes widened. "But who? Why?"

"I don't know. I thought you might have some idea."

"I?"

The actress stared at Anya as slowly her composure returned. She leaned forward, lowering her hand to clench it on the arm of her chair. Bluntly she asked, "What is it to you? Why are you concerned?"

It was an excellent question, one Anya had managed to ignore until that moment. She snatched at the first thought that occurred to her. "The attack was made on my property. Naturally, as his hostess I would have felt some responsibility if he had been killed."

"And why was he there on your property?"

"A—matter of business, livestock," Anya answered with silent appreciation for Madame Rosa's invention. It was proving most useful.

Simone lifted a brow. "You wouldn't know anything about the duel he missed while he was sojourning with you?"

"Men don't talk about these things," Anya said evasively. "But could you tell me who his enemies might be, and why they sought to kill him?"

The actress was silent for a long, considering minute. "My association with the gentleman is not of long standing."

"Still you must know something?"

"Ravel isn't one to talk much; he's more a man of action."

A small reminiscent flitted over the other woman's face that made Anya's fingers curl until her nails dug into her palms. She made no comment, however, but sat waiting for the actress to go on.

"He's a strange one, coming and going at odd times, with some most peculiar friends. It wouldn't be surprising if he had enemies, considering the life he has led, men who have been bested in duels, or their relatives; men who have lost to him at the gaming stables, or who have disagreed with his political views such as supporting that madman Walker. I'm afraid I couldn't name them for you, however.''

Anya nodded. Keeping her voice carefully noncommittal, she asked, ''What kind of man is he, from your point of view?''

Simone leaned back in her chair. ''Generous. Demanding. Inventive. Strong.''

Anya had the feeling she was being baited. It was effective, for the softly musing tone of the other woman's voice conjured up images in her brain that burned with white heat, spreading a burning ache throughout her body. There was the sound of the door opening somewhere behind her, doubtless the maid returning. Ignoring it, she said abruptly, ''Would you say he is honorable?''

''In his way.''

''Is he capable of murder?''

''Murder!'' The actress sat up straight once more.

''Is he?''

There was the scrape of a quiet footstep at the doorway. ''Why don't you ask me?'' Ravel said.

The quadroon maid who had summoned him, breathless now with her haste, slid into the room behind him and scuttled across to disappear into the back of the house. Anya rose to her feet, aware as she did so of Emile stepping forward in a protective gesture.

Ravel looked from Anya to Jean's brother, the expression in his black eyes as cold and flat and bitter as yesterday's coffee. Even after the time they had spent together, the things they had shared, she still thought him a murderer. The idea was like a knife twisting, ripping inside him. He heard again the scathing sound of her voice, saw the proud tilt of her chin, and he wanted to make love to her then and there, to force her to recognize what he felt for her, to make it matter to her. The desire was an ignoble one and he knew it for such, but it was no less entrancing for that.

Anya could think of nothing to say, could not force words through the constriction of her throat. What had prompted her to ask that question? She wasn't sure. She had wanted to startle Simone, to get an unstudied reply, perhaps to test her own judgment of Ravel, the judgment that though he might kill in self-defense, he would not deliberately take a life.

"What is it?" Ravel asked, a vicious undercurrent in his voice as he watched Anya. "Have you lost interest in hearing the answer? Or is it just embarrassment for being discovered here? Are you afraid that I will be so base as to spread abroad the news of where I found you, or even use it to bend you to my will? Is there nothing, no crime, of which you will absolve me?"

Before she could answer, Emile spoke. "I think we had better go, Anya."

"Oh, has the impropriety of her being here finally dawned on you?" Ravel inquired, turning to the younger man. "What a pity it didn't do so sooner."

"You need not vent your spleen on Emile," Anya said. "He was as reluctant as you could wish. But if he had not brought me, I would have come alone."

"I can imagine."

"Ravel, *mon cher*," Simone said, rising and moving to entwine her arm with his, "how fierce you sound. There is no need for such heat. We were only having a comfortable chat."

The other woman looked at Anya with a fixed, significant gaze. It was not difficult to understand the silent message. Simone felt the need of her assistance in preventing the challenge that she feared might result from this meeting she had brought about. It was an all-too-real possibility, one terrible to contemplate. Anya put her hand under Emile's elbow.

"I think you are right, Emile," she said, "we had better go. Mademoiselle Michel, it was kind of you to talk to me."

"It was my pleasure. Perhaps we will meet again."

Anya smiled, at the same time putting pressure on Emile's arm so that he moved beside her toward the door. 'Yes, perhaps so."

Ravel let them go. What was the point in trying to keep them? The last thing he wanted was to hear more of Anya's opinion of him, or to cross swords with Emile Girod. God, but he was weary. His head ached, the penalty of doing too much, too soon, and the places on his back where bits of red-hot coals had burned through his shirt stung under his coat. Shrugging a little to ease them, he moved toward the window that overlooked the court-yard.

"It was gallant of you to come so quickly," Simone said, "especially since it's been some time since you were here."

"Your maid seemed to think it urgent." The words were offhand as he drew aside the drapery, looking out. Below in the courtyard, Anya and Emile emerged from the stair entrance and walked toward the gate where his carriage stood waiting for him.

"Was it that, or was it the card I sent, her card, that brought you?"

Ravel turned his head. "Do you really want to know?"

"No," Simone said the word hoarse, strangled, as she met his hard gaze, "no, I don't." Swinging around, she picked up her heavy brocade skirts and walked from the room, slamming the door that led to her boudoir behind her.

The dying rays of the setting sun painted the sky with the late-winter colors of lavender-blue and gold. The color was reflected onto the sides of the plastered buildings and in the water standing in the gutter in the center of the street. It flickered along the lacquered side of a passing carriage and glowed in the glass of a shopwindow. Anya stared at the radiance around her with a furious scowl.

Ravel Duralde might or might not be a murderer, but he was certainly a scoundrel. He had made love to her, shut her away for his own pleasure, then when she had escaped and confronted his mistress, come running hotfoot to save the woman from a potentially distressful situation. What had he thought she was going to do to his mistress? Call her foul names? Horsewhip her? She would not so demean herself, and she would like very much to tell him so! Damn men and their touchy tempers and deadly impulses that made it necessary to tiptoe around them, even save them from themselves!

Not that she seriously thought Ravel would have allowed himself to be put in a position of having to meet Emile. She had seen the look in Ravel's eyes when he saw the young man, when he had absorbed the resemblance to Jean.

No matter, he had no business reprimanding her as if she were a convent miss unused to the ways of the world. It was no concern of his what she did, whom she visited, or whom she chose as her escort.

Emile reached to put his hand on her fingers that clutched his arm. "Slow down, Anya. You'll wear yourself out, and people are staring."

She swung her head to look at him without comprehension; then she realized that she was striding along with her head down as if she had a far destination to make and a short time to reach it. She checked, moderating her pace. "Sorry," she murmured.

"I understand that you are upset, but it seems to me it's out of proportion to what took place back there. I have a feeling there's more to this than you have told me. Don't you think I should know what it is, if I may get myself killed because of it?"

"I suppose so," she said unhappily.

She got no further. Her attention was caught by an abrupt movement ahead of them. The neighborhood they were in was not the best, being an area where gambling dens and drinking houses had filtered in among the more respectable establishments. What she had seen was the sudden swing as a man, who had been standing staring at her from where he lounged outside the doorway of a barrelhouse, ducked back inside. He had been big and burly and dressed in nondescript and wrinkled clothing, no different from the half dozen others who were hanging around that door. She might have passed him by without a glance if he had not moved. Instead, she registered his flight from the corner of her eye, saw the fringe of rust red hair under his bowler hat, and knew him immediately.

"That man," she said on a gasp, stopping so suddenly her hoop and petticoats swung against Emile's legs, "that was the leader of the gang who tried to kill Ravel!"

"What?" he exclaimed. "Where?"

"In there," she cried.

Without waiting for more, Anya picked up her skirts and ran toward where the man had disappeared. She pushed through the knot of men around the door, ignoring their muttered comments, not stopping to see if Emile was behind her. She stepped inside the dim, low-ceilinged room. The sickly sour smell of spilled beer, wet and foul sawdust, and uncleaned spittoons struck her like a blow in the face. The walls were lined with beer barrels stacked one on the other. Long tables, the tops scarred with knife carvings and ringed with the imprints of beer glasses, and with benches on either side for seating, sat in a solid rank in the center. Across the back was a bar made of rough planking laid on barrels, with glasses stacked in precarious pyramids behind it. To the right of the bar was a sagging door, just closing. Anya scanned the room, but none of the score or more men at the tables was the one she wanted. She started toward the rear door.

"Anya, wait!" Emile called.

She paid no attention. Pulling open the door, she stepped through the narrow opening. Her skirts dragged on the rough frame and she felt the cloth tear, but she had not time to be concerned. She was in a dirty and noisome court, the corners of which were used as a privy judging by the smell. She could hear running footfalls, however, and catching the upper hoop of her cage crinoline, she lifted her skirts high and plunged after the man. Rounding a shed at the back of the court, she came upon a gateless portal in the high wall that gave onto another street.

Emile was calling her. Lifting her voice as she stepped through onto the side street, she shouted, "This way!"

The street was empty. It was a back avenue, for it was unpaved and the banquettes were still made of wood. The rows of dilapidated houses that fronted it sat silent, with only here and there the glow of a lamp in a room. Nothing moved. Then from somewhere on the right came the squawk of a disturbed cat. The animal came streaking from an alley with its eyes wild, its fur standing in a ruff down its back, and its tail twice normal size. There was a growled curse, followed by the heavy thud of running steps. Anya, her shirts billowing over her hoop and the hem flying, sprinted in the direction of the sound.

A block. Two. Around a corner to the left. Anya's bonnet flew back, held only by its ribbons as it bounced against her back. She could hear footfalls behind her, though Emile had stopped wasting his breath trying to stop her.

Ahead of her was the raucous whine of music from a fiddle and a barrel organ and voices raised in laughter. She could see lights that were brighter now that the last of the sunset was fading and twilight closing in. It was toward the cross street from which they came that her quarry was heading; it must be. Breathless from the press of her stays that constricted her lungs, Anya forced herself to run those last yards.

She came abruptly into the light. Slowing her pace, she glanced around with her senses suddenly alert. There was something odd in her surroundings. She had taken little notice of the streets she was traversing and in any case few of them had posted names; still she did not like this place.

Her attention was diverted by the sight of the leader of the thugs, the man they called Red. He was shouldering his way through a crowd of men standing around the door of a house where a woman stood on the balcony. He looked back at her once, then slid inside. With the fire of determination in her eyes, Anya started after him.

"No you don't!"

The voice came from just behind her. Her arm was caught in an iron grasp and she was pulled around to face Ravel. She stared at him in surprise for an instant before she jerked at her arm, pushing at his chest with her free hand. "Let me go!"

"You need a keeper!" he said through set teeth. "What in the name of hell do you think you're doing?"

"He went in that house over there, the leader of the gang who was at Beau Refuge. Let go of me, or I'll lose him!"

"And just what were you going to do if you caught him? He fastened his hand on her other arm, giving her a shake.

"He can tell us who the boss is!"

"How were you going to persuade him to do that? Beg him prettily?"

"What kind of idiot do you think I am? I mean to find out where he's hiding and bring the police back to drag him out!"

Her arms were growing numb from his grip. The unbreakable strength of his hold filled with her such frustration that she felt like screaming. There was a strong urge, near uncontrollable, growing in her to kick him like the tomboy hoyden she had once been, or else to claw for his eyes.

"The police," he said, his tone edged with acid sarcasm,

"don't come here except in the broad light of day and in force. Look around you. This is Gallatin Street."

She ceased struggling. Her eyes were dark blue with doubt as she stared up at him. Slowly she turned her head.

Up and down the street around her was one barrelhouse and barroom after another, with their filthy sawdust spilling out the doors. The men moving in and out of them, weaving along, were sailors and stevedores and steamboatmen and men with the look of backcountry trappers and farmers. They were a rough lot, dirty, unshaven, reeling drunk. Among them she saw a thin and feral-looking creature who carried a set of leather thongs at his waist, the dreaded strangling cords that were known to deal quick death to any greenhorn stupid enough to wander into the area. The women who traipsed the wooden banquettes were little better. Hard-faced, dressed in ill-fitting and tawdry finery from which their bodies spilled in wanton display, there could be only one name for them. Even the woman on the balcony where the leader of the thugs had vanished was posturing and posing, now lifting her too-short skirt as high as her hipbone to give the crowd below a quick view, now bending to hold the railing and shake her shoulders so that her full and pendulous breasts spilled out of the low neck of her sleazy gown and had to be stuffed back in again. There could be little doubt that the door below her led into a bordello.

Anya moistened her lips. Keeping her voice firm with an effort, she said, "You could go in and bring the man out."

"And leave you here alone? You would be flat on your back with your skirts above your head and a line forming before I was out of sight."

She flashed him a fiery glance. "You need not sound so pleased at the prospect! Emile could stay with me. Where is he?"

"I sent him back to bring my carriage."

"Your carriage? When I want to go home, I can walk!" She was in truth exhausted by her long day and the night that had gone before it, an exhaustion she had not acknowledged or even felt until that moment. The last thing she would do, however, was admit it.

"I can't." His voice was hard, final.

"You mean," she said slowly, "that you are just going to leave? You are going to let the leader of those men get away? Why did you come, then? What are you doing here?"

"I followed you, what else? There is something we need to discuss."

Her words thick with fury and yet as cold as if coated with hoarfrost, she said, "I fail to see what it can be."

"Do you now?"

He released one arm then to hail Emile, who was hanging out the window of an approaching carriage as he watched for them. Anya could have broken the grasp Ravel retained in that moment of inattention, but what was the point? She stood still, hearing the echo of his words, hard and undisturbed, in her mind. What could he want of her? It was an unsettling question, but not nearly so threatening as the others that crowded in upon her. Surely Ravel's concern for her safety was exaggerated. That being so, why had he shown so little interest in running the leader of the thugs to earth? Why had he allowed the man to escape?

The inside of Ravel's carriage, a fairly new equipage, smelled of fine leather and the shellac glaze of the side walls, with just a hint of tobacco. It bumped and swayed on its springs over the rutted street. The pace the coachman set was brisk, as if he was not anxious to linger on the most notorious street in the city. After a short time, they reached a paved thoroughfare, and the going was smoother.

Ravel threw a glance at Anya. She sat upright with her bonnet that she had removed in her lap. The stony set of her features gave him a tight feeling in his chest. He wished he knew what was going on in that agile brain of hers, and at the same time was afraid he knew too well. She was maddening, and also unbelievably desirable with her hair escaping from its pins, her cheeks pink with anger and exertion, and the soft, rounded contours of her breasts straining against the bodice of her gown with every deep breath. If it weren't for Girod sitting across from them he might very well chance her rage, press her down upon the leather seat, and kiss her until she was too starved for air to resist him.

That would be the only way he was likely to have her after today. Unless his gamble paid off. Luck, however, as he knew

well, was no lady. She was a teasing trollop attracted only to
those who scorned her, a bitch who laughed and turned away
from those who yearned for her most.

The carriage drew up before the townhouse. Sitting forward,
reaching for the handle to open the door, Emile said to Anya,
"I'll see you inside."

"Stay where you are," Ravel said, his voice firm with authority. "My coachman will take you wherever you want to go.
I'll see to Anya, since I need to speak to Madame Hamilton."

Anya sent him a quick, curious stare, aware of a sense of
portent in his words.

"Now see here," Emile protested. "It is my responsibility
to see Anya—Mademoiselle Anya—safely inside. She is in my
care."

"Your care?"

Ravel's question held such biting irony that Anya saw Jean's
brother flinch. She put out her hand to lightly touch the wrist of
the younger man. "It's most gallant of you, but unnecessary. I
will be perfectly fine."

"If you are sure," he said, the stiffness of offended pride in
his tone.

"I'm very sure."

Ravel waited for no more, but pushed open the door and
stepped down, handing Anya out. At his order, the carriage
pulled away. He thought of offering Anya his arm, but the likelihood of her taking it seemed slim. She started under the *port
cochère* of the townhouse and he moved easily to walk at her
side.

"Do you actually have business with Madame Rosa?" Anya
inquired in a sharp undertone as they mounted the stairs to the
upper rooms.

"Yes, I do."

What it could be, she could not imagine, nor could she summon the will to care. She was tired, so very tired. Still there
were certain duties that must be observed. There was a light
burning in the salon, and rather than stalking away to her own
room, leaving Ravel to be tended to by the servants, she felt
obligated to see if her stepmother was able to see him.

Madame Rosa sat reading a novel, with her half-spectacles

that she sometimes used perched on her nose and a paper knife with which to slit the pages in her hand. She looked up as they entered, then removed her feet from the footstool on which they rested, sitting up straight.

"I was beginning to be worried," she began, then stopped as she caught sight of Anya's disheveled state. Her features stiffened. Laying her book and paper knife carefully aside, she took off her spectacles and got slowly to her feet. "Where is Emile?"

Ravel stepped forward. "I am afraid I persuaded him to allow me to escort Anya inside instead. I hope you will forgive my presumption, and my intrusion, Madame Hamilton."

"Yes, certainly, M'sieur Duralde," Madame Rosa answered.

The older woman's manner had little warmth and less cordiality, but she was sufficiently in command of herself to be polite. There was also in her shrewd gaze a measuring quality. Ravel drew a deep breath and took his pride in his hands.

"I realize what I have to say may come as a surprise—then again it may not. Either way, I trust you will consider it well and remember recent obligations. I have come to request from you, madame, formally and with all due respect, the hand of your stepdaughter Anya in marriage."

Chapter Thirteen

"No!"

The answer came not from Madame Rosa, but from Anya. She had not meant to speak, would have thought herself incapable of it for the pain welling up inside her. That single word, resonant with anger and revulsion, seemed to vibrate in the air as she stared at Ravel with her teeth clenched and her head high.

"Why?" His voice was dangerously soft though his narrowed lashes hid the expression in his dark eyes.

She opened her mouth to annihilate him, to say that she had no intention of falling in so easily with his need for vengenace. Something about him as he stood with his hands on his hips in the center of the small, elegant room stopped her. It was not easy to make her stiff lips pronounce the formal reply, still she managed it. "We should not suit."

"Anya," Madame Rosa said, a shade of anxiety in her tone as she looked from one to the other, "do not be hasty. Sit down and let us discuss the matter."

"There is nothing to be discussed. M'sieur Duralde has proposed as duty demands, and I have refused. That is the end of it."

Ravel made a soft sound of disgust. "Duty has nothing to do with this, and well you know it."

"Oh, yes, I know," Anya said, giving him a long, straight look.

There were times when being a gentleman was a great inconvenience, Ravel thought, holding to his temper with difficulty. He longed to either strangle Anya with her own shining hair, or else throw her over his shoulder and take her away to some place where he could hold and caress her until her cold eyes filled with

warm and languorous desire and her heart and mind were open
to him as he had dared dream once, on a chaise lounge at Beau
Refuge, that they might possibly be. His mind was lamentably
centered on one thing today, or so it seemed. Dear God, what
was the matter with him? Why did she obsess him so? She had
beauty and pride and courage, but so did a thousand other
women. He was mad to court humiliation, possibly the ruin of
carefully made plans, even death, for her sake.

He turned to Madame Rosa. "Your stepdaughter is in danger
because of me. I want the right to protect her, as well as make
just recompense for having compromised her good name."

Madame Rosa said to Anya, "That does not seem unreasonable to me."

"Because you don't know him," Anya cried.

"And you do, after a mere few days?"

"As well as I wish to."

Anya swung away from them, moving to put down her bonnet
and strip her gloves from her hands. Polite, she must be polite,
she told herself with compressed lips. It was pointless to scream
and rail at him, and if she did she might start to cry and that
would never do. What would her answer have been she wondered, if he had come with words of love and desire instead of
cold reason? She shuddered to think of it. There was a weakness
in her character where he was concerned; she might well have
fallen for such a trap.

"Anya," he began, his voice firm and yet with a raw note in
it that seemed to tear at her fragile composure.

"No!" She whirled to face him, slapping down the gloves
she held upon the small table beside her. "No, I'm not going to
marry you, Never! Do you understand me?"

She despised him. There was no reason, then, not to show
himself entirely despicable. "Never is a long time. What if I
were to say to you, marry me, or your half sister's fiancé dies?"

She stared at him with the color draining from her face.
Through stiff lips she said, "You wouldn't."

"Wouldn't I?"

"It's inhuman. You couldn't kill a man for such a reason, I
know you couldn't."

"Your trust is touching, if misplaced."

Trust. That was the ingredient that was missing in her relationship with this man. There were things about him she did not understand, things she suspected him of hiding. And yet she was as certain as she could be of anything that he would not be able to deliberately destroy Murray because of her. He might challenge him in the heat of anger, and match swords or pistols with him if it was required, but to carry a vendetta so far was not his way. It was astonishing how sure she was of that much, when she was sure of nothing else.

She lifted her chin. "It doesn't matter. This is a bargain already concluded between us, or so I thought. As I remember it, you swore you would not seek Murray out. If I cannot depend upon your word given then, how can you expect me to do so now?"

Somewhere in the back of his mind there stirred reluctant admiration for the firmness of her stand, for the logic of her mind and the way she spoke. It was short-lived. He had played his last card and there was nothing left for him to do except leave the game. He should have known how it would be, and yet it was hard to accept that the physical intimacy they had shared, the sweetness of her surrender, had meant nothing. His gaze rested on the firm curves of her lips, and the memory of the feel and taste and scent of her was like a bleeding canker inside him.

"I don't expect it," he said, the words quiet yet with an undertone of steel. "From you I expect nothing at all. But of one thing you can be sure; this isn't the end of it."

The door closed behind him. Anya stood still, staring at nothing.

Madame Rosa, her gaze pensive upon her stepdaughter, spoke finally. "Ah, *chère*, was that wise?"

With a visible effort Anya roused enough to give the older woman a weary smile. "Perhaps not, but it was necessary."

"Was it not also a trifle—hasty?"

"Who can tell?" Anya shook her head as if to dismiss unpleasant possibilities, then as a thought struck her, went on. "What did he mean by 'recent obligations'?"

Madame Rosa gave her a bland look. "Did he say that?"

"It appeared he expected the reminder to guarantee your approval, even your championing of his cause. Has it?"

"*Chère*! What are you saying?" Madame Rosa's tone throbbed with her distress. "You must know I want only what is best for you."

Anya sighed, rubbing a hand over her eyes. "Yes, I do know. Forgive me."

They said no more. Anya went slowly from the room. In her own bedchamber, she tidied her hair. Attracted by the fluttering of a moth at the French doors, she moved toward them, pushing them open to step out onto the gallery that overlooked the courtyard.

The last of the twilight had faded and dark had fallen. There was a blaze of light and the bustle of activity around the kitchen on the lower floor across the way, and the smell of shrimp and oysters simmering in a rich sauce and sugar being turned into caramel floated upward. It did not tempt Anya's appetite. She did not think she could face dinner. She would have something light in her room after she had bathed away a little of her weariness; then she was going to bed and sleep the clock around.

"Anya, is that you?"

The nearest pair of French doors opened and Celestine looked out. She had been dressing for dinner, for she was wearing a wrapper of pink challis and her hair spilled down her back. She looked very young and appealing, and also troubled.

"Yes, *chère*."

Celestine opened her mouth to speak, then, as she caught sight of Anya's face in the lamplight pouring through the doorway, said instead, "Oh, what has happened now?"

"Not a great deal," she said in wry tones. "Did you need something?"

"Only to talk to you for a few minutes."

Anya, catching her half sister's quick glance over her shoulder at her maid, assumed the matter was one of some little delicacy. She had often been the repository of Celestine's girlish confidences over the years, and could not refuse to listen now. "Of course. Would you like to come to my bedchamber when you are dressed?"

"Never mind," Celestine said, her gaze still searching Anya's face. "It isn't important."

"Are you sure?"

"In the morning will do just as well."

"Tomorrow is Mardi Gras," Anya reminded her.

Celestine gave her a bright smile. "Yes. Are we still going into the street?"

There was nothing Anya felt less like doing at that moment than joining a crowd of boisterous merrymakers. She could not spoil Celestine's pleasure, however. "We are indeed."

"Lovely. I thought you might have changed your mind after . . ."

"No, nothing has changed," Anya said as Celestine paused in embarrassment.

"I will see you in the morning, then," the other girl said happily.

Anya agreed and, when Celestine had gone back inside, turned to reenter her own bedchamber. She had lied. Everything had changed. Everything.

Three hours later Anya lay in her bed staring up into the darkness. She was too tired to sleep. Her bath had refreshed her, but, though she had lain for some time in the hot water scented with oil of damask roses, it had done little to relax her. She was so tense that the muscles in her legs quivered and she had to force herself repeatedly to unclench her jaws. Through her mind ran over and over again the image of the brutish faces of the men who had laid hands on her at Beau Refuge. She had been made to feel vulnerable, unable to protect herself, and she did not like it. She had always thought of herself as strong and self-sufficient, and to be handed such graphic proof that it wasn't so was unsettling, incensing, it made her long to smash something. Ravel was a part of that rage. He had shown her that she was vulnerable also to the needs of the flesh, and for that she would not easily forgive him.

Her life had been so uncomplicated before he had come into it. There had been no danger, no violence, no perilous emotions to shake her image of herself. There had been no complex questions of right and wrong, guilt and innocence, no decisions that might bring life or death. There had been no man to impose his will upon hers or to stir longings better left unawakened.

Echoing in her mind in an endless refrain were the things Ravel had said in the salon earlier, and the answers she had made. The arrogance of the man was beyond belief. He had tricked her into forfeiting her chastity, caused the destruction of her property, tried to hold her captive, and abused her on a public street, and still he thought she would accept with gratitude his condescending proposal of marriage. That she had caused him bodily injury, held him prisoner, and left him open to the attack of his enemies made little difference; she had refrained, in the main, from offering him direct insult.

Around her the house was silent. Activity had ceased in the courtyard as the servants finished their chores and found their way to bed. Somewhere a dog barked. Now and then the sound of a carriage rolling past in the street filtered through the thick walls. She had heard Celestine and Madame Rosa retire soon after dinner. If Madame Rosa had told Celestine of the events of the evening, then they must each have much to mull over. Anya wondered what Celestine thought of the proposal. It was likely that in her place, her half sister would have felt forced to accept it—though Celestine, being highly conventional, would never have placed herself in a position where it had to be offered.

Marriage. If she had accepted Ravel as her husband, there would have been orange blossoms and cream-colored satin, a betrothal bracelet, a wedding basket of gifts, and the blessing of a priest. There might have been a wedding journey to distant, curious relatives, followed by the return to the house on Esplanade. Then what? Nights of passion and days of contempt? A life with a stranger who would come to resent his social and legal imprisonment as fiercely as he had resented his captivity at Beau Refuge?

But beneath it all was an even more disturbing line of reasoning. If she could be so sure now that Ravel would not deliberately set out to harm Murray as a means of revenge, then what of seven years before when he had met Jean with a sword in the moonlit shadows? If Jean's death had been nothing more than a tragic accident, if the words she had screamed at Ravel had been false, then it was possible that she was to blame for what he had become. It could be that what had happened to her was her own fault.

She turned her head on her pillow and flung her arm over her eyes. She did not want to think anymore. She would give anything to be able to stop. There was oblivion in Madame Rosa's orange-flower water if she chose to seek it. A few minutes more, and she would ring the bell and ask a maid to bring the opiate. She had to sleep, somehow.

A soft scratching sound came from outside the French doors leading to the gallery. Anya started so violently that the bed shook. She sat upright. The windows were firmly closed against what Madame Rosa considered to be the dangerous fumes of the night air, but they were not locked. Beyond them there was the glow of moonlight pouring into the courtyard. Against that light, silhouetted on the muslin that covered the windows, was the dark shape of a man. Even as Anya watched, he reached for the handle of the door and began to press it down.

The glass-paned door panel eased open. The man put his head inside, then slid noiselessly into the room. He took a step toward the bed. Another. Anya jerked free of her paralyzed stillness. She opened her mouth to scream.

"Mam'zelle?"

She let out her breath in a sigh. "Marcel, you frightened the wits out of me!"

"I'm sorry, mam'zelle, but you did say to come to you at once when I had information. I didn't know whether to wake you or not."

"It's all right." she said quickly. "You have news?"

"I think so, mam'zelle. I went to the stables of M'sieur Ravel as you said. At first his people would say nothing, but then I thought to share with the coachman a bottle of rum. It happens that every Monday night for the past two months M'sieur Ravel has ordered his carriage for ten o'clock and had himself driven to an address on Rampart Street."

"A quadroon?" Anya asked, her brows drawing together over her eyes.

Rampart was well known as the street where the men of the city housed their mistresses, most of whom were beautiful women of one-quarter Negro blood and three-quarters white. The practice, known as *plaçage*, had been outlawed some eight years before, but the result had been merely to strip the women and the children of such unions of the legal rights they had once enjoyed, not to abolish the custom.

"But no, mam'zelle. It is a house where he meets with other men, two dozen or more in number. The coachman has seen them when he returns for m'sieur two hours later."

"I see," she said, her tone thoughtful.

"Today is Monday."

Her head came up. "The time?"

"Just half past ten."

"Why didn't you follow him?" she cried.

Marcel's voice held a hint of reproof as he answered. "There was no need. I know the house, and I thought, mam'zelle, that you might wish to see."

She flung back the covers. "You are right of course. Wait for me outside—no, find a carriage for hire. I don't want to wake the house having ours brought out."

"There is one waiting," Marcel said with dignity.

Anya laughed, a soft sound of relief caused as much by the prospect of doing something, discovering something about Ravel at last, as for Marcel's efficiency. "Very well. I will be with you in a moment."

They dismissed the carriage in front of a house several doors down from that where the meeting was being held. It was obvious that the men in attendance must have done the same, for there were no vehicles lining the street to attest to their presence. Lamplight glowed through the slats of the shutters that covered the windows of the white-painted shotgun house Marcel indicated, but no sound came from it, nor was there any movement around it. The street itself was dark here, the only light coming from a far corner where a lantern hung by its bail on a leaning wooden pole. Those who lived or visited on what had once been the back street of the Vieux Carré did not care for too much illumination shed upon their comings and goings.

So empty and quiet was the street indeed at this hour that Anya felt conspicuous. With Marcel at her right hand, she kept to the shadows as much as possible, moving from one dark patch to another. She had not troubled to don stays or a hoop and had put on only the minimum of petticoats, so that she moved with ease and a steady, confident stride. As they came nearer the small house, they slipped between two of its neighbors in order to approach from the rear. A cat emerging from under a set of back steps almost beneath their feet hissed and fled into the night. Anya, brushing past an enormous evergreen cape jasmine bush, stepped into a spider web and had to stop to wipe away the webs that clung to her face, tangling in her lashes. Marcel stepped on what was apparently a child's discarded hoop and stumbled against Anya. By reflex action, she reached out to help him, but caught his injured wrist in its sling, so that he drew breath with the sharp sound of pain. Her whispered apology resounded like a stentorian shout in her ears. They moved on, rounding a corner. The lighted house lay just in front of them.

Anya came to a halt. She stood staring at the shotgun cottage with a cold feeling inside her. Her disenchantment with the scheme upon which she and Marcel were embarked had been growing since they had left the carriage. To spy upon Ravel seemed ignoble, if not downright dangerous. But the truth of the matter was that she was afraid. Afraid of what they might discover.

What did it matter, after all, what Ravel did? She need never see him again if she wished; she had gone for years before without meeting him face-to-face. If she found out something to his discredit she would be faced with the dilemma of either permitting him to continue or else doing something about it. It was not a decision she cared to make.

Still, it would be cowardly to retreat now, when she was so close. Suppose she learned later that he was engaged in something clandestine, something that would hurt others? How would she live with the knowledge that she might have prevented it? And how could she live with the doubt?

It was with a distant feeling of being driven that she moved toward the side window of the room at the front of the house. Marcel, without being told, drifted toward the back door.

It was logical to assume that there might be a guard posted if this meeting was for a reason that was less than aboveboard. There did not appear to be any sign of one, still Anya looked around a last time as she crouched under the window. Seeing nothing, she rose to her full height and peered through the crack where the shutters, warped and loose on their hinges, came together in the middle.

She gave a soft exclamation. Seated directly across from her was Gaspard, Madame Rosa's faithful cavalier. He was leaning forward with a frown of concentration on his lean face and his hands propped on the silver head of his cane that stood between his feet. His presence was so unexpected, so incomprehensible, that it was a moment before Anya noticed anything more.

When finally she dragged her gaze away, she saw that the meeting room was furnished as a salon of incongruous elegance, with Louis Quatorze pieces, silk-hung walls, crystal girandoles, and a soothing blue and cream decor of the same refinement as that of Madame Rosa or any other Creole lady. There were nine men in her line of vision, though she thought from the rumble of the voices that there were several more that she could not see on either side. Some were seated, some stood leaning against the walls. Ravel was standing beside a commode table with the fingertips of one hand resting on its inlaid surface near a gavel. As Anya watched, he picked up that symbol of authority, turning it idly end over end as he listened to a man speaking on his left.

Then in that masculine gathering there was a small stir. A woman, moving with deft grace, came from the back room of the cottage with a silver tray and began to collect the empty liqueur glasses that a few of the men held or that sat here and there. She was no servant, however. The silk gown she wore was in the latest mode and draped over a generous-sized hoop, and her hair was tastefully arranged. The delicate application of cosmetics enhanced a vivid natural beauty. Her manner was gracious and unaffected as she moved about the room, as if she were perfectly at home. Which she was, of course. Her skin was the light creamy brown color knows as *café au lait*, the badge of the quadroon.

The woman stepped near Ravel, picking up his glass that sat on the commode table. She said something to him, perhaps a light apology as she moved on in front of him. He turned to reply, giving her a brief smile that seemed to hold a special warmth.

Pain gripped with the feel of steel claws inside Anya's chest. Damn the man! Was one mistress not enough for him? Were his appetites so demanding that he not only had to keep an actress under his protection and seduce every woman who crossed his path, but support a beautiful quadroon *placée* as well? He was depraved, an immoral monster who obviously felt he was entitled to every prerequisite that wealth afforded in a city like New Orleans. She wondered if Simone Michel knew about this quadroon, and if she did, how she felt about sharing her lover.

So great was Anya's indignation that it was a moment before the discussion taking place among the men inside took meaning. The words were muffled, not always distinct, but she could make out enough to guess the rest. First one and then another spoke, with Ravel taking little part for the moment.

"—the arsenal behind the Cabildo. It's poorly guarded, hardly more than a skeleton force in the hours after midnight and half of them asleep. The arms and ammunition there would give us a decided advantage. Gathering up our hunting guns and ancient family muskets is all very well, but we need more."

Arms. Weapons. That was what the thugs at Beau Refuge had been after. There was no time to consider the implications of that memory. Other men were speaking.

"Artillery. Nothing less than artillery will win the day."

"That seems a little drastic."

"So is the situation. It will take a lot of convincing before— "

"You are speaking of much killing, m'sieur."

"It may be that's what it will take."

Anya caught a flicker of movement from the corner of her eye. She turned her head. Marcel was beckoning her from the rear of the house. He called in a sibilant whisper, "This way, mam'zelle! Hurry!"

What she was hearing was of such potential importance that she hesitated, turning back for one last look through the crack between the shutters.

At that moment there came a thunderous knock on the door of the shotgun house. It was followed at once by shouting: "Police! Open up!"

The men inside started out of their seats with consternation in their faces. An instant later there was pandemonium as they fled in every direction. The candles in the girandoles were extinguished so that darkness closed down. In the last fading glow Anya saw a man swinging toward the window where she stood, wrenching up the sash. She stumbled back, turned to run. The shutters crashed open and a man hurtled headfirst out of the window. He somersaulted and his heel struck Anya at the knee. She went down, a small scream catching in her throat as she fell. The man bleated with surprise, but did not stop. He jumped to his feet, blundering off in the dark.

The dark forms of other men came pouring out of the window, sprawling, becoming entangled, leaping up to sprint away. Anya scrambled out of their reach and raised herself to her knees.

From the front of the house there rang out a yell of triumph. Anya turned her head to see a pair of men rounding the corner. A distant shaft of lamplight glinted on their painted caps and on the spontoon clubs they waved in their hands. She had no reason to fear the police, and yet there was nothing to say that they would believe she was not party to the meeting that had been taking place.

"Mam'zelle," Marcel cried, then he was beside her, hindering as much as helping with his one good hand as she struggled to stand upright despite her skirts wrapped around her knees.

There came a soft, fluent cursing from out of the darkness at the rear of the building. Dread seized Anya as she recognized the voice. Abruptly Ravel appeared beside her. "That way," he snapped to Marcel, giving him a shove toward where he had come from; then he spun to meet the two policemen who were upon him. He swung a hard fist, connecting with the chin of the man in the lead. As the man fell, Ravel wrenched the spontoon from his hand and, on the backswing, struck a blow that made the second man howl and clutch his elbow. Immediately Ravel sank the end of the club up to his fist in the policeman's belly and, as he bent over, gave him the coup de grace on the back of the neck. He did not wait for more. Catching Anya's arm, he jerked her into violent flight.

Behind them there came a strangled shout followed by the pounding of footfalls. The muffled explosions of guns firing shook the night. Ravel did not look back. Anya, dragging her skirts high above her knees the better to run, had no time to do anything other than follow his example.

They dodged around a clothesline pole and skirted a cistern

on piers before plunging between two houses. A dog ran out to bark at their heels until Ravel snapped out a shard command that made the animal whimper and veer away, slowing to a trot. Men and women put their heads covered with nightcaps out of bedroom windows. Lights blossomed behind closed shutters. Still they ran on, jumping drains and flower beds, leaping low fences and clipped shrubbery, swinging around the ends of porches.

Anya gasped for breath, yet there flowed in her veins in that headlong plunge through the night a mixture of terror and exhilaration and rage that made her feel as if she could run forever. No obstacle was too wide or too high, no stretch of deserted street or corridor between buildings was too long. She had shaken off Ravel's hold that was throwing her off-balance, and raced at his side unimpeded. It hardly mattered where she was running to or why, only that she and the man at her side were winning, leaving their pursuers behind with their heart-jarring effort.

They were pounding alongside a wall. They turned a corner. Ahead of them was an opening in the wall. "In here," Ravel said, and without hesitation she complied.

Sanctuary. Silence. It enclosed them. When Anya would have halted, Ravel reached for her hand and drew her deeper inside until they came finally to where a weeping willow, symbol of mourning, grew against one of the four great walls. She had never been here at night before. Her chest rising and falling as she fought for breath, Anya leaned against the wall that behind her held in ranks the burial vaults known as ovens. Raising her head, she looked out over the cemetery, one of the many that were similar in New Orleans, but the first to be called the City of the Dead.

The tombs, like small houses above the ground, were made of marble and plastered brick decorated with weeping angels and crosses and inverted torches, with pediments and columns and wrought iron. They gathered the light of a rising moon to shine whitely in the darkness. So closely set together were they, as if for company, that there was hardly room to walk except for narrow paths between the rows, like small streets, and a wide walkway around the walls. So little room was left, in fact, that hardly any new burials were made here.

The above-surface tombs and the thick walls of vaults that surrounded the burial ground were a Spanish custom transplanted to New Orleans, but one so useful due to the waterlogged nature of the soil that it had become entrenched, and was seen even in the cemeteries of the American section.

Anya had not been here in years, not since she had come as a child on All Saints' Day with Madame Rosa to help put armfuls of chrysanthemums at the monuments of her stepmother's relatives. She had played hide-and-seek among the tombs and traced with her small fingers the names and phrases chiseled into the marble, *ici repose*—here lies; *famille A.B. Plauche*— A.B. Plauche family; *morte, victime d'honneur*—dead, a victim of honor. Madame Rosa had never allowed gruesome tales of graves and malevolent specters, and so Anya had always felt that the spirits who inhabited such places, if such there should be, were benign presences with souls at peace.

There was no peace in the man beside her.

"You have," he said with vitriol in his voice, "the most damnable talent for thwarting me and interfering in my affairs that I have ever been called upon to endure. I couldn't believe it when I heard Marcel call to you back there. I couldn't believe it, and yet it seemed so surely where you would be and what you would be doing that it made a terrible kind of sense. I can understand what witchlike genius you used to find out where I was, but if you had to come, why in the name of all that's holy did you bring the police with you?"

Anya turned her head, staring at him in blank surprise. "I didn't bring the police."

"Don't lie!"

She faced him with her hands on her hips. "I'm not lying!"

"Who else would lead them there?"

"Lead them? Why should that be necessary? With so many meeting regularly there must be hundreds of people who know the time and place. It wasn't hard to discover."

"Who else but you would have a reason to send the police, then?"

"How should I know? Maybe your fancy quadroon mistress.

Maybe your kept actress. Maybe both, if they found out about each other!"

It was a moment before he answered, and then there was a strange timbre in his voice. "I have no quadroon mistress."

"Don't lie!" she said, flinging his order back at him in the same precise tone.

The words measured, he repeated, "I have no quadroon mistress."

"I saw her! I saw her dressed in her silk and lace, smiling at you as if she couldn't wait for everyone to leave." She had not meant to say those things, but her wrath had bubbled up inside her, forcing them out.

"You're jealous." There was savage satisfaction tinged with amazement in his tone.

"Jealous?" she exclaimed. "I'm disgusted. You are vile and corrupt, a murdering scoundrel and a blackmailer who tricked me into your bed and tried to use me to make yourself respectable."

"That may be," he said, taking a step toward her so that he towered over her, "but while you were in my bed you enjoyed it."

"I didn't!" There was a tremor in her voice as a peculiar convulsive shudder ran over her.

"Oh, you did. And even if you would rather die than marry me, even if you would like to see me rot in jail, you are still jealous of any other woman you think I might put in that bed."

She took a step backward, alarm and something more leaping inside her as he advanced upon her. "Don't be ridiculous. I have no grudge against you!"

"No, certainly not," he said in dry sarcasm. "By the way, a surgeon removed the stitches from my scalp today and told me my broken pate is healing nicely."

"That was an accident!"

"So you said. But it was a small price to pay when all was said and done." His voice slowed, becoming seductive in its hard depth. "I give you leave to try breaking it again, if it pleases you. There has never been anything between us but hate and distrust, and sometimes the sudden bright flare of—what? Desire? Lust? Whatever it is, it can be a partial recompense for what we have done to each other. If we permit it.''

Behind her was a corner where the wall turned. She glimpsed it from the periphery of her vision, but before she could step around it, Ravel blocked her way. There was so much tension in the air between them that the night seemed to vibrate with it. She could sense the sheer masculine power he held in control, feel the warmth that radiated from his body. The surface of her skin tingled with an awareness so strong it was like pain. Her muscles tensed as if expecting a blow. She stared up at him with her lips parted and moist and the silver-blue sheen of moonlight in her eyes.

"No," she whispered, the faintest ghost of sound.

His laugh was ragged. "You are the devil's own daughter, Anya Hamilton, the scourge of my soul, my personal nemesis sent to hound me to hell and back. Do with me what you will, but I must have you. And if I must, what better place than here?''

He reached for her, his hard soldier's hands closing on her upper arms. She could not tell if it was anger or lust or desperation that drove him, but as he pulled her against him a matching force exploded inside her. For a single moment she resisted, twisting in his arms; then with a volte-face that would have shocked her to the core if she had stopped to consider it, she flung herself against him, sliding her arms upward to clasp them around his neck. She lifted her lips to met his firm mouth, and a small sound of gladness escaped her as she felt its stinging heat. The nipples of her breasts hardened, pressing into the satin of his waistcoat and the hard muscles of his chest underneath. She could feel the studs of his shirt against her breastbone and the pulsing firmness of him through the thickness of her skirts. A primal ecstasy swept in upon her, erasing thought and time and place, leaving only a searing sense of need and a strange, ravaging joy.

Ravel took the onslaught of her response, absorbing it as a thirsty man might some pure, sweet liquid, reeling with its potency that like fine brandy seared deep into him, driving into his loins to send the consuming ache there flaring higher. The firmness of her breasts against him, the slender turn of her waist and the swelling curves of her hips under his hands brought both rich pleasure and torment. There had never been and would never be another woman who could drive him to such dizzy heights or so easily breach his defenses, one who could wound or heal, save or destroy his very being if she so willed, if she ever discovered her power. She was magic, the taste and feel, the warm female-and-rose scent of her, an enchantment he sought with blind craving, without the will or wish to escape.

The clothing that separated their bodies was an intolerable barrier. Anya lowered one hand to slide it beneath his frock coat, smoothing over the muscles that swathed his chest and rib cage to clasp the ridged strength of his back. Undulating against him with slow movements, she brought her other hand down to slip it between them, working at the buttons of his waistcoat. His soft indrawn breath was both reward and spur, and she moved quickly on to the fastenings of his shirt. When it hung open with the gold studs dangling in their holes, she spread the edges and, with her fingers spread wide, pressed her palms to the soft furring of hair on his chest with deep sensuous delight, finding the flat nubs of his paps and teasing them to hardness.

With a deep sound in his throat, he shrugged out of his coat and threw it on the ground. He drew her down with him to kneel upon its silk lining. He pulled away the snood in which she had confined her hair in her haste to follow him. The silken tresses fell about her in a tangled, shining curtain. He wrapped them around his hands and brought her mouth to meet his once more in a deep invasion. His tongue twined with hers in sinuous play, the rough surfaces abrading each other, savoring, exploring. At the same time, his fingers traced the high collar of the velvet jacket she wore and her gown underneath, finding the loops and the row of tiny buttons that held them closed from the neckline to the waist. With patience and dexterity he released them one by one until he reached and passed the softly rounded curves of her breasts where, maddened by the task and the warm vibrancy of her body, he suddenly inserted his hands and pulled, tearing the last buttons free, tearing also the camisole she wore beneath.

Anya gasped as the firm globes of her breasts were released into his warm, caressing hands. She was drowning in sensation and moonlight, awash in dark seas of perilous longing. Her skin was hot with the fever of exertion and desire and her blood flowed molten and throbbing in her veins. As Ravel bent his head to taste the apricot rose nipples he had uncovered, she pushed aside his shirt, exposing the sun-browned width of his shoulders that were defined by shadows and gilded silver-gold by the moon. She threaded her fingers through the vital waves of his hair and leaned to nuzzle his ear, touching her tongue with small catlike licks to its convolutions.

He released her with a lingering wet and warm caress and straightened to unfasten the buttons of his trousers. She reached out, not to help, but to trace with tingling fingertips the long strutted shape beneath them, to brush upward to the hard flatness of his belly with its thin line of dark hair and, in an absorbed and intuitive gift of pleasure, to follow the opening vee of trousers and underdrawers to where his manhood sprang forth.

His chest swelled, and with urgent strength he pressed her down, brushing her skirts high and stripping away her pantalettes so that the gently turned lengths of her legs gleamed pale and perfect among her petticoats. In suspended fascination, he smoothed along the taut muscle of her thigh to the shape of her knee and the sweetly turned calf below. He bent his head to flick the sensitive bend of her knee with his tongue, easing upward over the fragile inner surface of her thigh, and higher still to the shadowed and secret juncture of her body, lingering there.

A paroxysm of desire caught her and she writhed with it, consumed by the sudden onslaught of violent rapture. She clutched at his shoulders, digging her nails into him, pulling him toward her. In answer to that silent plea, he raised himself above her, his eyes dark with passion as they searched her face. She met his gaze, her own naked, without armor, softly beseeching. He positioned himself for entry, gently probing her readiness. She caught his waist and with a soft cry drew him hard and quick and deep inside her, wanting, needing to feel his strength and power. He recognized that need and met it without reserve, plunging into her with firm, sure, and endless strokes. Gooseflesh rose along the surface of her skin in shivering reaction to the immensity of her gratification. She surged against him, holding, rocking, meeting his driving power in a ravishing frenzy. With limbs entangled and breaths mingling, panting with effort, they moved together in the most ancient of exorcisms, most wild of moonlight rides and midnight comforts. There in that place of serene and careless death, they were marvelously, violently quick with the turbulence of life. Between that quiet rest and this rampaging intoxication of the spirit, between the glory and pain that was life and that entombed nothingness, there was no choice.

Ravel seemed to touch some sensitive inner trigger, again, again. She tensed, gasping, then called his name as she was taken by the silent grandeur of a brilliant and annihilating internal explosion. He buried his face in her hair, still generously striving, his skin dewed and glistening with his effort. "Ah, love," he whispered, "ah, my love," and thrust deep, deep into her being.

Chapter Fourteen

꿈 꿈 꿈 *It was some time later when Ravel and Anya* left the cemetery. They had gone less than three blocks when they were met by Ravel's carriage with Marcel on the seat beside the coachman. Marcel, after eluding pursuit, had circled around to the saloon where he knew the coachman was waiting for the hour to pick up his master. Together, they had proceeded slowly to the rendezvous so as to give the excitement time to die away. They had been around the area twice, searching, before coming upon Ravel and Anya.

The relief at seeing Marcel free and unharmed was enormous. Anya had been afraid that with his wrist in a sling he would be handicapped enough to be caught. She would have done everything in her power to secure his release, but it might have taken several days and a great deal of effort to arrange the proper style and amount of inducement for the proper officials. The police, the manservant said, had been so taken by surprise at the sudden flushing of their quarry that no one had been caught. Even the quadroon, the woman who lived in the house, had been spirited away safely.

Hearing the last, Anya acknowledged the possibility that Ravel had spoken the truth when he denied the quadroon as his mistress. She knew enough of him to realize, on reflection, that had the woman been his responsibility, he would not have left her side in the crisis. She recognized also with grim self-knowledge that in her concentration on that particular point she overlooked the main issue.

What had been the purpose of the meeting at the house of the quadroon? What was so dangerous about it that a corrupt police force had been called upon to intervene? When the carriage reached Madame Rosa's townhouse and Ravel got down to escort Anya to the gallery outside her bedroom, she taxed him with the question.

He watched her for a long moment. "You never give up, do you?"

"It isn't in my nature," she said, and heard the unhappiness in her voice with some surprise.

"Suppose I said the meeting had nothing to do with you, that it poses no danger to you and yours."

"In other words, it's none of my affair?"

"Exactly."

She made a helpless gesture. "I can't just leave it like that."

"Why not?" he asked, the words quiet but with an undertone of steel. "What is so important about what I may be doing that it would drive you to something like tonight's escapade?"

She had constructed a trap for herself. What answer could she give him other than the truth, which was that she had a compulsive need to understand him? The obvious question then was why that should be so. It was one she had no desire to examine, much less answer.

"Call it curiosity," she said.

If her answer failed to satisfy him, he did not show it. "A motive known for its danger."

There were others more perilous. "Is that a warning?"

"The consequences," he said deliberately, "could be worse next time."

Consequences. It was a cold description for the transports they had shared. Had it meant no more than that to him, another small revenge? Had the words he had spoken meant nothing except as a means to assure her acquiescence?

With a lift of her chin, she said, "The consequences for whom?"

"For both of us."

He turned then and walked away. Anya watched him go, watched the proud set of his shoulders, his long, easy stride, and the way the moonlight caught blue gleams in his hair as he descended the stairs. She watched him, and the hollow ache beneath her breastbone swelled, threatening to consume her.

Ravel forced himself to walk, placing one foot in front of the other, though the effort made his muscles stiff with cramps and his brain felt like hot jelly inside his skull. He wanted nothing more than to go back and force Anya to listen to him, to hear and understand what he had to say instead of rushing defenses of hate and fear into place against him. He had come near, so near to renewing his proposal. But what was the point in giving her the chance to throw it back in his face once more? He should accept defeat and bow out with what grace he could muster, but he would be damned if he would. She was his. He would make her see it if he had to destroy them both to do it.

The night was far gone when Anya finally slept. Even then, her endlessly turning thoughts would not allow her to rest, but brought her awake at odd intervals. When she rose at mid-morning there were dark shadows under her eyes and a look of strain about her face. She drank her coffee, but had no appetite for the hot rolls and butter brought to her bedchamber with it, nor could she summon the energy to get dressed.

She was standing at the open French door with her coffee cup in her hand, staring out into the courtyard, when a light tap came on the door that connected her room to that of her half sister. Immediately it opened and Celestine swung inside. "Do I disturb you, *chère*? Is now a good time to talk?"

Anya made a conscious effort to cast aside her low spirits and thrust her own problems to the back of her mind. She gave her half sister a warm smile. "Of course. Would you care for coffee?"

"I had mine ages ago, but I'll have another roll if you aren't going to eat yours."

"Help yourself."

Celestine did not wait for a further invitation, but perched herself on the edge of the bed beside the silver tray with its cream-colored linen napkin, small silver coffeepot, and napkin-covered basket. She unwrapped the rolls and selected one, taking a bite.

"Now, what seems to be the problem?" Anya asked.

Celestine looked at her, then lowered her lashes. She swallowed. "There is something I wanted to ask you."

"Well, what is it?"

"It's a personal thing, and perhaps you won't wish to tell me."

"How can I know until you ask?"

Celestine looked up, a frank look in her brown eyes. "I don't want to embarrass you. You are very American sometimes when it comes to such matters."

"Ah," Anya said, beginning to see the trend of the conversation, "those matters. What is it you want to know? I thought surely Madame Rosa had explained things to you."

"Well, yes," Celestine said, looking uncomfortable for the first time. "She told me what happens and why when a man and a woman make love. She told me that I must be guided by Murray and that I must strive to please him, but she did not say how a woman feels about it."

"I suspect that depends on the woman."

"Come, Anya, you know what I mean! I have heard the whispers that say you were intimate with Ravel Duralde. Is it nice? Will I like it? You must tell me, for soon I will be married, and then if I don't like it, it will be too late!"

Anya looked at her half sister with a lifted brow, ignoring the faint heat of her own flush. "Second thoughts?"

"No, no," Celestine said, pulling apart the roll she still held and balling the dough between her fingers. "Only, so much seems to depend on the man."

"Yes." Anya's tone was reflective as her thoughts went back to that night in the cotton gin.

"Did you enjoy it?" Celestine persevered.

Anya took a deep, steadying breath, then said slowly, "As it happens, I did."

"But what was it like? Tell me! Don't make me keep asking questions and more questions."

"It was—" Anya stopped. What could she say to make the other girl understand, to explain the tumult of emotions and the changes they had wrought within her? What words could she use to make her see the wonder of it without causing alarm?

"Anya!" There was exasperation in her half sister's tone.

"It was a thing of incredible intimacy, lying so close with nothing whatever between us, our bodies perfectly fitted, interlocking. It was a deep and profound pleasure, and at the same time it was exciting, wild and free.''

Celestine looked a bit surprised, and most intrigued. "Maman said it would hurt.''

"A little, but Ravel helped to make it less.''

The other girl bit her lip. "I wonder if Murray knows how to do that.''

"I'm sure that he will take great care, knowing how he feels about you.''

"Yes, I suppose.''

"Don't start worrying about it. Even if it isn't perfect at first, I understand it usually gets better.''

"I was just thinking—''

Celestine stopped and sat staring into space. Anya, in mystification, said, "What were you thinking?''

"I will wager Emile Girod knows. He probably had lots of experience abroad.''

"Possibly,'' Anya agreed, then added as she remembered Emile's rather pompous strictures on the conduct expected of girls of good family, "though I somehow doubt it included many untried females.''

With a scowl and a flounce on the bed, Celestine abandoned that line of discussion, reverting to the original topic. "But how strange to think of you and Ravel Duralde together the way you describe. You hardly knew each other, much less were in love. How can it be?''

Anya turned away, moving to the French doors. "I don't know.''

"Would it be the same, do you think, with any other man?''

"No!'' The answer was instant and instinctive.

"Perhaps,'' Celestine said, watching her with wide eyes, "perhaps it was love between you after all, one of those sudden passionate attachments like star-crossed lovers in an opera.''

"More likely it was simple lust,'' Anya answered, her tone hollow.

"Is that possible?''

She made a sudden gesture of impatience. "How should I know? My own experience is not that wide!''

Celestine jumped down from the bed and came toward her,

putting her hand on Anya's arm. "I didn't mean to suggest that it was, truly I didn't!"

"I know you didn't," Anya said, turning to give her half sister a quick, fierce hug. "I know."

Anya rang the bell for her maid, and she and Celestine talked of other things while the mulatto girl who answered helped her into a morning gown and dressed her hair. Sometime in the afternoon, she and her half sister would don their costumes and go into the streets, but the time was not yet.

The excitement of the day was building, for they could hear the sound of merrymaking coming from the street, but it would reach a peak only as darkness began to fall and the torchlight parade of the Mistick Krewe of Comus came in view. Then would be the best time to join the revelers for a few hours. They could not tarry long. They had received cards of invitation for the Comus Ball to be held at the Gaiety Theater immediately after the parade. The cards were much coveted since the ball would not only be the social event of the season, but also an occasion to see the costumed figures from the floats at close quarters as the ball was sponsored by the same men who had organized such stupendous entertainment for the city.

In the meantime, the day was fine, warmed by the golden light of the subtropical winter sun. The French doors from the salon out onto the gallery overlooking the street were thrown open, and Madame Rosa ordered a table of refreshments and a row of chairs placed outside, where those who wished could view the passing scene in comfort. Many of their neighbors had done the same, and there was much calling back and forth from balcony to balcony, and much visiting to drink a glass of wine or sample some special trifle of pastry or savory. Nearly everyone had a Mardi Gras cake, a yeasty sweet glazed with sugar icing in yellow, green, pink, and purple, and into which a bean had been baked that was supposed to confer a year of good luck upon the finder.

There was no lack of entertainment in the street below. Costumed figures strolled along arm in arm, cavaliers and red Indians, priests and corsairs, gypsies and queens, Venetians, Turks, Chinese, South Sea Islanders, and Eskimos. A pair of ladies of most peculiar gait, surpassing homeliness, exaggerated coquettish gestures, and wearing hoops so large they nearly filled the street were obviously gentlemen in disguise. They were accompanied along the street by the sound of smothered giggles and the calling of florid compliments.

Another troupe of women were viewed with less noise, but no less curiosity, at least on the part of the ladies. Painted, bejeweled, handsomely and rather ostentatiously gowned as courtesans with demi-masks, or else wearing the masculine costumes of Canal Street dandies, boisterous sailors, or goggling greenhorn flatboatmen, they were easily recognizable as women from the bordellos. They were not seeking custom, but rather enjoying the one day of the year when their presence was tolerated in the more respectable part of the city. To complete the world-turned-upside-down aspect of this day, it was possible for ladies, with perfect propriety, to venture into the higher class of bordello to further satisfy their curiosity. Many took advantage of the open invitation, though all were heavily veiled or masked, and few admitted it.

As the day advanced into afternoon, the streets became more crowded. The sense of gaiety and merriment increased. This was a day dedicated to laughter, a day to cast off care and escape from an identity that might be burdensome, assuming one that was fanciful, light, and free. It was a day of license and of catharsis, a day of purest pleasure without thought of tomorrow.

Many of the maskers, having fortified themselves for the strenuous festivities at various wineshops and barrooms along their way, were beginning to be a little tipsy. These, along with the few who were abroad without mask and costume, and also the few Negroes in the streets, were the targets for the young boys who by time-honored tradition pelted them with small paper bags of flour that burst on contact. Some even threw bags of the white powder up at the galleries before taking to their heels. The flour, brushed from costumes and swept from gallery floors, fogged in the air, sifting down to cover the streets like snow.

Murray, arriving toward teatime, had his new silk top hat knocked from his head by a well-placed flour bag while he was only a few feet from Madame Rosa's door. The flour also showered down over his face and right shoulder. He was still wiping at the flour and brushing his sleeve as he came into the salon.

Anya had deserted the gallery. She could not seem to enter into the spirit of the day, and as the sun waned and their side of the street was covered with shadow, she had felt cool. A small coal fire burned in the grate and she curled up in a chair before it, picking up the book that Madame Rosa had been reading and had left beside the chair. Celestine came inside, going to her room to dress for the evening; still Anya read on. She had just been telling herself for the tenth time that she really must go and make herself ready, when Murray entered. She put her book aside and rose with grace to greet him. Seeing the flour, she insisted that he remove his coat and gave it to the maid who had let him in, along with his hat, to be brushed. At the same time, she asked the girl to inform Celestine that her fiancé had arrived.

"You are very thoughtful," Murray said as he tugged at his shirt sleeves in a vain attempt to straighten the wrinkles that had formed under his coat. He seemed a bit ill at ease, which was not surprising. A gentleman seldom if ever appeared in his shirt sleeves before a lady not a member of his immediate family. She remembered with a pang that no such compunction had troubled Ravel.

"Not at all," she said.

"You are also, if I may say so, a most unusual woman."

Anya glanced at him uncertainly. Woman, not lady. Had the term been used purposely? Was it her imagination, or was there a shade of familiarity in his tone beyond that of a future brother-in-law? She had been expecting to hear something of the sort since her return, though not specifically from that quarter. It was inevitable that the story that had been circulated as protection would not be believed by everyone, but she had expected more faith, or perhaps more concealing guile, from her half sister's fiancé.

"I can't think why you should say so," she answered repressively. "Madame Rosa and Gaspard are out on the gallery, if you would care to join them."

"I will wait for my coat, unless you prefer to be alone?"

What could she say? She returned to her chair and seated herself upon it. "No, no, pray sit down."

He took the settee that was placed at a right angle to her chair beside the fire, and leaned back in a relaxed pose. "I understand I have you to thank for the cancellation of my meeting with Duralde."

"Who told you?"

He smiled with a flash of dimples as he shook his head. "Two people who are to be united as one cannot have secrets from each other; Celestine told me, of course. Besides, I had a special interest."

"Yes, I suppose so. It—seemed the right thing to do at the time."

"I had not realized you were so concerned for me."

Her shrug was as casual as she could make it. "The truth is I have not been rational on the subject of dueling since—well, since Jean's death."

"I see."

Did he? There was warmth, but apparently nothing more in his eyes as he watched her. She said, "I would hate to see Celestine's happiness destroyed over such a minor affair."

"It wasn't minor to me. However, it's over and done. But as you are on our side, so to speak, I wonder if I could prevail upon you to use your good offices in my favor? I cannot bring Madame Rosa to a serious discussion of our marriage. She smiles and nods and agrees that the waiting is hard, but always finds some excuse why the date we have chosen will not do. Can you not make her see that we are impatient to be together?"

Again she glanced at him, listening for the innuendo behind the words. She could not grasp it. No doubt it was in her head, caused by her own awareness. She gave him a rueful smile. "Madame Rosa can be quite wily when she wishes, I know, and she seldom responds to cajolery. You had best humor her; she will come around eventually."

Before Murray could answer, Gaspard stepped through the French doors from the gallery. He lifted his brows as he saw them together before the fire, but moved forward to exchange bows with Murray. With the formalities out of the way, he looked about him in a vague manner. "Madame Rosa sent me for her shawl. It should be here somewhere."

Anya found it where it had slid of its own silken weight from the back of a chair to lie behind it. She knelt to retrieve it, then turned with it in her hands to where her stepmother's friend stood in the middle of the room. Gaspard took the shawl from her without meeting her eyes, shaking out the heavy silk with its edging of fringe and folding it with precision before draping it over his arm.

Certainly there had been nothing remotely familiar in his manner toward her on this day. He had, instead, been ill at ease in her presence. The only explanation she could find was that he knew she had seen him at the meeting in the house on Rampart Street, and he did not quite know what to make of it.

Anya, watching his movements, was struck by how at home he seemed in the salon. In just the same way, he had appeared at home in the salon of the quadroon woman. There was a good reason for the impression. With the exception of the color, Madame Rosa's salon, with its taste and refinement, was almost precisely like the other one Anya had seen the night before. Nor was the cause hard to find. Gaspard had guided the furnishing of both, had helped choose wall hangings and draperies, furniture and bibelots. He had put his touch on the salon of the quadroon on Rampart Street as surely as he had this one. The only difference was that he had paid for the first. It followed that the quadroon, then, was his mistress, not Ravel's.

Not Ravel's.

Gaspard turned and walked back out into the gallery, still Anya stood staring after him as if transfixed.

"Is anything wrong?" Murray asked.

"No," she said, with a sudden brilliant smile. "No."

"What should be wrong?" Celestine asked as she swirled into the room at that moment and gave her hand to her fiancé. "It's Mardi Gras and you are here at last! I thought you were never coming!"

"How should I fail so lovely a lady?" Murray held her hand, smiling at her above it.

In her court gown of russet panne velvet from the Louis XIV period, over panniers ornamented with loops and skeins of pearls, Celestine was magnificent, and very much aware of it. "Such gallantry! I am overwhelmed."

Anya watched her half sister flutter her lashes at Murray and felt inside her a strange sense of suspension. They were so young, those two, and relatively untouched by the sordid crosscurrents that swirled around them. Their only thought was for the iron bands of convention that held them. Their worries were so few. Their courtship would proceed by slow degrees, culminating in a year or two in a beautiful wedding at the cathedral, followed by a night of innocent and virginal exploration. There would be a small house on some quiet street in the American section, then in time would come children and day after day of quiet, ordinary pleasures, of companionship and content. There might never be moments of stupendous ecstasy, but neither would there be times of black despair.

"But come, where is your costume?" Celestine was saying to Murray. "I thought you were going with Anya and me into the streets?"

"Are you sure you want to go? It's no place for a lady. There was a boy throwing rotten eggs not far from here, and two rowdies have been arrested for accosting a woman and pulling her into an alley near the square. I myself was pelted with flour on your very doorstep."

"You should have been in costume; then you would have been safe. As for Anya and myself, we will have you to protect us. Also Emile Girod."

"Emile?" Murray asked, frowning.

"Don't look like that," Celestine said, twining her arm in his. "Anya needs a man's arm to cling to in the crowds also."

"I didn't know you had invited him," Anya said, a note of inquiry in her voice.

"He sent a note this morning," Celestine began.

Murray grunted. "He invited himself, the dandified Parisian coxcomb."

"*Mon cher*!" Celestine said in amazement.

"I'm sorry," Murray said, his face reddening. "He just rubs me the wrong way."

"I didn't realize. Perhaps we can send a message, tell him not to come." Celestine sent Anya a helpless look.

Anya tilted her head as the sound came of footsteps on the stairs. "I believe it's too late."

Emile swaggered into the room in a manner entirely in keeping with his musketeer costume. His dark wig was luxuriant, his mustache appropriately curled, his hat gorgeously plumed and the cuffs of his gloves sewn with jewels. He swept the assembled company a deep bow, pointing his toe and keeping his hand on his sword as he dusted the floor with his hat brim in the prescribed manner. Still, that sword was not a toy but a weapon.

Celestine waltzed forward to drop a curtsy. "How fine you are, I vow! We are quite a matched pair, but what became of the Cossack uniform Anya and I heard you order? I quite expected to see you as a daring Russian officer."

"I woke this morning and did not feel Russian," Emile said with a grand gesture.

"In fact, you felt like d'Artagnan?"

"At the very least."

"Perhaps we should be grateful," Murray said with a tight smile, "that you did not feel like Adam."

Emile gave Murray a hard glance that flicked over his shirt sleeves. "At least I did not array myself as a clerk."

There was a moment of silence that vibrated with strain like an abruptly plucked harp string. Celestine looked from one man to the other with mingled fright and excitement in her eyes and her hands clasped before her. Anya, with nightmare visions of yet another challenge rising in her mind, stepped into the breach. "Murray is doubtless going to wait to surprise us. It's too provoking of him, since he will have seen our finery first. It would serve him right if I also refuse to change."

"Oh, Anya, no," Celestine moaned in distress and disappointment.

"You are quite right, no indeed," Anya reassured her. "I am to be a goddess, and I'm so looking forward to it that I mean to be a deity as long as possible. But since I have not yet begun to dress, Murray might have time to return to his lodging to change."

"It hardly matters whether I do or not," he said with an irritable movement of his shoulders.

"Of course it matters!" Celestine cried.

Emile made a move toward the younger girl, as if he meant to comfort her, but checked as Anya put a hand on his arm. Anya, her tone brisk, said to Murray, "Oh, come now, this is not a day for wrangling. You need not go with us at all, if you prefer. But if you are going, make up your mind; shall it be with a costume, or without?''

Murray had fallen in with the custom of masking and costumes readily enough for the ball a week before, but now with attention focused upon his attire, he had discovered within himself the American reluctance to appear ridiculous or to suspend reality long enough to enjoy a masquerade. Either that, or he was jealous of Emile's ability to appear natural and even rakish in his new identity.

Emile was doing nothing to mend the situation, perhaps out of pride or possibly from a simple inability to back down. Rather, he stood at attention with his hat under one arm and his hand still braced on his sword hilt, every inch the preening and haughty musketeer stoically awaiting the outcome of the discussion.

It struck Anya with sudden force that neither man was Jean. Despite the characteristics they shared with him, they were each their own man. She had foisted her expectations upon them, unrealistic expectations of resemblance to a paragon who in the past seven years had grown kinder, sweeter of nature, and more noble than any human could be. She had tried to re-create the romance she had shared with him in the attraction between the American Murray Nicholls and her half sister, and had invested so much of herself in it that the thought of Murray being killed in a duel had been like the prospect of losing Jean again. It was possible that she had been a little mad. Certainly it seemed so now, now that she knew and accepted one central fact. Jean was dead.

Jean was dead and she felt the loss as a faint, sweet ache, one that she would never quite banish. And yet she was alive, passionately alive. Ravel may have been right; she may have been burying herself, trying to disguise from herself with constant work and the cultivation of an image both spinsterish and outrageous that she could not mourn Jean forever. If it had been true, it was so no longer. Ravel had shown her that she was a living, breathing woman, and for the fact, if not the method of it, she must be grateful to him.

Celestine, a hurt look on her face, began once more to remonstrate with Murray. Her fiancé appeared to be weakening though his expression was harassed. Emile, acquiring tact in the face of Celestine's distress, began a minute inspection of his fingernails.

Abruptly, and with rueful exasperation, Murray agreed to go and find a costume, even if it was only a domino. With Celestine smiling and clinging to his arm, he moved toward the door to take his departure. The danger appeared to have been diverted, and with a sigh, Anya excused herself to the room at large and heartlessly abandoned Emile to the position of witness to the mending of the lovers' quarrel while she went away to dress for the evening.

Her costume had been delivered from Madame Lussan's shop, carefully packed in tissue paper. Anya's mulatto maid had pressed the two large pieces of cloth, one of white linen and the other of soft, lightweight lavender wool woven with a silver stripe and embroidered in purple, then hung them away in the armoire. While the maid took the two pieces out and laid them reverently on the bed, Anya stepped into the bath that was waiting. She did not linger since she did not want to be tardy. Minutes later, the maid was placing the linen cloth that formed a long tunic known as a chiton around her. Anya turned this way and that in front of the mirror, frowning as she looked at it. The fit of the garment was less than satisfactory. The problem was her undergarments. The chiton required a soft, draped appearance, one that was incompatible with stays. The sleeves, open at the shoulders and along the arms except for a series of small brooches, also exposed the capped sleeves of her camisole. The only solution was to remove everything except her pantalettes.

At last she stood ready. The chiton clung to her arms and shoulders and the proud curves of her breasts in loose, natural folds that were caught at the waist by a girdle of silver mesh tied with silver cords ending in purple silk tassels that swayed below her knees. The wool toga known as a himation was draped around her for warmth, covering her left arm and leaving her right free. On her feet were sandals that left her toes bare. Her hair had been dressed in loose waves that hung down her back, held only by a filet around her forehead. To cover her face was a demi-mask of cloth of silver.

The long flowing lines of the garment gave her a look of grace, and she felt delightfully free of confinement. At the same time, she was doubtful about appearing in public in them. The nightgowns most women wore, herself included, were, if not more modest, at least more concealing. They also failed to impart this sense of wanton awareness of her own seminakedness underneath them. She held up her mask before her face and tried a smile. Her eyes seemed to glitter through the almond-shaped holes, and there was in the curve of her lips a peculiar enticement.

She turned sharply from the mirror. It was only a costume. There would be dozens, perhaps hundreds, of other women this evening who would be unencumbered by stays and hoops and petticoats. If the truth were known, her greatest fear was not for how others would view her, but for the effect the costume might have upon her own nature. She had discovered as much as she cared to about her sensual needs, as much as she could live with in anything near comfort.

The four of them, Celestine and Murray, Anya and Emile, left the townhouse a short time later. The streets were much more crowded now, though carriage traffic had slowed. Streetlamps had been lighted early, so that their glow reflected yellow in the flour that caked the banquettes and lay in well-tracked trails over the thresholds of every shop and house. Here and there were spots of pink and green where *dragées* had been crushed underfoot.

Everywhere there was color and sound and movement. Paste jewels glittered and spangles gleamed and the light played in bright hues over the costumes. Two Negro women dressed as small girls, with their hair in pigtails and their skirts nearly to their knees, went giggling past on this evening when all classes mingled. They were followed by a clown who walked with a rolling gait and a pair of capering harlequins. Salome danced past with the head of John the Baptist most realistically done in plaster upon a silver platter and her naked limbs gleaming through her drifting veils. There were dairy maids and shepherdesses and Spanish señoritas in plenty, as well as enough Russian senators to fill a forum and enough pirates to man a fleet of ships. Cleopatra was carried past on a litter with Nubian slaves at the four corners. Napolean strutted past with Josephine on one arm and his other hand thrust into his shirtfront. Troubadours in doublets and hose, with ribbons on their arms and an upturned hat laid hopefully in front of them, sang on a street corner. Further along, a one-man band went through incredible contortions to render a brisk version of "Oh! Susanna!", and on the next corner a sailor danced a hornpipe to the music of a concertina.

The air carried a rich medley of smells from the vendors of peanuts and pralines, of gumbo and fried shrimp and oysters on buttered bread, of oranges and bouquets of violets in filigreed papers and bunches of the herb vetiver that was used to scent linens and underclothing. Also, from the open doors of restaurants, came the delicious aromas of seafood bubbling in stews and sauces, beef being braised, roast pork turning on spits in its own crisp and crackling skin, and pastries and bread browning in brick ovens. The two women and their escorts had forgone dinner in order to partake of the bounty available, and so as they walked they bought bowls of thick, spicy gumbo and the brown rounds of pralines with their rich taste of milk and sugar and pecans.

The brief flare of anger between the two men was forgotten as if it had never been. They had laughed and talked and pointed out costumes that were beautiful or droll or grotesque to each other, succumbing to the infection of the general excitement. In a few hours the day would be over and Ash Wednesday with its repentance would be upon them. The cares that had been pushed aside for the moment would return in force. But for now there was the pleasure of the moment and the joy of being alive. There was the escape from the dreary routine of life, from the duties and obligations that beset mortal men and women. There was this short time when nothing mattered but fun and laughter, along with the possibilities that lay in taking on a new identity and the adventure that waited around the next corner. For now, for the hours that lay just ahead of them, it was Mardi Gras. It was enough.

Chapter Fifteen

🦋 🦋 🦋 *A clatter of hoofbeats came from behind them* and they had to step aside for a troop of Bedouin Arabs who raced by with their robes flying in the wind of their passage. They were met with cheers and greetings, partially because they had been a fixture of the day for some years and partially because they threw great handfuls of bonbons and *dragées* to the people along their route as they went. Behind them came a number of other vehicles from cabriolets to carriages to furniture wagons, all tearing along at great speed with maskers leaning out the windows and over the sides or perched precariously on top. Chasing after them with red faces and pumping arms were a gang of young boys who scrambled for any of the candies that had been missed, and after the boys came a pack of mongrel dogs with flapping ears and wagging tongues and tails.

Murray sidestepped the shower of *dragées* that came their way, but Emile reached to catch a few, which he handed with great ceremony to Anya and Celestine. It was a strange thing, but the candy-coated almonds never tasted so good as when eaten on Mardi Gras day, and as they walked on, Anya crunched them between her teeth with gusto.

Ahead of them came the sound of a polka. The music was being made by three Negro minstrels playing banjos. A cluster of people had gathered around them and a few couples were circling and dipping to the perfect toe-tapping tune. Emile turned to Anya with a sweeping bow and offered his arm. She gave a delighted laugh and, with a light heart, curtsied and allowed herself to be swung into the street in the rollicking dance. Over Emile's shoulder, Anya caught a glimpse of Celestine tugging a self-conscious Murray into the street also.

Emile's hold was firm, his rhythm natural and sure, easy to follow. It was a pleasure to be in his arms, a part of the gaiety and the joy of the night, with the music propelling her, lifting her spirits like the sparkle of wine in her veins. It had been years since she had felt so light and free of care, and it seemed that never had she been quite so vital, so deliciously reckless.

The music came to a strumming finish. Anya and Emile halted with a final swing directly beside Celestine and Murray. As a slower waltz began at once, Emile turned to Celestine and, bowing, presented his arm. The girl glanced at her fiancé. Murray nodded his permission, though it seemed his smile was stiff. Celestine did not hesitate, but went into Emile's arms, giving herself up to the night and the music as surely as Anya had done. Anya, seeing it, smiled a little at the effect of Mardi Gras.

"Shall we?" Murray asked, the words abrupt.

Anya turned to him in surprise since she had expected him to retreat with relief to the banquette. She curtsied in mock formality, however, and accepted his embrace. They moved in perfect three-quarter time. Regardless, Murray lacked the Creole ability to feel the music; his performance had a mechanical sense about it, as if he had once learned to waltz by counting in his head. It might possibly have been that he was concentrating on other matters, however, for after a moment he spoke.

"Do you think he likes her?"

She followed the direction of his gaze that was fastened on Emile and her half sister. She was in no mood for emotional crosscurrents. Her answer was light. "How can you think so? For tonight he is my gallant."

"He's always around."

"He is a family friend of long standing and a sociable man. Why should he not visit?"

"I think your stepmother encourages him. It wouldn't surprise me if she is secretly hoping he will win Celestine's affections."

"Madame Rosa is not so conniving!"

He looked down at her, a skeptical light in his hazel eyes. "You think not?"

"In any case, it's Celestine who is important. Do you imagine that her affections can be so easily won over?"

"I don't know," he said with unhappiness shading his voice. "She's so young. I would give anything if our betrothal could be announced."

A betrothal was not official until it was celebrated before the proper gathering of friends and relatives and with offerings of food and wine. After that it was as binding as the marriage contract. To break it at that stage was practically unheard of.

"She is young, yes, but there are many girls her age who not only are married, but already have children. You must trust her."

He sighed. "Yes, but it isn't easy."

Anya could only agree. The waltz ended and they all walked on; still Anya found herself thinking of Murray's morose and jealous uncertainty. She had always thought of him as being confident within himself, easy of temperament, happy. Was it simply that she had foisted the image upon him with her need to make him like Jean, or had it been a pose, a mask he wore as did so many others, herself included?

They were all masqueraders in their different ways, people hiding their pain, their weaknesses, their vices, even their frightening strengths behind carefully constructed fronts, concealing these things from themselves as well as others. She herself, wrapped in her role of tragedy, pretending she needed no one because she was so afraid of being hurt again. Madame Rosa, whose indolent image not only prevented her from having to do the things that displeased her, but also covered her strong will that allowed her to direct the lives of others. Playful, sweet, innocent Celestine, who had a deep sensual streak that would one day be the delight of her husband. Gaspard, who was less the dandy and dilettante than he affected to be, disguising his virility behind a social facade. Emile, who behind his sophisticated and courteous mien was both more primitive and more credulous than he knew. And Ravel, the Black Knight, who despite his past was as tender as he was tough, at least as generous as he was self-seeking, and not half so unconventional as he was painted.

Where was Ravel? What was he doing? She had expected somehow to see him, or at least hear from him. It seemed so unlikely that he would leave the situation between them unsettled, unfinished. For herself, it was a constant disturbance at the back of her mind, a nagging ache that she had done her best to ignore as the day wore on.

Not to think of it at all was impossible. She had turned the fact of the meeting she had witnessed over and over in her mind but could come to no conclusion.

What had been the purpose of it? The possibilities were many, for clubs of various kinds, from the Freemasons and young men's benevolent societies to the heroics of the volunteer firemen, were a favorite occupation of the men of New Orleans, who had little else to occupy their time during the winter season.

On top of these were the political groups with a cause, such as the Democratic party members who were opposed to the notoriously corrupt Know-Nothings currently in power, and perhaps the Vigilance Committee with the same purpose. Another group might be one she scarcely believed in, that shadowy coalition of influential men whose purpose was to control the commerce of New Orleans and, by extension, the entire Mississippi Valley.

Then there was the Mistick Krewe of Comus that had evolved into a closed social organization known as the Pickwick Club, with meetings the year around. The last had rented for themselves a large and handsome house on St. Charles Street as a male retreat and gathering place.

That was the trouble. Of all the groups Anya could bring to mind, there was not one that did not have its accustomed location for meetings, a location that was more spacious, more convenient, and more comfortable than the house on Rampart Street. Why then had the men she had seen collected together in that house?

A simple answer presented itself. Rampart Street was quiet, it was discreet, and it was not unusual for strange men to come and go there.

The glaring question then, the one that eluded an answer, was, which of the possible groups might be subject to police harassment? Which of them would be most likely to contain members who would swiftly fade away at the arrival of the police Charleys?

The answer seemed to depend on the part played by the police the night before. If they had been protecting the citizens of New Orleans, then it was likely that there had been a report of criminal activity of some kind at the quadroon's house. If they were acting as the tool of the city government, then the meeting must have been of a political nature. It was possible also, supposing that the meeting had been of neither character, that it might be highly significant that the Charleys had shown such incompetence they had failed to detain a single man who had attended that meeting.

Ravel and Gaspard. They seemed such unlikely allies. Anya had not been aware that they knew each other, except perhaps on the most superficial level. What could they have in common, what goal did they share. She wished she knew.

Anya's attention was caught by a woman in the habit of a nun, who was waving to her from across the street. Anya stopped, and the woman came toward her. As she neared, the eyes behind the woman's mask were wary and she reached up to draw her black veil closer around her face.

"Mademoiselle Hamilton?"

"Yes?"

"I thought I could not mistake that hair, so shining and not quite gold or brown or red, but something in between."

Anya suddenly knew the voice. Clear and carefully modulated, it belonged to the actress Simone Michel, Ravel's mistress. "Yes, and you are—"

The woman interrupted her. "Could I speak to you on a matter of importance? You can catch up with your friends in a few moments."

There seemed no reasonable objection. Besides, the only likely subject of conversation between them was Ravel, and Anya could not deny a strong interest in whatever Simone Michel had to say on the subject. "I'll be along shortly," she said with a smile to the others.

They moved off, glancing back over their shoulders and at each other with some curiosity. The actress watched them go. When they were out of earshot, she asked abruptly, "Have you seen Ravel today?"

"No, I haven't," Anya answered just as shortly. "Have you?"

"No. I don't like the way he disappears lately. There have

been some odd tales concerning his vanishing act last week, some that concern you, my fine lady, but I think there's more to it than that.''

"Such as?''

The actress did not answer for a moment, as if judging whether to trust Anya. At last she said, ''I think whatever he's doing is dangerous. There are people who want him stopped because he's a gambler, a man who thrives on calculated risks, a natural leader. I don't know what you feel for Ravel, or he for you, but I think you should know what you are letting yourself in for if you get mixed up with him.''

''Close association doesn't seem to have harmed you,'' Anya observed.

"I wouldn't say that. However, I remain in the background; I know my place, you see. You apparently don't.''

Her place. She had none, nor was it likely she would ever have any. ''What is the danger? What are the risks he's taking?''

"I can't say for sure. All I know is that it's outside the law.''

''Then who are the people who want him stopped?'' Stopped. That was a nice euphemism for dead. She had known of the danger since the firing of the cotton gin, but it still seemed a thing beyond belief when spoken of here on this crowded street in the midst of noisy music and laughter.

"I don't know, not with any certainty. They are very careful to remain behind the scenes.''

"But you can guess, surely, since you have said so much?''

"Guessing could be a dangerous business also.''

"I see,'' Anya said with slow emphasis. ''Then the only reason you spoke to me at all was to warn me away from Ravel Duralde. Did you really think I would frighten so easily?''

The actress lifted her chin. ''I have watched you becoming drawn into something you know nothing about. I'm warning you because—because for some peculiar reason I like you. And also because if you run into trouble I will feel better knowing my conscience is clear.''

It could be true. There was no opportunity to test it, however, for the actress turned in a swirl of dead black skirts and walked away. Anya watched her blend with the crowd and disappear along a dim side street, and the main thing she felt was frustration. She had been close to an answer to her question, if only she had known it, if she had not lost the chance by her own defensiveness. And what had caused that defensiveness? The answer was simple. She had been jealous of the knowledge the actress had seemed to have about Ravel's movements, jealous of the implied confidences between them.

Jealous.

She couldn't be, shouldn't be. But she was.

Jealous.

Also stupid. She had no claim on Ravel Duralde and wanted none. He was everything she most disliked in a man. He was a professional killer, a glory-seeking soldier, a reckless gambler, a deceitful despoiler of women. The best thing that she could do would be to forget what had happened, forget what the man was and was not. Forget what he was going and why. Forget Ravel. But could she?

Could she?

So uncomfortable were her thoughts that her impulse was to escape them. She started walking along the banquette once more, searching the revelers ahead of her for Celestine and the two men. They were not to be seen. She rose on tiptoe, trying to see above the crowd. An Arab in a flowing burnous came up behind her, jostling her so that she stumbled off-balance. She moved out of his way with only a bare glance in his direction.

The man put his hand on her arm, giving her a push toward a nearby doorway. She looked down and saw that his fingernails were dirty and broken. His mask was some kind of thick veil drawn across the bridge of his nose, leaving his eyes and forehead free. He grinned at her above it and gave her another push.

Anya snatched her arm free and stepped smartly away from the man, placing a passing pair of men in monkey costumes between her accoster and herself. She was more irritated than afraid. She was a woman without the protection of a male escort, a servant, or the company of female friends, and in the easy atmosphere of the holiday it was not surprising that she should meet with some annoyance.

As she moved on, however, the man followed her. She increased her pace. He did the same. She wove in and out between what appeared to be a family group consisting of papa, mama, and nine children ranging in ages from a teenage boy taller than his mother to a baby in the arms of its Negro nurse. The Arab, rudely pushing aside a small girl dressed as a fairy, moved after Anya. The irate papa shouted at him, but he paid no attention.

Draping her himation more closely around her, Anya picked up her skirt and dodged across the street in the path of a dray loaded with whiskey barrels. The driver cursed and hauled on the reins, but she made it. It was a moment before she could catch her breath to look back. When she did, there were two Arabs crossing after her behind the dray.

Where were Celestine and Murray and Emile? How had they got so far ahead of her? Anxiously she stared down the side streets as she passed them. There was no sign of her half sister's russet velvet or Emile's plumed hat. The tale Murray had mentioned of a woman being attacked nagged at her. The men could hardly do that on the open street. In any case, she had no proof they meant her that kind of harm. More likely, they thought it a fine joke. Or else her costume was more suggestive of the hetaerae, the courtesans of ancient Greece, than even she had thought. She expected the two would grow tired of the chase, whatever its purpose, in short order.

Three, not two. A third man in Arab costume came at her from a side street. She swerved away to cross the intersection on the diagonal. Even as she did so, she realized that she was being herded away from the more crowded streets. That would not do. She had to double back.

Her breath was coming in short gasps. There was a pulling pain in her side. Her sandals were rubbing blisters on the sides of her feet. Her himation kept sliding down, threatening to trip her, and the tassels that banged against her shins kept getting between her legs. The maskers she passed turned their heads to look at her as if surprised at her haste, but there were no expressions on their disguises, only blank appraisal without promise of succor. If she stopped to explain, to ask for help, she might be caught, with no one to come to her aid.

She needed a weapon, but what would avail her against three men? A pepper pot pistol designed to shoot once from each of several small barrels? A sword and the skill to use it? A cane knife and the strength to send it flailing back and forth? She had nothing, could see nothing that would be of use.

The fourth man came from around a corner ahead of her. Once more she struck out away from them, racing across the street to reach the opposite corner, fleeing down the cross street.

This was no ribald jest, no accident. The men in the Arab costumes were after her. Their flowing burnouses had been chosen in all likelihood because they were already present in abundant numbers. Using them, the men could converge on their quarry in good order, but without attracting undue attention.

There was something horrifying about those faceless, shrouded figures. They seemed unreal, the silent and relentless figments from a nightmare. All she could think of was escape, to run faster and faster. She had lost track of where she was, where she was going. She could still hear the music and sound of the crowd that was congregating on Royal Street where the parade would pass, but it was growing fainter. Her heart thudded against the wall of her chest. The wind from the river was cold in her face. Her hair flew around her. Every step was agony.

She tripped on a sagging corner of her himation and staggered, catching at an iron post that supported a gallery overhead to keep from falling. Behind her she heard a loud guffaw.

That sound. She had heard it before on the night of the fire. The men in the Arab costumes were not sadistic wraiths bent on harrying a lone female. They were the thugs who had tried to kill her and Ravel at Beau Refuge, the men who had destroyed her property and terrorized her people in the quarters. That they dared set out in pursuit of her like coursing hounds after a rabbit brought the reviving power of rage boiling up inside her. She would not be caught. She would not be manhandled again or treated like some levee doxy.

She heard the rattle of the cabriolet before she saw it. The vehicle turned a corner and came toward her. It was not as ancient as most, and the mare that pulled it had a look of raw-boned strength. It was moving at a smart clip, but not excessively so. Flinging her himation over her shoulder, Anya made a wild dash into the street toward it. Behind her there came a yell and the thud of running feet.

The cabriolet's horse, startled by her sudden appearance and flying draperies, reared and whinnied. The driver sawed on the reins, rising in his seat while his hat tumbled from his head. Anya ducked under the mare's flailing hooves and reached for the edge of the kick board as she set her foot on the step and pulled herself upward.

"What the bloody hell—," the driver began.

Anya did not trouble to answer. As she landed beside him, she reached across for the whip in its socket. It was long and snaking with a tasseled end. She drew it back and sent it cracking toward the thugs, once, twice, three times. They yelled and scattered. The mare jerked forward in her harness at a run. Bouncing and sluing, the cabriolet raced down the street with the men in burnouses pounding after it. They shouted and cursed at each other as they fell slowly behind. Anya cracked the whip above the back of the mare a final time.

"Here now, here now, you dumb bitch," the driver hollered as he brought his mare under control.

It was impossible to tell whether he was talking to Anya or the horse, but she didn't care. She had escaped. Whatever the plans the thugs had had for her, she had foiled them. Reaction and exultation shuddered over her. She controlled them with a strong effort. She wasn't safe, not yet. The men knew what she looked like and the direction she was going.

How had they recognized her in her costume and mask? Had they too noticed the color of her hair? How could that be when, as far as she knew, they had never seen it at close quarters except at night or when it was covered by a bonnet? It was true there might have been other times, but the thought of them watching her, spying upon her, was not one she liked to consider. But perhaps they had heard when Simone Michel had called her name?

The actress had not only spoken her name aloud, but had separated her from her escort. Had it been a coincidence, or had Simone's show of concern been as false as the jewels that she wore on stage? It was all too possible. The things the actress had said were nothing Anya had not already known or guessed. All her reluctance to say more might have been feigned merely to make what she had said more intriguing.

And yet if that were true, what was the purpose? Ravel had

spent time with Anya, yes, but against his will. The intimacy there had been between the two of them was no threat to Simone. He had not, apparently, severed his relationship with the actress. Why then? In addition, even if the actress had pointed her out, what could the connection be between Simone and the thugs who had been at Beau Refuge? How had she known them in order to make use of them?

It was just barely possible that the incident tonight and the burning of the gin had a common thread, but the only one that she could see led to Ravel. Someone called "the boss" had ordered their deaths that night at the plantation. What would have happened to her tonight? Would she have been attacked in an alley, or would she have disappeared into the bordellos of New Orleans like hundreds of other women? Or would she, perhaps, have been found in a day or two floating in the river? And all because she had involved herself with Ravel Duralde?

There was no time to think of it. They were on Chartres Street, for the cabriolet had clattered past the cathedral and the Cabildo. Chartres ran parallel to Royal, the street down which the parade would come as it made its way from St. Charles and Canal Streets. At the intersections could be seen the press of people on that other thoroughfare. Somewhere in the milling mob was Celestine and Murray and Emile. Celestine would be frantic, worrying about where she could be, why she had not caught up with them. Should she try to find them, Anya wondered, or should she return to the townhouse?

The driver of the cabriolet settled the question for her. Whether out of curiosity to view the parade that would be coming at any moment, or because he thought he might find a passenger in the crowd, he swung his vehicle into the next cross street, making toward Royal.

The cabriolet slowed. There were people crowding the banquettes, spilling into the street here. Along Royal itself there was a solid line jostling each other, elbowing for position as they waited to see what the Krewe of Comus had for them this year. The galleries overhead were full to overflowing. The buzzing of voices was like a giant disturbed beehive, nearly drowning out the distant sound of banjos and concertinas. People craned their necks, looking up the street, inching further and further out into it from either side until only the open gutter down the center divided them.

The cabriolet driver pulled his mare to a halt and turned to Anya. "All right, me lady, what is it this is all about?"

He was not young and his voice held a lilt of Ireland. In his lined face there was sympathy as well as interest. Anya said, "You saw those men. They—well, I'm more grateful than I can say for your aid."

"I'd say you had a mortal close call. You might think on that before you go a-wandering off by yourself again."

"Yes, I will," Anya said as she gathered her draperies around her, preparing to alight. "I'm sorry if I caused you any inconvenience, and I wish that I could pay you now, but I came out without my purse. If you will present yourself at Madame Hamilton's townhouse in the morning—"

"Hush, now. I don't want pay, but I would trouble you for the return of my whip."

She still had it in her hand. Flushing, laughing a little, she handed it over then clambered down. Standing in the street, she thanked him once more then turned away.

"Take care," he called, saluting her with the whip.

She waved, and where there had been cold fear inside her before there was a small core of warmth. Despite the danger and treachery of the world, there were still kindly people in it.

They were few on this night, or so it seemed. She had not gone fifty feet before she saw a man in a burnous. He stood leaning against a wall, watching her. He made no move toward her, still her breath caught in her throat and she turned from him, threading in haste through the crowd, her head up as she searched for Celestine and the two men.

They were not to be seen. It crossed her mind that they might have been surrounded, spirited away somewhere as she undoubtedly would have been. No, she must not be foolish. There would have been too great a commotion caused by any attempt to take men like Emile and Murray. But where could they be? Where?

She stopped. There was no point in running hither and yon looking for them and wringing her hands. Surely there was little that could happen to her here in such a large gathering of people, the thickest part of the spectators. There was even a Charley standing on the nearest corner, swinging his spontoon by its thong behind his back. His very purpose was to keep order and prevent undue disturbance.

"It's coming! Comus is coming! Here it comes!"

The cry ran through the crowd. Hard upon it came the thin sound of music. It grew, becoming the ring and thump of a brass band, while as a counterpoint could be heard the melodious whistling of a calliope. There came the first glimpse of the bright glow of torchlight. In its beams, far up the street, there was a shifting motion that could be seen above the throng.

People moved toward the light like the drawing of a tidal surge by the power of the moon. Children squealed with excitement and women exclaimed. Young boys crawled through the legs of their elders to reach the front of the line, though some few were hauled back by their suspenders in the fists of indulgent fathers who then hoisted them to their shoulders.

Closer and closer came the parade. The music grew louder, blaring out above the ring of iron wheels and the clatter of horse and mule hooves on pavement. The crowd shouted and applauded.

There was wonder and amazement in the faces around Anya. Sighs of awe and pleasure sounded on all sides. The restless masqueraders had expected something grand after the parade the year before that had featured "The Demon Actors in Milton's *Paradise Lost*." On that night over a hundred terrible and grotesque characters, led by the winsome young god of revel and mirth, Comus, and by the prince of darkness, Lucifer himself, and including dreadful Pluto and pathetic Proserpine, the three Furies, the three Harpies, and scores more infernals on down to Charon and Chimera, had seemed to rise up in floods of light from the ground itself. The spectacle before them was less alarming, but much more satisfying.

This year instead of only Comus and Satan riding on a single cart, seated among outlandish scenery built on a platform while the other demons pranced on foot behind, there were dozens of carts decorated to look like chariots forming a long series of *tableaux roulants*. Never in the history of Mardi Gras marching had such a thing been seen before.

In the lead came a large transparency, or panel of tightly stretched and brightly colored translucent silk that was lighted from behind by a lantern with an enormous reflector. Illuminated were the words in beautiful flowing script:

> . . . *Marry, but you travelers*
> *May journey far and not look on this like again.*
> *Here you do behold the gods and goddesses;*
> *Presently you shall see them*
> *Unfold themselves.*

Directly behind this came another transparency that heralded the theme of the parade, *The Classic Pantheon*.

First in line, as was only fitting, rode handsome Comus crowned with flowers, magnificent king of the day in white and gold. Behind him came mighty Momus, son of the night in sable and silver, followed by two-faced Janus in his temple that was inset with the Four Seasons. Another great illuminating lantern, as well as long and stretched-out double lines of Negro torchbearers dressed in white suits, showed Neptune in a chariot shaped like a seashell and drawn by dolphins, then Flora in a bank of flowers pulled by butterflies; Ceres drawn by her oxen; Bacchus pulled by leopards, and Silenus precariously jogging on an ass. Next came Diana the Huntress in a chariot drawn by stags, and with the nine Muses behind her, then Vesta with her altar of fire; Destiny on his winged dragon, and Cybele, mother goddess of Asia, drawn by lions. Still they came on. There was Jupiter pulled by eagles and behind him Juno led by peacocks, with Iris the rainbow on one side and Argus the hundred-eyed on the other; Venus, goddess of love, was drawn by swans; Aurora stood with her winged horse; Apollo of the Sun, engulfed in swaths of gold, was drawn by the golden Sun, followed by Atlas carrying the world on his shoulders. Hercules was next, then Mars in his war chariot, and Minerva drawn by owls.

Cart after cart, they rolled into view, shining with gold and silver and paste jewels, awing the crowd with the marvelous effect created from papier-mâché, jigsawed wood, cascades of feathers and drapings of satin and silk, with sheets of gold leaf and barrels of paint. The hours of work expended were beyond counting, and it was easy to believe that a sum in excess of the rumored twenty thousand dollars had been spent by the Krewe of Comus.

Capering around the burdened carts were figures in the costumes of satyrs and nymphs, fauns and cupids. They were clustered particularly close around the next chariot in line, that of Great Pan, god of Arcadia, deity of armorous love, patron of pastoral poets.

Pan wore on his lower body a partial costume that had haunches covered with long white hair and the cloven feet of an Asian goat. From his shoulders swung a cloak of forest green wool held by a gold cord looped around great jeweled brooches, though his chest, broad and burned by the sun, was bare. Small gold horns sprang from the dark, tumbled curls that fell over his forehead, and twined in his hair were gold and green leaves of the vine. His face was covered by a gold demi-mask through which his eyes gleamed with lascivious joy. Unlike some of the other gods, who showed a tendency toward corpulence, Pan was lean and fit, his chest padded with muscle. Most of the others were also content to allow the mule hidden under the trappings of their mythological animals to be led, but Pan, his strong arms outstretched and corded with strength, was driving his own chariot pulled by real milk white goats. That he was a general favorite was plain from the cheers that rose along the route as he passed.

Anya applauded with the rest, her gaze upon Pan. She looked away to see what would come next, then looked back again, her attention irresistibly drawn. Pan was watching her, his gaze on her streaming hair, his smile devilish. She drew in her breath. It was Ravel. The god Pan was Ravel. She laughed aloud in sheer surprise.

It was at that moment of complete distraction that she felt the stir near her, heard a woman give a cry of stifled outrage. A man shouldered his way through the crowd and lunged at Anya. His hand closed on her arm, dragging her toward him. Caught off guard, she stumbled and his other arm clamped around her, holding her to the scratchy wool of his Arab burnous.

She cried out, bringing her free hand up to claw at his face. He snatched his head back and grabbed her other wrist in a bone-grinding hold. Anya stamped on his instep with her heel and had the satisfaction of hearing him curse. Before she could do it again there was a second Arab at her side and a third. They grasped her arms, drawing them back.

Twisting, struggling, she called out, "Help me!"

The Charley on the corner turned and looked, but it was as if he were blind or she were invisible. A small space began to form around her as people drew their children back out of harm's way. An elderly gentleman stepped forward with his cane upraised, as if ready to do battle for her. He was joined by another, younger man.

The first Arab winked at her would-be rescuers. "Don't be hasty, friends. She's only a whore 'at got outa line."

"No! I'm not! I'm not!"

Behind them there was a sudden clamor and commotion, but there was no time to heed it. The Arab shrugged. "Who you gonna believe?"

Hard and clear ringing with vicious irony, there came a new voice. It belonged to Ravel, who answered, "The lady, friend!"

Anya felt a sob of relief welling up inside her, though she could not see Ravel for the man who held her. His presence was plain, however.

A man in a burnous was sent sprawling backward into the crowd. There came the sharp crack of a blow to the chin and another reeled into the road. The Arab who had first grabbed her pulled a knife from under his robe. In a single fluid movement, Ravel caught his arm, twisted, and brought it down on the hairy white knee of his goat-god costume. There was a muted crunching sound and the man howled. The knife fell to the banquette. Ravel kicked it away so that it skittered between the feet of the spectators.

Swinging around then in a blur of dark green wool, he reached for Anya, clasping one arm across her back and the other under her knees as he lifted her high. He sprang with her from the banquette to where his chariot waited with the reins held by a patient faun. He handed Anya up, steadying her until she could stand in the bower of greenery that was his tableau, then swung up beside her. He took back his reins and braced his feet, then turned to circle Anya with his arm, drawing her against him.

He stared down at her, his mouth grim though there was a bright, bold light in his eyes. "Are you all right?"

She was not all right, nor would she ever be again. Her heart was a solid and enormous ache in her chest, and the hurtful press of tears was behind her eyes. She trembled inside with a strange glad terror. She was a fool, for she had fallen in love with an amorous god and the fates were not kind to mortal women who dared such a thing.

She smiled, her lips tremulous, and reached up to straighten the vine leaves that had been tipped most beguilingly over his left eye by his exertions. "Your crown is crooked," she said.

The touch of her hand, that small gesture and expression of concern, made the blood that flowed through Ravel's veins feel effervescent, as if it were hot and foaming champagne. He could no more resist the impulse to bend his head and press his mouth to the tender curves of her lips than he could stop the beating of his heart.

Around them the applauding crowd erupted into wild cheers, into hurrahs and cries of "Bravo."

Ravel lifted his head, and his eyes were dark with promise as he held Anya's soft blue gaze. He turned, and with one hand slapped the reins upon the haunches of his white goats. The parade of Comus rolled onward once more.

Chapter Sixteen

🦋 🦋 🦋 *To ride up and down the streets and around* the squares of New Orleans until the very end, playing nymph to Ravel's Pan while smiling and accepting the accolades of the interested watchers along the parade route, was a great temptation. It was also impractical. The men who portrayed the gods and also, in the old Greek theater tradition, the goddesses of *The Classic Pantheon* must eventually make their way to the Gaiety Theater, there to take their places for the grand tableaux that would be a feature of the Comus Ball. Anya had no part in that arrangement, nor was it right or fair to expect Ravel to make one for her. It was necessary for her to return home, take off her mask, and don her ball gown. The masquerade was over; to attempt to prolong it was useless.

Accordingly, Anya requested that when the slow-moving line of chariots passed Madame Rosa's townhouse, Ravel pause long enough to allow her to alight. He looked down at her, his arm tightening around her. It was strange, she thought, how much a demi-mask could hide, even when the eyes themselves were visible.

"You need not worry," she said. "I'll be safe there."

"Are you certain?"

"What do you mean?"

It was odd that he had not asked who the men were who had been menacing her, or why. It could be assumed they were the same men, for the same reason as before, because she could identify their leader, but he had no way of knowing unless he had some understanding she did not possess. Or unless he had sent them.

No, she would not think of that; to do so would be too swift a descent from the magic pinnacle of loving and perfect accord she had so recently reached. If it seemed a coincidence that the men attacked her on Mardi Gras day, on Royal Street as the parade was passing, it was simply because it was the first op-portunity that had occurred since the incident at Beau Refuge to separate her from her escort.

"I mean," he said slowly, "that perhaps you should consider who might gain if something should happen to you."

"That's ridiculous. The only reason I'm in any danger is be-cause—"

"Yes?" he said softly.

"Because of you," she finished, but with much less certainty in her tone. There seemed no connection whatever between Ravel and her pursuit by the Arabs. And yet there had to be. She had no enemies. None at all.

"There is no reason that I know of why any activities of mine should constitute a peril to you," Ravel said.

"But those men, they were the ones who tried to kill you. I'm almost sure of it!"

Was that their purpose?"

"Of course it was! Why are you trying to suggest otherwise?"

"For your protection," he said with quiet incision.

"Then again," she said, her voice stifled, "if they weren't the same, your presence was very convenient."

When he answered, his tone was deliberate. "As much as I might be tempted to have you mauled and terrorized for the plea-sure of rescuing you, it seems a rather drastic means of courtship."

They were nearing the townhouse, the vehicle slowing as with corded arms he pulled on the reins. "Why? Gratitude must surely be as acceptable to you as a reason to be wed as any other. You were willing enough to marry me for mere duty."

"Would you have preferred it if I had declared undying love and passion?"

The irony in his tone was like the flick of a whip in her vulner-able state. "Oh, infinitely," she said, summoning scorn to help disguise her pain, "so long as some pretense had to be made."

"Interesting. If you are sure the sense of duty was a pretense, what reason do you think I had for proposing a marriage be-tween us?"

"The same as most, money and position."

"I have enough of both to suit my needs."

"Respectability?"

"Ah, that's a prospect, isn't it? I thought respectability was what I was offering you."

"Did you indeed!" she said wrathfully. The chariot had stopped. She gathered up her skirt, preparing to alight.

He put his hand, warm and strong, on her arm. "I have lived without respectability most of my life. Why should I feel the lack of it now?"

"Most of us want the things we can't have." Her gaze was dark blue and steady.

"True," he said, soft amusement in his tone as he released her, "but there is a basic fault in your reasoning, if you will look for it."

She descended with what grace she could muster from the chariot. On the banquette, she turned, ignoring the curious stares of those around her as she answered him in scathing tones. "If I discover it, I will let you know."

"Do," he said with the greatest affability, and, slapping the reins he held over the backs of his goats, rolled away.

There was no time to think about his meaning, however, or to regret the discord that always seemed to arise between them. Nor was there time to bend her mind in earnest to the reasons for the attack upon her. Servants, hanging out the attic windows of the house to watch the parade, had pulled in their heads and run screaming into the house with the news that she was found. She was met on the courtyard staircase by Celestine, her face red and blotched with tears. The other girl flew to throw her arms around Anya, while Emile and Murray came down more slowly behind her.

"Where were you?" Celestine cried. "We looked everywhere, but it was as if you had disappeared from the face of the earth! We only just now arrived back here to see if you had returned."

Anya explained as best she could between exclamations of horror, sympathy, and concern. By the time she was finished, Celestine was wringing her hands.

"But you might have been killed, or worse! I can't think how we came to be separated so completely, except that we turned aside to look at a cunning bonnet in a shopwindow, then saw ahead of us another woman in a costume similar to yours so that we thought you had passed us by. I told Emile and Murray that it wasn't you, that you wouldn't wear that cloth thing over your head like a washerwoman, but they insisted."

"A thousand regrets, Mademoiselle Anya," Emile said, his gaze earnest as he possessed himself of her hand. "I will never forgive myself for leaving you, for exposing you to such fear and anguish. But how intrepid of you to defeat them. I am all admiration! Never, but never, have I heard the like."

"If you two are going to make such a fuss," Murray said in practical tones, "you might at least let her come into the salon where she can sit down."

"Indeed, yes," Madame Rosa said from the landing. "I'm sure she is exhausted after such excitement. And I believe we could all do with a restorative."

The tale had to be told again, with embellishments, for her stepmother. Celestine, a distraught court lady, sat on the settee beside Anya, holding her hand as if she meant never to let go of her again. Madame Rosa occupied a sturdy chair nearby, with Gaspard, his face creased with worry, behind her chair. Murray had removed the black domino that he had worn over his normal clothing. He sat on Celestine's other side, while Emile took a side chair, sitting forward with his elbows on his knees, his embroidered gauntlets and his cavalier's hat thrown aside, and with his soft brown curls in disarray.

"How fortunate Duralde was able to come to your aid," Gaspard said.

"Yes, he was quite the hero," Murray agreed.

Emile struck himself on the knee. "I should have been there!"

Anya looked down at the glass of dry sherry that had been placed in her hand. Ringing in her mind was Ravel's suggestion that she consider who might benefit from her disappearance. It was unbelievable that any of the people in that room would harm her. She knew them so well. They were the warp and woof of her life. With the possible exception of Emile, it was inconceivable that they should not always be there.

It was true, of course, that there might be some cause for envy against her. She was her father's principal heir. The laws of succession in Louisiana were based on the French laws of the Napoleonic Code that had been devised from old Roman law. They set up strict guidelines for the division of property, protecting women and children and making it impossible for a man to disinherit his family. Property that was acquired during a marriage was considered to belong to both man and wife equally. On the death of either spouse, half the property went to the children. Therefore, on the death of Anya's mother, Anya had inherited half of Beau Refuge. On the death of her father, his second wife, Madame Rosa, retained use of any monies accumulated during her marriage to Anya's father, but the remaining half of the plantation itself had been divided equally between Anya and Celestine. Anya, therefore, owned three-quarters of Beau Refuge, three-quarters of her father's fortune. Even the townhouse had been bought by Anya since her father's death, for the pleasure of Madame Rosa and Celestine. Anya called it her stepmother's in her mind because Madame Rosa stayed there far more than she did and had supervised the furnishing of it, but in truth her stepmother and half sister might be said to be living on Anya's charity.

There had never at any time been any sign of resentment for that fact. She had always been generous with the profits Beau Refuge engendered, had even depended for many years on Madame Rosa's sane and sensible advice for investment of them. Neither her stepmother nor her half sister had the least desire to usurp her place. It was, in fact, much more comfortable for them to allow her to do the work that provided the means for them to live.

As for the others, Emile was simply Jean's younger brother. He might have a grudge against Ravel, but that had nothing to do with her. It was true she hardly knew him; he had been away so long and had seldom been a part of her circle, still what she had seen of him she liked. Murray was Celestine's beloved fiancé, a nice, ordinary man from a nice, ordinary Midwest background. He had a great deal of quiet charm, and modest ambitions in his work as a law office clerk; he intended to stand for the bar soon and had mentioned the possibility of going into politics. If he was not particularly suave nor voluble in the manner of Creole gentlemen, he pleased Celestine, which was recommendation enough.

Then there was Gaspard, fastidious, elegant Gaspard, who did not appreciate Murray and who kept a quadroon mistress on Rampart Street while assiduously playing the part of faithful and indispensable escort to Madame Rosa. What reason he might have had to see Anya dead during the gin fire she could not fathom, but it was possible he realized she was aware of his quadroon, possible also that it was a secret he would go to great lengths to keep. Still, if that were so, surely the man would not have used his love cottage as a meeting place? For all the masculine humor concerning the impossibility of women keeping a secret, men were hardly more likely to hold such information sacred.

Anya, studying Gaspard as she considered his case, recognized suddenly that he was watching her with a pensive and rather ironic gaze. She looked away and, propelled by a peculiar embarrassment, came to her feet. "It's sweet of all of you to be concerned, but I truly don't need coddling; I'm perfectly all right, I assure you. Isn't it about time we made ready for the ball?"

Celestine did not release her hand. "You are sure you feel like going?"

"I wouldn't dream of missing it, nor would I think of depriving any of you. I feel terrible enough already for being the cause of most of you failing to see the parade of Comus properly. It was—quite beautiful."

"We will have to hurry if we are to be in time to see the tableaux" Madame Rosa said.

"Exactly my point," Anya declared, her brisk air only a little strained around the edges. "Has anyone ordered the carriage?"

Her ball gown was of soft teal blue satin with a black lace bertha, a black satin waistband accenting the waist, and rosettes of black lace around the hem of the enormously full skirt. There was no time for an elaborate hair arrangement; she had her maid dress it in deep waves around her face and a simple figure eight at the back decorated with a spray of teal blue velvet leaves tied with black steamers. Her jewelry was a parure of aquamarines and diamonds that included earrings, necklace, and a pair of bracelets. Anya was standing, allowing her maid to fasten the right bracelet, when it suddenly came to her what Ravel had meant by his parting words so short a time before.

She had accused him of proposing a marriage, using the conventions as an excuse, to gain the respectability he could not have in any other way. What was it she had said, something about wanting the things one could not have? For him, however, the subject had not been respectability, but herself. He had wanted her. And yet, the painful truth was that he had already possessed her in the physical sense, therefore he had proposed marriage in order to make the possession permanent. In his peculiar way, he was saying his motive for requesting her hand had been desire, just that and nothing more.

She did not know whether to be gratified or enraged or pained, and was in fact each in turn. One thing was certain: despite her blithe promise to inform Ravel when she had discovered his meaning, she would not be mentioning the matter to him.

The enormous hoops worn this season under ball gowns were collapsible, still there was scarcely room for more than two ladies with them on in a single carriage. For comfort's sake, Madame Rosa did not aspire to such enormous width, she claimed to believe such ostentation unbecoming in a widow. Her embonpoint was such, however, that she needed at least half a seat so as not to feel crowded. It was usual then for only four persons, two ladies and two gentlemen, to ride in a carriage. The Hamilton party had for some time contained the awkward number of five, three of them ladies; therefore two carriages were needed for most outings. Their number was ordinarily divided so that Murray and Celestine could ride together in the Hamilton carriage with Anya as chaperone, while Madame Rosa and Gaspard came on in a second carriage belonging to the dapper Frenchman. The addition of Emile caused complications. He had shown no sign of feeling the odd man out, and so it was to be assumed that he had constituted himself Anya's escort for the evening also. How then was their party to be allotted carriage space? There seemed no help for it but to separate Gaspard and Madame Rosa.

It had been much more simple in the old days, Anya thought as she proceeded toward the salon with her evening cape over her arm, when everyone walked to the ballroom with a maid behind her carrying her dancing slippers.

"How prompt you are," Gaspard said, turning from the window as she moved into the room, "and how lovely. We have been assigned to the first carriage, along with M'sieur Girod. We will go as soon as he returns so that seats may be saved at the theater for Madame Rosa and Mademoiselle Celestine. I fear time may be critical; it's going to be terribly crowded.''

Anya agreed easily enough. The arrangement might not be what she would have chosen, but it was logical. A small silence fell. In an effort to make conversation, Anya said, "How late it seems, to be setting out.''

"Yes, the result of waiting for darkness to begin the parade. Everyone must see it first before attending the ball, and you must admit it is much more impressive by torchlight.''

"Oh, yes. The effect would not have been at all the same without it.''

She sounded as ill at ease as she felt. Why did not some of the others come? She straightened the folds of her wrap, a cape of black velvet. Her head came up in sudden alarm as Gaspard took a deliberate stride toward her.

"Come, Mademoiselle Anya, this will not do. We have known each other too long for this tiptoeing around. You obviously feel you know something to my discredit and are being painfully discreet. Come and sit down and let us discuss it.''

"You—you want to talk about it, to me?''

His thin lips moved in a wry smile. "It's not something of which I am ashamed, and I pay you the compliment of thinking that you will understand.''

Because she was not precisely an innocent herself? No, she must not be quite so cynical. Moving to the settee, she maneuvered her skirts so as not to crush them and seated herself.

"I believe—that is, I am led to understand,'' he said, sitting on the edge of his chair and crossing one ankle over the other, "that you saw me at the home of my mistress.''

Anya inclined her head in agreement.

"The woman has been under my protection for some time, since we were hardly more than children. Such arrangements usually end when a man marries; I never married.''

"But you have been escorting Madame Rosa for years!''

"True. One thing does not exclude the other.''

"Are you saying you love both of them?''

"In different ways,'' he agreed, unperturbed.

"Indeed.''

"You need not scoff. One is comfortable, uncomplicated,

quite earthy, the other stimulating to the mind but soothing to the soul."

Which was which? Anya stared at him, fascinated by this glimpse into the complicated emotional life of a man who had always seemed so simple. "What if you were to marry Madame Rosa?"

"That hardly seems likely."

"Why not? Have you ever proposed?"

"The time never seemed right."

"Oh, come, that isn't much of an excuse!"

"Perhaps not," he agreed, "but I have never cared to jeopardize the standing I have with her."

"So you do nothing."

"Does that seem cowardly? I assure you I have thought so myself often enough."

"It seems," Anya said forthrightly, "as if you were loath to disturb the nice arrangement you had established for yourself."

"I can see why you think so, but can you tell me, this moment, whether Madame Rosa would accept me if I were to chance the question?"

Anya opened her mouth, then shut it again. A frown drew her brows together. With surprise, she discovered that she could not with confidence give him the assurance he seemed to require. "You will never know unless you try."

"Yes, but my fortune is not large, my home not so impressive as Beau Refuge. What have I to offer her except my homage?"

"Your love?"

"And if that is not enough?"

"If it is, what then? What of the woman on Rampart Street?"

"I have not visited her at night, except for the meetings, for five years. She would not be surprised to receive a settlement, though for now she serves to protect Madame Rosa from the malicious tongues of the gossips."

Devotion took strange forms. So did confidences. Anya could find nothing to say to the one she had just been given. She grasped at the reminder of other involvements.

"These meetings, what is their purpose? What is it about them that caused the police to put a stop to the one that night?"

"I can't tell you that."

"You mean you won't."

"If it pleases you to put it that way. It would be best if you applied to Duralde for an answer."

Madame Rosa, moving with a stride that was quiet for her size, spoke as she came into the room. "An answer to what?"

"Ah, *chérie*, utterly chic as always," Gaspard said, rising without haste and going toward his inamorata. "An answer? Why, to the question of what Comus means to do next year to surpass this evening's spectacle."

The carriage ride to the theater seemed long. The earlier events had cast a pall over the evening. Anya's two escorts, Emile and Gaspard, were solicitous, but not talkative. The vehicle swayed over the flour- and confetti-strewn streets. Celebration of the day was still going on, though with less joy. Women and children had gone inside for the most part. The maskers they passed were mostly young men or members of the rougher element.

Their carriage rolled in and out of the thin yellow pools of gaslight, the flickering radiance striking in peculiar angles of light and shadow across their faces. Anya caught herself glancing often at her stepmother's favorite escort. The things he had said disturbed her mind. He had not slept with his quadroon mistress for five years. Did he mean to imply then that he reserved that pleasure for Madame Rosa? It seemed so strange to think of it, but looking back, Anya knew it was possible. Five years of discretion. Five years of pretense. The course of love, it appeared, did not grow smoother as one grew older. Pride and stubbornness were not restricted to the young; if anything they hardened into more rigid masks to hide behind. Desire was balanced by an equal and paralyzing fear of rejection that must lead to self-ridicule.

But to think of Gaspard, so urbane and pleasant and sartorially perfect, silently coming and going, silently pleasing and taking pleasure in Madame Rosa while concealing his love for her. So many years slipping away, safe but only half-lived. And Madame Rosa herself in her constant black, declining into complacent widowhood, not knowing how he felt. It was pathetic when all that was needed was a bit of forthrightness.

All?

There was no risk greater than forthrightness concerning matters of the heart. She loved Ravel, but it was impossible for her to go to him, not knowing how he felt in return; impossible to say, "I've changed my mind, I will marry you after all." There was no guarantee that he still wished to be her husband, or that if he did, it would be for the right reason.

Reasons. Anya leaned her head back against the velvet seat and closed her eyes. Desire was the one he gave, but was it so uncomplicated? Could it not be he wanted her also for revenge, for position, to right the wrong he had done to her as convention demanded, to expiate his guilt over Jean's death, to gain control of Beau Refuge, to reestablish his mother if not himself, even perhaps to save her from the menace he had caused?

Ravel might once have been a straightforward young man. However, driven by the past, he had become a hardened mercenary and an opportunist. He had become rich and gained a degree of power. Far from being the outcast she once had thought, he seemed to have found his way to the inner circles of American business and social community as epitomized by the Mistick Krewe of Comus. It would not be unusual if in the process he had come to feel that his desires were paramount, that any way of achieving them was perfectly valid.

That being the case, perhaps she had been right, no matter how he tried to deny it. Perhaps the attack and his rescue of her this evening were too timely indeed. Perhaps she was supposed to be frightened into turning to her protector. How desperately he must want her, then.

Gratitude had been mistaken before for love; was it possible that was what she felt now, what she had been meant to feel?

And if she did truly care for Ravel, if it was love that caused her such pain at this moment, could she allow herself to be used as he wished? If he should ask again, could she marry him in the hope that what she felt could counterbalance all the old wrongs and the betrayals, and that with the heat of the passion that could flare between them they might forge a life worth living?

Chapter Seventeen

🎐 🎐 🎐 *Crisp's Gaiety Theater had closed during the* winter and reopened under new management and with a new name. Officially the Varieties Theatre, it was still known affectionately, to a populace unused to the change, as the Gaiety. Whatever it might be called, a vast number of people had converged upon it this evening. The press of carriages was so great it was difficult to get near the door. Around the entrance, the crowd of uninvited persons clamoring for admittance, including ladies in elaborate toilettes shaking their fists and screaming like apple women, was so thick that Anya felt lucky that her card of invitation was not torn from her hands and that she and Gaspard and Emile were able to push inside without having their clothes ripped from their backs. The near hysteria outside was ample indication, if any was needed, that this was the year's most fabulous social gathering.

It was not the only ball of consequence by any means. Most of Creole society was at the Orleans Theater where another glittering *bal masqué* was in progress. The Young Men's Benevolent Society was also holding a mask-and-fancy-dress ball where, it was rumored, members would appear in the scarlet silk costumes of Chinese mandarins of the Celestial Empire Club for a series of drills and pantomimes. There had been cards available for both these other affairs, but it had been decided that the Comus Ball offered the most exciting prospect for the evening.

Within the walls of the theater, the orchestra that played lilting melodies was nearly drowned out by the hum of voices. The tiers of seats above the wooden floor that covered the parquet sparkled and glittered with jewels and silk and satin from the gowns of the ladies. There was scarce a dark color to be seen, for the gentlemen were all either taking refuge in the refreshment room, called the ''crush-room'' or else standing at the back of the boxes to permit their wives and daughters the comfort of the chairs. Along those rows of white shoulders and brilliant and costly gowns there was a constant movement as the ladies plied their fans in the warmth caused by the mild day, the mass of bodies, and the heat of the gaslights.

The assigned seats for the Hamilton party, in a box very nearly on the stage itself, were taken as Gaspard had feared. It seemed that budging the occupants, the stout wife and two plump nieces of an American planter from upriver, might be an impossible task, but Emile managed it by dint of excellent manners and guile. As they stood near the box, he discussed the best seating in the most idle of conversation, but in a carrying voice. It was so warm near the dress circle where the lights were brightest, was it not? Quite stifling as the theater became crowded, and of course it was a good distance from the exits in case of fire or other catastrophe. Theaters burned with distressing frequency; it was taking one's life into one's hands to attend at all. And it was such a short time ago, a matter of a few years, that the floor over the parquet had collapsed at a ball, killing and maiming several ladies while a number of others had been trampled in the panic because they were so far from the exit. *Sacrebleu*, but he had not realized the young ladies from the country were listening; he would not have alarmed them for anything! But he did know where there were three chairs quite near a window. He would personally escort the younger ladies, one on either arm, if they cared to see them?

One niece was plain and mousy, the other rather bold, with china blue eyes, white-blond curls, and a tendency to simper and flutter her lashes. They were neither of them immune to Gallic charm when administered with all the bows and complimentary flourishes that Emile could assume. They moved. Anya and Gaspard took their places. Anya spread her cape on one chair and placed her fan and opera glasses on the other. She was not sanguine about her ability to hold off a determined feminine invasion, even with Emile's aid, but she intended to try.

The siege was brief. Celestine and Madame Rosa arrived in short order. Emile and Gaspard remained talking and pointing out acquaintances until the ladies were settled, then prepared to take their leave, to go and repair their forces in the crushroom. Murray was inclined to remain behind, until Celestine told him frankly that he might as well go as stand over her, cutting off the air. The gentlemen were not out of sight before a girl Celestine's age, with whom she had attended convent school, waved from the next box then pranced around to show them the ruby betrothal bracelet she had just received.

Madame Rosa, taking advantage of Celestine's lack of attention as she gossiped with her friend, turned her back on her daughter. To Anya she said, "Now you may tell me without the trouble of evasion what you and Gaspard were talking of earlier."

Anya searched her mind, saying in a vague, rather offhand manner, "We were speaking of Ravel, and the marvelous parade."

"Please do not dissemble, Anya. I may be approaching middle age, but my hearing is most acute. I distinctly heard some mention of my name and the question of marriage in the same breath."

Gaspard had not asked it, but Anya knew he expected her to keep his confidence. She would have liked to do so, but Madame Rosa had been her friend and confidante for many years, the repository of her childish secrets, sharer of her girlish wedding plans, and listener to her adult strategies for making Beau Refuge produce more handsomely. It was not easy to withstand her.

"It wasn't important," she said.

"I disagree. It disturbs me to think of you and Gaspard talking of me behind my back."

"It wasn't like that. It was just—just idle conversation."

"If that's so, why won't you tell me what was said?"

"Gaspard would not be pleased. Perhaps it would be best if you asked him," Anya said, a shade desperately.

"I shall, never doubt it, but I would also like to hear it from you."

Anya frowned. "Surely you don't think there was anything clandestine between us—it's too ridiculous!"

"Then you will explain to me what makes it so," Madame Rosa said with patient tenacity.

An idea flickered across Anya's mind. It seemed to present an avenue of escape, or at least a means to gain information she wanted in exchange for her betrayal of Gaspard. "There is something that has been troubling me. I asked you about it once, but you could not seem to clarify the problem. Perhaps now that you have had time to think about it, you can."

Madame Rosa pursed her lips, then said with caution, "It's possible."

"It concerns Ravel and the words he said to you in connection with his proposal of marriage. Explain them to me, and I will tell you what Gaspard said."

If she had hoped that Madame Rosa would demur for the sake of protecting Ravel, allowing her to protect Gaspard in return, she underestimated her. Madame Rosa sacrificed Ravel at once. "Of course, if I can."

"It was when he was requesting my hand," Anya said, slowly bringing the scene into focus in her mind. "He said to you that he trusted you would 'remember recent obligations,' as if you would know what they were, as if you were obliged to him in some way important enough to sway you against your will to hear his suit."

Madame Rosa's features tightened, and almost in an involuntary movement, she looked over her shoulder at her daughter. "Yes. Yes, I remember."

Until she brought it to light again, Anya had not realized how disturbed she had been over that incident. Suddenly nothing was as important as learning the answer, not her future relationship with the man who might become Madame Rosa's husband, nothing. Anya felt her stomach knot inside her as she waited for her stepmother to continue. When she did not, she said in strained tones, "Well?"

"It is a matter of some delicacy, one that concerns other people."

"Of course," Anya had expected nothing less; still she frowned as Madame Rosa glanced over her shoulder once more.

"I think you know I have not been happy with my Celestine's choice for a husband."

"I knew you had asked her and Murray to wait before making a formal announcement," Anya answered with caution.

"I hoped the attachment would fade, end of its own accord as do so many. So far it has not."

"Celestine has a tender heart."

"Yes, and Murray is a most attentive lover. She can hardly breathe without him there."

Anya lifted her brows. "Is that a fault?"

"There may be few women who would call it one, still I cannot be happy with him for Celestine."

"But why? What is it about him you dislike?"

Madame Rosa shrugged plump shoulders, her smile wry. "I don't know. Perhaps it's because he wants to take my daughter from me. Perhaps it's because he's an *américain*, instead of a Creole, and lacks polish. Perhaps it's because he reminds me of an ill-trained puppy, boundlessly fond, always underfoot, and prone to chewing the legs of the furniture when your back is turned."

Anya could not help laughing. "Come, Madame Rosa!"

"It was only a fancy. Still, I thought that if Celestine saw her young man in a situation of some delicacy, one where the need for courage and the mien of a true gentlemen were paramount, she would discover he was not what she wanted, either."

Anya's mind leaped ahead to the obvious conclusion. "The challenge at the St. Charles Theater ball."

Madame Rosa gave a heavy nod.

"But how was it arranged? How did you persuade Ravel to act?"

"That part was simplicity itself. I sent him a note, asking him to call. When he came, I told him what I wanted, that I wished him to force a quarrel upon Murray. At first he refused; it was against his principles. Then he learned that I knew of the meetings he and Gaspard were attending."

"You know?" Anya leaned quickly to catch the older woman's arm.

"*Chère*, you are hurting! Of course I know."

"What are they for, what is the purpose?"

"Gaspard told me it was for the Vigilance Committee. I see no reason to doubt him."

"Vigilance—" Of course. The group of men opposed to the corrupt Know-Nothing party. Anya was flooded by a relief so immense that tears sprang into her eyes. A moment later, they died away. "I can't believe Ravel would allow himself to be blackmailed."

"Nonetheless, he did just that. It was his idea to approach Murray through you. Celestine seemed the obvious choice, but he thought that while a man will rise to fight for his fiancée as a natural thing, he will be more likely to back off from a challenge over his fiancée's sister, particularly a half sister. And yet Celestine's affection for you is such that she would be deeply offended by such a failure."

Anya nodded. So now she knew what the obligation was, knew also why Ravel had broken the unspoken pact that had existed between them all those years, the pact not to see or speak to one another. Why was she not happier?

"You were wrong," she said. "Murray rose wonderfully to the challenge. He was every inch the protector."

"Yes," Madame Rosa said with a sigh.

"How could you do it? One of them might have been killed, and at your instigation. How could you have lived with yourself?"

"I never thought Murray would screw his courage up to it, never intended it to actually come to a duel. Once the thing was put in motion, there seemed no way of stopping it. Except that you found a way. You intervened. You injured Ravel and destroyed his reputation, leaving me under even more of an obligation to the man. How could I refuse my permission for him to address you then? It was impossible."

"He made it so."

"You abetted him."

"I can't think how you came to see Murray as a coward. Only remember how he shot the man that night when those thugs attacked our carriage."

"Apparently I was wrong," Madame Rosa said, her voice carrying an unusual snap. "And now you must tell me what it was that Gaspard was saying to you."

Anya hesitated only a moment. She had agreed, and she could not deny that it would be interesting to see her stepmother's reaction. "In the main, he was telling me all the reasons why he had never asked you to marry him."

"He likes matters just as they stand, with his social and private lives neatly separated, with me in one and his quadroon in the other."

"You know about her?"

"I am not a fool."

"Perhaps not, but you are wrong about Gaspard, also." A qualm assailed Anya for what she was about to do. To meddle in other people's lives was never wise.

"Am I?"

"He would ask you to be his wife if he thought you would accept. His quadroon is no more than a screen to protect your good name. He loves you."

What Anya expected Madame Rosa to say or do, she could not have said. To blush and stammer was not in the older woman's character, any more than violent rage and fulsome threats would be. Still she had somehow anticipated something more than she received.

"Does he? Does he indeed?" Madame Rosa said. With that she turned away, unfurling her fan to wave it languidly before her face as she listened to the chatter of her daughter and her friend.

Anya was left to her own thoughts. Ravel and Gaspard, members of the clandestine Committee of Vigilance. Could it be true, or had it been only a tale concocted to pacify Madame Rosa? Would the present administration, with its stranglehold on the city, be so bothered by the activities of a small group of men such as she had seen at the house of the quadroon that the police would be sent to break it up?

Vigilance. The word implied watchfulness, unceasing care. No doubt the motives of some of the committee were of the highest, and yet, it might be nothing more than an excuse to wrest the law from the public appointed officials and administer it themselves. What, in such a case, was to prevent them from bending it to suit their own purposes? Could they be trusted not to use it to enforce their personal prejudices, to pursue their personal vendettas, to accomplish their personal gain? It could not be denied, however, that it was time something was done. There was such chaos in the government that those elected to administer it were using it to do precisely all those things she feared the Vigilance Committee might do, except on a larger scale. The officials were for the most part Americans, men who had come to make their fortunes in the richest seaport in the world, men who had used the rough-and-tumble tactics of Northern politics to push aside the Creoles who ran for public office as a duty, not a career; to take over the slow-moving, laissez-faire system of hotheaded arguments followed by genial agreements over coffee and wine and to whip it into something more nearly resembling a bull-and-bear fight, noisy, bloody, and without finesse. And of late they had taken to hamstringing the bull to be certain the call went in favor of the bear.

But if Ravel was indeed a member of this secret committee, how did that explain the men who had tried to kill him? Or her? Was there any connection between the thugs at Beau Refuge and those who had held up the carriage in which she had been riding on the night they had seen Charlotte Cushman as Queen Katherine? Could that possibly have been an attempt on her life, just as the attack of the Arabs had been later?

No. She must not give way to such uncontrolled fantasies. Robbery had been the sole purpose of that first attack. It had come because they had strayed into the back streets while avoiding the jam of carriages near the theater. There was no need to look for deeper explanations; it had been merest happenstance.

Her attention was distracted by the appearance of a man on the wide theater stage below. For some time there had been discreet bumps and scraping sounds behind the velvet curtains that closed it off. Now all was quiet.

As the audience noticed the tall man in evening clothes on the stage, the sound of voices and whispering, the rustling noise made by a large, anxious gathering died away to a few quiet coughs.

The man lifted a gold flutelike whistle to his lips and blew a long and melodious note. At the top of his voice he cried, "When you next hear that sound, it will be the signal for the midnight repast. Now it heralds the opening of the Second Annual Tableaux Ball of the Mistick Krewe of Comus. As captian of the Krewe I bid you welcome and wish you joy of the Mardi Gras season. Let the revels begin! Behold, the gods and goddesses in their appointed places!"

With one arm outflung, the captain backed away from the center of the stage. The curtain swished open. Drawn-out cries of pleasure sounded everywhere as a scene of glorious light, brilliant color, and beauty appeared before them. In this first tableau, entitled *Minerva's Victory*, perhaps a quarter of the deities seen that day were presented in reverse order of the parade, all with their mythological background scenery and other symbols of their divinity around them. Gilded and burnished, heaped with flowers and surrounded by fearsome and beautiful beasts, they stood in poses of grandeur or hauteur. Above each one was the beautiful painted transparency lighted from behind that identified him.

So it went as the tableaux, one after the other—*Flight of Time, Bacchanalian Revel, Comus Krewe and Procession*—till the total of four, were unveiled. It was like seeing life-sized works of art, each magnificently staged for the maximum effect to be gained by color and proportion and the mix of the good and the evil, the sublime and ludicrous.

What prodigies of effort had been expended, what sums of money had been squandered to present this illusion. There were those who shook their heads and muttered under their breaths, "What a waste, what a waste." But there were others who watched with bright, glowing eyes and full hearts, accepting the joy of the moment and the sheer wonder of the creative flight, celebrating the glory of being alive and a part of the magic.

Slowly the voices of the audience rose again.

"See, there is a bat, such a monster he is!"

"Look at the swans!"

"Poor Atlas, carrying such a heavy weight."

"Pegasus does look just as if he could fly!"

"How did they do it? How did they do it?"

Ravel was in the next to last tableau. Anya sat and watched him in his costume of the goat-god Pan that should have been ridiculous but was not, and a smile that she could not seem to banish played around her mouth. What a fine god of love he made, as handsome as such a god should be, and yet unsettling in his darkness as love itself was unsettling. The pose he had assumed was perfect, both beseeching and threatening, tender and lascivious. He moved not a muscle; still the fluttering lantern light of his transparency shone gold on the vine leaves twined in his blue-black hair, and polished to the sheen of brass the planes of his chest, glinting among the fine dark whorls of hair that grew there.

He did not see her, could not look anywhere but straight ahead as he held his stance, and she was grateful. Why did she have to love him? Why did the mere sight of him make her burn with the kind of yearning she had hardly dreamed of less than two weeks ago? She felt drawn to him, as if to be apart were wrong, as if she had never been quite free of him for seven long years. It was almost as if they were caught, both of them, in something beyond their control, perhaps one of those old myths of love and hate, jealousy and destruction, played out for the amusement of a vain god, and from which the only escape was death.

At last the curtains closed. The music, softly playing all this time, swelled. Next would come the march of the maskers. Excitement suddenly crackled like lightning around the room. The ladies, both young and old, in the tiers of boxes straightened, patting their hair and smoothing their flounces. Some of them would be chosen as partners for the costumed members of the Krewe in their parade around the room. Afterward they would break from the march to dance. There were rules, however. No gentleman in evening wear could descend to the floor; no gentleman in costume could ascend to the boxes. The way that ladies were chosen was by having their names called out by the captain so that they might descend to meet the man hidden behind his mask who had chosen them.

The grand march led by Comus began, the maskers making a circuit of the floor to provide one last full look at their grandeur. There was a brief pause; then the first lady's name was called.

There were shy smiles of embarrassment, cries of delight, and squeals of triumph as one by one the ladies took their places. Some were wives, some daughters and nieces, some, since the Krewe was young, were mothers. Most were sweethearts, each giving the man who met her at the edge of the parquet a close, questioning look, as if to be certain he was who she expected. It was entertaining to watch them, and to laugh at the confusion as the club members assigned to the task of finding the ladies called by the captain scurried here and there, repeating the call again and again, until they were red in the face and wore identical looks of harassment to the point of near apoplexy. It was difficult not to smile at the expressions of anxiety of pique or assumed indifference on the faces of the ladies as they waited to see if they would be chosen or left to sit alone and deserted when the music began.

"Miss Hamilton! Miss Anya Hamilton!"

The call started some distance away and came closer. Anya went still. Ravel. She had not expected it, not after the way they had parted. The call came again. She sat paralyzed. What could he be thinking of, to link her name with his so publicly after all the gossip? There was little hope that people would not recognize him. Compared to the others, he had scarcely any costume or mask on at all.

Madame Rosa nudged her. "What are you waiting for? Go on."

"How can I?"

"It's carnival time. How can you not?"

How indeed? Anya rose to her feet and made her way down from the box. Ravel waited at the edge of the floor. As she saw him, her heart started to pound. Her fingers trembled slightly as she placed them on his wrist that he offered correctly, formally, to her.

He inclined his head, his gaze warm as it moved over her, noting the faint flush across her cheekbones and the way the teal of her gown reflected in her eyes; the proud tilt of her head and the soft hollow between her breasts revealed by her décolletage. He had not been sure she would come down; it wouldn't have surprised him if he had been left standing there without a partner when the march began. He felt as if he had won a victory, though he was not sure over what. Now if he could only manage to prevent himself from mauling her here under the fascinated gaze of the old ladies in the boxes, and, incidentally, dance in some fashion in these damned boots made like cloven hooves, he might count Lady Luck on his side once more. Turning, he led her out to where the line of march was forming.

"I suppose you know," Anya said in low tones, "that you

have just confirmed all the worst suspicions of everyone who has heard of our peculiar escapade."

"I thought I figured as the gallant rescuer of your family home? What could be more natural than that, having seen you in delicious dishabille battling the flames, I am now enamored?"

"Dishabille? I was fully clothed and you know it!"

"I do, but all the busybodies with the busy imaginations weren't privileged to see you as I was, and it's their duty to think the worst. Besides, it was only by the most fortunate stroke of timing that you—"

"Never mind! If you can't be brought to see that this is doing neither of us any good, then you can't. I won't waste my breath on you."

"Good. You can tell me instead if you have discovered the error of your thinking. And you had better stop glaring at me, or you will give the busybodies even more indecent ideas."

She gave him a smile of molasses sweetness. "I realized very soon what you meant, but I have yet to make up my mind which is worse, to have received a duty proposal or one that sprang only from your overheated male needs."

The march began. With the couple following them treading on their heels and the one before them lagging behind, it was a moment before he could answer. When he did, there was resignation in his tone.

"I should have known that you would put the worst possible construction on anything I said."

"In this case it was already there! But you need not trouble to repeat the offer. You will no longer find an ally in Madame Rosa. I know why she did not refuse to allow your suit last time, why she spoke for you. Such blackmail, as clever as you may think it, won't work a second time."

"Now who," he asked, his voice deadly in its softness, "said there would be a second time?"

"Oh, won't there be? Then I am very much obliged to you!" Her eyes were as dark and cold as the ocean's depths.

"You have not, I trust, allowed Murray to learn Madame Rosa's part in the arrangement that led to our clash?"

"Certainly not!"

"Good. I somehow doubt that he would be properly understanding. It would be the very thing to bring him after me, breathing righteous fire and determined to take up where we left off."

"I wish that I had permitted him to meet you! I doubt that you would be so smug now." No one was able to make her quite so angry as this man. No one.

"No, indeed," he said with the greatest goodwill. "With any luck at all, I might even be dead."

The march was over. The orchestra plunged immediately into a waltz and the marchers broke up, turning to each other and moving close to glide away on the music. Ravel gave her no chance to refuse the dance. He clamped his left hand at the slender turn of Anya's waist and clasped her left hand in his right. They swung into the waltz, moving, swaying, turning together, their bodies perfectly attuned.

Dead? The word gave Anya a cold feeling deep inside. No, it could not be. He was so vital; he had such strength both in body and mind. That it could all be ended in an instant did not seem possible. But it was possible. Like the pagan god he personified, once so powerful, he could cease to be. Nothing would remain except the memory of him in the minds of a few and some carved letters on a tombstone.

What then of the love she felt, the love that, like her heart, beat inside her as if frantic to escape? What would happen, she wondered, if she suddenly said, "I love you, Ravel"? Would he believe her? And if he did, would he laugh? Would he take advantage of her? Would he be unmoved, or worst of all, moved only to pity?

He was not the only half-dressed man in the room—there were the fauns who had accompanied him and the satyrs of Bacchus—but he was easily the most magnificent. Half the women in the boxes had their opera glasses trained upon him, and most of them would cheerfully sacrifice their good names for the honor of being called out by him at this Comus ball.

What was there about women that, no matter how staid they pretended to be, delighted in a rake? Like moths to a flame, they enjoyed fluttering near the danger. She must not be a silly moth.

''Is your mother here tonight?'' she asked, running her gaze over the women in the boxes once more.

''I could not persuade her.''

''She wasn't too ill to come?''

''No, no. The truth is, her literary circle meets this evening and she preferred to be there. Her illness is more of an inconvenience than a bar to doing what she wishes. Her heart is a little weak, possibly, but I've discovered that it gets weaker when there is something she wants me to do.''

''Such as remaining in New Orleans instead of joining William Walker in Nicaragua last fall?''

''The very thought brought on severe palpitations. She's a wise lady, if a little devious.''

The warmth in his voice gave Anya a curious feeling in the region of her heart. ''Your mother saw the parade, I suppose?''

''She did, and pronounced my costume vulgar but effective.''

''A woman of taste,'' Anya said, her tone demure.

Effective it certainly was. To be so close to him in public while he was half-naked was making her feel decidedly overheated, a heat that seemed to radiate from the lower part of her body, affecting her as if he were mighty Pan himself.

Ravel, glancing down at the soft color across her cheekbones, murmured, ''I'm glad you like it.''

Anya searched her mind for something, anything, to change the subject. ''I don't believe I thanked you for coming so gallantly to my rescue this afternoon.''

He shook his head. ''You will do so now at your own peril.''

''My life means a great deal to me; it would be the basest ingratitude not to express my appreciation.''

''It also means much to me.''

She absorbed that in silence as they whirled with her gown belling out around them, almost obscuring the lower part of his body in teal silk. His forest green cloak swung from his shoulders, and the metallic cord that held it, his mask, and the leaves of his crown caught the lamplight so that together they made a swirling kaleidoscope of grace and color and bright gold reflections.

Slowly there grew between them a sense of unity, of restraints lifting, enmity receding. They moved with one accord, as if every muscle and fiber was guided by the same impulse. However much or little else there might be between them, this physical harmony could not be denied. It carried its own pleasure, its own genuine gratification.

His arms were strong, his hold and his movements sure, his feel for the rhythm true. For that brief space of time Anya gave herself up to him with inescapable and implicit trust. He would not betray her or himself here, this she knew.

Lightly, tirelessly, she floated in his arms, following him by instinct and with precision, so that to Ravel she seemed a part of him, bone of his bone, flesh of his flesh, as if parting would be a severance. He never wanted to let her go. Never in this life.

It was right, a perfect melding, a free blending of spirit and mind and body, a thing of fate and unconscious will, grand and beautiful. It was also impossible to sustain.

The music ended. There was a spattering of applause. Around Anya and Ravel the dancers made polite noises and began to move toward the boxes as each lady was escorted back to her seat. Dazed and reluctant, Anya and Ravel stepped back from each other. Once more Anya placed her hand on his wrist. She glanced up at the box and saw Celestine sitting with her elbows propped on the railing and a look of longing on her face. Madame Rosa was gossiping with a friend while Gaspard hovered behind her. Murray and Emile were nowhere in sight.

To break the strained silence that gripped them, Anya said, "What a pity Celestine isn't able to dance."

"There's something wrong with her?"

"No, no, only that she knows no one here except Murray and Emile, who are in evening wear and may not take the floor."

"I could have her called out."

She looked at him sharply, but his attention was on the shadowy alcove toward which they were moving, the alcove that held the short flight of steps leading to the box. "You could, of course, but would it be prudent?"

"I'm growing a little tired of being prudent."

"I thought a moment ago you were worrying about Murray's righteous anger?"

"A moment ago you were also wishing me on the field with

him. Tell me, if such a thing really happened, what would you do this time to save him?''

"Don't talk nonsense!''

"Perhaps it's sense. Perhaps it would be better to go back to where we began and make an end of it.'' He looked down at her, his eyes through the slits of his mask dark and opaque.

"You're trying to frighten me.''

"Would you be frightened, Anya?''

"You swore you would never be the one to force the issue between you and Murray!'' There was a tightness in her chest, so that she could not get her breath.

"Nor will I be. All I propose is a waltz, or perhaps a polka, with a lady who is being neglected.''

"It's sheer provocation!''

He smiled with wicked charm, though there was something watchful behind his eyes. "Now, if I were to take you in my arms and, while tasting your sweet lips, release about half the buttons of that lovely but constricting gown you are wearing, that would be provocation.''

"That,'' she said between her teeth, "would be suicide. I would kill you myself.''

"It might be worth it.''

They were nearing the alcove. As if driven, Anya said, "Ravel, you really wouldn't provoke Murray, would you?''

"Give me an alternative.''

"What do you mean?'' Something in his manner alerted her, so that she sent him a dark look.

"Promise me other, more personal, entertainment.''

The color drained from her face as she took his point. She waited for rage to erupt inside her, but instead there was only a spreading ache. There was something here she did not understand. His words, the way he said them, did not sound like him. It was as if he no longer cared what she thought, as if he wanted to offend her, and yet there was more to it than that.

Who was he, what was he really behind his mask? The gold metallic cloth of it gave him a hard, almost foreign appearance, as if she had never known him. It was like an ambush he was hiding behind, hiding from her, hiding from himself.

He sensed her withdrawal from him, the flicker of puzzled

fear within her, and knew a piercing regret. He almost reached out to her, but stilled the impulse, as he must. For an instant only he permitted himself to wonder what it would be like to have her concern directed toward him instead of against him. It was not a vision he could hold to for long.

In choked tones, Anya answered, "I'll see you damned first."

"You did that long ago, my darling Anya, so there's no need to hold yourself above what we both know would be a pleasure—"

She could not find an answer, but neither was one required. A man, his form obscured by the dimness until that moment, stepped from the alcove. It was Emile. His color was high and his eyes overbright, but his manner was exquisitely polite as he bowed.

"It's Duralde behind that mask, I believe, and annoying Mademoiselle Anya again. For too long you have persecuted her unchecked. It's time you were stopped."

Ravel's eyes widened a fraction and he breathed a soft oath as he faced Jean's young brother. A moment later, all visible signs that he had been taken by surprise were gone as he stood at ease in his outlandish costume. His voice was calm when he spoke.

"And you propose to do it?"

"If I must."

"Even knowing it will mean her ruin when the gossips are done? Your concern for her is touching beyond belief."

"Your continued pursuit will have the same effect."

"Meaning?" Ravel inquired, his tone soft.

"Meaning you are unfit to associate with her, unfit for any society except that of the *canailles américaine* such as those who have staged this affair tonight."

"Emile, no!" Anya cried, regaining her voice that shock and horror had taken from her.

"No, indeed," came the corroboration as Murray moved quickly down the steps and stepped onto the edge of the dance floor. "As an American, I take exception to being called such a name."

Emile barely glanced at him. "I will give you satisfaction when I am done with this renegade dog."

Anger came finally to Anya's rescue. "Don't be idiots, all of you! There is nothing whatever that requires this."

"I must request that you leave us, Mademoiselle Anya," Emile said, his tone polite. "This is not a thing of women."

"It certainly should be, since I am involved! It's ridiculous, barbaric, and I will not stand by and see any of you killed because of it, or because of me!"

"You cannot prevent it."

Gaspard, apparently attracted by the sound of raised voices, opened the door of the box and came down the alcove stairs to join them. His tone of voice quietly censorious as he surveyed the three younger men, he said, "What madness is this? You will disturb the ladies, to say nothing of doing Mademoiselle Anya irreparable harm."

"Yes," Emile said. "Let us go elsewhere."

"What's the point?" Murray asked. "We can settle this right here, right now. It's a question of who will take the dueling field first."

"Nonsense," Gaspard said testily. "Things are not done this way."

"I demand satisfaction," Murray insisted.

From behind them there came a cry. Celestine stood at the doorway of the box. She stared at the tense group below her, looking from one man to the other with her hands clamped to her mouth. Abruptly her knees gave way and she fell to the floor in a swoon.

Emile made an abortive gesture toward her, but halted as Madame Rosa went to the girl's aid. His face grave, he looked at Murray. "You may demand nothing at this point, m'sieur. That privilege belongs to Duralde."

"That is perfectly right," Gaspard approved.

"Spare me the punctilio," Ravel said to Emile. "I will not fight you."

"One assumes there is a reason?" Emile inquired.

"You are Jean's brother."

"An accident of birth. I am also Mademoiselle Anya's defender."

"It makes no difference."

"Perhaps it will make a difference if I assume that role,"

Murray said. "As her future brother-in-law I demand that right. Will you now meet me?"

"This is not possible," Emile said hotly, turning on Murray. "If you wish to issue a challenge, you must wait your turn."

"Gentlemen, gentlemen," Gaspard pleaded, making imperative gestures for quiet.

It was a farce, a deadly farce. Anya closed her eyes, then opened them to look toward where Celestine had fallen. Madame Rosa was there, loosening her daughter's bodice and the stays underneath. The eyes of the two women met and in them there was both scorn and despair.

"If he has been forcing himself upon Mademoiselle Anya again," Murray was saying, "I will be delighted to have the opportunity of chastising the scoundrel. If it need be after you, then well enough."

"That is, of course, if I am alive," Ravel said, his voice mocking under the pleasantry. "On the other hand, it's perfectly agreeable to me if you two would like to exchange shots or cross swords first, after which I will face the one left standing."

Emile drew himself up even more stiffly than before. "This is not a matter for humor, Duralde, nor will I be cheated of a meeting with you. If you will not deign to resent my insults, then I demand satisfaction for your insolent attitude toward the lady who was once my brother's betrothed."

"Oh, very well!" Ravel said in sudden explosive wrath. "Let us have a grand exchanging of cards and civilities before we each gather our friends to watch us try to kill each other! Tomorrow is Ash Wednesday. If we die, then we will not have to face forty meatless days. If we survive, how better to start the Lenten season than by having something worthwhile to repent?"

Chapter Eighteen

🦋 🦋 🦋 *The captain's whistle blew at midnight for the* unmasking and the call to supper at the second ball of Comus, but the Hamilton party was not there. Celestine, the moment she revived from her faint, began to cry and could not stop. Even if there had not been the possibility of attracting the notice of the curious, the merriment around them seemed crude and insensitive and the strained civility of the men toward each other unbearable. Mardi Gras had lost its savor. It was time to go home.

At the townhouse, Anya changed out of her ball gown. She did not dress for bed, but rather pulled on an ordinary morning gown over a petticoat or two and went to see about Celestine.

Her half sister had been put to bed, and lay clutching a handkerchief in one hand and a bottle of smelling salts in the other, while Madame Rosa sat beside the bed smoothing her hair back from her tear-damp face. She had been fairly quiet, but at the sight of Anya, fresh tears began to course down her face. Such copious grief so exacerbated Anya's own fears and the tightness in her throat that her voice was sharp as she approached the bed.

"Good heavens, Celestine, if I didn't know better, I'd think one or all of the men were already dead! Do try for a little self-control!"

"I'm trying, but I'm not like you!" Celestine answered from behind her handkerchief, the words thick due to her reddened and stopped-up nose.

"I've never seen that turning myself into a fountain helped a thing, if that's what you mean."

"Yes, I am aware! I wonder sometimes if you have any feelings at all."

294

"Now, Celestine," Madame Rosa said, at the same time giving her head a small shake as she frowned across her daughter at Anya.

"It's true!" Celestine said, wiping at her streaming eyes. "I don't see how she can hold her head up, much less stand there dry-eyed, when it's all her fault."

"My fault?" Anya echoed.

Celestine sent her a look of angry despair. "They are fighting over you, aren't they?"

Anya opened her mouth to tell the other girl that she was the cause and Madame Rosa the instigator of the entire chain of events. She closed it again. She could not betray Madame Rosa, nor could she place that burden upon Celestine.

"You don't deny it. It's true, then. This is where your want of conduct has brought us. Shameless, shameless. How we are ever to hold up our heads after this, I don't know."

"Celestine!" her mother exclaimed. "You don't know what you are saying."

"Yes I do. If Murray dies, or Emile or Ravel, any of them, it will be on Anya's head. I hate her, I hate her."

"That will do!" Madame Rosa said in a voice that finally silenced her daughter but caused the younger girl to throw herself over in the bed, burying her face in her pillow in a fresh bout of weeping. Above the noisy, hiccuping sobs Madame Rosa said to Anya, "Pay no attention. She's upset and doesn't mean a word of it; I'm sure she will beg your pardon in the morning. For now, it might be better if you leave her to me. The best thing you could do, I think, would be to go and talk to Murray. If you will, you can see to it that he goes home."

Gaspard and Emile had gone, but Celestine's fiancé was still waiting in the salon. He was pacing up and down when Anya entered. He came toward her at once, his face creased with worry.

"Is she going to be all right?"

"Yes, of course," Anya answered. "It was just such a shock."

"I know, I know, and her heart is so sensitive. I would like to see her, but the sight of me just seems to set her off again."

Anya gave him a rueful smile. "Yes, I have that same effect.

It's natural, I suppose. You had best leave us. There is nothing you can do here, and I'm sure you have much that must be attended to since the meeting is to be in the morning.''

"Yes, yes indeed," he said, a stained look in his eyes.

"I would like to wish you *bonne chance*," she went on, putting out her hand. "I cannot see the necessity of such meetings, but I am not ungrateful to you for—for acting as my champion.''

"It's nothing, a matter of—"

"Of honor. Yes, I know, but all the same you have my appreciation and my prayers for your safety.''

He bowed over her hand, his smile troubled. "I can ask no more.''

When he had gone, she closed and locked the door behind him, leaning her head against it a moment with a weary sigh. Straightening, she moved to blow out the lamp that burned on a side table. Just as the light faded, she noticed one of the muslin curtains caught between the panels of a set of the French doors overlooking the street. It was too much trouble to relight the lamp. Surefooted in the darkness, she stepped to open the doors to release the curtain. Even as she did so, she realized that with all the coming and going on the gallery during the afternoon, one of the jalousie shutters had not been closed for the night. She leaned to catch it, pulled it toward her, then stopped with it in her hand to take a deep breath of the fresh evening air.

Her attention was caught by a movement across the street. A man, hovering in the shadows under the gallery across the way, drew back into the doorway under the overhang. At the same time, there came the sound of footsteps as Murray emerged from the *porte cochère* of the townhouse just beneath where Anya stood and started along the banquette under the gallery. The carriage was available, but apparently he preferred to walk.

The man who had been watching waited for several seconds, until Murray had nearly reached the next cross street; then he stepped from the doorway. Keeping to the shadows of the opposite side, he set out after Murray. He made no attempt to overtake him, but kept the same distance between them.

With a frown between her eyes, Anya watched the two men recede along the street. Her first thought had been a footpad, some ruffian strayed into this more respectable area of the Vieux

Carré. She had dismissed it almost instantly. The way the man following Murray moved, his size and carriage, was familiar. It made no sense, and yet she would swear that it was Emile Girod.

She was imagining things, she told herself, she must be. What possible reason could Emile have for following Murray? Still she stepped out onto the gallery to keep the two men in sight a little longer.

Murray came to the next intersection and crossed it. The other man did the same a moment later, passing under a gaslight hanging on a bracket at the corner. It was Emile.

Anya stood for a second longer. It was all her fault, Celestine had said, this meeting and the enmity between the two men. If that was even partially true—

She turned abruptly and stepped into the house, locking the shutter and French doors before moving from the room with swift steps. She was in her own bedchamber with her hand on her cloak in the armoire when a sudden idea came to her. Whirling, she avoided Celestine's room, from which could be heard the murmur of voices, going back to the salon and through it to Madame Rosa's bedchamber. From her stepmother's armoire she took a widow's black cloak and bonnet.

Once outside the house on the banquette, she stopped to put on her borrowed apparel. The dark cloak was voluminous and a little short, but covered her admirably and was nearly invisible in the dimness. The bonnet not only was designed to conceal the face from the sides, but had also a long length of veiling that hung down in front as added protection from prying eyes. Feeling as disguised as she ever had in a Mardi Gras mask, Anya set out after the two men.

She moved as swiftly as she dared, even running for the first block since there was no one in sight, neither her quarries nor other late revelers. She feared that the pair she sought had made a turning, and so peered down every side street but saw no sign of them. It had not taken her long to prepare herself and leave the house, but when someone was moving away in a straight line, a few minutes could make a great deal of difference. She was beginning to ask herself where they might have stopped, which house Murray might have chosen to enter, perhaps to speak to some friend about being a second for the coming duel, when suddenly she caught a glimpse of Emile ahead of her. After a moment she saw the crown of Murray's top hat. He was just threading his way through a group of noisy women of the streets dressed as clowns, still on the same side of the street she was on.

She slowed at once, keeping to the shadows in a rather self-conscious imitation of Emile. Ahead of them was a brightly lighted building with the surrounding streets lined with carriages. It became apparent within a few more yards that this was the destination of Celestine's fiancé. It was the St. Louis Hotel.

There were two hotels of particular distinction in New Orleans. One was the St. Charles on the street of the same name, a hotel patronized primarily by English and Americans and considered to be an American stronghold. The other was the St. Louis at the corner of Royal and St. Louis Streets, which housed the Creole planters and their families when they came to town and also most other businessmen from France. Both were establishments of luxury, comfort, and a great deal of elegance. Both had magnificent ballrooms, public rooms, barrooms, separate dining rooms for men and women, and a number of attached shops. The St. Louis had in addition a skylighted rotunda said to be the most beautiful in America. Every day from noon until three as many as half a dozen auctions were held simultaneously in this great open space, selling everything from cotton and tobacco and sugarcane to consignments of fancy merchandise such as ladies' bonnets; from the property and household goods of bankrupt planters to choice slaves.

The main entrance to the rotunda was from St. Louis Street and the direct thoroughfare from Canal called Exchange Alley; however, the doors leading to the hotel lobby opened onto Royal. It was toward this Royal Street entrance that Murray was heading. He passed under the gaslights that illuminated the long row of arched windows fronting the hotel on the lower floor and turned in under the portico that was supported by four enormous fluted columns.

Anya watched Emile saunter across the street and enter the hotel in his turn, swinging his usual cane with an air of nonchalance, so that its silver knob flashed in the light. She stood for long moments with the inside of her bottom lip caught between her teeth; then, dropping the veil of her gray-black bonnet over her face, she moved after him.

She was just in time to see Emile disappearing up the great curving staircase that led to the public rooms on the second floor and from there on up to the bedchambers on the top two floors. Keeping her head slightly bowed, she crossed the main lobby to mount upward also, trailing her fingers along the walnut banister. She kept her lowered gaze on the turned posts of the railing so that her bonnet brim would conceal her face should he happen to look back.

By the time she reached the landing, Emile was standing before the etched glass door of the barroom. It was too late to turn back for he had already seen her. His glance was cursory, however, without a hint of recognition. It seemed likely that he would pay her more attention if she should stop. She kept moving with slow steps. As she neared, she held her breath, waiting for his sudden startled recognition. It did not come. He did not even glance in her direction, so intent was he on his own quarry. Just before she reached him, he stepped into the barroom, moving to one side. Anya looked into the crowded place as she passed, but could see nothing of Murray.

A lady did not enter a barroom. The need to know what was happening inside, what reason Emile had for following Murray, was so great that Anya was tempted to throw propriety to the winds and chance the prohibition. She would be firmly escorted out, she was sure, but she would have a chance to look around before that happened.

The trouble was, she would also draw attention to herself. That she did not want, though less because of the conventions than for fear of disturbing the odd situation she had stumbled upon, and also out of a disinclination to appear ridiculous by being caught spying in so flagrant a manner on two men close to her family. She was forced to content herself with the prospect of making another slow pass before the door.

Chattering voices impinged on her absorption. They belonged to a trio of women emerging from the ladies' ordinary, the dining area reserved for women and their invited guests. Of middle age, with graying hair and plump bejeweled fingers, wrists, and throats, they were dressed in ball gowns, as if they had come from a *bal de société*. As they reached the barroom door, they halted and one of them raised a hand in imperious summons. From the comments exchanged, it appeared that they were ready to turn homeward if they could pry their husbands from their drinking. Good-humored and yet a trifle impatient, they stood waiting.

Anya moved in behind them, looking over their shoulders. She took a step to the left, then one to the right. There. There was Murray, standing at one end of the bar near another man with the look of an American. The two men had their heads together as they talked, as if they did not want to be overheard. Even as Anya watched, however, the other American reached into his pocket and took out a purse. He called a busboy to him, a sullen-looking young man with lank blond hair and a pock-marked face. He spoke to him and gave him a coin. The blond-haired youth took it and went toward a back door, removing his ankle-length apron as he went. The man extracted another coin from the purse and threw it down on the bar. He and Murray stood talking for a few minutes more, then turned together toward the door.

There were a number of tables and scores of men between Anya and the two men. She calculated the distance to the ladies' ordinary and also that to the stairs, and chose the stairs. Heed-less of the stares of the three ladies waiting for their husbands, she moved with more haste than dignity toward the staircase and down it to the first turning. She slowed then, though the re-mainder of her descent was still swift. Rounding one of the large circular newels at the bottom, she descended a few more steps and passed through a doorway that led toward the hotel's ro-tunda. Here she paused, listening.

The face of the man with Murray had been familiar, but she could not quite place it. She did not think it was anyone she had seen lately, nor any of Murray's friends she had ever met at various social events. That was odd; a man usually chose his friends to be his seconds, since they would be more likely to look after his interests in matters of the duel. Perhaps the man was a surgeon preferred by the Americans? It was required that one be present on the field of honor.

The footsteps of the two men descended the marble treads of

the stairs and continued out the hotel door. Anya waited with strained patience for Emile. The seconds ticked past. What was he doing? She had left her place, putting a foot on the short run of steps back up to the lobby, when she heard the clatter of his hurried descent. Stifling a mad urge to laugh aloud, she drew back out of sight until he too had stepped through the hotel doors held open by a pair of obsequious doormen. As soon as he was out of sight, she followed.

The hour was growing late. Most of the balls had ended and people were wending their way homeward. Even the hordes of riffraff, the women from the bordellos and their rougher customers, were slowly reeling off toward their more usual haunts. Parties of drunken men staggered here and there. Now and then a shiny carriage with a liveried coachman on the box rolled past or a man on horseback with a cloak thrown carelessly around a wrinkled costume trotted toward his lodgings. Trash and refuse littered the street. A few men and women in rags picked at it here and there, scavenging. No one molested Anya; no one even seemed to see her. The sight of a widow was so common, and so respected, in New Orleans that she was nearly invisible.

It appeared for a time that Murray was retracing his route, perhaps returning to the Hamilton townhouse. He passed it by with scarcely a look, however, going on another two blocks before he turned right, heading toward the river. Anya, her feet aching from walking in her dancing slippers, thought seriously of turning into her own gateway, of dropping away from this strange chase. There seemed no reason behind it, not that she had had much time to think about it. The only thing that kept her on the trail was the sure knowledge that if she did give up, she would never be able to rest for puzzling over what Emile was doing. Curiosity. Ravel had warned her against it once. How long ago that seemed.

The block slipped past. It was instinct, not any consciously recognized landmark, that told her suddenly where she was heading. She had been this way not too long before, and in the darkest hours. Her heart leaped in her throat and she looked around at the barrelhouses and the signs that advertised gambling in the upper rooms. Ahead came the faint sounds of music and drunken shouts and the gleam of light. If Murray did not call a halt soon, they were all going to run into Gallatin Street.

He did not stop. Ahead of her, Murray and the man with him turned left and were swallowed up in the noise and blaring, romping life of the city's most notorious area. Anya saw Emile pause on the corner and she halted, waiting for him to go on. He did not move immediately, but stood with his feet spread, grasping his cane in both hands like a weapon as he gazed after the other two men.

The silk of Emile's top hat and the satin lapels and fine cloth of his coat caught the light, and it occurred to Anya how out of place he looked there in his evening clothes. The precaution he had just taken was a natural one to a man going into territory he knew to be dangerous. Murray, on the other hand, though dressed in much the same way, had turned into Gallatin Street as if it were like any other.

A frown drew Anya's brows together. Did Emile's action indicate that he knew the place and the need to be on his guard well, or only that he was wary in an area known for its unsavory reputation? Did Murray's apparent lack of concern stem from ignorance of the street's seamy character, or from the contempt of familiarity?

Why in the name of all the saints was Emile following Murray? What did he expect to gain? It seemed foolish, nearly as foolish as her trailing after them both, and yet there was something about it that so intrigued her that she could not bring herself to turn back, in spite of the impulse to do so that clamored inside her.

A cart rumbled past carrying whiskey barrels, one of which was leaking into the street. Down the narrow banquette came a sailor with his arm around a hard-faced doxy. He was a mountain of a man in a striped jersey, and the woman still wore a man's costume that made her look like a country yokel. They made a zigzag step around Anya, and the sailor gave her a leering grin through her veil as he squeezed one of the doxy's breasts. On the opposite side of the street just down from where Anya stood, two drunks singing a bawdy song about a girl named Biddie at the top of their lungs, both carrying demijohns of drink, staggered out of a barroom. They began to make their way up toward Gallatin. A man with shifting, squinting eyes and his hand inside his coat as if clutching a weapon rounded the corner on that side. He was moving with a loping stride. Seeing the pair, he gave them a wide berth, stepping out into the street and back again, before charging on into the darkness.

This was no place for her. In sudden decision, Anya picked up her skirts, preparing to turn around and go home. What stopped her was a sudden move made by the two drunks. They suddenly angled across the street a short distance ahead of her. They were still singing, but seemed much better able to make their arms and legs work. They were nearing Emile.

Jean's brother turned his head and saw the pair coming. He stepped back out of their way in a gesture of both good manners and good sense. They bore down on him, swinging their demi-johns, caroling and laughing at their own coarse ditty. As they neared him, they released their hold on each other and with expansive good humor reeled over to clamp their arms around Emile.

The movement was too quick, too hard. The singing broke off too sharply. Anya opened her mouth to cry out a warning. It was too late. One of the swinging demijohns caught Emile a smashing blow on the side of the head. He sagged between the two men, his crushed hat flopping to the dirty street. One of the men jerked his cane from his flaccid fingers. Between them they half dragged, half carried him across the street, out of Anya's sight.

She started forward, all thought of her own danger forgotten. If she could see where he was taken, she might bring help. There came a whisper of sound behind her. She caught a whiff of beer and stale sweat; then rough hands caught at her, dragging her into a hold like a steel barrel hoop that confined her arms inside her cloak. Something hard and sharp prodded her side.

"Keep quiet, dearie, or I'll slit you open like gutting a fish!"

It was the sailor and his doxy. The woman held the knife while the man squeezed Anya to his oxlike, hair-matted chest.

"Release me at once!" Anya's fury was real if rather breathless from the hard pressure of the sailor's arms. It was also directed at herself for walking into this trap, a trap that must have been set by a coin handed to a busboy.

The woman laughed. She jerked her head toward Gallatin and the sailor began to shove her in that direction. Anya set her feet, only to be lifted in such a viselike grip that the air was expelled from her lungs. She felt her stays and her ribs bend, and black dots began to dance before her eyes. The woman spoke, an indistinct sound through the rushing noise in Anya's ears. The sailor's grasp shifted downward to her hips and she was heaved up and over his shoulder. Blood poured into her head in a dark tide, so that her eyes and nose ached and she could not see. She caught her breath, only to have it jolted from her again as the sailor began to move. She clung to consciousness with fierce concentration, but could not seem to move as she was carried in the same direction Emile had been taken.

They entered a building, mounted stairs of rough wood, went down a corridor bare of carpet and with whitewashed walls. The woman knocked on a door and it was opened.

"Put her there." The voice was amused, triumphant, shockingly familiar.

She was deposited none too gently in a hard wooden chair. The sailor stepped back and, at another terse order, he and the woman left the room. The figure of a man stepped toward Anya and reached to jerk free the bow that tied her bonnet. The headpiece with its obscuring black veil was whipped from her head and thrown to one side.

She was in a bedchamber, if it could be called by so exalted a name. The only furnishings were a plain iron bed, a table with a pitcher and bowl, and the chair in which she was seated. There were no window coverings, no decorations on the walls, no rugs to soften the bare wood of the floor. Such severity was suitable for only two purposes, either a monk's cell or a whore's room in the cheapest kind of bordello.

There were four men in the room. One of them was Emile. He lay on the bed with his eyes closed. His hair was matted with blood and there was a frightening pallor in his face. She thought his eyelids quivered as she looked at him, but if so it must have been a spasm of the nerves for he was not conscious. The foot of the bed sagged under the weight of the man Murray had met in the barroom, while leaning against the wall near the head was another man that Anya recognized with a fatalistic lack of surprise, a man with rust red hair trailing from under a bowler hat, the man known as Red who had shoved her into the gin room at Beau Refuge. Standing in front of her with his hand on his hips and a satisfied smirk on his face was Murray.

"I had no idea," he said, "that you would make it so easy for me."

Her head was pounding in time with her heart and it was difficult to focus her eyes. She was proud of the evenness of her voice as she spoke, however. "That was not, I assure you, my purpose."

"Oh, I don't doubt it. You are a meddlesome and altogether infuriating female. Fascinating, I will admit, but impossible. Life will be much easier for me without you."

Her head was beginning to clear; the sudden leap of fear caused by his words was a powerful goad. She stared at him, then gave a nod. "I see. You think you will be able to manage Celestine."

"I know it. She loves me."

"Madame Rosa does not."

"She will be prostrate over your disappearance for some time, and when she recovers, she will need someone to depend on."

"You underestimate her, I think."

He shrugged. "If she becomes too troublesome, there can always be a severe case of food poisoning. She does love her food."

"And you will control all of Beau Refuge since Celestine, as both my next of kin and also her mother's, will inherit."

"Exactly."

"What a loving husband you will make."

"Oh, yes, I'll love her. She is a very lovable girl."

Oddly enough, she believed him. In his way, he cared for her half sister, though his first aim was to use her for his advantage. That did not stop Anya's blood from congealing at the thought of Celestine in his hands. "You aren't married to her yet. It seems to me her affections have been, shall we say, less warm these last few days."

Murray jerked his thumb over his shoulder at the bed where Emile lay. "Because of him, you mean? I will attend to that."

Had she endangered Emile with her words? Surely not. Emile

had undoubtedly suspected something or he would never have set himself to spy upon Murray. For that reason alone, Murray could not longer afford to let him live.

She gave him a clear look. "Well, that's one way of besting a dueling opponent."

He reached out quite casually and slapped her. The blow flung her head to one side and she tasted blood as her teeth cut her lips. She only prevented herself from falling off the chair by catching the side of it with one hand.

Using that hold for leverage, Anya pushed herself up with rage in her eyes. Doubling her fist as Jean had taught her to do long ago, she struck for the point of Murray's chin. He turned his head at the last moment, but stumbled backward under the force of the hit. Crashing into the bed, he grabbed at the footrail to save himself.

The thug called Red gave a crack of laughter. "I tol' you to watch 'er!"

"Why, you bitch," Murray said, rising slowly to his feet. He came toward her.

"Later," the man from the barroom said. The single word was spoken with impatience and cold authority. It sent more terror coursing through Anya's veins than anything Murray had said.

Murray stopped in place. "But Mr. Lillie—"

"The one we want is Duralde."

The stiffness went out of Murray's shoulders. He did not pull his forelock like a serf before his master, but it was in his expression.

Mr. Lillie. Chris Lillie. Anya had seen him once at a distance. It had been at a political rally. He was the Tammany Hall politician imported by the democrats but now aligned with the Know-Nothing party that was behind the present corrupt government. Graying, well fed, with the thickened features of a former pugilist, he sat with knees apart and a bored look on his face. Just beneath him, half under the bed, lay her black bonnet. Its veiling nearly concealed what looked to be Emile's cane.

She stepped behind the chair in which she had been seated, holding to its back for support. Her voice soft as she faced

Murray, she said, "You fraud. Just a struggling law clerk, but one with ambition. What is the price of advancement? Ravel's head? You were willing to risk a great deal to gain it, weren't you? Even your own life."

"There was little risk."

"On the field of honor?"

"There are ways to better the odds."

It was his vanity that made him answer her, that and possibly a desire to strike at her in words if he could not attack her physically. The blows were telling. With the dawn, in a few short hours, he would be meeting Ravel. Somehow, someway, the contest would be weighted in Murray's favor.

"Such honor," she said in scathing tones. "What will happen to your position as a landed gentleman if anybody finds out? You'll be finished."

"They won't find out."

"Ravel has fought duels in Central America in two different military expeditions, been in every kind of dirty battlefield situation, and been held in prison with every kind of thief and trickster. You may find that he knows more of how to better the odds than you do. You may be in more danger than you know."

"I may," Murray answered with a sneer, "but it won't help you."

She had made her own blow count. For just an instant there had been a flicker of fear in Murray's eyes. Perhaps Madame Rosa was right; perhaps he was a coward. Why had she never noticed before now how weak his mouth was, and how hard his eyes?

Before she could think how to use her suspicion to advantage, she intercepted a quick, thoughtful glance in her direction from Chris Lillie. For a long moment, she could not think what she might have said to catch his interest. Then it came to her. Ravel. Central America.

Her eyes blazing with relief and pure exultation, she stepped from behind her chair to accuse Murray and Chris Lillie at the same time. "But that's it, isn't it? That's why you want Ravel dead, and have from the beginning. He's a danger to you. It's his experience as a soldier and an officer with the Cuban expedition and with William Walker in Nicaragua that frightens you.

If he should use it to turn the Vigilance Committee into an army, your stranglehold on the city could be broken. The Know-Nothing party would be thrown out, trampled in the dust by the stampede of voters able at last to get to the polls without hindrance.''

"Smart, too, ain't she?" the redheaded man observed.

Murray started to answer, but Lillie cut him off with a hard, chopping gesture. He stood up and, without a glance toward Anya, walked to the door. Murray hesitated, then followed him.

"You coming back," Red called after Murray, adding in a suggestive tone, "later?"

"No." Murray's hazel eyes were like cracked marbles as he stared at Anya. "You know what to do."

"Make you any difference what happens before?"

"Not in the least." Celestine's fiancé smiled, a cold movement of the lips.

The door closed behind them.

Anya looked at the man still leaning against the wall. "I will pay you well if you will let us go."

"Yes, and have just a whale of a time watching me hang afterward."

"Touch me and you'll also hang."

"Maybe. Maybe not. I always wanted to have me a lady."

"Enough to die for the pleasure?"

"Well, now," he said, and there was hot anticipation behind his eyes as he pushed away from the wall, "it's not me who's goin' to die."

Anya backed away, keeping her eyes upon him. "Nor am I."

"Is that so?"

"You can bet on it."

"Against my own self?"

"That's your choice."

A little more, a little further away from the bed, away from the end of it where her bonnet lay. He was big and he was strong as he stalked her. She had to be sure. She sidled along the footrail, letting her fingers trail along the iron bar at the top.

"What you running away for? There's no place to go."

Wasn't there? "You expect me to just give up?"

"Might as well. Might even find it worked out better."

"And pigs might fly."

A cruel smile bared his teeth. "I do like a woman with a tongue in her head."

"Oh, do you?"

"I do. Sassy women fight back and that makes it more fun. But try anything smart with me like you did with Nicholls and you'll be glad to git the whole thing over."

"How kind of you to warn me," she mocked.

He made some answer, but she did not hear. Grasping the end of the iron rail, she swung like a banner unfurling around the end and dove for the floor. The jarring fall set her head to pounding once more, but she whipped over, rolling, sliding under the high bed, stretching toward her bonnet on the far side—and the cane that lay under its veiling. Emile's sword cane.

The man called Red cursed, growling threats as he plunged after her. She heard the crashing thud as he flung himself down on his knees beside the bed. He was reached for her, catching her skirts, bunching them in his hands and tearing them loose at the waist as he pulled.

Her fingers touched the cane, sent it rolling. She hitched toward it, panting with the effort. She was pulled backward. She looked up and saw the bed ropes on the bed, with the thin mattress bulging between them. Was the bulge moving? There was no time to tell. She was being dragged from under the bed. She grasped at the ropes above her, curling her fingers around them, holding tight. She kicked backward and heard a grunt as her foot connected. There was a slight release of the aching pressure on the skirts at her waist. She hunched forward again.

She could not reach the cane. She tried instead for the bonnet, catching the veiling, yanking it in her direction with a sharp tug. The cane came with it. She had her fingers on it. Had it in her hand.

Red gave a mighty wrench. Her shoulder scraped over the floor and the skin was torn on her fingers that were twisted in the bed ropes as she was pulled half the length of her body from under her cover. The man must have had his foot braced on the side rail. Desperately she put both hands on the cane and turned the head. Nothing happened. Again she tried as she had once seen Emile do in a darkened carriage. Nothing.

She was being hauled into the open on her side. Hard hands were on her hips, sinking into the flesh. If the cane was not a sword, it could at least be a club with its heavy silver head. As her shoulders cleared the bed, she suddenly bent double. Her head came into the open. She reached with her left hand and grabbed the shirt front of the red-haired man squatting over her, yanking him toward her with all her strength. As he leaned forward, she brought the head of the cane from beneath the bed, ramming it under his chin with the force of her pain and rage behind it.

She heard the crack of hard silver metal on bone, heard his teeth snap together. His hold loosened and he rocked back on his heels. Instantly she shoved away from him, scrambling to her knees, pulling herself up by holding to the bed. She was only half on her feet when he caught her skirts.

She struck at him but he fended off the blow and nearly yanked the cane from her hand before she wrenched it free. Grunting, he hauled himself up hand over hand on her skirts, drawing her toward him at the same time. She feinted with the cane but he was ready for her, reaching for it.

Behind him there was a movement. Emile was awake, raising himself with difficulty to one elbow. He shook his head as if to clear it, focusing on Anya.

He was weak, too weak to help her. Anya brought the cane down on Red's hand that was wrapped in her skirts. He did not seem to feel it. She jabbed at him with the ferrule and he laughed, grabbing for it. His fingers closed on the metal end for a long moment, but using both hands, she wrestled it from his one-handed grasp.

"I'll git it. I'll git it, I'll use it to beat your pretty—"

Anya ignored the rest of the threat. On the bed behind Red, Emile was reaching out, his fingers spread and trembling. His eyes were clear and in their depths there was a plea. What was it he wanted? The cane? But what could he do with it in his condition?

Red caught her wrist, wrenching it. In another second he would have the cane. She would have only one more chance to use it. One more.

To use it or give it up to its owner. To take her last chance, or let Emile have it. The decision must be made quickly.

Anya reached for the cane with her left hand. As Red let go of her skirts to grab for that arm, she threw the slender stick, arching, toward the bed. She saw Emile reach for it; then her view was blotted out as she went slowly to her knees, compelled by the grinding pain as her wrists were slowly twisted behind her. Through a red haze, she heard a click.

Red gave a hoarse, whistling grunt and went stiff. His grip slackened, his arms flopped down, then slowly he keeled to the side to strike the floor with a solid thud. There was a small slit in his neck. It was hardly bleeding at all.

Anya looked toward the cane in Emile's hand. From it there protruded a six-inch blade. She met his eyes and he gave her a gallant smile. He said, "Forgive me. On this cane there is a button."

Chapter Nineteen

 Whether because Murray had been confident of the ability of the leader of the thugs to deal with a woman and an unconscious man alone, or because it was Red himself who had been so sanguine, there was no guard outside the door, no one in the entire bordello who made the slightest effort to stop them as they left it. The sight of a woman helping along a man somewhat incapacitated was too common to draw attention beyond an ironic lift of a brow because they were going out instead of coming in.

The difficulty, Anya found, was in finding transportation. There were no cabriolets in this port of the city, and no one wanted to stop for what was apparently a woman of the streets and her drunken customer. Anya could have walked, but Emile was not in so good a case. At last she was able to beg a ride for them on the tail of the cart of a butcher who had been delivering sausages to what passed for restaurants on Gallatin Street. His cart was caked with grease and smelled like something long dead, but he took them to the door of the townhouse.

Madame Rosa was aghast at the sight of them. She did not waste time exclaiming, however, but rang for the servants and soon had Emile in bed in a spare bedchamber. A doctor was sent for, who, on his arrival, declared with the greatest possible firmness that M'sieur Girod was not capable of appearing on the field of honor at dawn. The affair must be canceled. There could be no other choice.

Anya waited only long enough after that for Emile to pen a note of regrets and apologies. She had changed her torn gown and ordered the carriage brought out. Leaving Emile in Madame Rosa's capable hands, taking his note with her, she left the town-

house once more. Ravel must be warned, and though she could
have explained how matters stood in a message of her own, her
restless fears would not allow it.

In the courtyard she found not only the landau, but Marcel
on the box beside the coachman, with a musket propped against
the seat beside him. He would not permit that she go alone. If
she had so little concern for her own safety as to set out so
foolishly as she had earlier, then someone must take care of her.

Anya felt the press of time too much to argue; moreover, she
was glad of the gesture of protection. Giving the coachman the
order he seemed fully to expect, she climbed into the carriage
and sat back on the seat.

There were yellow gleams of light showing through the shutters on the lower floor of the Duralde house. It was a relief to
see them; Anya had not liked the idea of waking the entire house
in order to speak to Ravel. She would have done it, but she
preferred a quieter entrance.

Marcel went with her to the door and lifted the knocker for
her. When the door swung open, Anya half expected to see a
butler or some older housekeeper, but it was Ravel himself who
stood there. The light was behind him, so she could not see his
face, but she thought from the sudden stillness of his form that
she was the last person he had expected. He wore no coat and
the sleeves of his shirt were rolled to the elbows. His hair was
tousled, as if he had been running his fingers through it, and in
his right hand he held a pen with the nib still wet with ink.

He had been writing his will, or perhaps some last instructions concerning his affairs for his mother or his man of business. It was an obvious precaution under the circumstances; still
it gave Anya a suffocating feeling in her chest.

"I will wait for you in the carriage, mam'zelle," Marcel said,
and melted away into the darkness behind her.

"What are you doing here?"

Ravel thought he had relegated Anya to a corner of his mind
so as to concentrate without distraction on the matter at hand.
The sight of her on his doorstep showed him what a fool he was
to think such a thing possible.

Anya's answer was as stark as Ravel's question had been.
"There are a number of things I must tell you. May I come in?"

He stepped aside with the stiffness of reluctance.

Setting the soft curves of her mouth in firm lines, Anya swept past him. The light was coming from a sitting room to the right. It was fitted out as a study with not only a grouping of chairs and small tables, but also a set of glass-fronted bookshelves and a desk with a top of tooled and gilded Spanish leather. Anya moved toward it. Ravel entered the room behind her and closed the door. Moving to the desk, he sat down on the corner as she took a chair to one side.

His voice dry, he said, "I am at your service."

The mask was gone. The man who sat watching her was the same one she had known so briefly at Beau Refuge. For that much she was thankful, even if there was little warmth or welcome in his expression.

"Emile will not be able to meet with you in the morning," she began, and took the note entrusted to her from her string purse to hand it over. Keeping her voice even with an effort, she told him how Emile had followed Murray and been struck down, was taken prisoner then escaped, though the tale was somewhat incomplete. Her own part in the events she omitted. It had no bearing on the duel, and she had a distinct aversion to speaking of her near assault by the man called Red, or of hearing yet again that she was in need of a keeper.

Ravel listened in silence. The lamplight gleaming on her hair and shimmering in the intense blue of her eyes was a distraction, and he transferred his gaze to the toe of his boot. His frown deepened, becoming grim and thoughtful by turns.

Finally Anya said, "Emile has no grudge against you, no ill will whatever. He accepts that his brother's death was an accident. His challenge this evening was made because he thought to forestall Murray. He had been watching him and asking questions about him. It had begun to look as if Murray meant to use the duello in some way as an excuse to kill you. Before he could speak to you about it, he saw Murray lying in wait for you at the ball. Because of the friendship Jean felt for you, and because of lessons you gave him once with a sword when he was a younger brother tagging after you and Jean, he stepped in as a delaying tactic, meaning to apologize and explain later."

She came to an end, her gaze upon Ravel's face. She waited

for some comment. When it was not forthcoming she said, "You aren't surprised."

He looked up briefly. "No."

"Not even that the duel with Murray will be fixed in some way to his advantage?"

"Given the rest, it seems a logical step for him to take."

"What are you going to do about it?"

"Do? I will meet him."

"You can't! It would be like walking into a trap. You don't know how he is going to arrange the thing."

He gave her his full and exasperated attention. "What would you have me do? Fail to put in an appearance? I can't do that, not again."

"Death with honor, is that it? You would rather die than face the whispers and sniggers?"

Darkness rose in his eyes. He took a deep breath, trying for patience. He had insulted Anya on the dance floor at the Comus ball in the hope of giving her such a disgust for him that a scene like this could be avoided, a scene he had guessed would come as soon as he had seen Murray waiting for him to return Anya to her seat. He might have saved himself the trouble.

"You don't understand," he said, his voice low. "It has nothing to do with what people will say; I am bound by my given word to uphold a certain level of conduct. To fail would be to fail myself. Call it pride, call it stupidity, and most men will agree it's both those things. But it is also a code to live by."

It was a code that required courage and integrity, one that defied the mean grasping after life at any cost. Without it, would men remain gentlemen? Or would it be the same: some men would adhere to the principles by natural tendency, while others would use them for their own ends and discard them when they ceased to be profitable?

"There must be something that can be done!"

"What do you suggest?"

That was of course the question. The police could not be called in, for they were ranged with the Know-Nothing party Murray was being used to protect. To go to Murray and confront him would be useless; he would only deny everything and possibly hint that it was cowardice that caused the accusations.

There was really only one thing that Ravel could do, if he would not avoid the meeting.

"Your seconds—," she began.

"They will check the field thoroughly, you can be sure of that. In the end, Murray will have to face me, alone. It will be just the two of us."

"Is that supposed to be a comfort? I saw him perfecting his prowess with a sword in Exchange Alley. I also saw him shoot a man once, in the dark; the ball went through the heart."

Murray had shot the thug that night when their carriage had been held up. "My God," the man's confederate, a man very like Red, had bawled, and it had not been because of the smoking pistol in Murray's hand. It had been because he had been appalled at their unlucky choice of vehicle, because he had recognized Murray and knew the dead man had been shot to keep him from showing that he had done the same.

"I didn't know," Ravel said softly, "that you needed comforting."

There was nothing in his face to show that it mattered to him one way or the other. She got to her feet, turning away. "I—I feel responsible. If I had not interfered—"

"If you had not interfered, I might be dead. If this meeting is to be rigged now, the first would have been rigged."

She sent him a quick glance from under her lashes. "A strange meeting," she said, her tone laced with bitterness. "Madame Rosa wanted you to show up Murray, but he wouldn't back down because it was such a good opportunity to be rid of you. There you were, both apparently fighting over the attentions paid me, when in reality I had nothing to do with the motives of either one of you."

"That isn't precisely so," he answered, his tone measured. "I agreed to Madame Rosa's request primarily because it gave me an excuse for doing something I had wanted to do for a long time."

"Meaning?"

"I approached you because I was tired of avoiding you, tired of watching you avoid me."

"But you were masked," she said.

"It was easier that way."

Had it been easier to let fall his figurative social mask while wearing a real one? Had it seemed less dangerous to break their pact of mutual avoidance in secret? If it had not been for Murray's interference, would she ever have known who the man in the mask of a knight had been?

When she made no answer, he went on. "But you must not blame Madame Rosa for what happened. There was more to it, even, than that. It was in the interest of the Vigilance Committee to be rid of Murray Nicholls, either through forcing him to back down in public so that he was ruined in New Orleans, or by facing him with sword or pistol. He was in far too deep with Lillie, and was too close to attaining a foothold in the Creole community through your half sister, to be allowed to remain. I was not an unwilling accomplice."

For a brief time he had thought Anya might be involved with Murray and Lillie; the way she had abducted him had been so convenient for their purpose. The idea held a certain humor now, though once it had been less than amusing.

Anya turned toward him, caught the faint flicker of his smile. It was chilling, coupled with what he had said. "And if I had not stopped the meeting, what then? Would you have been a willing assassin?"

Assassin. Murderer. Heartless killer. He had heard the accusation before, long ago. A white line appeared around his mouth, and when he spoke there was a raw edge to the words. "I have never been privileged to see Nicholls wield a sword or shoot a man, but I have made it my business to know something of him, including his skill with weapons. My purpose was and is to encourage him to leave the city for the sake of his health. In exchange, he would have had, and still will have, a chance to kill me."

An excellent chance, one Murray intended to better. "Yes," she agreed, her gaze steady, "but does that make it right?"

"To use a rite with ties to ancient chivalry in a base manner for a worthy cause? No, but it is sometimes the only way."

"That's what you're still doing, isn't it? You're still doing the work of your Vigilance Committee, not simply upholding your honor."

"Few things are simple."

She watched him for long moments, letting her gaze touch the strong bronze planes of his face, the width of his shoulders, the masculine beauty of his hard hands. Inside her rose an impulse, growing, burgeoning until abruptly she could contain it no longer. She moved toward him with a soft rustle of her skirts. "Here is one thing that is very simple. Come away with me now. By dawn we could be well along on the road to Mississippi, or to Texas if you prefer. From either place we could take a ship to Paris, or Venice or Rome. You offered once to marry me; I will be your wife if you will come with me now."

It was a temptation such as he had never known. The need to snatch her up and drive away with her before she could change her mind or marshal some damnably intellectual excuse was like claws tearing him apart inside. Nothing he had ever done, not facing screaming hordes of Nicaraguans nor being led into the torture chamber of a Spanish dungeon, required the self-command it took to look her in the eyes and appear indifferent.

"Such a sacrifice," he drawled. "You must love your little half sister very much, or is it Nicholls himself?"

"Or you."

He flinched from the words as from a blow to the heart. "Don't! You may pledge your immortal soul and it will not stop this meeting. Nothing will stop it this time."

He had no use for her love; he did not want it. The tears rising behind her eyes made them luminous. "Very well then! Go to your senseless duel! Face Murray and attempt to kill him if you must. But when you find yourself lying on the wet grass with a bullet in your chest, remember I warned you!"

She whirled from him and ran to the door, pulling it open so recklessly that it banged against the wall. She was through it and across the entrance hall in an instant.

Ravel stared after her with an arrested expression on his face. He leaped up. "Anya!"

The only answer was the slamming of the front door. By the time he reached it and flung it open, the carriage was drawing away. On the point of racing after her, he stopped.

Desolation settled in a hard, hot knot inside him. It rose into his eyes, clouding their dark surface. A soft sound left him and his shoulders sagged. Perhaps it was better this way. He went back inside and closed the door.

Anya sat upright on the carriage seat with her arms crossed

over her chest and her eyes burning as she stared into the dimness. Her thoughts raced inside her brain, and they were not pleasant. The vehicle had not gone two blocks before she reached up to knock with her knuckles on the roof. The panel connected to the coachman's seat slid open.

"Yes, mam'zelle?" Marcel asked.

"Take me to Elijah and Samson's house," she said.

"But mam'zelle!" he protested with sudden anxiety in his tones.

"Now, please," she said softly.

The panel slid shut.

They sat their horses in a dense thicket of scrub brush and vines. They needed its concealment, for the sky in the east was turning a lighter gray with each passing minute. The four of them, Anya and Marcel, Samson and Elijah, did not talk. They watched the road in front of them that, covered with white sea shells crushed by countless wheels, lay like a long pale arrow pointing back toward the city, and they listened for the sound of a carriage. Three had gone by already. The first had held an upright older man who might have been a surgeon, the one after that had contained Murray and his friends who would act for him as seconds, and the last had been occupied by men who must have been Ravel's seconds.

Anya had dressed for this outing in the leather skirt and mannish frock coat that were her riding habit, and had put her hair up in a coronet of braids. She did not expect what would take place shortly to be a rough-and-tumble affair; still she meant to be prepared, especially after having her clothes half torn off of her earlier.

As the minutes stretched, she thought about the man for whom they waited. Her anger toward him had faded, becoming chagrin and regret that were so painful she had to clench her teeth to prevent herself from crying out. She had offered herself to him, offered her love, and he had refused her. She wished the words had never been spoken. She should have known what his answer would be, and would have if she had not been too upset and off-balance from the events of the night to think. He had made his proposal before out of duty. By her rejection, she had released him from the obligation. He had desired her in a purely physical

manner for a time, had even, perhaps, needed her in order to
heal the scars from wounds she had inflicted unintentionally
years ago. It had not taken long for him to appease his needs.
Now he wanted no more of her.

Well enough, she would accept it. She had injured him, had
damaged his honor, and she had made recompense in the manner of his choosing. He was in danger once more at least partially because of her, and she would remedy the matter. After
that, it would be over. They would return to their polite pact.
They would avoid each other when possible, speak only when
necessary. They would look at each other when they were forced
to meet and turn away as if they were strangers.

But sometimes when he was not looking Anya would watch
him, the way his lashes shielded his eyes, the curve of his mouth
when he smiled, the negligent grace of his movements. She
would watch and remember, and she would bleed inside.

There was a carriage coming. It was a phaeton buggy traveling at great speed, trailing a long plume of white dust. There
was only one man in the open vehicle. Marcel stared at it hard,
then turned to give the signal. It was Ravel. He was alone,
driving himself. The four of them gathered their reins. Anya
repeated her quiet instructions.

The buggy bowled past. They allowed it to gain a small distance, then set out after it. No attempt was made to come up
with it, but they kept it well in sight. The dust fogged around
them in a choking cloud, but they did not falter.

The road they were on ran from the city straight out some
two or three miles to the Allard plantation. On that property,
just across Bayou St. John, lay the twin oak trees a convenient
pistol shot apart that were known as the dueling oaks. The meeting ground was a reasonable distance from town, quiet and private, and far enough from all habitation that there was little
danger of accidental injuries. For these reasons, it was here that
most affairs of honor had been settled for the past twenty years.
The list of men who had injured, maimed, or killed their man
on that field comprised most of the respectable male population
of New Orleans. Those who had not set foot under the oaks did
not count.

They were nearing the bayou. The trees grew thicker on the

sides of the road here; the new leaves, opening at the tips of their branches due to the last few warm days, appeared colorless, like a wreath of fog in the gray light, while the clutter of vines and shrubby growth at their bases was still black.

It was from that dark cover that the firing came, streaking the dawn with explosions of orange and red. Terror leaped in Anya's chest. She had expected an attack, some attempt to stop Ravel's carriage, but not this cowardly ambush from cover. With a shout of rage that strained her throat she spurred forward. Only slightly behind her, Marcel and Samson and Elijah did the same.

The buggy did not stop, but rather picked up speed. There was no cracking whip, however. It was running away, out of control. Now from the thicket came a trio of men. They clung to their mounts like men unaccustomed to the saddle, kicking their horses into a run as they set out after the speeding buggy. They either had not seen Anya and her men, or chose to ignore them. It was a mistake.

Beside Anya, Samson fired. The weapon he carried was no pistol, but a double-barreled shotgun loaded with ounce balls. It roared like a cannon, setting up thunderous echoes. One of the horsemen ahead threw up his hands and catapulted from the saddle as if struck in the back by a huge fist. The others looked over their shoulders. One turned to shoot with the pistol he held in his fist. The bullet whipped past with a whistling sound. Elijah, yelling an angry oath, fired his own shotgun. The man with the pistol pitched from his horse and was caught by a foot in the stirrup. His horse reared and whinnied, trying to jar him loose. He jerked free and flew to land in the ditch. The third man crouched low on his horse, flinging looks of wild fright over his shoulder. At the first break in the trees, he veered from the road and plunged away over the plowed fields.

Marcel, riding with the agility of a jockey, moved ahead. He was coming closer to the buggy, closer. He flew past it, reached for the harness of the horse.

They saw him check, draw his hand back. The buggy was slowing of its own accord. By then Anya was riding even with the driver's seat. Ravel was on one knee, bracing against the kickboard. He had lost his hat when he had thrown himself to one side to avoid the shot that had torn a hole the size of a man's fist in the leather upholstery where he had been sitting, but he was unharmed and he had his horse back under control. As the vehicle drew to a stop, he regained his seat. Anya and the others reined in their horses.

Anya could not speak. She sent a glance to Marcel. He interpreted it in an instant from long practice. Turning to Ravel, he said, "You are all right, m'sieur?"

"As you see," Ravel said shortly. "Tell your meddling mistress that she may now go home, before she gets hurt!"

"Ah, M'sieur Duralde," Marcel said, his tone gently chiding, "I would not be so unwise. You must give her that message yourself."

Ravel turned to Anya. Before he could speak, she said in clipped tones, "Save yourself the trouble. We were on our way to view a duel. I believe you are heading the same way. If our company does not offend you, we will ride with you."

He could not refuse without at least an implied insult to the men who had just rescued him. Still, he tried once more. "Don't think me ungrateful, for I'm not. There are few who have ever done as much for me. It's just that a duel is no place for a woman."

She would not allow herself to be warmed by his gratitude. "You think I will faint at the sight of blood? I have been present when women were brought to bed for childbirth. By comparison, any bloodletting at this affair can only be paltry."

"I would remind you that should anything happen to me, your danger will increase."

"I have my guard."

"Yours, or mine?"

"Ours. Does it matter?"

He looked at her for a long moment before a faint smile tugged at his mouth. He shook his head with slow incredulity. "I don't suppose it does."

"Shall we proceed, then?"

They did. In a short time they had crossed the bayou and come to the two huge old oaks. Beneath them the dry grass of autumn, mixed with the new green of winter grass, was wet with dew. Morning mists lay upon the surrounding fields, shrouding the carriages that sat waiting. Voices were muffled, ringing with a curious dullness as the men gathered in two knots at either end of the field talked among themselves. The sky was lightning almost perceptibly. A breeze, little more than a breath of air, moved the topmost leaves of the trees. A bird sang and then, when there was no answer, fell into abashed silence.

Anya and the men with her dismounted. Marcel took Ravel's reins as he alighted from the buggy. Ravel's seconds started toward him. Murray, with his back rather conspicuously to the road, began to turn. He caught sight of Ravel.

Anya saw the face of the man who was engaged to Celestine turn white, then red again, saw his mouth fall open, then close so tightly that his lips seemed to disappear. Murray whipped his head to stare back down the road as if expecting to see his men. Then slowly, as if just registering her presence, he turned back to stare at Anya. There was malevolence in his eyes, but she was untouched by it. Lifting her head, she smiled.

Ravel barely noticed Murray except to follow his gaze directed toward Anya. Ravel saw her smile, the bright pride and glory of it as she stared at the man she had risked so much to save before, and his footsteps faltered. Had there been any truth at all in the story she had told him in the early hours of the morning, or had it been a tale of nonsense concocted to prevent him from appearing on the field? An assassin, she had called him, which might have been the only true indication of her sentiments she had given. Why else would she speak of love, except to sway him to do what she wanted?

But what of the thugs, hired by Murray to attack him in order to even the odds? Had she routed them out of nothing more than a sense of fair play? It was not impossible; he had benefited from her essential fairness before.

Anya and Murray. She might despise the things he did and try to stop them, might have relinquished all hope of intimacy between them for the sake of Celestine, but she would not deny what she felt for him. That was her way, the way of many women who loved unwisely.

The formalities began. The seconds tossed a coin among them to see which representative of the two men would have the privilege of giving the signal to begin. To the losing seconds went the choice of which direction their man would face, though there was little difference as to smoothness of the site or angle of the sun on either end of this field, another reason for its popularity. To Ravel, as the challenged man, went not only the choice of time and place, but also of the weapon with which the contest would be decided. It was to be swords.

The blades were brought out, a matched pair of small swords in a case lined with white satin. The blades were of Toledo steel, elaborately chased, and the hilts were inlaid in Arabic designs in gold and silver. To Murray went first choice of the blades, as was customary since the swords had been provided by Ravel. He took one gingerly in his hand, hefting it for weight and balance, slicing the air with it a few times. His movements were jerky and there was a frown between his hazel eyes. There could be little doubt that he had never meant matters to go this far.

The sound of another set of wheels grating on the shell-covered road drew Anya's attention. A closed carriage drew up a short distance away. A man stepped down and, with all the nonchalance of one out of his morning constitutional, strode toward where she stood. Perfectly dressed in the black that might be suitable should the occasion turn out to be a somber one, it was Gaspard. Anya gave him a strained smile of greeting.

"Madame Rosa sent me, so that I may tell her what happens," Gaspard said in low tones. "I would have come for myself if she had not. I feel as responsible as she does."

"You?"

"It seems to me that if she had to choose someone to show up Nicholls, it should have been me."

His pride was hurt, Anya thought. For the second time in as many days, she saw him as a man instead of merely Madame Rosa's perennial escort. "Perhaps she valued your company too much to risk even the possibility of losing it?" she suggested.

Gaspard gave her a searching look, as if fearing ridicule. After a long moment he said, "Possibly."

Anya's attention was drawn irresistibly by the business at hand and she turned away. The seconds were directing the principals as to where they must stand, Ravel to the right, Murray to the left. Once in place, they could not move until the signal to begin was given, on pain of being cut down with pistol or sword by the opposing seconds. The two men removed their coats and rolled their sleeves to the elbow. They took up their stances, their swords held loosely at their sides in their right hands, their left fists behind their backs. The seconds moved to their places near the duelists they represented.

The morning grew brighter. The rising sun sent its first rays above the tree-lined horizon. They danced and sparkled in the dew. They splashed the white linen shirts of the two men with yellow and gleamed with iridescent fire along the blades the duelists held in their hands as they swept them up in a salute. They caught the drift of the white signal handkerchief as it fell to the grass like a snowflake out of its proper climate.

The blades of the two men came together with a sharp, musical chiming, tapping, testing. The men circled warily, feinting and parrying as each searched out the strength of the other's wrist, the depth of his knowledge. They shifted back and forth, leaving trails in the wet grass. Each watched for an opening, dividing his attention in these first moments between the face of the opposite man and the tip of his sword.

Slowly the tempo increased. Murray lunged and Ravel parried, giving ground, then in a sudden display of skill, pressed the younger man back. He did not pursue his advantage, but recoiled, holding his guard. Emboldened, Murray attacked, using one clever stratagem after another. Ravel defended himself with each appropriate countermeasure, sometimes deflecting a wicked ruse with a device so brilliant that it brought murmurs of admiration from the men watching.

Regardless, time and again Ravel failed to follow through. It was as if he held himself in check, keeping the full range of his skill in reserve.

Gaspard said in puzzlement, almost to himself, "What is he doing?"

Anya, watching with her heart choking her, could find no answer.

Perspiration appeared in a sheen on Murray's forehead. The breathing of both men grew deeper. In the intense quiet, the scuffling of their footsteps in the grass was loud. Their shirts, growing limp and damp in the moist morning air, clung to their shoulders and upper arms, and their trousers were molded to the muscles of their thighs. Ravel's hair curled over his head, falling toward his eyes, and he flung it back with a quick impatient jerk of his head.

Baffled rage crept into Murray's face. He redoubled his efforts so that his blade darted and sang. He made a sudden lunge that Ravel parried in seconds at the last moment. The small swords scraped in a shower of orange sparks. Then in an instant Murray whirled the tip of his blade in a riposte and leaned in extension toward Ravel. There was an odd movement, almost a hesitation in the swordplay, as if Ravel began a defense and deliberately abandoned it. When Murray drew back, there was a red stain on Ravel's sleeve.

The seconds ran forward and thrust a sword between the two men, knocking Murray's blade aside as he tried to thrust again at Ravel, who was already dropping his guard. The two men disengaged. Ravel's representative bowed to Murray. "In keeping with the code, sir, I must now ask you if honor is satisfied."

There was a greenish tinge to Murray's skin and a hunted look in his eyes as he stared at Ravel. His victory had been a fluke; he had been allowed a small bloodletting and he knew it. His role now was to declare himself satisfied and permit the contest to end. It was apparent that he would like to comply, but either he had more courage than suspected, or else he had more to fear from capitulating than he did from continuing. His answer, when it came, was bald.

"No, damn you!"

Ravel's seconds exchanged a grim glance among themselves, but had no choice except to step back and signal that the match resume.

Again the clanging swordplay began, the attack and parry and riposte, the advance and retreat. But now the concentration of the two men was more circumscribed, fastened only to the glittering tip of the other man's sword. Their breathing was harsh. Ravel's movements, however, took on the lithe, controlled quality of long practice, as if he could go on at the pace he was setting forever.

And it was he who set the pace. Murray was overmatched; if it had not been plain before, it was now. He was a competent swordsman, but he was facing a master. Only some wild piece of luck, some mistake by Ravel, could give him a victory. A dozen times Ravel could have drawn blood, could even have killed him, still he contained himself. As Murray's rage and fear increased, his sword arm began to tremble and his lunges became wilder, more violent.

There was a movement so swift Anya could not follow it. The swords grated together with a sound that tore at the nerves, sliding along each other until the hilts met with a furious clang. The two men strained against each other face to face, wrist to wrist, knee to knee.

Murray, panting, demanded, "What do you think you're doing, Duralde?"

"Giving you satisfaction. Isn't that what you wanted?"

"I want you dead!"

"Denial, they say, is good for the soul."

Ravel spared a brief look at Anya where she stood with her hands clasped in front of her and her eyes wide as she watched them. What she had found in this tainted specimen of manhood he did not know, but if it was possible, he would preserve him for her. It would be far better if he removed Murray, better for New Orleans, better for Anya. He lacked the courage. It was not that he was without the will to strike the final blow; he could so easily end the fight and Murray's life. But not in front of Anya. He could not bring himself to kill the man she loved, could not bear to face the condemnation in her eyes, not again.

It would have better if he and Murray had been equally matched, if there had been more danger. He cursed the conceit in Nicholls that had allowed him to think he was a swordsman because of a few lessons in Exchange Alley. Instead, it was the same as it had been so often in the past; Ravel's skill learned in a thousand passages at arms with the master who had been his stepfather had given him an unfair advantage. To bring to bear all the ancient moves, tricks, and wily subterfuges that he knew would remove the element of honor from the contest, turning it instead into a rite of murder. And though it was a betrayal of his friends and the cause he supported to refrain, he must, because Anya was there. He could not play the assassin, or even the role of scourge that he had been given, certainly not while she watched.

Anya met Ravel's glance, as swift and lethal as the flick of a sword, and felt that it struck deep inside her. She saw the desolation behind it, the futility and the pain, with a terrible recognition. It was just so Ravel had looked when she had accused him of murdering Jean all those years ago. Here on this field, she was his *bête noire*, a reminder of the inescapable past. That was his handicap, the thing that kept him from exerting his expertise, from protecting himself fully from the man trying to kill him. A small miscalculation, a moment of inattention, and it could be fatal.

Murray wrenched himself backward, stumbling, slipping in the dew-wet grass. The movement was so familiar that it sent a shiver along Ravel's spine. Just so Jean had slipped in the dew on that night, here on this very field, under these old oaks with their swaying moss.

The duel could not continue like this. It must be ended one way or another. He waited, poised and patient, until Murray recovered, then in a crackling display of technique, with his blade winking like silver, snicking, slithering, grittily scraping, he began to advance upon his opponent. Murray gave ground, defending himself with teeth clenched and sweat pouring into his eyes. It availed him little. Ravel's wrist was as tempered and pliant as his sword, and both were directed by vivid thought and implacable will.

There was a feint, a riposte. The blades ground edge to edge. Ravel's swirled, adhering, bending, prizing. Murray's grip was broken and his sword spun end over end, landing in the grass with a dull clatter.

Once more the ritual was observed. It was obvious to everyone assembled there on that field that Ravel could as easily have spitted Murray. When the younger man refused to accept his defeat, when he once again declared himself unsatisfied, the rumble of the discussion among the seconds and the attending surgeon was loud. Nevertheless, at a gesture from Ravel, Murray's small sword was retrieved and wiped dry. The match went on.

What would Ravel do now? The answer was not long in coming. The swords tapped like the ringing of a set of bells, they flashed like lightning, crossing, leveling, and when the two men drew apart, there was blood on Ravel's opposite arm.

Once more he had allowed himself to be nicked. The wound was deeper than the first, for it was fast turning his sleeve to crimson. Surely now Murray could not refuse to stop.

He could. He did. The surgeon tied a strip of bandage around Ravel's arm and the two men faced each other again.

A shudder ripped over Anya. It was followed by another and another. The clash of the blades grated on her nerves so that she wanted to scream. How much longer could it go on? There must be something she could do, but what? What?

Gaspard shook his head. "Never, but never, have I seen anything like it. It's magnificent!"

Anya turned her head to stare at him as if he were mad. "What are you talking about?"

"Wait. Wait and see," he answered, and gave a low, admiring laugh.

Anya turned from the older man, watching with straining eyes. Another injury, this time in Ravel's side as he twisted, leaping back to avoid a violent thrust. The question was a mere formality. Murray gasped out his refusal, but there was jubilation in his eyes. Oblivious of the hard stares of Ravel's seconds, he was waiting for a moment of misjudgment, for the mistake that would give him the chance to finish the other man. He gripped the hilt of his sword tighter as the duel continued.

Slowly Anya began to grasp Gaspard's meaning. It was so simple and yet so clever; so noble and yet so diabolical; so obscure, yet simply rooted in the essence of the code duello.

What Murray did not seem to realize was that with every drop of Ravel's blood he shed, he was coming nearer to his own ruin. This was a contest of honor, not of endurance or skill. Murray's stubborn insistence on satisfaction in the face of his opponent's magnanimity was branding him as lacking in the instincts of a gentleman as surely as any revelation of his recent activities would have done. If the object of this meeting was to discredit Murray, then Ravel was succeeding.

But how far would he carry his sacrifice? How much blood must he lose before he would consider his task accomplished? With so many injuries, as small as they might be, how long could he retain the control to permit Murray to slash him only where he himself chose? And was his purpose truly what it seemed, or was there in it also an element of expiation? Expiation for the death of another young man here on this ground seven years ago?

Chapter Twenty

🗲 🗲 🗲 *Faster now the wounds came, a slice to the* shoulder, another thrust to the arm, a scratch on the cheek an inch below the eye. It seemed it was Murray who chose the sites and Ravel who only avoided drastic results. Ravel's seconds had moved in concert toward him once, as if to halt the fight, but he had stopped them with a dogged shake of his head. The men acting for him were at a loss. So far had this contest gone beyond the bounds of the code that they finally ceased to intervene with the question of satisfaction. Murray's seconds, though they should have joined with the men of Ravel to halt the duel, were of his own stripe; they stood back, openly gloating.

Ravel's parries were slowing; his hair was wet with perspiration. His breathing was as hard as Murray's, and with every heave of his chest, the spreading red of his blood seeped in wider splotches across his damp shirt. Murray, his lips drawn back in a feral grin, aimed a thrust at Ravel's breastbone. There was a blur of motion, a singing of steel, and when the two men parted, Ravel's shirt was torn and his chest had a small slash, but Murray had a gash on his neck. He slapped his left hand to it, then stared at his reddened fingers in disbelief. Ravel stepped back, lowering his sword. There was a sudden silence.

"Murderer! Bloodstained butcher!"

The screams came from behind Anya. She turned in time to see Celestine tumble from the closed carriage that had brought Gaspard.

"Mother of God," the older man said under his voice, "I had forgotten her."

Anya started toward her half sister, but Celestine fended her off. Tripping over her full skirts, the younger girl stumbled to-

330

ward the men who faced each other. "Stop it!" she screamed. "Stop it! I can't stand any more!"

Murray saw Ravel's stunned distraction, his lowered guard, saw also his own opportunity. He gathered himself, stealthily raising his sword. He drew a soft breath.

To Anya it seemed like a tableau, a scene of frozen motion representing some fable of life and death and the fine balance between the two. Celestine with tears running down her face, nearly between the two men. Ravel off guard. Murray intent on his advantage. The bloodied swords. The old oaks. The startled seconds. Gaspard, gaping. The clear morning sunlight.

How had they come to be there? The causes were many, but a portion of the blame was hers. That being so, she must mend matters as best she could.

It was instinct that guided her, however, not slow and rational thought. Before the answer was clear she was moving, launching herself after Celestine, crying out her warning.

"Ravel, watch out! Kill him! End it, for the love of God!"

Her shoulder and one hand struck Celestine in the back. Together they plunged earthward. A yard of singing death passed so close over the back of Anya's head that she felt the wind of its flight, felt it and knew that Murray would have been glad if it had found her.

Then came the resonant clang of blades engaging, the hard ring, the furious scrape and clatter of a strong, deliberate attack. There was a swift-drawn breath, a grunt. A second muttered in amazement. Anya swung her head in time to see Murray stagger back and fall sprawling in the grass. His hand still holding his sword twitched, and then he was still.

It was done, over. A vast weariness settled upon Anya. She felt as if moving were beyond her strength. The seconds crowded around and three men offered her their hands to rise. She accepted that of the man nearest. The other two men lifted Celestine, who took one swift look at Murray then cast herself into Anya's arms, sobbing. Over the girl's shoulder, Anya looked to where Ravel stood. A second had taken his sword, and the surgeon, muttering under his breath, was cutting away his blood-soaked shirt. Ravel did not seem to notice; his black gaze was

upon Anya, and in it the same fierce, burning concentration he
had brought to the duel.

Gaspard was there, his words soothing and yet as bracing as
those of a father as he took a part of Celestine's weight. He turned
with the younger girl toward the carriage, urging her along, away
from the scene of carnage, and with Anya supporting her on the
other side, managed to place the stricken girl in the closed vehicle.

He turned then to Anya. "Come, *chère*, get in and let us go
home. Your man can bring your mount. There is nothing more
to be done here."

"Yes, in a moment," she answered, and turned to walk back
toward the men under the oaks.

The surgeon had dressed the most serious of Ravel's cuts and
cleaned the others with carbolic. The smell of it hung on the
air, masking the scent of blood. Murray's seconds had dis-
bursed, carrying his body to his carriage, making ready to depart. Ravel's men drew back at her approach in a display of
conscious sensibility. The surgeon looked at Anya, then tossed
his roll of bandaging into his bag, snapped it shut, and after
dividing a bow between her and his patient, moved briskly toward where the seconds had gathered.

The morning sun exposed the dark shadows of sleeplessness
and worry under Anya's eyes, but made her skin appear translucent
and turned her braided hair into a shimmering aureole around her
head. She stood before Ravel with her back straight and her head
at a proud angle, though there was contrition in her eyes.

"I'm sorry," she said.

"For what?"

His tone was brusque. If there was not such an interested
audience around them, if he did not feel quite so covered with
gore, he would snatch her in his arms and taste her soft lips
before he forced her to explain why now, after all this time, she
should care whether he lived or died.

"For everything. For the words spoken in grief and malice
seven years ago. For interfering between you and Murray. For
whatever it was I did that made you let Murray carve you like a
choice piece of—"

"Even," he interrupted, "if I am not?"

"Even so."

He stared at her a moment, his dark eyes searching her face. "There is a matter unsettled between us, one made even more imperative after this morning. A matter of marriage."

Pain burgeoned inside Anya, but she kept her voice steady, and even managed a faint smile as she repeated the answer he had given her so short a time ago. "Such a sacrifice. There is no need, not for my sake."

"I have no use for sacrifices."

"I am to believe that, after what I saw here? No, we will forget it, if you please. We have hurt each other enough; there is nothing that requires us to go on doing it. I care not at all what society thinks, nor do you. That being so, we are free to go back to the way we were. Shall we agree on a new pact? When we meet it will be as friends, polite, distant friends who bow and smile but do not meddle in each other's lives."

"I would rather," he said, his tone grinding, "be your enemy."

It was a moment before she could speak. To cover her distress, she turned swiftly from him and picked up the hem of her leather skirt. Over her shoulder she said, "As you wish."

Ravel stood with his muscles hard cramped in the effort to prevent himself from reaching out and snatching her back. Let her go. It was what she wanted, wasn't it? She had made that clear.

Celestine was not inconsolable. In fact, her spirits improved and her grief receded in direct proportion to the speed of Emile's recovery. When she was coherent, she explained to Anya that it had not been Ravel she had called a bloodstained butcher at all, but Murray. She had discovered on Mardi Gras night, as Emile had thrown down his challenge to both Ravel and Murray, that it was the gallant Frenchman she loved. It was that sudden knowledge and the predicament of having two men in her life about to meet each other on the field of honor that had rendered her senseless.

Then as she lay abed at the townhouse, Emile had been brought in with his skull cracked. Madame Rosa had, reluctantly, told her of the perfidy of her fiancé. Celestine had realized what a monster he was and how he had used her. She had been torn between the desire to remain at Emile's side and the need to know if she was to be released from so horrible a man, as well as a frighteningly urgent need to see justice meted out to him for what he had done to both Anya and Emile—and herself. She had begged a place in Gaspard's carriage.

Then had come that terrible duel. It had appeared that Ravel was allowing himself to be slaughtered for some strange reason having to do with men's stupid sense of honor. She had feared that Murray would finally kill him and be free to finish what he had begun with Emile, to persecute and endanger Anya, even to force her herself to marry him as she had pledged. She had gone a little mad.

Now it was over and they could be easy again. Emile was mending nicely and seemed to enjoy having her sit with him, read to him. Yesterday he had caught her hand and carried it to his lips, calling her his lovely angel. Murray had never called her an angel.

Madame Rosa was vindicated in her distrust of Murray. She did not, however, make the mistake of denouncing him to her friends and enjoying her triumph, which would of course have called for explanations that could only besmirch her daughter with the same filth that had covered him. With dignity and reserve, she expressed her regret over the death of the young man on the field of honor. Her daughter, she said, had been prostrate, but was trying to rise above her sorrow by making herself useful in the sickroom. She was always well chaperoned, naturally. She, Madame Rosa, would be sorry to see the Girod boy leave her house when his injury permitted him to be moved. He was so very agreeable as a patient, and was having such a salutary effect upon Celestine, not only in overcoming her grief but in helping her become more mature and responsible. It was most comical to watch her persuade him to take his medicine and rest as the doctor ordered.

With Celestine more or less in seclusion and Anya refusing all invitations, in part to save her stepmother embarrassment but primarily out of a disinclination for frivolous amusement, it fell to Gaspard to escort Madame Rosa to the few entertainments available during the Lenten season. They seemed, perhaps, a little more overtly affectionate, a little more satisfied in each other's company, but of the prospect of a closer relationship there was not a sign. There was nothing, apparently, to keep them from going on as they were indefinitely.

It was fortunate, Madame Rosa said after a few outings, that the duel and Anya's part in it had occurred on Ash Wednesday, since the balls and parties of the winter season were at an end, and many people had left town. There was talk; it would have been useless to expect there to be none, but it was not nearly so rabid as it might have been earlier. Most people seemed to agree that Anya was eccentric and headstrong, if not immoral, and that it was unlikely she would ever find a man who could endure her wild ways. There was also much interest in the fact that Ravel Duralde, the other party in the stories circulating, had dropped out of sight. There were some who swore that he had left the country, while others, who claimed to have it from eye-witnesses of the duel, said that he was so mutilated his health was impaired and he was recuperating at some Northern spa. Still another story placed him in the country where, it was whispered, he had every intention of becoming a recluse like his father.

Anya listened to the stories and the gossip concerning Ravel and herself that were brought by Madame Rosa, but they hardly touched her. It was as if they concerned other people. She heard Celestine speaking volubly and without end of how she felt about Emile and Murray, and she was glad that her half sister was not as devastated as she had feared, was glad that she appeared to be in reach of happiness, but wished only that she would talk about something else, anything else. In a vague way, she was relieved that Madame Rosa's social round seemed little affected by what she had done, that life was going to go on just the same. Still, her sole impulse of any strength was to have done with the last of the obligations that tied her to New Orleans and to get away, away from the mess she had made of things, away from her longing for Ravel Duralde, away from her barely expunged guilt over Celestine, away from her concern for Madame Rosa. Away, she just wanted to get away.

Beau Refuge, beautiful place of refuge. It was more than just a name, it was an ideal. Anya longed for it, for its quiet that soothed her and its routine that absorbed and rejuvenated her; for its peace that would allow her the time to remember, for its memories.

For the moment, she tried not to think of Ravel. She did try. But it was difficult when every hour brought some reminder, when nearly everything that was said had some reference to him, or when the way those around her avoided mention of his name made it plain he was on their minds. Even the single visitor announced for her in the week that followed the duel was a piercing reminder.

She entered the salon to find Madame Castillo standing in the center of the room. Ravel's mother was beautifully dressed in a walking costume of gray velvet and with a small hat of the same material tipped forward on her dark curls. Her face was haggard, however, and there were new lines of worry in her face. Anya went forward with perfect politeness to offer her hand though there was a gripping in her stomach and she could feel the blankness of her own features.

Madame Castillo spoke first. "I hope you don't mind that I have come, but I had to see you."

"Certainly. Please sit down. May I offer you refreshment, a glass of *eau sucre* or perhaps a little wine and a few cakes?" The amenities served to give her time to recover her poise.

"Thank you, no." The older woman sank down upon the settee. She looked for a moment at her gloved hands clenched into fists on her knees, then raised her head to meet Anya's gaze. "It's about Ravel. Have you seen him?"

"I assume you mean since the duel. No. No, I haven't."

Madame Castillo closed her eyes. "I was afraid of it."

"He—he is gone?" It was impossible not to ask.

"Since the day after that morning when they brought him home. I would not have you think me an alarmist, but once before he left like this. I did not see him again for four years."

Once before, when Jean was killed. Anya made a helpless gesture. "I understand, but I have no idea where he may be."

"I thought he might have given you some idea of his destination, might have at least communicated with you."

"No." Her voice was flat.

"Forgive me, but I find it difficult to comprehend. My son has never been irresponsible. Even when he was younger, seven years ago, he left behind a letter for me. He is most considerate of those he loves, so much so that I now find it beyond belief that he would not let me, or you, know where he was going!"

The words reverberated in Anya's mind so that it was a moment before she could grasp them. "Those he loves? He has no love for me."

"Don't be foolish." Madame Castillo's tone was sharp. "He

has loved you for years, since you were his best friend's be-trothed. Why else would the things you said to him the night Jean was killed have such power to destroy him?''

There was a swelling, choking feeling inside Anya's chest and she could hear her own heartbeat fluttering in her ears. She whispered, ''It can't be true.''

''I assure you it can. It is.''

''But why didn't he tell me?''

''Perhaps he had some reason to think it wouldn't matter. But it does, doesn't it?''

The dazed look Anya gave her was answer enough. ''If you had not come, I might never have known.''

''Now are you certain he said nothing, gave no hint of where he might be going, when last you saw him?''

Anya shook her head, looking down at her hands.

Madame Castillo frowned. ''It's so perplexing. I heard him speaking to his valet the night before he left. It seemed odd at the time, though I was not really attending. It can't think it was important or see how it might pertain at all to his whereabouts, but I could swear he asked for a chess set—and a chain.''

Slowly Anya lifted her gaze to meet that of the other woman. A shiver ran along her nerves and she suppressed it. A chess set? A chain? Was it possible? No, it couldn't be. He would not go to Beau Refuge, not for love. No, and not even for revenge; he was not that kind of man. Was he?

''I would rather be your enemy!''

''What is it, *chère*?''

Anya moistened her lips. ''Possibly nothing. But—it may be I can find Ravel.''

It had been midafternoon when Madame Castillo made her visit. The early darkness of February was falling by the time Anya could have her things packed, make her arrangements to leave town, and say her adieux to Madame Rosa, Celestine, and Emile. No one tried to dissuade her. They had become so used to her hurried departures and unexpected arrivals that it caused scarcely a ripple. In any case, she had sighed often enough for Beau Refuge in the past few days that they had been in almost hourly expectation of her setting out for the plantation.

The good weather they had enjoyed through Mardi Gras and

beyond had not held. There was a chill wind blowing that crept into the carriage. It carried in its breath a presage of rain, though for the moment the moon shed enough light to see the road. Anya huddled under a fur rug against the damp cold and prayed that the rain would not come until morning. By then she would have reached her home. By then she would know if Ravel was there. By then she would have discovered, once and for all, what, if anything, he felt for her.

He might have loved her once; that would explain much. It did not mean, however, that he loved her still. It would be amazing if he did, after everything she had done to him, all the trouble she had caused. Her motives had been of the best, but he could hardly be blamed for failing to believe it.

She thought of him as he had been when they played chess together, or when she had bartered with him for a hairpin, the way he had smiled, the teasing, caressing light in his eyes. Dissembling devil. He had only pretended to be her prisoner. But how handsome he had been, and what pleasure she had taken in the feeling that he could not escape her. Only a part of what she felt, if she were truthful, had been the satisfaction of vengeance. She had quite enjoyed thinking that he was in her power, even while she had feared what he would do if released. Human beings were strange creatures.

She would not feel that same way now in the same circumstances. Or would she? If the means presented itself and she knew it would end this uncertainty, she might be tempted to confine him once more. Admitting it, she was not quite certain what kind of woman that made her, except an honest one.

The miles jolted by. Anya sat staring into the dark, thinking and also trying not to think in an endless round. Now and then a shiver rippled along her nerves. She was not sure whether the cause was cold or excitement, dread or anticipation.

She tried to think of every eventuality. If Rável was there at Beau Refuge, would she be gracious and receptive and wait for him to declare himself. Would she be impetuous and run into his arms? Would she be tongue-tied and miserably aware of how they had parted, ready to take fright to find offense so that nothing was changed, nothing resolved? If he was not there, would she sit down and wail, or would she calmly greet Denise, calmly walk upstairs and put herself to bed, calmly blow out the lamp, and then wail?

Dear God, would this journey never end?

It did at last. The carriage rolled along the drive under the spreading arms of the oaks, black at this midnight hour, and pulled up before the house. It sat dark and silent. If there was anyone there, they had gone to bed, including Denise.

Marcel, who had come with her as a matter of course, the most faithful man of her acquaintance, got down from the box and opened the carriage door. Stiffly Anya climbed down. She glanced at the house with her lips pressed to prevent them from trembling. When Marcel said that he would ride to the stables with the coachman to bed down the horses, she agreed with a weary nod. Gathering up her skirts, she trudged up the steps to the upper gallery and pulled the rope for the bell at the door. She heard it ringing on the back gallery. While she stood waiting for Denise to come and let her in, she turned to look around her, pulling her cloak closer around her against the tug of the wind. Below her, Marcel set her baggage on the lower gallery, then climbed back up beside Solon, the coachman. The carriage moved away down the drive.

Denise did not come. Anya turned from comtemplating the night and reached once more for the bellpull. It was then that she noticed the great front door was standing ajar.

What was Denise thinking of? Anyone could walk in. Or had the latch been broken somehow during the thievery of Murray's men? She didn't remember such a thing, but surely it should be repaired by now, even so? Such scolding questions were a distraction from the odd sense of unease that crept in upon her.

This was her home. There was no reason for her to hover about on the doorstep. Marcel would be returning at any moment, and in any case, she no longer had anything to fear.

She pushed open the door and stepped into the main salon. When her eyes had adjusted to the inside, she could see well enough with the gleam of moonlight. The room was full of squat shapes of furniture made colorless and ghostly in the dimness. There did not appear to be a lamp anywhere close. Instead of searching for one, she moved with the ease of long familiarity through the room to the door that connected with the dining room. Here, it was darker since the room, being in the center of the house, had no windows. She passed through it quickly, just touching with the tips of her fingers the backs of the chairs lined at the table. Beyond the dining room was the back sitting room, with her own bedchamber opening from it to the left. Anya moved toward the last room as toward a sanctuary.

Her hand found the knob, she turned it, pushed open the door. She stepped inside. Gooseflesh rose on her arms. She hesitated, listening. She could hear nothing. Her heart was thudding against her ribs. There was a tight feeling around her forehead, as if a tight band were fitted there. A light. She needed light to banish this fluttering of nerves. She moved away from the door toward the washstand where a lamp always sat with matches in a holder beside it.

Hard hands caught her forearms, clamping them to her sides. She was whirled, lifted with hard arms at her back and under her knees. She kicked, arching against the chest of the man who held her. It made no impression. A few jarring steps, and suddenly she was dropped.

Even as she gave a strangled cry, she struck the soft resilience of the feather mattress of her own bed. Her bearings returned in an instant, and she tried to roll. The mattress gave and a heavy and confining weight landed across her waist. She pushed at it, felt a hard muscular shoulder, felt also the thick padding of a bandage. She went still.

Swiftly her right arm was caught. The hard and warm fingers upon it moved to her wrist. There was a musical jangle and a sharp clicking sound. Something cold and heavy confined her arm. The weight upon her lifted, the bed rocked on its ropes, and she was alone.

She lay in unmoving disbelief for an instant; then with a yank of her arm she tested the shackle that held her. It gave only a short distance before stopping with a dull rattle. The chain was fastened to the post of the bed.

She raised herself on her elbow, straining her eyes in the darkness. Her voice vibrating with fury, she said, "Ravel Duralde, I know you're there! What do you think you are doing?"

There was a soft popping sound and yellow-orange light flared at the washstand. Ravel stood holding a phosphorus match in his hand. He reached for the globe of the lamp and, when he had removed it, touched the flame to the wick. The leaping fire as it caught gave his face the glazed look of a demonic mask in porcelain, an appearance that faded as he replaced the globe and picked up the lamp, moving toward her. He placed the light on the table beside the bed before he spoke.

"What do you think?"

"I think you're insane!"

"You may be right."

He turned to look at her, and at the expression in his dark eyes a frisson that had nothing to do with fear moved over her. She swallowed. "How did you get in here?"

"Denise let me in. I told her I was your guest and that you would be returning at any moment. She has left me to wait up for you these past three nights. She thinks the way you have kept me kicking my heels is extremely bad mannered, but finds my patience endearing. It is all most unconventional but about what she might expect from the two of us."

"I'm sure," Anya said tartly. "Do you know that everyone thinks you have disappeared, even your mother? You might at least have left her a message."

A smile curved his mouth. "Still concerned for my mother? Let me set your mind at ease. I told her in detail where I would be, and what I meant to do."

"She—she knows?"

"It was she who suggested that if you failed to leave town within a certain time she might send you to me."

A trap, and most carefully laid. What an idiot she had been to believe a word of it.

He moved to sit on the edge of the bed, drawing up one knee to brace himself though he was careful not to block the light shining on her face. "She also told me how she would see to it that you came."

Anya held his gaze as long as she could. Lowering her lashes, she said tonelessly, "Did she?"

"There were many possibilities, many emotions she might play upon," he said, his voice taking on a deeper shading, "among them hate, revenge, remorse, compassion, guilt. But there was only one she would use, just one. If you did not come for that reason, you would not come at all."

She made no answer; she could not for the hard lump forming in her throat.

"Tell me why you came, Anya," he urged, his voice soft.

She tried to move her arm and the rattle of the chain brought a small surge of anger, enough to muster defiance. "What does it matter? You have what you want!"

"It matters, sweet Anya; oh, yes, it matters." He reached to touch her cheek with one knuckle, taking pleasure in the smooth texture of her skin. His attention was caught by the gleam of a pin holding the thick braids of her hair, and he leaned to pluck it out and toss it to one side. His hand warm and gentle upon her hair as he probed for others, he repeated, "Tell me."

There was no escape. His will was relentless; she had seen that much, if there had ever been any doubt, beneath the dueling oaks. He required nothing less than capitulation. He would have it, then, but only at a price.

"I came," she said, swallowing on tears, "because I was sorry for what I had done to you."

"Remorse. No, that isn't it." He drew her braids over her shoulders and began to release the tresses, spreading them over her breasts.

She put her free hand on his shoulder, touching the bandaging lightly. "Because I felt your pain and, knowing I was the cause, longed to ease it."

"Compassion," he said, and trailed his fingers along the row of buttons that closed the neck of her blue velvet traveling costume. Still there was a tremor in his touch.

"Because I had made you an outcast once and would not have it happen again if words of mine could prevent it, because I wanted to say to you that you had misunderstood, that it was not you Celestine meant to accuse of murder, but Murray."

"Guilt. I've carried enough of it with me over the years to know it." He shook his head.

Beneath his fingers, her buttons had opened to the waist. Her camisole strained over the curves of her breasts that were pressed upward by her corset. With intent concentration, he smoothed over them with one knuckle, watching as the nipples tightened under that gentle, persuasive caress.

On a difficult breath, Anya said, "I came because to stay away would be to give you a peace you don't deserve."

"Vengeance," he said, "is mine."

"And because you refused to honor the pact I offered, because there is something between us that has been there for seven long years and will not go away!"

"Hate," he said, and the word was no more than a whisper.

"Not hate," she answered, and looked at him with tears shimmering in her eyes.

"Anya—"

There was such pain, such doubt in that quiet word that her tears spilled over, making heated tracks in her hair. Her voice husky, she asked, "Have you hated me, all this time?"

His face hardened and he reached to catch her arms, giving her a shake. "I have loved you with every ounce of my being and every soulless beat of my heart since first I saw you, and well you know it! You have been the dream I sought, chaste and unsullied, the one bright beacon that kept me sane and gave me hope in a filthy and vermin-infested Spanish prison and in the rotting heat of a Central American jungle. Unworthy as I was, I could not give up hope of having you, though death itself kept us apart. You were my luck, my secret joy, my talisman, the one symbol I honored, until you placed yourself in my hands. After so long, how could I resist the need to have you? But knowing your sweetness, I was damned. There was nothing I would not do, nothing I will not do now, to have you again and again, to hold you always in my arms as I have held you in my heart."

She required no more in a declaration. "If you can love me, can I not love you?"

"You can and you will. I will see to that if I have to keep you shackled to me for the rest of your days."

"There is no need," she said, her eyes clear and deep blue as she met his black gaze. "I love you, now."

"Anya," he whispered. "Can you? You wouldn't lie?"

"How can you think it?"

"How do I dare think otherwise, when I've waited so long?"

Tears shimmered as they welled into her eyes. She reached to touch the hard plane of his face with gentle fingertips. "Oh,

Ravel, I've waited, too, though I did not know it. Take my love now, please, for I can wait no longer.''

He lowered himself beside her, easing over her to her left side so that his own, less injured right arm supported him. There was reverence and a ravishing gentleness in the way he drew her to him. He molded her mouth to his, savoring the pure rapture of her surrender.

The moments passed. With slow delicacy and care, he removed her clothing layer by layer until she lay naked beside him. Gently, endlessly, he lavished upon her a seven-year store of sensual delights, tasting her skin, teasing, seeking to give her pleasure, succeeding beyond imagining.

Anya, drowning willingly in sheer sensation, still had the sense of being confined since her right wrist was chained and her left hand trapped between their two bodies. Her inability to move, to do anything other than writhe under his ravishing caresses, was disturbing on more than one count.

Against Ravel's ear, she whispered, ''This is lovely, but it would be better without the chain.''

''Are you sure?'' There was a hint of laughter in his voice that indicated his perfect awareness of what he was doing.

''I promise.''

''By all means, then.''

He took from his pocket a small key, then heaved himself out of bed with a quick grimace of the flexing of sore and sliced muscles. Fitting the key into the lock, he released her from the shackle, then dragged the chain from the bedpost and flung it on the floor. He discarded his clothes and bent then to blow out the lamp. When he turned, Anya's arms were outstretched, welcoming. With soft words of love and blind joy, he came to her.

The moonlight creeping into the room shed its cool radiance upon the moving forms upon the bed, gilding their bodies so that they had the look of a pagan god and goddess disporting themselves in splendor. It touched the chain that lay upon the floor, shining on sinuous links with the precious gleam of purest gold, sparkling on the bracelet with the faceted glitter of diamonds and sapphires that formed the wrist shackle.

Anya did not notice. Ravel did not care.

Author's Note

꙾ ꙾ ꙾ *The Vigilance Committee as described in Prisoner of Desire* was an actual organization. It was formed in the early spring of 1858 in response to the corruption of the Know-Nothing party, and numbered approximately a thousand members. The known leader was a former officer of the United States Army, Captain Johnson Kelly Duncan, age thirty-two, and many officers and members had served with William Walker in Nicaragua. The group engaged in an armed altercation with the New Orleans city government on June 1, 1858, following the seizure of the lists of registered voters by Know-Nothing rowdies for the purpose of striking from them the names of opposing voters. Incensed by this flagrant act, the committee gathered in the Vieux Carré at midnight on June 2, where they took possession of the Cabildo, the city jail, and the arsenal on St. Peter Street to the rear of the Cabildo. They armed themselves with the muskets and other weapons from the arsenal, hauled several pieces of artillery into place commanding the approaches to Jackson Square, and formed entrenchments of cotton bales and paving stones.

On the following morning, notices appeared in the papers urging men to join with the committee to inflict "prompt and exemplary punishment upon well-known and notorious offenders and violators of the rights and privileges of citizens," and to help free the city of the "thugs, outlaws, assassins and murderers" who infested it.

Waterman, the mayor of New Orleans, sent the police with warrants for the arrest of the committee, but the members refused to submit. An attempt was made to call out the state militia, but the number of men responding to the call was insufficient to dislodge the committee. The mayor, conceding defeat, met with Captain Duncan and accepted the demands of the committee, granting them legitimacy by appointing them special police for the purpose of keeping order and guarding the polls on Election Day. Waterman then took up residence in the Cabildo for his own protection.

In the meantime, a large mob of Know-Nothings and various other rowdies had gathered. They were sanctioned as a special army by the city government and given permission to take weapons from a sporting goods store. After a great deal of milling around Lafayette Square and firing into the air to work up their courage, they charged the defenses of the committee. They were quickly routed.

The situation remained volatile, however. The two groups of armed men faced each other in the streets for five days as pledges were made and rescinded and speakers alternately urged peaceful disbandment or war to the finish. Eleven men were killed, five in various clashes, six from mysterious causes that may have stemmed from the pledge of the committee to rid the city of undesirables.

The election, held on June 7, was one of the most peaceful on record, though the result was as expected, with the Know-Nothings carrying the day. Shortly thereafter, the Vigilance Committee put down their weapons and abandoned their posts. A few were arrested but were soon released; others left the city for a time before returning and taking up their lives. Captain Duncan remained in New Orleans where he was active as a civil engineer, surveyor, and architect. When the Civil War began, he joined the Confederacy as a colonel, but was almost immediately promoted to the rank of brigadier-general and given the command of Forts Jackson and St. Philip below New Orleans on the Mississippi River. He was taken a prisoner of war when New Orleans fell in 1862, and died a year later.

The second parade of the Mistick Krewe of Comus, with the theme *The Classic Pantheon*, took place on February 16, 1858, and occurred substantially as related. This parade should be recognized as the first of the great processions that had evolved into the parades as we know them today. The march of Comus the year before, in the costumes of characters from Milton's

Paradise Lost and with a single tableau cart, or float, was a forerunner, but lacked the size and magnificence that would qualify it as the prototype.

The second parade of Comus contained more than thirty floats representing the "heathen gods," as a contemporary newspaper account called them. Among the gods depicted was Pan, though there is some doubt as to whether the man costumed as a pagan god of love rode on a cart or walked among his fauns. Lacking a reliable guide, the descriptions of the costume worn by Ravel and his bower of greenery on a cart pulled by white goats are my own invention. Under most circumstances, I am a willing slave to provable fact, but, being inescapably romantic and reposing implicit faith in the lenient and gracious spirit of Mardi Gras, I feel that the shades of maskers past will forgive the substitution and even, perhaps, agree that if this isn't the way it was, it's the way it should have been. . . .

Jennifer Blake
Sweet Brier
Quitman, Louisiana

About the Author

Jennifer Blake was born near Goldonna, Louisiana, in her grand-parents' 120-year-old hand-built cottage. She grew up on an eighty-acre farm in the rolling hills of north Louisiana. While married and raising her children, she became a voracious reader. At last, she set out to write a book on her own. That first book was followed by thirty-four more, and today they have together reached over ten million copies in print, making Jennifer Blake one of the bestselling romance authors of our time. Her most recent novel is *Joy and Anger*.

Jennifer and husband live near Quitman, Louisiana, in a house styled after Southern planters' cottages.